...lood and Lightning
...VEL BY Micki Janae

...978-1-953103-44-4 (trade paperback)
...978-1-953103-45-1 (Epub)
...ary of Congress Control Number: 2024932770

...110

...edition

...cation Date: October 8, 2024

...C Coding:
...9000 - Young Adult Fiction / Legends, Myths, Fables / Greek & Roman
...46120 Young Adult Fiction / People & Places / United States / African American & Black
...19020 Young Adult Fiction / Fantasy / Dark Fantasy
...01000 - Young Adult Fiction / Action & Adventure / General

...R ILLUSTRATION:
...rine Massa: www.catherinemassa.com

... DESIGN:
...esign International: www.katgeorges.com

...BUTED IN THE U.S. AND INTERNATIONALLY BY:
...m/Publishers Group West: www.pgw.com

... Rooms Press | New York, NY
...hreeroomspress.com | info@threeroomspress.com

OF
BLOOD
AND
LIGHTNING

OF
BLOOD
AND
LIGHTNI

A NOVEL

MICKI JANA

THREE ROOMS PRESS
New York, NY

For hardheaded, disobedient,
angry Black girls everywhere
<3

OF
BLOOD
AND
LIGHTNING

PART ONE:

THE HOLY
SEVEN

CHAPTER ONE

An empty universe, and the tall, powerful man that waits at its edge.

He's wearing a royal blue toga, and there are lashings on his back. I approach him. There's something invisible between us. Something tugging me closer.

As I walk, drums pound in the rhythm of my feet. The man must not hear it, or me, because he doesn't turn around. Not until I'm close enough to see the ridges of his scars.

He towers over me by at least two feet. Each part of his body is powerful and massive, like he could crush my head between both of his giant hands. The stench of ozone and honey wafts around him, and something else too, something nearly intoxicating. He doesn't say anything. His eyes speak for him: blue and piercing, filled with some glowing light. They cast over me like lighthouses, searching for something in a violent storm.

"What is this?" I ask him.

He doesn't answer. Lightning wraps around his shoulders and spirals down his arms like thick straps of rope. It gathers into his hands in boiling pools of blue electricity. With his right hand, he reaches into his waistband for the handle of a sword.

My feet are rooted in place. Heat boils beneath my skin, like I'm going to catch fire. I try to scream, but my mouth is wired shut.

He pulls out his sword and aims it at the sky. Blue lightning wraps around the blade until a jet of electricity fires overhead. Gray clouds gather above us, swirling into a vortex of heat and blue light. The darkness is absolute, but it cowers in the presence of this man's power. The earth, if it's the earth, trembles beneath us. Then, it speaks.

"He who splits the sky. He who calls lightning from blood."

The man lowers his sword, but the storm remains. He aims it at my chest this time. At my heart.

"You will split the sky," he says. "You will call lightning from blood."

He drives the sword through my chest and the world goes black.

"OPHELIA."

My aunt Cherice reaches back with a gentle hand, rousing me out of sleep. I blink at the influx of sunlight, bright and unyielding. It feels wrong. Today isn't the day for birdsong or blue skies. There should be storm clouds and buckets of rain, so much lightning that every living thing flees the Earth to escape its wrath. Instead, New River, North Dakota comes around the bend of a winding, gravel road in all its sun-soaked glory.

"We're here, honey," Cherice says from the passenger seat, her voice small.

The welcome sign must have been recently painted because it's surrounded by two rows of bright red caution tape. Beyond it, the road splits into a small, clustered town of storefronts, old banks, and service stations. From the top of the hill, I can see Mercy Park and the city library sitting right beside it, shrouded in a flicker of fairy lights. A shallow creek trails all the way from the park to the elementary school on the edge of town. Every sign and street corner is familiar. Technically, this is home, but I haven't called it that in a very long time.

It's bittersweet. On the one hand, being in New River makes me feel like a kid again. The last time I was here, everything was so much bigger than me. Every building scraped the sky. Every tree was the long, spindly hand of God. Not now though. Now, I recognize it for the ugly, dull, dead-end town it is. New River is North Dakota's tar pit. Most people aren't unlucky enough to be born here, so they stand half a chance. If you're born in New River, you die in New River.

The only upside is that the summers aren't so hot here. In Austin, they were sweltering and oppressive. I turn over in my seat, closing my eyes. Some part of me had wanted to stay awake to see us drive into town. Now that we have, everything just feels more final. It's the door you can't open. Once you're here, you can never ever go back to where you were, no matter how badly you want to.

I could never see myself missing Austin before. I hated the heat too much and how big everything was. A city like that made you feel like something was swallowing you. Now, all I wish I could do is travel back two weeks and sit out on the deck my father built. It's just dawning on me now that I'll never get to do that again, any of it. There'll never be another day when I come home and my father is waiting for me.

"Ophelia." Janus's voice. It's the first time he's spoken since we loaded up the car last night.

I keep my eyes closed. "Yeah." I'm not looking, and they almost sound the same.

"I just wanted to say thank you," he says.

I press my forehead against the window, feeling the tension between my skin and the glass. "For what?"

"You've been really strong these past few days. I appreciate it."

I don't know what to say to that, so I don't say anything at all.

The car finally jerks to a stop in the four-car driveway of their massive house. It's a two-story monolith of rich, coffee-colored brick, and dark, ink-blot windows. The grass is perfectly manicured and lines a long, graveled path to the front door.

Janus kills the engine. Cherice opens her door first, and then the two of them are climbing out of the car. If I don't get out of this car, none of this is real. I follow their lead reluctantly, tugging my bags onto my shoulders.

"Oh no." Janus takes my suitcase from me and carries it up to the house without another word.

I'm not prepared for how quiet and gloomy their house is, even after they start flipping lights on. Something about the high ceilings makes me feel like this house is going to swallow me whole.

Cherice goes straight upstairs without a word, but Janus lingers in the foyer with me. He doesn't look much different from the last time I saw him. He looks like my dad. I stare down at my shoes. It used to be comforting that I could look into my uncle's face, and see all the things he shared with my father: the same wide, flat nose; the same rich, dark skin. Now, it feels like the universe is playing some sick joke on me.

"You're in the guest room," he says, his voice low. "Well, not the guest room anymore."

"Thanks."

We climb the stairs in silence and then the long stretch of hallway to the empty, bland room that now belongs to me. There's nothing on the walls. The only furniture filling the room is the massive, king-sized bed in the middle, a desk and vanity pushed up against the wall, and a TV. Janus sets my bags down by the door, but I don't bother retrieving them.

As soon as I sit on the bed, my chest caves in. There's a million tons of pressure right above my heart, pressing down like something wants to bury me in a sinkhole.

And thankfully, Janus says nothing.

He nods once before leaving the room, shutting the door behind him. I listen as his footsteps recede down the hall until they're quiet. Something hitches in my chest—hot and brutal. No matter where I go—death always finds me.

This is it, I'm thinking. *I'm going to die.*

But it's worse than that. It's worse than anything I could ever imagine. And as much as I beg and plead, I don't die.

CHAPTER TWO

FIVE YEARS AGO, MY FATHER DECIDED that Thanksgiving dinner was going to be a two-person affair. I was old enough to remember the smell of my grandmother's house, when we'd all gather for dinner. Her and Grandpa, Janus and Aunt Cherice. The twins too, back when they were here. The memories are spotty, but on a good day, I can still see the massive spread of ham, collard greens, and dressing laid out on a long dining table. In my mind, the globs of butter melting against Grandma's homemade yeast rolls were like dollops of sunshine, cut straight out of the sky. When she'd bring out the massive saucer of canned cranberry sauce, it felt like we were in the presence of some gelatinous god.

For a long time, it was really hard when the holidays rolled around. I knew I'd never experience those moments again. There were too many pieces missing, and my father couldn't be persuaded to change his mind. He was stubborn like that. Eventually, Thanksgiving regained some of its color. It couldn't come close to the same warmth from those early memories, but it was enough to sustain the two of us. We learned how to cook together, even though neither of us could ever get anything to taste like my grandmother's. There were no more big house parties, and the holes in our family were too deep to plug, but we bridged all the gaps as best we could.

I wake up to the sound of Cherice vacuuming outside my door. The clock on the nightstand reads 8:45 am. I can't remember the last time I knew what time it was.

I close my eyes again. I'd been dreaming. Something about a field of bright, yellow honeysuckle, spreading out for miles and miles around me. They towered above my head like giants and caught the sun in their velvety, green hands.

Then, memory.

When I open my eyes again, fifteen minutes have gone by, and sleep still hasn't come for me. I reach blindly for my phone before dragging it off the nightstand. July is almost over, but not without a fight. It's been daylight for four hours, and the sun won't be setting anytime soon.

Pale slats of light spill into my room, casting scattered bits of rainbow across the carpet. I throw off my sheets and crouch down beside the window, watching specks of dust float by in a lazy river of light. The air is warm against my knuckles, like something's trying to hold my hand. I pull it back and stumble into the bathroom.

My reflection shocks me. Whoever this girl is, she shouldn't be here. She's not me. She looks haggard and defeated, like she's just been crushed by some terrible adversary. I tug on one of my twists and catch a whiff of my armpit.

"Fine," I mumble, starting the shower.

I root around in my bag for the toiletries I packed: a large bottle of leave-in conditioner, my moisturizing shampoo, and a wide-toothed comb. I can't remember the last time I washed my hair or exactly how long these twists have been in. They were already two weeks old when I pinned them up for Dad's funeral.

Steam fills the bathroom like fog. I peel my clothes off and step into the shower. My joints ache. I scrub myself clean with the expensive body wash Cherice keeps in the once-guest bath, now mine. Then, I untwist my hair and massage conditioner into my scalp. I work through the knots slowly, until the tub is speckled with clumps of dark curls.

When I'm done, I wash my hair and dry myself in front of the mirror. As the steam clears, my hair frames my face like a halo. I don't look like my father's daughter, not like this. I used to sit in front of the mirror for hours, trying to work out what my mother might have looked like. She was the greatest mystery of my life, and then I stopped caring. As much as I try not to, I search for her now. Dad never kept any pictures. He never even told me her name. Whenever I asked him about her, he always just told me that she had to go away. Nothing else. Ever.

I push away from the vanity and pad into my room. I don't bother unpacking. I just pick clean clothes out of my luggage and tug them on. Some part of me considers climbing back into bed, but my hair's wet. For better or worse, I'm locked into this now.

I sit at the vanity with a bottle of conditioner and a tub of green styling gel. It takes three hours to work through my hair: first detangling, then carefully parting gridded lines with the pointed handle of a comb. By the time I've woven my hair into fresh twists, both of my hands are cramping.

Something about being clean and fresh makes me avoid my bed now. For two weeks, it had held me like a cocoon as the days passed. I felt so safe there, sheltered in the sheets, but that's over. I can't rot in bed forever. Not really.

Downstairs, Cherice and Janus sit quietly in the living room with the TV off. Janus thumbs through a massive book with a faded cover. When he sees me, he closes the volume, his eyes flaring in surprise.

"Hey, you're up," he says. "I like the hair."

"Thanks."

Cherice looks up from the loveseat, knitting needles in hand. There's a red hue to her eyes, like she just stopped crying.

"It looks nice," she says, her voice weak. "Are you hungry?"

I squint at the wall. When was the last time I ate? Before the funeral? At one of the gas stations we stopped at on the way here? I can't remember. In fact, I can't even really remember the funeral, much less the days that preceded it. Only bits and pieces: the sound of something falling downstairs, my father's lifeless body sprawled out in our kitchen. Things get murky after that. All I remember after finding him are the stark white walls of a hospital room.

"No," I tell them. "I think I need some fresh air. I've been inside too much. Can I take the car?"

Janus's smile is weary. "I think that's a good idea." He digs around in his pocket and pulls out a bundle of keys. "You can drive right?"

"Yeah."

He raises an eyebrow. "Are you sure? You have a license?"

"Yes, I have a license. I've been driving since I was fourteen."

Dad didn't really believe in prolonging experiences. By fourteen, I'd already learned how to handle myself on the freeway. It only took two attempts, and the right front side of my Dad's bumper. It was a shame, though. He loved that car.

"All right." He tosses me the keys. "You should drive around town. See it in the daylight."

That strikes me as the last thing I want to do, but it's not like I had a plan to begin with. "Thanks."

"Are you sure you aren't hungry?" Cherice asks.

"I'm sure. I'll see you later."

By the time I'm out of the house, I already regret doing this. It's hot, but not nearly as hot as I'm used to. It should be nice, comforting. It's neither.

CHAPTER THREE

ON THE LONG, WINDING BACK ROAD that leads into town, dense forest rushes past me, smearing the world in streaks of green paint. The sun is high and bold and rains down shards of gold light through breaks in the trees. No one drives past me. No one drives behind me. It's just me, and this car, and each groove in the asphalt, rattling beneath the tires.

It's as much beauty as New River is willing to give me. When the trees give way and a small, dust-coated town comes into view, it loses all its luster to an inglorious flood of memory. Austin was home, sure, but New River is different. I was born here. I took my first steps here. I can still map out the route to my childhood home but the thought of it painfully tugs at my heart.

Everything changed after we moved. Austin took me into its arms and that was that, but I think there'll always be a part of me that belongs to this tiny, quiet town. I lived here until I was twelve, until we had a funeral one day and buried four people. Those losses should make being here more painful, like the twist of a knife. Somehow, instead, they warm me like a lantern and lead me right to Mercy Park.

The car stops before I can really think about it. At first, the door feels too heavy to open, then a memory appears: sometime in October, when the park was full of pumpkins. I see a man on a horse pulling a cartful of hay, but I can't remember how the hay felt against my skin, or even the lurch of the cart over all the fallen leaves. Maybe I hadn't ridden it after all.

Finally, I push the door open and step out. Thankfully, the park is deserted, except for the trees and a shallow creek that cuts them right down the middle. I take steps over a bridge I remember; water gurgles beneath my feet. On the other side of the bridge, a hiker's trail disappears into a wall of dense foliage. I sit on a bench a few feet away from the trail's open mouth.

The creek trickles past beside me, gurgling over a bed of rocks. Mercy Park is the only thing that's bigger than I remember. All around me, the trees tower like a halo of gleaming emerald. The sun sits right above the horizon, beaming like the eye of God. In my head, the wind catches around me, and I leave New River behind. I leave the earth and bathe in the cosmic rays of outer space. The only thing I wonder is if it'd be far enough away. Maybe if I go beyond Saturn, beyond the Kuiper Belt. Past Andromeda's spiraling arms, and into the cold, unforgiving embrace of deep space.

"Can I sit?"

A boy's voice pulls me back to Earth. He's tall and dark-haired, with grim, ocean-blue eyes.

I shrug. "Sure."

"Thanks." He sits at the opposite end of the bench with his backpack between his knees. He looks like we could be the same age. "You waiting on someone?"

I stare at the trees again. "No."

"Oh. Are you new here?" He asks. "I don't think I've seen you before."

"Sort of. I just moved back."

He throws out his arms in a lazy gesture of showmanship. "Well, welcome back to the place where nothing ever happens. Ever."

The dry mirth in his tone makes me smile. "I don't know. You still have elections."

"They're boring." He shrugs.

"Prom?"

"Boring," he says.

"Well, I guess I won't bother then."

Silence. Something scampers along in the woods to my right, rustling underbrush.

"You're starting at the high school?" he asks.

I nod. My father is dead, and I still have to worry about graduating. It seems so needlessly cruel.

"Senior?"

"Yep." I say flatly.

He snorts. "I feel you. Although, upside, nobody really cares here. Most people don't even finish junior year."

"Seriously?"

"Yeah. They go into family businesses. Live with their parents or right down the street," he says. "It's a pretty popular track."

"I think I'd rather blow my brains out."

His laughter flings from tree to tree. "You'd be very surprised. That's not really a popular sentiment around here."

"Yeah, I figured. I guess I just don't get it." I finally look at him. He's watching me with an intent curiosity.

"It's nothing really. It's the path of least resistance, but this place sucks. I'd rather take the resistance."

I turn back to the trees, smiling. "You're very optimistic."

He snorts. "So I've been told. I think it's my fatal flaw."

A moment of silence hangs between us.

"So what's your name?" he asks.

I shrug again, even though it's not that kind of question. "What's yours?"

"Roman," he laughs. "I think it's your turn again."

"I'm Ophelia. Nice to meet you, Roman."

"It's nice to meet you too, Ophelia."

More voices sound on the other side of the bridge. Four figures walk in from the parking lot. A boy with shoulder-length locs runs after another with golden hair as he races across the bridge. Roman points at them smiling, "That's Baxter and Cassius." The two girls following them—one with waist-length box braids, the other with caramel-colored skin—shake their heads, whispering something that sends them into fits of laughter.

"Roman tell him I'm right," the boy with gold hair says as he shoves against the boy with locs. "I'm always right. Tell him I'm right."

Roman frowns. "A, right about what? And B, Cass, I can't in good conscience lie to that degree on your behalf."

"I told you." The dark-skinned boy taunts.

Cass rolls his eyes. "Okay, but really this time. If Bruce Banner were to lose control of the Hulk under extreme conditions, *and* he just so happened to be in South Dakota, there's no way SHIELD could enact a contingency in enough time to save Mount Rushmore. Baxter thinks I'm full of shit, but you know what, good riddance. No one needs that thing anyway."

Roman blinks. "Are you having a stroke?"

"That's what I said." Baxter throws up his hands. "SHIELD is the most powerful government agency in the world. They have an anti-Hulk satellite. He's done."

Cass rolls his eyes. "There's nothing wrong with being wrong, Baxter."

The other boy's expression is smug. "As long as you can accept it, that's fine by me."

"Would you two please shut up?" says the first girl, as both girls cross the bridge. "You can't do this again. Not today."

"It does get exhausting," Roman says.

Baxter scoffs, jerking his head back. "Whose side are you on?"

"Olivia's," Roman says, laughing. "You guys can't seriously drag this out for another two months."

The caramel-colored girl at Olivia's side throws her head back in exhaustion. "Like why can't you argue about climate change . . . or the Silver Surfer?"

Cass scoffs. "We're already on an irreversible course toward planetary annihilation. And nobody cares about the Silver Surfer."

Baxter shakes his head. "Can't argue with that logic."

"Oh guys, this is Ophelia." Roman points in my direction. I freeze. "She's new here."

I offer them a half-hearted wave. Olivia waves back, and the girl behind her inserts, "I'm Alessia."

"I'm Baxter. 'Sup."

"Nice to meet you. I'm Cassius."

"Hi." I try to smile. "Nice to meet you guys."

There's a pregnant pause. Something in the air is alive.

"So." Cassius rubs his hands together, his eyes full of mischief. "You wanna go jump off a cliff?"

Even before he explains himself, I've already said yes. I'm not sure why. Maybe it's because beyond leaving the house and sitting on this bench, I hadn't really planned anything else.

Before I know it, I'm in the back seat of Alessia's minivan, shoved between Cassius and a smudged, tiny half-window, with Slipknot playing the whole way there. Roman sits up front with Alessia. Their conversation gets drowned out by the sound of Olivia and Baxter howling about the old sandwich they found under the middle seat. Cassius takes it all in with me, that glint of mischief still shining in his eyes. I think it might just be how his face looks.

"So when did you move in?" he asks.

"About two weeks ago." A cold shadow rips through me, but I try to ignore it.

"What made you decide to move to the shittiest hunk of nothing in the American Midwest?"

I shrug. "The scenery. I'm a huge fan of tumbleweeds."

"Okay." He rolls his eyes. " We don't even have those."

"I saw like seventy-eight of them on the drive in."

He laughs. "That's a really specific number."

"Mm-hmm. I counted."

It's not easy to see through such a tiny window, but the longer we drive, the thicker the trees get. It's another thirty minutes before the old van finally creaks to a stop. When we get out, the sky is a network of powder-blue veins tracing a crooked map above our heads. The trees tower like ancient green watchmen. At the clearing's north side, a tiny, wooden sign announces that we're five miles out from the "Leap of

Faith." I don't like the sound of that, and to my horror that's exactly where Baxter starts leading us.

I fall in line beside Roman. He doesn't talk, so I can hear everything—the crunch of stone and bark beneath our feet, the chatter of birdsong curling through the trees. Somewhere ahead of us, a river rushes by. As we get closer, it becomes overwhelming until we're all staring down the open face of a jagged, moss-speckled cliff. The trees break away on either side of it, revealing a massive, yawning chasm. It's not a river down below, but one of the largest lakes I've ever seen. The water is clear cobalt. I'm terrified.

"Absolutely not," I say, but everyone else is already taking off their shoes and socks.

Cassius laughs at me. "You can't say we weren't up front."

"I don't even have a swimsuit."

"You don't need one," Roman tells me. He shrugs off his jacket to reveal a black muscle tank underneath. "Imagine how much we limit ourselves by thinking we need swimsuits."

Again, if I weren't so terrified, I'd be in awe.

"Yep." Baxter says, "Sometimes all you need is grit, courage, and a pair of jeans."

I shake my head. "You're insane. There's no way. We're too high up."

Alessia shrugs. "It's okay, Ophelia. We do this all the time. It's completely safe."

"That's not comforting."

"Don't worry," Roman says. "You don't have to jump if you don't want to. We're gonna come back up for our shoes anyway, so we can come get you."

"Although," Cassius interjects, dragging out the word. "You'd have a lot of fun and be much, much cooler if you jumped."

"Are you peer pressuring me?"

His smile is too wide to be anything but sincere. "Is it working?"

"No." I turn away from the cliff, crossing my arms. "No it's not.

"Shame." He shrugs and kicks his shoes back toward the tree line. That smile is still there, but the mischief in his eyes is coupled with something else, something wilder. "Well, see ya."

With that, Cassius hurls himself off the edge of the cliff. The others cheer, but my stomach drops to my feet and I cover my eyes. I count ten seconds between him jumping and the sound of his body hitting the water. He howls the whole way.

Only a few seconds after he lands, Alessia takes a running leap and swan dives, her arms out to slice the air. The cheering grows louder as she sinks into the water. I watch her this time. The jump looks as bad as I think it will, but down below, in the water, the two of them bubble with triumph. And no one else seems deterred.

Olivia jumps after her, screeching the whole way down, and then Baxter. He takes a running leap too and lands four somersaults before his body hits the water. He comes up sweeping locs out of his face, his mouth wide open in laughter.

"Yo!" He shouts up the mountain. "Let's go, Hartfield."

Roman rolls his eyes, but even he can't conceal his excitement. Whatever heaviness he carried in the park is gone now. The light in his eyes is electric.

"Hey," he says. "No one's gonna make you jump if you don't want to, but it really is like flying."

Before I can ask him what he means, he's already jumped off the cliff. I watch him enter the water too, his body coiled into a cannonball. He comes up for air, cheering, as water drips down his face. The others crowd around him, their voices like a roaring army against the rounded walls of the mountain.

Like flying.

I'm an idiot, so I take off my shoes and then my socks. I kick them a few feet away before finally turning to face the cliff. Somehow, even though I know I'm going to jump off of my own free will, I'm still afraid of falling.

"Oh shit, she's gonna jump," Baxter shouts from the water. He starts chanting. "Jump! Jump! Jump!"

A part of me seriously wants to step away from the edge and apologize for being a coward, but another wants to fly. It's stupid. It's so stupid, but they're cheering, and for the first time in two weeks, I'm not rotting in that damn bed.

I don't let myself think. I close my eyes and jump.

Through the wind. Past the cliff's grasping, clay red arms. Over the chasm and the wide yawn of its mouth. And just for a second, as my body plummets to the water, it does feel like flying.

CHAPTER FOUR

By THE TIME SUMMER ENDS, I'VE leapt from the cliff sixteen times.

I wasn't expecting that day in the woods to lead to more. I've never been the type to make friends easily, but there are exceptions to any rule. I don't know if friends is the right word for it, but it's the only one I have. Who else shows up to your house every day in a creaky, old van at the crack of dawn and won't take no for an answer?

On the last day of summer, instead of returning to the cliff, Alessia drives out to a junkyard on the edge of town. Past the splintered old black perimeter gate, dunes of gravel rise to the sky in ash-gray heaps. A whirling wind calls throughout the Yard, filling it with sound. It's clear that no one's been here for a while. The main building is a block of old wood and ugly, chipped paint. A few feet to the right, at the mouth of the junkyard, is a fire pit that looks recently used.

"Maverick," Baxter and Cassius laugh at the same time.

They run off down a gravel-lined path and come back carrying two logs each. After setting them down around the used fire pit, they retreat back the way they came.

"Ophelia!" Olivia pats the space beside her on one of the logs, but Roman comes rushing in front of me, whining.

He pokes his bottom lip out. "No, I need to show her the thing."

"What thing?" I ask.

His eyes are almost childlike. "You'll see. Come on."

We leave Olivia and Alessia by the fire, and Roman leads the way through the Yard. It seems impossible that something can be this big and so empty. The only light comes from the row of streetlights lining the perimeter, but they flicker as we walk past, casting the Yard in and out of darkness. Roman and I keep pace in silence.

It's only when we get to the very back of the Yard, where the perimeter gate comes back into view, that I see it: a rickety old water tower, draped in darkness.

I shake my head firmly, crossing my arms. "Absolutely not."

"You gotta get a new line." Staring up at the massive tower, he grabs hold of the ladder and starts pulling himself up.

"You're insane."

His laughter drifts down to meet me. "Of course I am. I'm climbing the water tower by myself. Get up here."

"Is this legal?"

Another laugh, but nothing else. He's already halfway up the tower and I still haven't made up my mind. It doesn't look secure at all, but aside from some light creaking, the tower holds beneath him. He pulls himself to his feet at the top and pumps his fist, his voice filling the air.

"Why do you people like climbing things and jumping from high places?" I shout. "Does that not seem strange to you?"

He shrugs. "It's a rush. Rushes are nice."

"That's because you're an adrenaline junkie. I'm not."

He laughs again. "Okay, but do you like looking at pretty lights?"

"Of course. What self-respecting person doesn't like pretty lights?"

"Then get up here," he says, "It's the best view in town."

In the distance, I can see the others laughing by the campfire. The smart decision would be to return to them and let him have the water tower all to himself. But he's leaning over the edge of the platform, his eyes hazy and dazzling.

I sigh and set one reluctant hand to the base of the ladder. Roman cheers me on as I make my way up. When I get to the halfway point, I know I've gone too far. There's an impossible distance between me and the earth.

"Hey!" Roman calls, "just don't look down."

And of course, on cue, I look down. By the time I reach the top, my back is slick with sweat.

He pumps his fist. "You did it!"

"Shut up. Now where's the—*oh* . . ."

My breath catches. The tower's platform overlooks New River in all its sleeping glory. The forest is a castle of shadow and foliage. In the distance, an ocean of sparkling lights stretches from east to west like a wall of fire.

"What's that?"

"Fargo," he says. "They haven't used this tower in forty years, but it's the best place to be at night."

"No kidding. You can see everything."

His expression is smug. "I told you. And I'm not an adrenaline junkie. I just like adventure."

"Right, so like I said."

He rolls his eyes, smirking. "Whatever. I'm glad you like it."

"Thanks for showing me." I really do mean it.

After watching a shooting star fall across the sky, we climb back down the tower. Back at the campfire, they pass around bottles of Bud Light, chilled from an ice bath in the red cooler by Baxter's feet. He offers me one, but I wave my hand.

"Beer's disgusting. It tastes like dog piss."

He quirks one of his brows. "How would you know what dog piss tastes like?"

"I don't," I shrug, "but I know I'm right."

Olivia laughs and reaches around him to pull out a blue wine cooler. I take it from her and sit at Roman's side. His eyes look like balls of deep blue flame in the firelight, and they're still filled with that childlike wonder.

"So what do you think about New River now?" Alessia asks.

"Oh, easily the worst place I've ever lived in," I say.

She snorts. "I thought the same thing when I moved here five years ago. I haven't really been convinced otherwise."

"Hey wait, it's not all bad." Baxter casts his arms wide, gesturing to the broader world around us. "In a town where nothing happens, the possibilities are endless."

Olivia chugs the last of her cooler and reaches around him for another one. "Thank you, Langston Hughes."

He bumps her with his shoulder, but he's laughing.

For two weeks, I've been able to escape the oppressive cloud of grief. At least when I'm with them. When I'm alone, that shadow creeps in again, hungry. Listening to them laugh around the fire makes me feel safe. It's a welcome reprieve, but I know it's only temporary.

"Oh! I wanted to do something." Roman pulls another bottle from the cooler and raises it between us. My chest tightens when he gestures to me with the neck of the bottle. "To a new friend. And to the last summer."

Alessia laughs. "Corny. So, so very corny."

"On most occasions, yes, but I think Roman has a point this time," Baxter says. "Next week's senior year. After that, we graduate, and then there's no more summer. It's just life."

Roman looks pleased. "Exactly, which is why we should remember it."

Olivia shrugs and raises her wine cooler. Reluctantly, Alessia follows her lead. Then Baxter, Cass, and me too. It's not ideal at all, but this is the last time summer gets to mean something. Our last night before staring into a world of infinite possibility. I'm not sure what the world looks like for me anymore. For so long, it was a life I thought I'd share with my father. I'm not unrealistic. I knew that at some point I'd have to lose him, but I never thought it would be so soon. I'm not ready.

We finish our drinks and then Baxter gets an angry text from his father. He kisses Olivia goodbye before leaving in a hurry. Then she has to go too and it's only the four of us. Cassius looks out on the dark still shadows surrounding us, something in his eyes I haven't seen before. They normally glitter with mischief; this is something darker.

"Have you guys gotten your schedules yet?" Alessia asks, checking her phone.

"No." Cass's voice is flat and distant.

"Yeah, I got mine," Roman says. "When did you pick your classes? Was it after the deadline?"

"Yeah." She tosses her phone into her bag. "Don't tell me I have to pick it up the day of."

"If it was after the deadline, then I'm pretty sure you do. What about you, Ophelia?"

"Yeah, I'm getting mine day of," I say. "I'm what's considered an 'emergency transfer.'"

Alessia laughs. "I'm sure you'll love it." She picks up her bag in one, swift motion. "All right, guys. I'm heading home. If I stay up too late I'll hate myself in the morning."

"See you later," Roman says.

"See you," I call.

Cassius is silent, his eyes far away. Alessia bends down and waves a hand in front of his face. "Hello? Anybody home?"

He blinks before really looking at her. "Shit, my bad. I'll see you later, Leese."

"Are you okay?" she asks. " You've got this whole 'Shining' thing going on."

"Yeah. Yeah, I'm fine." He doesn't even sound like he's convinced himself. "I'll walk you out. I'm leaving too."

"Boo!" Roman hisses, but Cass doesn't seem to care.

He grabs his bag and follows Alessia to the front gate, something frenzied in his step. Cass never seems disturbed by anything, but tonight it's like he's seen a ghost.

"That's weird," Roman says.

We sit around the fire a bit longer, before pouring our drinks onto the flames. Roman kills off the dying fire with a heap of rocks, and we walk back through the gate side by side. It's only then in the dark it feels creepy.

"Thanks for showing me the tower," I tell Roman.

He waves me off. "You're welcome. Any time."

"So, what do you think was wrong with Cass?"

He shrugs. "I don't know. I wouldn't worry too much though. It's just Cass."

Driving me home, something in his eyes seems disturbed.

"You okay?" I ask.

"What? Yeah, yeah." He rubs his eyes furiously. "I haven't been sleeping well. Nightmares."

"About what?"

He shrugs, but the shadow across his face won't leave. "It's stupid."

"Probably, but I still want to know." My chest warms at the sound of his laughter, even if it's strained.

"I don't know. It feels so real," he says. "Sometimes there's a guy there, sometimes I'm by myself, but in every dream I'm lost at sea."

The long drive back is quiet. The house is even quieter.

That night, I dream of a lightning storm.

CHAPTER FIVE

New River High is nothing short of spectacular. It is also a huge waste of money. The city's only high school is a towering mausoleum secluded in the swell of a tiny forest about thirty minutes out from town. Three brick buildings stand watch as New River's student population returns for another year.

When Cherice comes to a stop in the drop-off line, I almost tell her to turn around and take me home. This feels wrong. I was supposed to graduate in Austin, with my father in the audience, cheering me on from his seat. I don't want this milestone if I don't get to experience it with him.

Alessia's waiting on the steps. When she waves, I wave back.

"Is that one of your friends?" Cherice asks. Her voice hasn't picked up since we buried my dad, and it's obvious she hasn't been sleeping. The circles beneath her eyes have only gotten darker these past few weeks.

"Yeah. That's Alessia."

"She seems sweet. You should invite her to the house sometime."

I quirk an eyebrow at her. "Really?"

"Yeah. It's good that you have friends here. I hope it makes things easier."

I watch her drive away with a lump in my throat. Having friends does make things easier, but only when I'm not thinking about how hard things are. I'd managed to make it all the way through breakfast without thoughts of my dad, but that's as lucky as I get today. Already his shadow hangs at my back, matching each of my steps with his own.

"Uh-oh," Alessia says.

I frown at her. "What?"

"Sometimes you get this look, like you're somewhere else. Is everything okay?"

"Why wouldn't it be?" I watch cars turn into the parking lot to avoid her searching gaze. "This is the most exciting day of my academic career."

She rolls her eyes. "Right. Very convincing."

"Thanks. Hey, show me where the office is?" I ask.

Cement steps lead up to the school's entrance. It quickly becomes apparent that there's more building than necessary. The halls are wide, with polished wood and humming fluorescents. Voices clatter into clouds of echo as we walk to the front office, which is down at the end of the main hall, behind a set of glass, double doors. Alessia scans her student pass to get in.

A woman with a blond pixie cut talks into a telephone behind the front desk. She waves a bangled hand when we come in, gesturing for us to wait. We sit along the wall in padded maroon chairs. The office at my old school wasn't nearly as big as this one, even though they had four more secretaries and at least four times the student population. It wasn't as nice either. Everything in this office is either expensive dark mahogany or gleaming marble.

I gesture to the creme walls around me. "Very fancy."

"We had a gas main blow up a few years ago," Alessia says. "The school got the worst of it so they rebuilt."

"Oh god. That's terrible."

She shrugs. "It happened in the middle of the night. No school for the rest of the year isn't a bad trade off."

"How can I help you?" The woman behind the desk calls after hanging up the phone. She looks older than my uncle, and her perfume smells like something my grandma would've worn. Something sweet and heavy.

"Hi, I'm Ophelia Johnson. I came to get my schedule."

"Oh yeah. I heard about you." She roots around a filing cabinet for a few seconds before pulling out a manila folder. My name is scrawled along the label in purple ink. "This should have your full schedule and a map of the building. Welcome to New River."

The map is impossible to read, but thankfully Alessia helps me find my locker and my first class. It's English, on the second floor at the end of another long hallway.

"All right, here's your stop," she says, clapping a hand against the doorpost.

It's my worst nightmare. As soon as I walk into the classroom, Mr. Fuller locks eyes on me like a shark catching the scent of blood.

"Ms. Johnson," he greets, startling me. "Welcome to New River."

"Thanks."

"Come on. Tell us a little about yourself."

I stammer my way through an introduction, before taking a seat at the back. It's more or less the same introduction for every class until lunch. By then, I never want to say another word again but as soon as I step into the hallway, there's Roman.

"Hey," he says. I ignore the flock of butterflies swarming around in my chest. "What are you doing on the chemistry floor?"

I look around confused. Chemistry isn't even on my schedule. "This is the chemistry floor?"

He points up at the ceiling, where a black sign labeled "chemistry" dangles above our heads.

I press a hand to my forehead. "Why do you need a whole chemistry floor?"

"The mayor insisted." He shrugs. "Are you trying to find the cafeteria?"

"No?"

He rolls his eyes and cuts out in front of me, smirking. "Well, if you happen to change your mind, I'm heading there now."

"And I will just follow you for no reason."

The cafeteria is on the first floor. Four steam tables line the left wall of the room. Blackboard signs advertise meal options in blue bubble letters. Roman and I join a long line curving along the cafeteria's left side for chicken tenders and mac and cheese.

"So, how's the food here? Should I manage my expectations?"

"Actually, it's pretty good," he says. "Miss Sibil is an angel. Literally sent from the gods."

"Really?"

"Yeah. She used to work at the elementary school. Always gave me free snacks." A warm fondness washes over his face. "She's very sweet."

"That is sweet," I tell him. "I remember the elementary school. I had Ms. Thomas for—what was it—third grade."

He laughs. "That's crazy. I had Ms. Gause, right next door. When'd you move?"

"Middle school." My heart clenches. I ignore it. "What about you? You've been here your whole life. What's next?"

He lets out a labored breath. "Well, I've applied to Vanderbilt and NYU. Haven't really decided on the safeties yet."

"Impressive." I raise my eyebrows. "What major?"

He shrugs. "I'm undecided. My dad thinks I should go into Law, at least for the money. That just seems kind of soul crushing, so I was thinking either philosophy or lit."

"You know, being unemployed until the day you die really isn't that bad."

He laughs. "Yeah, he doesn't feel that way. He thinks it's dumb."

"He's a lawyer and he thinks philosophy and literature are dumb? Is he any good?"

He rolls his eyes. "He represents the corporate machine. If somebody so much as slips in a Target, he's their guy."

"Ah. I see."

At the end of the line, we both take ceramic blue plates that are hot to the touch. The steam wafting into my face carries the scent of fried tenders.

"So when is it my turn?" he asks.

"Your turn to what?"

"Interrogate you." He nudges me with his plate. "I don't know anything about you."

"You're a lucky man."

This time, he doesn't laugh. "I don't think so. I think I'd be luckier if I knew what your favorite color was. Or how you like your coffee."

"Maybe." I shrug. "Maybe not."

The others have already claimed a table in the corner of the room, on the right side of the cafeteria, but Cassius is nowhere in sight.

"Is he out in the field?" Roman asks.

Olivia cuts into a chicken tender with a fork and knife. "No. He went home."

"On the first day?"

Baxter nods. His expression is almost grim. "He said he felt sick during third period, and he's been acting weird since yesterday. I don't think he's sleeping well."

Roman cuts a look at me before lowering his eyes. "Does it have something to do with James?"

"I don't know," Olivia says, and then, quieter, "probably."

After that, everyone goes quiet.

"Who's James?" I ask, looking around.

Alessia swallows and sets down her fork. "Cass's step-dad. He's an asshole, so Cass doesn't really like talking about him. Some days are worse than others."

No one else volunteers to explain any further. I don't pry.

Eventually, Baxter and Alessia start arguing about carbon dating, while Roman makes the case for why he should know my favorite color until the bell rings, ending our lunch period. By the end of the day, I've finally caved and told him it's purple. All things considered, he really wouldn't make a terrible lawyer. He seems satisfied and volunteers to drive me home.

"That's sweet, but it's really okay." I tell him. "My aunt's probably on her way already."

"Okay. Can I wait with you then?"

Butterflies again. I look down at my shoes, my cheeks warm. "Yeah, sure. I mean, if you want."

We talk until my aunt pulls up ten minutes later, looking more restless than this morning. She tries to smile at Roman when he introduces himself, but the strain around her lips betrays her.

On the drive home, Cherice's smile becomes a bit more genuine. "Who's Roman?"

I roll my eyes. "Nobody."

She doesn't look convinced.

"Okay. He's a friend," I tell her.

She makes an odd shimmying motion with her shoulders. I think she's supposed to be dancing. "A friend that likes you?" she probes.

"No. He's just nice."

"Right. Yep. I said the same thing about your uncle," she says. I groan into my seatbelt. I think she laughs, before getting serious again. "Okay. I wanted to talk to you about something."

I brace myself for the worst. "Okay."

"Your uncle and I are having a few friends over tonight. I don't want to tell you to stay out of the way or anything, but these guys are a bit . . . strange, and I don't want them to freak you out."

Well. That's not weird at all.

"I got you, Aunt Cherice," I tell her. "I have homework anyway."

"Already?"

"Already."

I shudder like I always do before entering the house, but today it has a kind of warmth to it. It smells like cooked beef and spices, and the lights are on. In the kitchen, the table is set with ten plates and ten royal blue napkins. Janus mans the stove with a "kiss the cook" apron tied around his waist. He looks proud of it.

"Check it." He gestures to the apron with a wooden spoon. "I got this baby for fifty cents at the Bargain Mart. A steal right?"

"I don't think you can steal something they were trying to get rid of. You sure it wasn't free?"

"Hater." He waves me off with a wooden spoon. "Did your aunt tell you about tonight?"

"Yep. I'm incognito."

"Thanks, Ophelia. It'll only be a few hours. I promise."

"I can still eat dinner, right?" I ask.

He pretends to think. "Well, no actually."

Then he smiles. We both laugh at the same time, and it feels good.

I do homework in the living room until Janus calls me in to take the heaping plate he made me. The table is loaded with platters of jasmine rice, grilled asparagus, and a pot of steaming beef tips. I'd forgotten how good Janus was at cooking. Cherice is another story.

Only a few minutes after I've finished eating, a car pulls up outside. I grab my stuff and sneak up the stairs. Before the house can fill with noise and bodies, I lock myself in my room to try to finish my homework. When I'm done, I get in the shower and start getting ready for bed. Going through the motions is enough to distract me, but eventually, unfortunately, curiosity gets the best of me.

By now, it's dark outside, but I can still see the row of cars parked in front of the house. They aren't regular cars. Each one of them is something sleek and expensive. Through my bedroom door, it's impossible to hear anything. I know I shouldn't. They'd been so nice about asking me to stay upstairs, but I can't ignore that voice in the back of my head anymore. What are they up to?

I give myself another two minutes to weigh my options before slowly pulling open my door. The floor creaks a little beneath me, so I slowly walk on the balls of my feet, until I get to the top of the stairs. I can hear voices now, but I can't make out what they're saying.

I step down until I'm just behind the wall. Light spills over the bottom step from a lamp in the living room, where they all must be sitting. I thought I heard laughing earlier, but I must have been imagining things. Whatever they're talking about, their voices are soft and urgent.

"It's unacceptable. We can't just take it. Not anymore. Not like this." The man's voice is harsh, like the edge of a serrated blade.

A woman chimes in. "I agree. They went too far this time."

"And it's not like we don't have the numbers. We could actually do something."

This time, I recognize Janus's voice. "And then what? Your daughters are next? Or Kenes's? Seriously, play it out for me. How does this end?"

"In blood."

My uncle scoffs. "So you do get it."

"No!" The other man's voice again. "Not ours. Not this time. They've taken too much. It won't be like that this time."

Cherice speaks. "Oh? Why not? The last time we felt all powerful and emboldened, I had to bury my children."

The silence in the room is painful. For a second, I'm afraid they can hear the sound of my breathing.

She continues, her voice trembling. "This wasn't a call to arms, Aaron. It's a warning. I know what you're thinking, and I'm telling you it won't work. You know that. Don't be stupid."

"Well somebody has to do something. Hell, if Jason were here, he would."

Janus's voice goes quiet with anger. "No, he wouldn't, and don't you ever presume to know what my brother would want. He moved across the country to escape this bullshit. You should consider doing the same. Be smart. Don't get yourself killed."

"*I* wouldn't do that, Janus."

"Man, what the hell are you trying to say?"

"Hey," the other woman interjects. "No one's saying anything. We're all on the same side here. But listen, first Ankippi, then Surias, and now Decatrae. These aren't isolated incidents. They're not rogues just trying to blow off a little steam. These attacks are organized. Someone's planning something."

I BACKTRACK TO MY ROOM AS quietly as possible, shutting my door with a soft click. Oh *god*. I've heard too much. I've heard too much, and I can't understand any of it. I don't even know who those people were, but they had Cherice and Janus terrified. That's one thing I'm sure of.

And that thing Cherice said about Iris and Irene—it sends dread through my spine.

We've had too many funerals. I was twelve, and middle school had become this new, horrid invention. I was home alone, doing homework, when my father came to break the news. I could tell something was wrong. Before he'd even spoken, the truth was already evident in the hard lines of his face. There'd been an accident, and there were no survivors. Not my grandparents. Not the twins.

But that's not what Cherice said last night. It was something else, something more sinister. And my father. Why were they talking about my father?

CHAPTER SIX

THANKFULLY, I'M SO CAUGHT UP IN my own head that
school flies by. Before I know it, I'm waiting on the steps with
Alessia and Baxter laughing behind me.

Olivia bumps me with her shoulder. "You're quiet."

"Sorry."

"No, it's nothing bad. You just seem like you've got something on your mind."

The secret meeting. The deaths in my family. And some
nameless, faceless "they," plotting something. I can't make
sense of any of it.

There are too many things that I cannot explain since
Dad died and I moved to New River. I thought it was just in
my head, but I'm becoming convinced that it's something
more than that.

"I guess I've just been dealing with a lot," I tell her. "I'm okay."

"Are you sure?" She asks.

"Positive." I try to smile. It doesn't work.

She presses her lips together. I think that has to be pity in
her eyes. "Okay. Just let me know if you need anything."

I'll totally do that. "Okay. Thanks."

"No problem." She waves. "I'll see you later."

I wave back. "See you."

Baxter waves at me from the end of the sidewalk, where she walks to meet him. They disappear into the parking lot before Alessia bumps past me.

"Hey, have you seen Cass today?" she asks.

I shake my head. "No. I didn't see him yesterday either."

"Yeah, I've been trying to call him, but he hasn't been answering."

"Who hasn't been answering?" Roman comes down the steps, his thumbs looped through the straps of his backpack.

"Cass," she tells him. "I've called him like six times today."

He pulls out his phone and scrolls through it. "Yeah, me too. He hasn't responded to any of my texts."

She shrugs. "I'll just go to his house."

"Wait, he didn't come to school today, either?" I ask.

Roman shakes his head. "No. Actually, I tried calling him last night, but he rushed me off the phone. He sounded nervous."

"That's not like him at all," Alessia says. "I'm gonna go check on him, all right?."

My phone dings. A message from Cherice:

Hey, could one of your friend's drop you off? We're in a meeting. Won't be home for a couple hours.

After the initial disappointment, a light bulb screws on in my brain. "Roman?"

"Yeah?"

"Would you mind taking me home today?"

"Of course." He pulls his keys out of his pocket and starts jingling them to a tune I don't recognize. "Leese, can you let me know what you find out?"

"Yep. I'll talk to you guys later."

Roman's car is at the back of the lot. It's an older, black Cadillac with warm leather seats. A strawberry-scented tree dangles from the rear-view mirror.

"Okay, so where am I taking you?" he asks.

"Green Groves."

"Oh! I knew a guy who lived there." He pulls out of the parking lot and onto the main road. "So, purple?"

I roll my eyes. "Yes. Lavender specifically. Why?"

"I'm just curious. What's so special about lavender?"

"Um . . ." The crushed lavender between the pages of my dad's books, the walls of my childhood bedroom. A dried-out stem, clutched between a set of tiny, brown hands. "I guess it's just pretty."

"Hmm." He glances at me. "You did the thing again."

"What thing?"

"You're a brooder," he says. "You brood."

I fold my arms, frowning. "I do not. I've never brooded. Not even once."

He laughs. "Whatever you say, Ophelia."

We pull up to my house twenty minutes later. Thankfully, the driveway is empty.

"Thanks, Roman. I appreciate it."

"No problem. I really don't mind at all."

And I think he really means it.

I watch his car leave the driveway and head back down the road we came.

Then I'm running. I don't know what I'm looking for, but I know I have to find it. I start downstairs, in the living room. If they were having a meeting, maybe someone dropped a memo. Then the kitchen, and the dining room, and the guest bathroom. Nothing.

I move upstairs to their bedroom. I start on Cherice's side, but it isn't until I'm looking through Janus's closet that something promising catches my eye. It's a thick book filled with hundreds of laminated photos. I recognize the man on the cover as my grandfather, about twenty-five years before his death. He's standing in front of a hot spring wearing an all-black jumpsuit. Something heavy but smudged dangles from his hip.

The label across the front of the photobook reads: THE 157TH BANQUET OF THE CURSED CHILDREN, 1986.

I sit on the floor at the foot of the bed with the book in my lap. I don't recognize most of the people. There are photos of men and women stopped in laughter, a table loaded with platters of food, a watch tower over the sea, and hundreds of people gathered in neat rows, dressed like my grandfather.

When I see my father's face, my chest goes ice cold. He's a kid in all of them, no older than twelve, but I'd recognize him anywhere. At any point in time. He's wearing the same all-black one-piece as everyone else, but it looks a bit baggier on him. There's an electric light in his eyes that I don't ever remember seeing when he was alive, even when he was smiling.

In one picture, he snarls at the camera, holding out a tiny, plastic sword. My grandma's in the photo too. She's standing behind him, her smile as wide and bright as the sun.

"Hey Nana," I whisper.

Janus is in the next one, only a little older than my dad. They're in each other's arms, smiling cheek to cheek.

I keep going through the photobook. Most of them are strangers, but my family pops up a lot. It's the last and final picture that makes my blood go cold. It's my grandfather, then a young man, standing on some kind of platform, over-looking a sea of black-clothed people. He's holding the sun, or at least that's what it looks like. The sword in his hand is full of light, and he aims it at the sky.

The label beneath is written: *House of the Cursed Children, 1986.*

CHAPTER SEVEN

At lunch, for the first time since the sun rose over this planet, our table is quiet. The lunchroom around us buzzes with conversation. It's easy to tune it all out with so many questions clogging my brain. I keep seeing my grandfather, standing over a sea of people with a sword in his hand. The light filling the blade. That's the image that's burned into my mind: that impossible light. There was no way they edited it, so where did it come from?

We're down two people today. Baxter, Roman, and Olivia sit around the table, picking at lunches they won't eat. Cassius and Alessia are nowhere in sight. I even tried calling this morning, but neither answered. I hate to think that something terrible has happened.

In my dreams, a storm swelled above me, choked with lightning, the same dream I've been having for the past two weeks, beneath the same storm that brewed when that strange man from last time met me on the way to New River. It was nothing. Just my brain making things up. But that's only if it happens once.

I shove my tray away, trying to clear my thoughts. It only makes me think of last night's discovery.

Why would my uncle have this book in his closet? Furthermore, what are the real connections between my family and the people in those photos?

I pull out my laptop, even though I know there's no point. You can't research something that's not on the internet at all.

In a jolting motion, Baxter stands up from the table. He's sweating, and he doesn't look steady on his feet.

"You good?" Roman asks, his voice low. Like the day I met him, there's a storm in his eyes.

Baxter nods, but he looks confused. "Yeah. Yeah, I just need to . . ." He grabs his bag with trembling hands. "I'll catch you guys later."

Without saying goodbye, he turns to leave at a frenzied pace. Olivia's already getting up to follow him.

"I'll let you guys know what's up with him," she says. "And let me know if you hear anything from Cass or Alessia." Roman nods.

When she's gone, I go back to scrolling. The only articles I found about any sort of ancient library are about the Library of Alexandria. When I search, "House of the Cursed Children," all I get are Amazon links for kids's books. Nothing that looks like it could be connected to that photo-book, and nothing that explains this gaping cavern of uncertainty between me and my family.

Roman's voice startles me. "Who are the Cursed Children?"

I shut the laptop and shove it in my bag. "No one. Hey, what do you think's up with Cass and Leese?"

"I don't know. She said she was going to check on him yesterday, and now she's not here. I'm worried."

"This isn't like either of them, is it?" I ask.

"No, not at all. I mean Alessia will vanish for hours, sure, but you can just never, ever get rid of Cass. And even when she's gone, she usually checks in." He shakes his head. "This isn't normal. It's freaking me out."

He stares at the table, thinking, before letting out a sigh. "I actually did get in touch with Cass last night, but he told me not to say anything."

"Why?"

"He wasn't making any sense. He kept talking about ghosts. He said he was having nightmares, but he thought they were real."

And again I see the storm. The man. His ash-gray beard and the heavy, chiseled lines in his ancient face.

"Did he tell you what he saw?"

He shakes his head. "He wouldn't say it. He said I'd think he was crazy."

"Would you?"

His eyes are like a violent hurricane. "I'm not sure."

Roman drives me home again today. Another meeting. He doesn't seem to mind, but like lunch he's quiet. I don't like it. I don't like any of this.

"Are you feeling okay?" He asks.

His question catches me off guard. "Yeah, why wouldn't I be?"

"Just checking. It seems like everybody's off today," he says. "Earlier, Olivia told me that Baxter's refusing to talk to her, and now she doesn't feel good either."

"Is it flu season?"

He snorts, straight-faced. "That's funny."

"Seriously though, try not to worry too much."

"Do you mean that?"

I shrug. "I feel like it's good advice."

"Right."

Like yesterday, the driveway is empty. It feels like I should try to reassure him before I leave, but I don't know how to do that. Anything I say would be empty and disingenuous. How could I possibly convince him not to worry when there's obviously so much to worry about?

"I'll see you tomorrow," I tell him, because I can't think of anything else.

He smiles, but I can spot a fake a mile away. "Yeah. I'll see you."

I wait until he drives away before going inside. I sit in the living room to do my homework, but I can't focus. After barely finishing a study guide for calculus, curiosity gnaws me down to the bone. I've pulled out my phone and texted Cass before I even know I've decided to.

Roman said you were having nightmares. What do you see?

Twenty minutes pass. Between each minute, I'm checking my phone, but he hasn't said anything. I try calling. The line rings and rings, until I finally get his voicemail. I make it about ten more minutes before kicking my bag away. Cherice and Janus aren't back yet, and if their meeting runs as long as last time, I should have another hour. I run down the basement steps.

When my grandparents died, Dad didn't take anything from their house. Everything they owned got shipped up here in huge brown boxes. I find them piled in a corner at the very back of the basement, beneath an old, yellowed sheet. I can tell from the dust and cobwebs that no one's touched anything since they were brought here. That doesn't make sense either. I always hated that Dad wouldn't let us keep anything, but he'd never explain why, and I could never convince him. Why wouldn't you want to at least have one thing that belonged to your parents?

The first box I open is full of books: old, thick volumes with yellow pages. They're all stuck together and nearly impossible to read. The first is the story of Heracles, with the Nemean lion carved on the front cover. The next is about Theseus. The one after is about Atalanta.

I open a new box, this one wrapped in layers of duct tape. Metal clinks as I set it down on the floor. Inside, dull blades with dusty hilts pile on top of each other. Each blade is carved with the sigil of a rising sun, only one of them has my grandfather's name on it. It's a long, bronze dagger, with a roughly cut ruby helming the hilt. In my hands, it feels heavy and warm, even though it's been in this box for years.

It's at the bottom of the box that the sun-sigiled daggers disappear. These are marked in a language I can't read.

Like the first, I push this box to the side and keep going. One is full of jewels: rubies and emeralds and huge chunks of glittering diamond. Another box is nearly overflowing with pieces of fine gold. These look much older than both the books and the jewels. The words carved along the edges are in the same language as those engraved daggers. On each one of them, dead center, is the profile of a king.

I'm reaching for another box when my uncle shouts behind me. He comes in like a streak of shadow, standing between me and the boxes in the corner. I've never seen him like that. His chest heaves with each breath. That look in his eyes could be terror, but it could also be rage. Cherice comes in behind me, her hands trembling. That *is* terror, like I've done something I shouldn't have.

"What are you doing down here?" Janus demands. Standing over me, his anger is a blazing tower.

"I just wanted to look through Grandma's stuff. Why are you yelling at me?"

"Ophelia, no." Cherice's voice is nearly too quiet to hear. "No honey, you can't do that."

"Why?" I stand up to look her in the eye. "Why would you keep their stuff down here under a sheet?"

"Because nobody needs to touch this stuff. Ever!" Janus starts closing boxes and stacking them back up. "I don't want to catch you down here, again. You understand me?"

"No, I don't. What is this stuff?"

"None of your concern." He's stacking the boxes so violently it looks like he might throw them. "I mean it, Ophelia. Don't come down here again."

"Why not?"

Cherice answers in a brittle voice. "It's danger—"

"No!" Janus shouts. "You don't come down here because I said so, and because this is my goddamn house! And in my house, this area is off limits. End of story."

He drapes the sheet back over the boxes, and it's almost like no one ever opened them in the first place. But I did.

"Okay, fine. But what's the House of the Cursed Children? Who were you talking to the other night? What's going on?"

Cherice looks like she'll faint, but Janus only grows more furious. So furious that he goes still and his voice is dead calm.

"Don't, Ophelia. Don't ask. Don't go looking. I'm serious, and I'm saying that for your benefit. Graduate, go to college, and live your life. Don't go down this road."

"I don't understand."

"Good. Now go upstairs."

I stare past him, at the boxes in the corner. Cherice drops a hand on my shoulder. Thankfully, her voice is calmer now.

"Come on, honey. You shouldn't be down here."

I follow her up the stairs with Janus behind me. As soon as the door closes, he pulls out his keys to lock it. He still looks angry, but I can see the fear more clearly, like the eyes of an animal that knows it's about to die.

"Why? Why can't I know?"

"It's for your own good, Ophelia." Cherice is still trying to stay calm. "Trust me. You're very lucky."

"And trust me, that's not a road you want to go down," Janus says. "Leave the past alone. For your sake."

CHAPTER EIGHT

TWO HOURS LATER AND I CAN still hear Janus's voice, trembling with anger and fear.

They didn't technically send me to my room, but I couldn't stay down there, not when his rage was filling up the house. I should have taken pictures of what I saw in those boxes. All I can remember now is the devastated expression on Cherice's face and the fire in Janus's eyes. He's never talked to me like that before.

I pace around my room, trying to wrangle my thoughts into something coherent. How could a secret like this exist right beneath my feet?

My phone rings. Cass's face flashes across the screen.

I answer after the second ring. "Hey."

"Hey. Why are you asking me about my nightmares?" he asks.

"I wanna know more."

"Why?" There's a steel edge to his voice.

"Because I've been having dreams too, Cass," I admit, finally, "and I don't know what's going on, but I'm freaking out."

He goes quiet. And then, "Baxter said the same thing. And Alessia."

52

"What? They're having dreams too. About what?"

"Baxter said he kept seeing this guy that looked like he was standing on the sun but he could never see his face," he says, "and then Alessia kept seeing herself covered in blood. And she had a sword."

A chill spreads through my chest. It's more similar than I anticipated, and if it's happening to other people, then it's not just some imaginary experience. We're all seeing things, like some kind of joint psychosis.

"And what about you?" I ask.

"What about you? What do you see?" he deflects.

"A storm. Now stop messing with me, Cass. What did you see?"

Another beat of silence. This one seems like it'll stretch on forever. "The dead."

"The dead? What do you mean?"

He sighs. "It might be better if I show you, but you can't freak out."

"Why would I freak out?"

He ignores my question. "If you can sneak out of your house in like an hour, meet me in the park. I'll show you."

"Wait, Cass. I don't have a car."

He sighs again. "One hour. I'll pick you up. But you have to be ready, and you can't think I'm crazy. I mean it."

"I won't. Promise."

I try prying over the phone, but Cass refused to say anything else. Apparently, seeing is believing.

I have to be honest with myself. This is a bad idea. Janus and Cherice are already on edge. Sneaking out seems impossible, and if I get caught, Janus might actually kill me. Or have a stroke. Whichever comes first.

The hour passes. I'm waiting with my shoes on when Cass's message comes through. This is a bad idea, yes, but that doesn't mean it isn't happening.

I open my bedroom door just a crack. The house is quiet and still. And dark too. There's not a single light on, not even in Janus and Cherice's room.

I step out into the hall, keeping my steps light. I stop in front of their door, listening. All I hear is Cherice's demonic snoring, and there's no sign that Janus is awake either.

Good.

It's been an hour since Cass called, and I still haven't figured out how I'm going to do this. I'd thought about jumping from my bedroom window. That idea lasted for all of three seconds. The next obvious choice was the front door, but I'd never get away with that. The basement door is locked, and there's no use trying to go out through the garage. The guest bathroom.

I hurry as quietly as possible to the downstairs bathroom. The window above the toilet isn't remarkable in size, but it opens without a sound when I pull it up. That must mean good luck.

After making sure the door is locked behind me, I climb onto the toilet and squeeze myself through the window. It's not graceful. I go out ass first and end up in the bushes. I pause in the grass until I hear the light rumble of Cass's truck.

I can see his smirk from all the way over here. It's a pleasant change from the past few days, but my cheeks burn with humiliation. People make sneaking out of the house look so cool and easy in movies. As it turns out, there's nothing cool about squeezing out of a window.

"Very smooth, by the way," he says when I get to the car.

"Shut up." I close the door behind me as quietly as possible. "So were you telling the truth earlier or were you just messing with me?"

"Yeah. I'm telling the truth."

A shadow falls over his eyes and whatever light was in them a few seconds ago is gone. Now he's more difficult to read.

"You saw the dead?" I ask.

He nods. "I can speak to them. I don't know how and I don't know why. I just woke up one day and . . ." he goes quiet, his voice falling flat. "Yeah."

We're quiet until we pull into the parking lot of Mercy Park. With the exception of the fairy lights in the trees, which are now starting to flicker, there is no other light or life around. No cars whizz past. No one walks the streets, warm with liquor and merriment. It's not that kind of town. It's always sleeping, even when the sun is up.

"Follow me." Cass says.

He leads us past the playground, over the bridge, and past the walking trail. Past the statue of some white man in an iron suit, past the fountain, and past the tree line too. By the time I think to ask where we're going, we're already deep in the woods. My stomach churns. Why would we need to be this deep in the woods?

"Please don't murder me," I say.

His laugh is genuine this time and ricochets against the surrounding trees. "You have my word. I just want to show you something, and it's important that no one else sees us. This should be far enough though."

I can barely see his face, even though we're only a few feet apart. He reaches into his pocket and pulls out a small knife.

"What are you—"

Wincing, he makes a tiny incision along the center of his palm. This time, I do jump back. His blood beads out, red and gold. When he raises the other hand, snapping his fingers, a bud of red flame catches between his skin. The sigil of a three-headed dog is carved into the back of his right hand.

"Don't freak out," he says.

He drops the flame into his palm, creating a haze of red light around us.

My mouth is hanging open. "What the hell's that?"

"I'm not sure. I just woke up one day and I was looking at my grandfather. He died two years ago." His eyes burn like binary stars. "Ever since then, I've been seeing dead people everywhere. Is there someone you want to talk to?"

My mouth goes dry as cotton. "What?"

"I told you I can talk to the dead. Give me a name."

My heart sinks. There's the obvious choice, but I'm not so quick to say his name. I don't think I could handle it, not this soon. Maybe my grandpa. I've always wanted to have just one more conversation with him. Sit on the porch one last time with a plate of cookies and two glasses of sweet tea between us, rocking our chairs in time to a cicada's song.

But I know that's not the right answer either.

"Rosa Johnson," I tell him. "That's my grandmother."

He nods before closing his eyes. When he speaks in what seems like some foreign tongue, his voice breaks into three pieces. *"Rosa. Johnson. Return."*

For a second, everything's so calm and quiet that I can hear that flame crackling against his fingertip. A howling wind rushes in from somewhere deep in the forest. Around us, the trees kneel in surrender.

A glob of silver mist wafts up from the fire in his palm. I'm crying. Even before her face is formed, I know what shape the mist is taking: those tiny, hunched shoulders, the ghostly skirt sweeping her feet; her hands, soft and wrinkled; her face, puckered and pruned like a sun-ripened peach. Rosa Johnson. My grandma Rosy, not here in the flesh, but here all the same.

"Grandma?"

She smiles at me and I can't help it. I fall to my knees. This can't be real, and yet here she is, watching me with what has to be love and recognition.

"Grandma," I say again. Not a question, but a triumph.

"Hi, honey. My Little Philly."

My chest aches. Here, an open wound, and an onslaught of memory: a small, brick house on the outskirts of New River, surrounded by a field of swaying grass. It's summer, I'm a little girl, and their house towers over me. I can see everything: the horses and cows, the sun burning a hole into the sky. My grandma, young and spry, running through the grass with me, chasing me. Or maybe we're racing. My legs are too short, but she lets me win.

"Run, Little Philly. I'm gonna get you."

"Oh god." I clutch a hand to my chest, but the other reaches for her.

We reach across time and her hand is warm. It makes me sob. All this time, all these layers between us, and her hands are still warm.

"Have you seen . . ." I can't finish the question, but she knows anyway.

Her smile is soft. "Yes, Ophelia. I've seen him. And he's good. He's real good."

"And Grandpa? And the twins?" My chest aches again. "How are they?"

"We're fine, Ophelia," she says. It sounds like she really means it. "The dead have no worries. The living, however, are a different story, and I'm so sorry we didn't prepare you."

"Wait, what?"

She doesn't stop talking. "Just understand that we wanted to keep you safe and we did the best we could."

"Grandma, I don't understand."

But she's already fading. Her form dissolves in the wind, carrying her voice with it. I just barely catch the last thing she says. "I've seen what's coming, sweet girl. Brace yourself."

And she's gone. Just like five years ago.

"Grandma," I call again, still sobbing.

Cass's expression looks taxed. Sweat coats his face and he sways on his feet like he'll fall.

"Ophelia," he says, his voice weak.

I fall to my knees. "No, where is she? I wasn't done." My fingers split the soil, like I'm trying to claw her free from the earth.

"Ophelia."

"Bring her back!"

He crouches down in front of me, looking me in the eye. "I can't. I can only do it for so long. It takes too much energy."

"But—"

"I'm sorry." He puts both hands on my shoulders like he's going to hug me. Thankfully, he doesn't. "I'm really sorry. I didn't know you'd lost so many people."

I resist the urge to curl into a ball in front of him. He didn't know because there was no point in telling anybody.

Talking about them, saying their names out loud—it wouldn't have made me feel better, and it certainly wouldn't have brought anybody back.

I want to say it doesn't matter, but that's not true. Not at all. "Take me home. I want to go home."

He studies my face for a second, his eyes soft. Full of apology. "Okay," he whispers. "Come on."

We hike back through the forest, his pace much slower than last time. The car ride back is just as quiet. I lean my head against the window, chasing the image of my grandmother in my mind. The memory's already losing its color. I can't remember everything. Not the way she looked, or if the buckles on her shoes were silver or gold.

Just her words and the warning in them: *I've seen what's coming.*

As soon as Cass pulls up to the house, I pull off my seatbelt like it's on fire.

"Ophelia, I'm really sorry," he says. "We can try again tomorrow if you—"

I shake my head. "No. Thank you for showing me, but I can't do that again. And thanks for driving me home."

I shove the door open and slide out of the car. I'm about to close it when he reaches across to stop me. "Ophelia. Wait."

"What?"

"How long ago did your dad die?" he asks.

My chest goes cold. "Why?"

He looks embarrassed. "I felt him. When we were talking to your grandma, it was like he was trying to reach out to you."

I clutch a hand to my stomach, but I don't throw up. "Really?"

"Yeah. I couldn't hear what he was saying, but I felt his love for you. And he had so much of it. I just thought you should know."

I don't know what to say. If I talk, I might spit my heart up into this grass. But I have to say something, because I can never repay him for what he's just done. "Um, thank you, Cassius. Really. I appreciate this."

He smiles. "Thanks for believing me. And hey, if you need anything, whatever it is—please let me know."

I shut the door to his truck, but he doesn't drive off until after I've squeezed back into the house through the window. Thankfully, the door is still locked and the house is still quiet. I sneak upstairs, my brain a storm of chaos. How could that have actually just happened? And what did she mean?

I've seen what's coming.

Maybe she was just confused. She seemed happy, so I know she had to be at least a little bit confused. But what Cass said was real. That blood-red sigil on the back of his hand was real, and so was the fire in his palm. There's no mistaking that, so what does it mean? My head pounds. As soon as I step into my room, all the energy trickles out of me. Whatever this is, it can wait until morning.

I kick my pants off and fall into bed. I don't realize how tired I am until I feel my body sink into the mattress, all the tension rising to the surface.

We lost everyone. My grandparents. Iris and Irene. And now Dad. It's like some cruel game where the worst thing that could happen to you happens five times. I try not to think about it like that, as a chain of tragedy that eats through us with vicious abandon, but now it's hard not to. The grief in Cass's voice was real, even though they weren't his losses.

OF BLOOD AND LIGHTNING

I close my eyes and try to imagine what it would sound like if Iris and Irene were still here. They'd be about eleven now, and probably even louder than they used to be. I can remember the sound of their feet pacing down the halls. The way their laughter would slip through the crack at the bottom of my door, beckoning me to join them. I want them to be here with me now.

Eventually, I fall asleep to the sound of phantom laughter.

CHAPTER NINE

All around me, the darkness is absolute. In all directions: above my head, at my feet. Wind rushes past me, like a thousand icy hands tearing at my clothes. I try to run, but there are no roads, no paths, no way out of this palace of shadow.

"Hello?" I shout.

Fear blossoms in the pit of my chest. I look down at my hands, turning them over. How do I know if they're real? I wring them together, feeling the warmth of my own skin. It feels like flesh, true and solid, and yet nothing about this can be real.

Not the darkness, or the broad-shouldered man now in front of me. When I look up, he's standing with his back to me. His lashed, bleeding back. The wind blows against his royal blue toga like a ship's billowing sails. He's much taller than me, with massive, dangerous biceps, and a deadly sword hanging from his hip.

I've been here before. Even before he turns around, I know the chiseled set of his jaw and the ancient, proud look in his piercing blue eyes.

The air is thick with honey and ozone. Above us, a black storm swirls to life, filling the darkness with arrows of lightning. Like before, ripples of electricity spill out from his shoulders and dance into the palms of his hands.

He raises a crooked finger, pointing at something over my shoulder. It's only then that I realize he isn't looking at me.

I follow his finger to the woman behind me, someone I'm sure I've never seen before. She's as tall as the man, maybe taller. Her brown skin glows like she's hoarding the sun in each of her cells. Like the man, her expression is calm, but the look in her eyes is urgent. She pulls out the sword that dangles at her hip and aims it at me. At my chest. Behind me, I hear the scrape of another sword being pulled free.

I try to move, but I'm stuck between them, with two blades aimed true to my heart. The woman—blazing with the light of a billion suns. The man who carries lightning in his palms. They stare me down, swords ready, some intent I can't read brimming in both of their eyes.

The earth speaks.

"She who rends the world. He who calls lightning from blood."

The woman echoes. "You will rend the world."

And then the man. "You will call lightning from blood."

I scream. I know what's coming. "Wait!"

But the woman speaks again, her voice echoing against this vast chasm of nothingness a thousand times. "Ophelia Johnson, the Order of Ruin is your birthright. Kneel to none."

In a surge of purple light and lightning, they both charge at me.

OUTSIDE MY DOOR, THE HOUSE IS quiet. The dream, if I can even call it that, sits like a lump at the back of my throat. All night I replayed it. Each time, the memory seemed clearer. I keep seeing them: the man's crooked finger as he pointed over my shoulder and the tall, defiant stance of the woman who knew my name.

I'm sure neither of them were speaking English, and yet I understood them. Perfectly. And even worse, in the quiet, still space of my room, I recite their declaration:

"You will rend the world. You will call lightning from blood."

The strange language molds itself around my tongue with ease. It's not any language I was ever taught, but I heard it yesterday, too, when Cassius commanded my grandmother to return from the dark.

It should be impossible, but I already know how blurred that line is. I spoke to my dead grandmother yesterday. I saw her face, molded by the mist from Cass's hands. I don't know what this is, or how I could wake up in a world like this. On the heels of my father's death, it all seems too cruel to be true.

Someone knocks and I pretend to be asleep. They come in anyway. I'm hoping it's Cherice, but my heart plummets when Janus eases into the room.

"Hey," he says, an uncertain edge to his voice. "I know you're not sleeping."

I open a single eye. He stands awkwardly at the edge of my bed, looking harmless. There's no sign of yesterday's rage, but I know it's in there somewhere. That kind of anger just doesn't disappear.

"Hi," I mutter.

"Look, I wanted to apologize for my outburst yesterday. "I know you don't understand how serious this stuff is, but you didn't deserve that," he says. "I'm really sorry."

"I accept your apology. What stuff?"

He sighs, everything in his eyes begging me to ask anything else. "It's better if you don't know. I know that's a really shitty answer, but it's the truth. I promise. One day, when you're older, when you're ready, if you want to know more I will gladly tell you. But I can't right now. For your sake."

"But why?"

"I can't—" he pinches the bridge of his nose, trying to breathe. "I can't tell you, Ophelia. He made me take a vow, and I won't break it. Not even in death."

"Are you saying my *dad* is the reason you won't tell me anything? Seriously?"

A hint of anger returns, coupled with a fierce wave of pride. Before things got bad, no one was closer than my dad and my uncle. In most of my memories, wherever my dad was, my uncle was always at his side. It was only after Grandma's death that they grew apart. Dad and I moved far away, and this terrible distance grew between us.

"Yes, Ophelia, and I will not break my word to my brother. I don't care where he is. I'm sorry. I know that's not what you want to hear, but that's my answer," he says. His tone is flat and final. "Now, are you going to school?"

"Do I have a choice?" I ask.

"You do."

"Then no. I'm tired."

"Okay. I understand." He gets up to leave, but stops in my doorway, softening his expression. "I'm sorry, Ophelia. Get some rest." Then he's gone. It's then that I make up my mind. If he gets to keep secrets, so do I.

Cherice comes in to say goodbye about ten minutes later. She doesn't look like she slept, but tries her best to act cheery.

About an hour after they've both left, I finally climb out of bed. The first thing I reach for is my laptop. Researching the photobook was a dud yesterday, so I'm not sure what I expect now. Everything I type into Google must either be too vague or too broad. None of the results look promising. I guess it would help if I had some idea of what I was looking for in the first place.

I press the pads of my fingers against my eyes, wondering if an answer will appear in the dark. What am I looking at, and what does it mean that any of this is happening to me? Well, I guess it's not just happening to me. Cass has been talking to the dead, and apparently, these strange dreams are plaguing all of us. Alessia's stopped coming to school, and I haven't seen Baxter since the day he stormed out of the cafeteria.

And then there's me. Twice now I've seen that man, but last night was the first time a woman visited me. When I woke up, I could smell ozone in the air and feel heat pricking in my fingertips. Maybe it was my imagination or just an empty echo of the dream. Or maybe it's worse than that. Cass can talk to the dead.

I kick my legs over the edge of the bed and stumble into a pair of jeans. Outside, Green Groves is quiet as always. In the backyard, overgrown grass scrapes my calves, blowing gently in a morning breeze. I can taste fall. Above my head, leaves have browned around the edges. Soon, summer will be a distant memory.

I don't know what I'm doing. I don't even know if there's something to do. My hands haven't stopped prickling since I woke up, but that's not necessarily an omen of great and terrible things. I hold them out in front of me. Yep. They look normal, nothing odd or strange at all.

But then, I fold my left hand like Cass did yesterday, thumb to middle finger, and snap. A jolt of electricity comes to life between my fingers. It's small, but it's there. I try it again and I'm convinced. I'm not imagining it. Blue sparks come to life against my skin. Like there are storm clouds in each of my cells, churning out thunder and lightning with each tiny shift of flesh.

"Holy shit," I mutter.

I clench both of my hands into fists. Heat breaks out across the back of my neck, along the top of my shoulders. By the time the air fills with ozone, lightning is dancing down my arms in thick, looping bands. It gathers in my palms, boiling in bright, blue pools. I clench them again, and the lightning stretches itself into a long, silver sword.

I've never held a sword before, but it feels like it belongs. Lightning races down the blade's spine; it beams like a stolen sun. Above me, a storm swirls out of the sky's pale blue nothingness. Thick black clouds coast over New River, soaking it with rain.

Every time I swing my sword, the storm finds a new voice. Thunder cut straight from the pounding in my chest. Lightning called from my blood.

CHAPTER TEN

FOR THE NEXT THREE DAYS, I stay home. After Janus and Cherice leave, I go to the backyard and spend the day building storms. Every flash of lightning or clatter of thunder is a work of my hands. It rains for three days like god is trying to flood the earth and no one else knows it's my doing.

I go back and forth believing it. Six months ago, the life I lived was empty of anything like magic or conspiracy. This is crazier than any dream I've ever had. People shouldn't be able to make storms or wield lightning.

And yet, on the third day, I find myself lifting the lawnmower over my head. I expected a struggle, but it feels light in my hands. I don't strain. It soars over my head, supported by nothing more than the strength of my ten-fingered grip.

Someone gasps, and my body turns to stone. Olivia gapes at me from the other side of the chain link fence.

"What are you doing here?" I shout.

"I came to check on you and also ask an awkward question, but I think I got my answer."

I glance up at the lawnmower, still balanced in my hands. "Oh?"

68

"There's some weird shit going on, man."

"Yeah. Weird shit." I set the lawnmower down as gently as possible and wipe my hands off. "You brought everybody else with you? I think we need to talk."

"No, but they're waiting. Let's go."

ABOUT THIRTY MINUTES OUT FROM TOWN, in the heart of the New River National Forest Preserve, the mayor lives in a massive coffee-colored mansion. Towering redwoods halo his property, concealing it from view. The house is much, much bigger than Cherice's and Janus's. Much colder too. Even on a day as pretty as this one, the dark windows offer no light or warmth as we arrive.

It's the guesthouse to the left of it, closer to the tree line, that seems to have all the color. Thankfully, that's where Olivia takes me.

Cass and Alessia lounge on the front porch, swinging in white rocking chairs. I lock eyes with him as we approach the house, a chill running down my spine. His eyes are concerned, and filled with the same apology as the other night.

"I thought you freaking died," Alessia says, only half-joking. "You in on it?"

"In on what exactly?" I ask.

She reaches into the air and pulls out a double-sided war ax. The handle is nearly twice as long as her legs. Both blades are the color of blood, with a wolf's head carved into the metal in white paint.

"It's like a magic trick." With a flourish, she pulls at least six more weapons out of thin air.

"Holy shit."

"Please do not encourage her." Olivia rolls her eyes. "Alessia, I told you that stuff is dangerous."

Alessia shrugs. "Obviously."

"Come on," Olivia grumbles, grabbing my arm.

She leads us into the house, which is bright with specks of gold light, scattered around the room, suspended in midair. They appear to be coming from Baxter's feet. He whizzes around the house like a comet, leaving flurries of gold light in his wake. Light pulses out from his skin like he's the sun; his smile is just as bright.

"'Sup Ophelia," he calls as he skates across the ceiling.

"'Sup, Baxter. You look different."

He slides to a stop in front of us, laughing. "I'm the fastest man alive."

Olivia shoves him hard in the shoulder. "But not the fastest person. I'm faster than you."

"We can race and settle this right now," he smirks.

Apparently, everyone else has found the silver lining. I'm not seeing any of the terror that plagued me the night I had that dream.

Then there's Roman. His eyes look sunken, like he hasn't slept in days.

"Okay, just hold on." Roman comes out of the kitchen massaging his eyes.

Alessia groans, throwing her head back. "Roman, please don't do that thing you always do where you suck the fun out of everything."

"I don't want to hear it. Just a few days ago you were freaking out about this shit, so what's fun about it now?" Roman scoffs, "and I don't always do that."

"Um, *superpowers are fun* about it?" she says matter-of-factly. "And I love you, but yes you do."

Olivia looks down at her shoes. "We used to place bets on

it. You bought me a bike in eighth grade and you didn't even know it."

Roman looks exasperated. "Were you betting on me or against me?"

Olivia says nothing.

"Look, Roman. There's nothing objectively wrong with superpowers," Baxter says.

Roman narrows his eyes in disbelief. "Oh, okay. And all that shit about war and death. Does that sound fun to you?"

Baxter stops smiling.

"The dreams. I was at the beach and a guy with a trident stepped out of the water. I thought he was gonna stab me—I mean, he did—but he said something first: *the Beasts of the Sea will unite and wage a Holy War.*" Roman recites, slipping into that ancient language as easily as I had.

Cass's expression goes dark. "*Your portion is a throne of shadow. The Heirs of Death will know your voice.*"

"So we all got weird prophecies?" Alessia says.

"*The Huntress's might will be the scourge of Paradise* was mine," Olivia tips her head, gesturing. "What'd you get, Leese?"

"It was short: *A Holy Spear will heed the call.* I didn't know what it meant so I've been ignoring it."

"Jesus," Roman hisses, dragging a hand through his hair. "Okay, Ophelia. What about you?"

It's right there, on the tip of my tongue. "*The Order of Ruin is your birthright.*" My mouth is bone dry, "*Kneel to none.*"

Roman throws up his hands. "See. Nothing about this is fun."

"All right just hold on," Alessia says. "Maybe there's a rational explanation to all this?"

Cass frowns. "Like what? We're the Avengers?"

"You're not helping," Roman chides.

Cass doesn't look apologetic. "All right, then. What do we do about it?"

"Nothing." Fear builds in my throat like bile. "We do nothing."

"Yeah, I agree," Olivia says. "This is way too weird."

"Oh come on," Alessia groans. "How many people get to wake up with superpowers?"

"I don't think that's the point, Alessia," Cassius says. "Cool or not, we don't know what any of this shit means. It could be dangerous."

"You don't know that," she scoffs.

"What about a Holy War doesn't sound dangerous to you?" Roman furrows his brows in disbelief. He turns to Cass. "Also, did you just agree with me?"

Cass waves him off. "I shouldn't have said anything."

"I'm just saying that simply having powers isn't the dangerous part," Alessia says. "That's all."

Cass scoffs. "That's delusional. You're delusional."

"You know what, let's just put it to a vote. Either we ignore this or do something about it," Baxter says. "I vote we do something about it."

I pinch the bridge of my nose. "What'd you hear?"

"*Ten thousand suns will wash the Earth in wrath.*" He doesn't seem as disturbed as the others. "I'm not gonna pretend I know what's going on here, but I don't think we should just ignore it. It might make things worse."

"I agree," Alessia says.

"Well. I don't," Roman scoffs. "I'm sorry. This is too crazy for me."

"Agreed." Cass locks eyes with me. "But I do wonder what this all means. It's not every day you dream about Holy Wars."

"What?" I squirm beneath his gaze.

"Your grandma," he says. "She told you to brace yourself. What did she mean by that?"

My grandmother's voice floats through my skull. I shake my head to clear her out. I'm not a fan of listening to my uncle, but hearing them talk about this turns it into something different, something bigger. Maybe it really is best not to go looking.

"I don't know. She never said anything like that to me when she was alive."

Baxter's eyes go wide. He watches Cass in disbelief. "So you really can talk to the dead?"

"Told you."

"Look, I say we leave it alone," I say. "I don't want anything to do with this. Olivia?"

"Olivia, come on," Alessia sighs.

Olivia shakes her head. "I don't know. It would be reckless to just dive headfirst into this without knowing anything at all, but I just can't ignore the fact that it's happening. I'm conflicted."

"Great, so we're tied." Roman rakes another hand through his hair, the storm in his eyes turning them dark. "But I don't want to do this. I don't want any part of it."

"Me either," Cass says.

Alessia doesn't bother trying to hide her disappointment. "Well, I think that's bullshit. Baxter's right. If there's something we're supposed to do, then why aren't we doing it?"

No one says anything. It's not an unfair question, but I can't do this, not when there's another mystery already on my hands. Not when I'm already carrying so much grief. New River was supposed to offer me peace and quiet. This isn't what I signed up for.

MICKI JANAE

"I'm sorry," I tell her. I don't miss the way Cass finds my eyes. "I can't. I'm out. Now who wants to take me home?"

Cass breaks my gaze as Roman volunteers. "I'm heading out too. I'll take you."

"Thanks."

"Guys, come on," Baxter says. "At least give it some time. Don't be so quick to write this off."

I shrug. "Sorry. I'll see you guys later."

Roman follows me out of the house, his expression wary. It doesn't look like he's slept well in the past few days, if at all. He's always had some kind of darkness about him, like there's a shadow at his back. This is different.

"You okay?" I ask him.

He shakes his head. "I don't know if that's the word I'd use. What about you? Got kinda heated in there."

"I just—I don't need this shit. Not right now." My throat closes like I'm going to cry. "I just need to catch a break." But I will not cry. Not here.

The softness in his voice catches me off guard. "Okay. Let's go to the tower."

CHAPTER ELEVEN

WE PASS A BOTTLE OF WINE between us. Our feet sway in the wind.

I haven't come to fully trust the water tower yet. It creaks in response to each one of our movements, no matter how small they are. I hook my hands over the bottom safety rail, frail as it is, and stare down at the world below. How high up is the drop? Would falling from a distance like this hurt? Would I even feel anything? How long would it take? Three seconds? Four? Would they feel like seconds at all?

Roman passes the bottle. I chug, trying not to think. Those thoughts only creep in when it's late like this. Usually, I'm alone. I don't know if being here makes things better or worse.

"What are you thinking about?" Roman asks.

The tower. The distance between here, where I'm sitting, and the rest of the Earth.

I hold up my hand instead of answering. Lightning crackles between my fingers, up from my wrist, down to my fingertips. I turn it over, filling the world with light. Above us, clouds rattle with thunder.

"I think I hate this."

He shrugs. "It's only been about seventy-two hours, so maybe that's a little extreme."

I scoff. "I thought you were firmly anti-superpowers."

"I'm anti-weird-prophetic-nonsense. Not exactly anti-superpowers."

He extends his hand. The air swells with the smell of salt and jasmine. Two bulbs of sea-green light come on in his eyes. In the center of his palm, ocean water swirls into a tiny, deep blue whirlpool.

"I think they're cool," he says. "I just don't like the implications."

"What exactly did you hear?"

"*You will claim the Seventh throne with ichor and sacrifice. The Beasts of the Sea will unite to wage a Holy War.*" His expression darkens, despite the city's sparkling light. "Ichor and sacrifice? I don't know what that means."

"Have you looked it up?" I ask him. "What about *Beasts of the Sea*?"

"I tried," he says. "Honestly, it almost sounds like we're talking about video games. It might not even exist."

"But it does."

He sits back and holds out his hand. "And yet it does."

I pass him the bottle and watch him drink.

"Before, you said you needed to catch a break." His tone is cautious. "I don't want to pry. It's your business, but . . ."

I lean my head against the rail. I know I can't avoid it forever, especially not now that so many other things are coming to light. I just hate saying it out loud. I hate thinking about it. I hate that it's true, that all of this isn't some kind of nightmare. It's as real as this cool metal railing in my hands.

"I moved back to New River because my dad died," I tell him. "It happened last month, out of nowhere. And I guess it feels like everything just keeps . . . happening, but all I want is for the world to stop. Like, if I could just get one day where the Earth doesn't spin, I might be all right."

For a long time, he's quiet. I refuse to look at him. I've been trying to avoid that look people get in their eyes when they find out you've been touched by death. Pity and cheap grief. They try to make you feel better, but all the platitudes just make it worse. Why would I care that there's a better place on the other side? A month ago he was with me. He was *here.* Close enough to reach out and touch. Why would I want anything other than his presence? What could possibly make that better?

"But things do keep happening," he says, surprising me. "You might just want to lie where you are and let the world grow over you, but things don't work that way. You have to keep living your life how you did before, but it's impossible, and yet you're doing it."

"Yeah." I finally look at him.

"I told you about my dad, right? This summer, we found out he's sick." He looks down at the ground, putting far too much faith in the tower's railing. "I keep thinking that one day it won't feel awful, but it never comes." He doesn't say it like he's talking about something you get over, like a cold.

"I'm sorry. I didn't—"

He shakes his head. "No, Ophelia, I'm saying I get it. I know you don't like talking about stuff like this, and I just want you to know that you can. You don't have to suffer in silence."

"Roman, that's really sweet, but it's okay. I wouldn't want to pile that shit on you."

77

He frowns. "You really wouldn't be. I mean it."

I take the wine from him and let it warm my chest again. "No I mean—it's just me, and that's not a very interesting story."

"Is that how you see yourself?"

"Well, I'm not exactly a showstopper."

"Do you not know how special you are?"

The question makes me squirm. I think of myself as a lot of things, but special certainly isn't one of them. I'm the type to disappear in a crowded room, not stand out.

I look away from him. His gaze is too intense. "Don't know if that's the word I'd use."

"You can quite literally call thunder and lightning from the heavens," he snorts. "Plus, the whole room lights up when you walk in. Everybody loves you."

I roll my eyes. "You're delusional."

"I'm not, but I guess you just can't see it, which is okay. Doesn't mean it isn't there." He smiles and city lights glimmer in his eyes, "but I can, and it's kinda like . . . magic."

"Well, thanks." I try to ignore the wild, fluttering sensation in my stomach. I hate it when boys call you magical on water towers and split bottles of wine with you. It's just not practical.

"You're welcome," he says, still smiling, "and thanks for coming here with me. I missed you."

More flutters and a jolt of electricity that has nothing to do with lightning, racing straight down my sternum like an arrow. I tug the wine away from him and down the last drop.

"Oh no," I laugh, turning it over. "I'm sorry."

"It's okay." He gasps and points at something in the sky, a wide smile breaking open across his face. "Hey, look at that." Above us, quiet stars stand watch over New River. It's a whole lot more than you can see in Austin. Without streetlights, skyscrapers, and traffic, you can see the entire galaxy from here.

"Draco," he says, tracing a great dragon across the sky.

CHAPTER TWELVE

Janus, Cherice, and I eat dinner at dusk now. Things have gotten better, in an odd sort of way. A quiet truce rules over the house. We can go out for movies now, and sit in each other's presence without struggling to fill up the silence. Janus's roaring laughter returns at some point, carrying through the house like smoke after a fire. One morning, I even wake up to the sound of Cherice singing in the hall. This kind of peace hasn't lived here in a long time, and every one seems better off for it.

But there's one condition, one line no one crosses: the boxes in the basement don't exist. I'm still not allowed down there. I don't ask about Dad's past or the House of the Cursed Children. My curiosity doesn't go away, but I've decided that I prefer a warm house to the truth.

It could be worse.

September goes by in a blur. It's a useless month anyway. When October sweeps in with all its fierceness, New River finally steps out of its shell. A swarm of orange lights overtake the trees in Mercy Park. The annual pumpkin patch appears overnight, with brightly decorated signs advertising it all over town. Storefronts sprout plastic mummies and life-sized statues of Dracula. It's the sleepiest town in the American Midwest, but something about the month of Halloween brings the whole place to life.

Apparently, it brings Cherice to life, too. When I come down for breakfast this morning, she's busy draping fake cobwebs over the fireplace. A six-foot inflatable witch perches in the corner, sneering with her one good eye. The boxes in the corner overflow with sprawls of plastic spiders and dull, orange Christmas lights. I don't recognize the tune she's humming, but it's nice to hear her voice.

Cherice used to sing all the time. Whenever we'd have a family dinner, or Grandma just wanted to hear a song, it was Cherice's voice that filled the room with the sound of cosmic glory.

"Morning," I call on the way to the kitchen.

Her smile catches me off guard. "Morning. Your uncle's making French toast."

I narrow my eyes, trying to read her.

"Everything okay?"

"Yes, everything's okay." She laughs, but it doesn't sound right. "I just love Halloween. It was the twins's favorite holiday."

I watch her, waiting for some sign of the darkness to return. I feel my own darkness, pressing against the inner walls of my chest, rabid and swollen, but she seems undisturbed. She returns to the fireplace, humming a new song this time.

In the kitchen, Janus is flipping the last of the French toast. The table is already set with platters of egg, smoked sausage, and syrup. I have to settle myself when he sees me. The light surging into his eyes is so much like my father.

"Good morning." He gestures to the pan with a spatula. "I'm almost done with this. Hope you're hungry."

"Starving." I take a seat at the table. "I didn't know you guys decorated the house for Halloween."

Unlike Cherice, sadness settles into his shoulders, and he breaks eye contact.

"It was Iris and Irene's favorite holiday," he says. "Their favorite thing was when we'd put little plastic ghosts all over the house. It was like Christmas. I guess when we do it now—I mean I know it's a little silly—but it feels like a part of them is still here."

"Yeah, it does. And it's not silly."

He smiles at me. I hate how miserable he looks.

We eat breakfast together, and it's the lightest the whole house has been in over a month. Cherice finishes first and volunteers to wash the dishes.

"Oh wait, I nearly forgot," she says, hands covered in suds. The same mischievous look from before is back. It's bright in Janus's eyes too, but he doesn't say anything.

"What?" I ask, looking between them.

"I'm forgetting something. One second." Cherice floats out of the room. Down the hall, I swear I hear her giggling.

"Okay, what's going on?" I ask. "You guys are being weird."

He shrugs, doing his best to appear harmless. "I don't know what you mean."

"Come on."

"I'm serious," he smirks. "I have no idea what you're talking about."

"Very funny."

"Okay!" Cherice comes whizzing back around the corner, clutching something in her hand. "We've been doing some thinking, and we think it's great that you're making friends. That said, we figured you'd need a way to get around."

I don't get it. "What?"

Cherice dances around the kitchen island until she's standing at my side. In a fairy-like motion, she sets something down in front of me: a thick lone, black-trimmed key.

"What is this?" I laugh.

Cherice laughs too. "It's yours." She gestures to the door with a jerk of her shoulder. "Come on!"

She runs off, out of the kitchen. I snatch up my bag to follow her with Janus laughing behind me. Sitting in the driveway is a sleek, candy apple-red sedan. I still don't believe it. Dad and I talked a lot about getting me a car at some point, but it was never an actual possibility. We only had one income, and even as a tenured professor, my father couldn't afford such extravagant luxuries as a second car. I'd resigned myself to bumming rides and walking everywhere for the next five to eight years, so I'm still not convinced that what I'm seeing is real.

"This is mine?" I ask, scrutinizing the key like it'll vanish into thin air.

"Yep," Janus says. "I had a car in senior year. I probably got into a lot more trouble than I should've, but it was a great time, and I think you deserve those experiences." His expression darkens a little, pinched with worry. "Just be careful. Never drink and drive. Or smoke and drive. And never drive after midnight. Wherever you are, you stay there. You understand?"

"Yeah, I understand." For once, I can't fight the elation that swells in my chest. "So this is really mine?"

Cherice rubs my shoulder. "Yes, honey. It's all yours."

I swallow the lump in my throat and smile. "Thank you," I tell them. "I don't even—thank you."

"You're very welcome."

I learned how to drive on long, winding backroads. My father would drive us far away from town, as if no amount of distance was truly far enough to be safe. Whenever he was satisfied with how empty the roads were, he finally let me get behind the wheel. The first few times, I nearly crashed the car. It seemed hopeless. It made no sense to me that people could control these giant, metal death machines. Until one day, I got in the car and it felt like I could fly.

After getting my license, I couldn't drive much. Sometimes Dad would let me take the car to a movie, or just out to clear my head. Now, with my hands on the wheel, I wish he could be here to see me.

New River races by in streaks of blue and gold. I crack the windows and let cool air fill the car. It really does smell like fall: earthy and warm, like tree sap. It's a beautiful day.

I park toward the back of the school's sprawling lot. It takes a few tries to catch my breath before I get out of the car. Olivia's waiting on the front steps, eating a banana.

She waves it at me. "Hey girl."

"Hey. Check it out." I jingle the keys. "Absolutely insane."

"Holy shit. You should show me later."

"Yeah, totally."

"Speaking of, you got any plans tonight?" She asks.

"No. What's up?"

"I was thinking we should meet up at the Yard tonight. Bax and I have been . . . working on something." She says it in a low voice like she's afraid someone's listening. "We wanted to show everybody."

OF BLOOD AND LIGHTNING

"Oh? Working on what?"

She looks around, and my heart drops a little. I'm hoping it's not what I think it is, but she flashes her hand. Silver wisps of light dance between her fingers.

I narrow my eyes. "I thought we were gonna leave it alone."

"No, we are, but it doesn't mean they go away," she says. "And if you take away all the doom and gloom, they're kinda cool."

"I don't know." I shake my head. "I've kind of been trying not to think about it."

Cassius and Alessia walk up next. These days, Cass doesn't seem to be missing as much sleep. This morning though, something else is weighing on him.

"What's up," Alessia greets.

Cass offers a half-hearted wave and Olivia clicks her teeth.

"Oh, I know that look. Mr. Raymond is on the warpath again."

Cassius rolls his eyes, his frustration hot and searing. "A half-empty box of cereal is suddenly the end of the world."

Alessia rubs his shoulder, trying to comfort him. It doesn't seem like it's working.

"It's okay, Cass," Alessia says. "You know it doesn't have anything to do with you. Not really."

"Yeah, obviously. I just—it's whatever." He shakes his head, pinching the bridge of his nose. "I was told we're meeting at the Yard tonight. Why?"

"No, don't be like that," Olivia groans. "We're just having fun tonight."

"Yeah, right. Okay."

"Cass I'm just as against this as you are, but you can't tell me you're not at least a little entertained," Olivia says.

"I don't know, Liv. I'm really struggling to see the silver lining in this one."

"You could probably punch a tank without breaking your hand," Alessia says, a manic smile across her face. "Or an airplane."

Cass furrows his brows. "Why would I wanna do that?"

"Just come to the Yard," she whines.

He shakes his head before catching my eye. "Are you going?"

Olivia nudges me, and Alessia pouts over Cass's shoulder. I never mind going to the Yard, but these powers are bad news. I'm not sure about a lot of things, but I'm sure about that.

"To watch," I say. "I will go to watch."

Cass looks disappointed.

"You don't even have to do anything, Cass. I swear. I swear," Alessia says, squeezing his shoulders.

"This is literally peer pressure."

I shrug. "You made me jump off a cliff."

He points an accusing finger at me. "I knew you were still holding a grudge about that."

My phone buzzes with a message from Roman: *running late, I'll be in by second period.* A second later, the bell echoes across the front steps.

"Holy shit." Olivia jumps up and loops her bag over her shoulders. "Hey, has anybody heard from Roman?"

Alessia looks uneasy. "Not this again."

"No, don't worry," I tell them. "He said he's running late. He texted me."

Olivia pulls out her phone. "Oh, I have to let him know about tonight."

"Yeah, maybe he can be the voice of reason," Cass grumbles.

Alessia ignores him and starts running up the steps. "Don't forget. Tonight at nine."

Cass and I exchange an uncertain look and part.

WHEN I GET HOME, A GIANT cobweb trails from the bottom right corner of the roof, all the way to the front left corner of the front yard. Dozens of glittering black spiders, each larger than a textbook, are scattered along the cobweb's dingy white frames. Beneath them, the yard is littered with dirty fragments of bone: an amputated foot, caught in the base of a rose bush, a gnarled hand, grasping through the soil. Gravestones scatter up and down the front yard, splattered ominously in what looks like ketchup.

With the sun setting just behind the house's dark shingles, everything is washed in the light of a dying day. I duck beneath a section of cobweb and walk up to the door with a chill at the back of my neck. I know none of this is real, but I hadn't expected it to be so life-like. There are bits of organ and viscera scattered in the bushes, and bloody footprints trail my own up the walkway. The steps are bordered with jack-o-lanterns, each carved into a horrified expression. The Grim Reaper meets me at the front door, staring out from the absolute darkness of his hood.

The foyer's not much better. A cardboard cut-out of Dracula has been wedged into the corner, blood dripping from the corner of his mouth like a red creek. The footprints from outside lead into the living room, where more cobwebs coat the fireplace. More boxes are sitting in the corner, so the house must still be under construction.

Thankfully, the kitchen is still normal. Janus and Cherice stand around the stove, tasting stew from the steaming pot between them.

I gesture outside with a wave of my arm. "Oh my god."

They cackle with laughter.

"I told you it was gon' get her!" Janus howls.

"God, Ophelia. You should see your face." It's the first time I've seen Cherice really throw her head back to laugh. And it's glorious.

Their laughter worms its way into my chest. It's not the first time we've all laughed together like this, but it's the richest. It's so thick in the air around us that you could catch it like a comet's tail and ride off to some other world.

I brush away a tear. "When you said you were decorating the house, I didn't know you meant this."

"Well, me neither. I was seriously just gonna do something low-key, but then that bitch Gloria on 10th Street decided I needed a crash course on the HOA statutes." Cherice jerks her neck back, indignant. "So yeah, now we have a big ass cobweb hanging off the side of our house. Happy Halloween!"

"And that's exactly why I married you." Janus wraps a hand around her waist and pulls her close, pressing a kiss to her forehead. "So how was your day, Ophelia?"

"Boring." I shrug. It actually was, so I'm not technically lying. Not yet. "What's for dinner?"

Janus beams with pride. "You'll see," he says.

Twenty minutes later, a platter of chuck roast sits between us on a mountain of diced carrots and soft, steaming potatoes. The bacon-wrapped asparagus beside them looks just as delicious.

"I was feeling a little creative," Janus shrugs. "It's no big deal."

Cherice kisses his shoulder. "It's the biggest, babe. You snapped."

"Thank you, thank you."

I'm waiting until we're finished with dinner to bring it up, but apparently, there's a second course. After sweeping our plates away, Janus brings out a Dutch apple pie and a tub of ice cream. We pass the ice cream around first, then the pie.

"Babe, is this homemade?" Cherice asks.

Janus scoffs. "Girl, hell no. This is Sara Lee."

I snort into my bowl. "Either way, it's really good. Thanks, Uncle Janus."

He winks. "No problem. It's my pleasure."

After a few silent minutes of scraping our forks, I finally find my courage. "So, it's not a school night."

Janus raises an eyebrow. "No, it's not. What's up?"

"So, it's not exactly a party, but my friend Baxter is throwing this get-together at this house. There'll be like six people max, and—"

He cuts me off, his eyes suspicious. "I don't know, Phie. Six is enough to start drinking."

"No, no it's not like that. We'd never. It's just like a—I don't know. We're gonna hang out, and it's gonna be totally safe because he's the mayor's son. We couldn't get into trouble if we tried."

Janus's gaze is hard and searching. Then he cackles again. "I'm just messing with you. Have fun."

"Wait," Cherice holds up her hand. "What time, who all's gonna be there, and when are you gonna be back?"

"Um, nine, just the same group of friends, and . . . maybe midnight."

She points a stern finger at me. "It better be midnight. I'm serious."

I finish my pie and ice cream in three huge bites and sweep my plate away and go upstairs to work on my homework.

A few hours and a hastily drafted essay later, someone knocks on my door. I shout for them to come in as I tighten my shoelaces and shrug into my jacket.

"Hey," Janus shoulders his way into the room and shuts the door like he doesn't want to be overheard. "I just wanted to tell you to be safe. Even sleepy ass towns like this one can be dangerous. If you trust your friends, stick with them and come back in the morning if you have to."

There's something in his voice that goes beyond surface level concern. He knows something. But even if I asked him, I'm sure he wouldn't tell.

"I got you, Uncle Janus. I'll be okay."

He holds out his pinky, dead serious. I laugh but oblige him.

"Just be safe," he says.

"I will."

CHAPTER THIRTEEN

I DON'T KNOW THAT I'VE MEMORIZED the way to the Yard until I'm five minutes out. The darkness out here is thick like ink, the road a wild, bending serpent. I follow its mouth through a black iron gate and park in front of the main building. From where I'm standing, I can see the warm glow of a campfire, but it's the light in the distance that catches my attention.

Streaks of gold and silver whizz past each other, launching sparks of light across the Yard. They move like bullets in the darkness, impossibly fast. Across from them, in a blazing haze of red flame, Alessia attacks the air with burning spears.

I find Roman and Cassius at the campfire, watching in a mixture of awe and worry. I sit between them and pull a bottle from the cooler.

"That's insane," I mutter.

Roman jumps. "Where'd you come from?"

"Did I scare you?" I smirk.

His cheeks burn. "I was distracted. And yes, it *is* insane. We're drawing too much attention to ourselves."

I furrow my brows. "Roman, we're the only people out here."

He points in the direction of the main station. "The 94 cuts through town right along there. If someone sees a bunch of lights out here they might call the police."

"Then we run away," Cass says simply. He curls one of his arms, flexing his bicep. "I could carry someone's car."

"Ridiculous," Roman mutters, shaking his head.

"Did you tell them that?" I ask him.

Roman rolls his eyes. "Obviously. They don't care. They have no concept of caution or restraint."

Cass snorts. "Did you seriously expect anything else?"

"Maybe not from Baxter or Leese, but I at least had a little bit of faith in Olivia," Roman says.

"Can't blame them." I hold my hand out to see what happens and a thin wave of lightning trickles down my index finger. "I hate to say it, but it's not like they're *not* cool."

"Of course, but it's like making a deal with the devil. There has to be a catch, right?"

"Like what?" Cass asks.

Roman shrugs. "I don't know. Maybe the more we use these powers the faster we age, or maybe they'll turn us evil."

Cass and I laugh, but I try to hide my smile when Roman doesn't. He rolls his eyes and chugs the last of his beer.

"I'm serious," he chides.

"I know you are, but you can't make it sound like science fiction." Cass's eyes flash the color of blood. "Necromancy is technically fantasy, by the way."

"My *point*," Roman hisses, "is that there's no way we just get to have superpowers. Even Superman had an Achilles's heel. Achilles himself was indestructible and part-*god*, and even that came with a catch."

A fuse clicks in my brain. Every night until I got too old and sick of it, my dad would sit at my bedside and read stories from these old, weathered books. Stories about heroes like Achilles. Stories about monsters. Stories about gods of death and war.

"Look, there probably—absolutely—is. I'm not saying you're wrong." Cass points across the Yard, to the streaking jets of silver and gold light. "I mean, you don't see me out there." I watch the shapes in the distance. Olivia, a comet of silver light; Alessia, and her instruments of war; and Baxter, a blazing sun racing to scorch the earth. "But," Cass continues, sipping from his bottle, "there's no legitimate harm I can see in messing around in an abandoned junkyard. We're not climbing the Eiffel Tower, so who cares?"

"I do," Roman says. "I don't like that I don't understand this, and you shouldn't either."

Cass sits back and stares off with pondering eyes. "Okay, maybe there's a way for us to figure this out without taking things too far. For science. We form a hypothesis, run some experiments, and see what we got."

My brain moves with synaptic lightning, rifling through each of the stories my father told me. A boy, having flown too close to the sun, falling from the sky. Fire stolen from Heaven. A war between gods, and the divine dynasty that would emerge from the victors.

"What is it?" Roman asks, watching me.

Wind tears past us as three figures join us around the fire, nearly blowing it out. Alessia, Baxter, and Olivia wield weapons and wear gleaming plates of armor. Alessia says something, but I'm not listening to her. The slant-eyed wolf painted on the breastplate of her armor looks alive in the firelight.

Of course. *Of course.* How hadn't I seen it before?

"Hold on, Leese." Cass holds up a hand to stop her before turning on me. "Ophelia, what's wrong?"

"I think I know what this is," I'm saying, but someone else interrupts me.

"Trespassing is illegal, you know. So is underage drinking."

The voice comes from the shadows to the east. I jump back behind the log I'm sitting on, but Alessia leaps ahead of us, a double-bladed sword in her hand. Olivia and Baxter flank her on each side, arrows drawn at the ready.

A man's silhouette takes shape. He's tall and stubbled, with fiery red hair tousled across his head in loose curls. He looks older than us, but not by much. His steps are casual and relaxed, but the others don't ease up. As he gets closer, he raises his hands in a show of surrender.

"Easy," he says, smirking. *"I'm not here for a fight. I need your help."*

My legs tremble. As he approaches, weights drop into my stomach. He speaks the language from our dreams.

"Who are you?" I ask, trying to keep my voice steady.

He finally steps into the firelight. Dark ink curls along his thumbs and thickens into wide bands that disappear into the cuffs of his jacket. More tattoos snake along his neck: dark sigils and runes that I can't read.

"I apologize for the intrusion, but I've been looking for you all. It's important." The light in his eyes goes out and he slips into English. "My name is Griffin. I am this generation's Vessel of Destiny. General Davis of the Sacred House requests your presence immediately. It's urgent."

No one expects Alessia to laugh, but she does and maybe we all should have. She lowers her sword a little and eases out of a defensive stance. "Vessel of Destiny? What the hell is that?"

He doesn't seem offended. In fact, he seems a little amused. "I am this world's only human connection to Destiny. When the Fates speak, they speak through me."

Olivia tilts her head. "Like a prophet?"

"Yeah. Like a prophet." He clears his throat. "Now, please come with me. There's a lot to discuss, and we need to do it quickly."

"Hold on," Olivia scoffs. "How do we know you're telling us the truth? Why are you here?"

"I'm sorry, can we go back a bit? The Fates are real?" I ask. "Like actually real?"

He smiles at me. "Oh yes, Ophelia Johnson. Whatever ideas you have about the world you live in, abandon them now. They've all been false."

I take another step back. "How do you know my name?"

"I know all of you. I know that almost three months ago the six of you inherited the powers of the Olympic Pantheon. I know that you're scared, but you were chosen to carry them. It's why we need you."

"For what?" Olivia asks again, narrowing her eyes. "You're here because we have the powers of Greek gods?"

Cass mutters sardonically. "So I was actually right about the Avengers thing. Great."

Griffin furrows his brows. "The Avengers are made up. This is real. I'm here because three months ago, the Fates went missing and are being held hostage. That's why we need your help. Our allies attempted a rescue operation when we sensed them in the Underworld, but whoever took them is very fast and very powerful. They're way stronger than we are."

Baxter scoffs, shaking his head. "There's no way. This is insane."

"Who's we?" Cass asks.

"I'm working with the Sacred House of Athena," Griffin says. "Like I said, we tried to rescue the Fates, but our operation failed. We need fresh eyes."

"And consulting a bunch of kids seems right to you?" Alessia looks around at us, her tone dark with mocking. "Anybody here have any experience with hostages?"

Griffin narrows his eyes, frustrated. "You're not just a bunch of kids. Right now, whether you like it or not, you're the most powerful people on this planet. The Fates need your help. They never need anybody's help, so you have to understand the position you're in. This is *serious*. Will you do it or not?"

Roman cuts his eyes from us to Griffin, before gesturing for us all to huddle around him. Griffin looks exasperated, but he doesn't complain as we deliberate in low voices.

"All right, whatever we do we all have to be on the same page," he says.

"Does anybody seriously buy this?" Cass scoffs. His tone is biting, but there's fear beneath it. "It's insane."

Olivia massages her temple with a trembling hand. I don't think I've ever seen her so unsettled. "It's insane that you can see dead people, so maybe this makes sense. He said we were chosen for this. Maybe he's right."

Baxter shakes his head. "This has nothing to do with those dreams. He's talking about an active hostage situation. What the hell are we supposed to do about that?"

He has a point. If the Vessel of Destiny can't even find the Fates, what are we supposed to do?

Roman's cheeks have turned a sickly shade of green, but he surprises me. "Maybe this is how we find out why this is happening to us. I mean, maybe this is *why* it happened."

"I thought you were very against this," Alessia scoffs. "Having powers is one thing, but we don't know this guy. We don't know if anything he's telling us is true."

Cass scoffs. "Oh, what? It's not fun anymore, Alessia?"

"I was against this, and honestly I still might be," Roman says, "but I also want to understand, and our first clue in three months literally just appeared out of thin air."

Olivia swears. "Damn it. That's a good point."

"I think you're right," I say, surprising myself too. "I think we should do it."

Griffin's urgency is real. I watch him standing by the fire, the way he tugs and twists his fingers like he can't keep himself still.

"Me too," Baxter says. "I wanna know why this is happening to me, to us. That guy seems like our best bet."

Cass watches Griffin through narrowed eyes For once, there's no humor to his expression. "I don't like this but okay. Let's do it."

Alessia shrugs, resigned. "If he's lying, I guess we can always just kill him."

Baxter winces. "Alessia!"

"What?"

We break out of the huddle and join Griffin by the fire. He's started pacing around it.

He doesn't look happy. "So?"

"We'll do it," Roman says, "but you have to tell us everything. No secrets, no lies."

Griffin is so relieved it looks like he'll pass out. "Of course. Full disclosure at all times. Now I need you to come with me.

The commanders of the Sacred House are waiting to meet with you. Tonight."

Cass checks his phone. "Tonight? My curfew's midnight."

Griffin blinks. "To be clear, you're the commander of fallen souls and you're worried about missing curfew?"

"Yes," Cass says simply.

Baxter rolls his eyes. "Just tell James you're spending the night at my house."

"I guess." Cass shrugs. "So how does this work, 'cause I didn't actually see you come in. Are you driving the invisible Batmobile?"

"No, but you'll see," Griffin says. Then he looks at me. "Oh, Ophelia, I was wondering if there was any way I could speak with your father as well. He was the last person to contact the Fates the night they were abducted. We've been looking for him, but his house was abandoned."

A tundra of grief turns my chest ice cold. My knees buckle, but I stay on my feet.

"What the hell are you talking about?" I hiss, suddenly angry.

His voice softens into something more cautious. "We have it on record that Jason Johnson contacted the Fates on the night of July 1st, about an hour before they were abducted. Maybe they told him something that can shed some light on what we're dealing with."

"No." I'm shaking my head; it makes me dizzy. I clutch a hand to my stomach, trying to steady myself. "No. No, he can't."

July 1st. His body on the kitchen floor, eyes wide open. The way I kneeled at his side, trying to pump life back into his heart. It didn't work. Even after I'd cracked his chest, I kept going. By the time EMTs finally arrived, by the time I finally called them, my hands were slick with blood. My father's body had been covered in it.

"Ophelia." It's Cassius. His voice is softer than usual.

"I'm sorry," Griffin says. "I don't understand. I know he hasn't really contacted anybody in our world in a long time, so anything he can—"

"Shut up," I hiss. Thunder rumbles above our heads. "He died that night. He's dead." Saying the words is like pulling out my own teeth. "He was a *history professor.* You don't know anything about him."

They're looking at me like I'm sick and pathetic. Maybe I am. My eyes burn with hot tears. I don't know if I want to scream or disappear.

"Oh no, I'm so sorry. I didn't know," Griffin says, and it sounds like he means it. "Your father was a legend. He still is. You should know that."

"What?" I drag my hands down my face, wiping away the tears that have just betrayed me. "What the hell are you talking about?"

He furrows his brows. "About fifteen years ago, demigods were at war with the Sons of Cronus. Your father fought alongside the Children of Ares and Athena. He led an army to victory in the last battle of the war and walked away from everything. Still, even now, he's our hero. We called him the Saint of Blood."

I want to throw up. I've known for months that there were things my family kept from me, but I would have never guessed something like this. My father liked long walks at sunset and glasses of red wine. He was just as normal as anyone else, at least in my memory.

But of course, my memories are lies. If the secret hoard in Cherice's and Janus's basement is any indication, everything I've ever known up until this point is a lie.

I take a deep breath and force it out. Everyone's watching me. I can't fall apart with everybody watching me. "Okay," I say, my voice finally steady. "Okay, the Fates. What if we can't find them? What happens then?"

A shadow casts over his face like he's seeing ghosts, too. "Eventually, whoever has the Fates *will* kill them. Then the universe ends, and we all die."

CHAPTER FOURTEEN

I ONCE SAW A MAN STANDING barefoot in the middle of the street, shouting into the rain.

His clothes were soiled and tattered. His shoes had split along both sides, exposing his feet to what had been a cruel winter. My dad and I were in Boston, and it was the first few hours before a snowstorm was supposed to hit. The man had posted up in the middle of a busy street, a dirty cardboard sign in one hand and a cowbell in the other. He kept shouting: *The end is near! The end is near!*

Dad and I laughed at the time, but now I shudder to think that perhaps that man had been a prophet after all.

I sit near the fire, my legs weak from the news. Around me, everyone's voices have fallen into the same muffled mash. I can't hear what they're saying; I'm not really here. It took some time, but eventually, the gravity of Griffin's words shackled me in place:

We all die.

People die all the time, every day; but this is different, so much different. And so much worse. The individual lives of every human being on this planet are now firmly in my hands. I turn them over in the firelight, searching for something capable. The world is going to end and I have to save it. Me and the people I jump off cliffs with.

It must be some kind of mistake. It has to be. Maybe the gods got it wrong. They should have given their power to someone important, not a bunch of kids.

Griffin argues with Baxter about something on the other side of the fire, but I've tuned them out. Without even thinking, I stand up and walk toward the dark, sprawling planes of the Yard. A sharp chill plunges down my chest. This isn't happening. I don't know how, but I've decided. Griffin is a hallucination. The past few weeks have been some kind of collective psychosis, and staying here would only mean I'm enabling them. I don't care what I said. I'm going home.

Goosebumps creep out along my shoulders. Behind me, something low and thin splits the air on an unstoppable course. Someone shouts, maybe Roman or Baxter. Lightning spikes in my feet, charging the earth. I pivot to the side and raise my hand, just in time to catch a small, jade green blade between my fingers.

"Man, what the hell was that?" Baxter demands, his shoulders squared.

"I'm sorry," Griffin says, breathless. "I had to prove to you that this is real, because we don't have time for delusions. This is happening to you, Ophelia."

"What are you talking about?" I hiss, closing the distance between us.

A bead of white light switches on in his right eye. "*Selective telepathy. You had doubts. I wanted to dispel them.*" He looks apologetic, but he's still smiling. "Seeing is believing. And now that that's settled, we have to go."

OF BLOOD AND LIGHTNING

"Okay, but how'd you find us in the first place?" Olivia asks. "It's freaking me out."

"An Olympic god hasn't walked this Earth for thousands of years," Griffin says. "I felt you as soon as you inherited their power. The power of a god is like a radio wave," he continues, "and when you started using them, you started sending those waves out. An ordinary mortal wouldn't be able to sense it or see the results of that power with their naked eyes. People with divine blood can. Depending on how powerful that blood is, they might even be able to track it, like me. As soon as I sensed you, I knew I had to find you."

Alessia shakes her head, laughing, "Look we're gonna do it, but I just don't get why you wouldn't find the Fates yourself, being that you're the one who's actually connected to them."

"Oh wow. That's actually an incredible idea. Why didn't I think of that myself?" He slaps his forehead, his expression dark with mocking. "Oh yeah, that's because I did. I knew they were taken the second it happened. And there was nothing I could do about it. Now, if you could save your questions for later, we're gonna be late."

"Where's this place at again?" Roman asks.

Griffin clenches his jaw. "Jasper, Wyoming."

"You want us to go to Wyoming?" Alessia laughs. "Tonight?"

"What?" he shrugs. "You got a term paper due?"

She stops laughing. "You're actually serious."

"Dead serious. Now are we going or not? I can have you all back before sunrise."

We each lock eyes across the fire, waiting for someone to say something. Roman sighs and pulls out his phone, which is as good an answer as any.

Cassius mutters as he pulls his out too.

"Story?" Olivia asks, already typing.

"My house," Baxter says. "Presentation for Clark."

I shake my head. "We already used that one."

"Oh. Marvel movie night," Roman says.

Griffin looks confused. "What's happening?"

"Parents," we all say at the same time.

When it looks like Griffin has exhausted all his patience, we kill the fire. Darkness only blankets us for a second. In the next, a ball of white light forms in the middle of Griffin's bridged palms.

"Should we all hold hands?" Cass asks.

Griffin snorts. "That's funny."

The light in his palm swells into a tiny sun, about the size of a bowling ball, before blasting out from him like a supernova. It washes over us, then a curtain of darkness falls across the world. The earth falls away in a swallow of air. I don't know if I'm floating or falling, and then my feet land against the damp ground.

It's another forest, this one a towering wall of evergreens. We're standing in the middle of a massive clearing, with the moon dangling in the center of the sky. More stars than I can count shine above. Nothing that looks like a house though.

Baxter sucks his teeth. "Are we meeting them here, or . . ."

Griffin shushes him. "Just wait for it."

A second later, a wall of air along the eastern tree line shimmers and falls away. It parts like a curtain, revealing a massive chain of interconnected buildings behind a black, iron gate. Sentries in black robes stand around it, in clusters of two and three. Griffin leads the way to the front, where the gates break open on their own. The sprawling lawn in front of us lays at the feet of dark, gothic buildings, their windows glowing with orange lanterns. More robed people wander over the grounds, some of them racing by on four-wheelers. At least twenty of them come marching along the western perimeter, led by a drill sergeant.

There's one huge building in the very center, with a stained glass dome. More than a dozen others are scattered around it, with the same domed roofs. The smaller ones, built like houses, are dark along the edge, while the building in the center is washed in streetlights. People urgently stream in and out of the double doors. It looks like everyone's on edge tonight.

"Welcome to the Sacred House of Athena," Griffin says, throwing out his hands. "Home to the Children of War."

"Holy shit," Alessia mutters. "So you aren't insane."

"Only a little. Come on."

No one stops us as Griffin takes us inside. The grand foyer is paved in beige marble. A high ceiling hangs above us, light striking from its glass chandelier. More people move around us, but none of them seem to care why we're here. The air is charged with electricity.

Griffin urges us on, up the double staircase, to a hallway lined with burgundy carpet. Brown doors line the walkway, each labeled with a bronze plaque. This must not be our floor though, because Griffin leads us to another stairwell around the corner. We climb and climb, until the gaping windows around us reveal a sprawling view of the facility. I can't see the clearing anymore. It's just a sea of dark forest, spreading out into infinity.

Griffin decides we can stop on the tenth floor. There are more doors on this one, but the plaques are blank. All except

the one at the end of the hall, which is labeled: *Chief General.*
We pass by it, before stopping at the door of what must be a
conference room. The glass is frosted, but I can see the
blurry outline of a long table.

Griffin stops before opening the door.

"Okay this is it," he says. "Pull up your big kid pants
because this is when it gets real."

Alessia glowers at him. "Just open the door."

He lets us inside with a sigh. Two people are already waiting
on the left side of the table. A dark-skinned young woman
with a severe expression; the man is much older, like he could
be her grandfather. He wears a golden robe, cut from thick
velvet, with dozens of black chains hanging from his neck. A
second woman sits at the head of the table and looks like she's
in charge. She's dressed for battle, in a black, armored one
piece, with dark locs framing her face. She's sitting down, but
I'm sure there's a sword dangling from her hip.

"Goodness. I thought you were gone for good this time,
Griffin," she says, her smile polite.

Griffin laughs. "Yet another day passes and death doesn't
visit me. Apologies."

"Please, I wouldn't want to get rid of you. Take a seat. All
of you."

Still following Griffin's lead, we each take a seat at the
massive, stone table. It's large enough for at least thirty
people. The floor up here is a pure, white marble. The huge
window at the front of the room offers a clear view of the
front gate, where the guards still stand and watch. At each
corner of the room, the statue of an armored woman
watches us. She wields a scepter, with a Greek helmet
beneath her feet.

"Hello," the woman at the end of the table greets. "I would first like to thank you all for making the time. I know it's a little late. My name is Chief General Makena Davis." She gestures to the woman at her side. "This is my Lieutenant General and Tactical Commander Atalanta Evans. And this is my Minister of Intel, Emilio Fueves. Welcome to the Sacred House of Athena. I apologize that we aren't meeting under better circumstances."

Their titles sink in the room like weights of gold. I can tell from the way they hold their shoulders back that these are very important people. If people like this are meeting me in the middle of the night, then it really has to be that bad.

"Well, it's nice to meet you all the same," Roman says, sounding unsure. "We were told that the Fates have been kidnapped."

Her polite smile remains. "Yes. Please, Minister Fueves."

The grizzled man right across from me doesn't look nearly as polite. He picks up a briefcase and takes out a bright red manila folder. The stamp across the front reads: URGENT.

"Approximately two months ago, on July 27th, the Fates were abducted from their home at around 11:45 pm. We were contacted on July 29th by Griffin Warren, the Vessel of Destiny." He flips through a few pages before continuing. "Exactly four weeks after that, we assembled a specialized extraction team, Minerva Squad One, and attempted a rescue them from the Underworld. The attempt was unsuccessful as the Fates are still well hidden. One month after our rescue attempt, the Vessel of Destiny made a divine connection to the Fates." He gestures for Griffin to continue.

Griffin's expression goes dark. "When I make divine connections, I become a conduit of Fate. It's like long-distance telepathy. I accessed their thoughts, and they were seeing their own deaths. I don't know when, and I don't know how, but I'm sure of one thing: if we don't find them they're going to die."

Cass is pale. The same haunted expression he's been wearing for the past few weeks drifts onto his face again like the dead surround us now. "So where do we start?"

"We're reasonably sure what their motive is," Lieutenant Evans says. "The house looked like they'd been searching for something. A couple weeks after the Fates's abduction, there were raids on Demigod libraries all over the eastern seaboard. They're looking for the Codex Sanctus."

"Well, what the hell is that?" Baxter asks, not bothering to hide the panic in his voice.

The General shakes her head. "We conducted an audit of our intel but found nothing. From witness statements and first-hand survivor accounts, we've concluded that it's both an ancient text and artifact. Lieutenant?"

"Thank you, General," she says, clearing her throat. "Our infiltration of the Underworld leads us to believe that it's been compromised. Since our operation failed, we haven't been able to make contact with Queen Persephone, or any of our other constituents down below. We believe that at this time, our best course of action is to locate the Codex Sanctus before our enemies do and use it to lure them into a trap. We'll propose an exchange: the Codex for the Fates."

Olivia waves her hand. "I'm sorry, I'm not trying to be rude, but how exactly are we supposed to do something that you haven't? Until a few weeks ago, I thought the gods were just myths. I'd say you're much better equipped than we are."

"Well, frankly, whoever has the Fates is much more powerful than we are." The General pulls out a file of her own, also marked: URGENT. "Demigods are organized into Houses by patron god. At first, I suspected the Sons of Cronus, but whoever's doing this is much more powerful and organized. We've been collaborating with the Southern House of Poseidon for tactical intel on our enemies. We don't know much about them yet, but they're highly trained and highly dangerous. When Griffin felt the presence of Olympic gods on the earth again, we knew you were our only hope."

A shadow falls across Cass's face. "And the whole end of the world thing? Is it true?"

The Lieutenant's expression is just as grim. "It is. The fabric of space-time is held together by destiny itself. The Fates are the metaphysical core of that destiny. If they're gone, our universe will cease to exist."

Hearing it a second time doesn't make it easier to stomach.

"Please help us save them," the General says. "Our Polis is at your disposal anytime. Use whatever resources you need. Effective immediately, I'm approving the six of you for security level Alpha-B. You'll have essentially unfettered access to any part of the facility and grounds, with very few exceptions."

The Lieutenant stands from her seat and disappears through a door to the left of the window. She comes back carrying an old, black briefcase with threads pulling up along the seams. She opens it against the table and starts lining things up in front of her: a mortar and pestle, four glass bottles of herbs, sealed with parchment and twine, and a box of matches.

She sprinkles herbs into the mortar before pulling a small, bronze knife out of her pocket. It looks like the same one Cass used to summon my grandmother. She makes a long incision along the middle of her palm and squeezes gold blood into the bowl. As she crushes the herbs, a strong aroma I don't recognize fills the room. When she's done, she gets up and walks over to me.

"May I see the back of your hand?" She asks, her eyes cold and distant.

I do as she says. She dips the pad of her thumb into the dark mixture and presses it against the back of my right hand. She closes her eyes, muttering under her breath. Red light washes over my hand. The dark mixture spreads out from her thumb, seeping into my skin. When she pulls her hand away, the image of a severed Gorgon head stares back at me. Medusa, in all her serpent-haired glory.

She goes around the room, repeating the process with the others. When she's done, she drops a lit match into the bowl. The mixture disappears, and she packs everything away.

"Thank you, Lieutenant," the General says. "From now on, whenever you need to come here, you'll be granted access. So what can we do to help?"

For once, Roman sounds like the calm one. "Do you have a library?"

THE TRIP TO THE LIBRARY IS another trek up the stairs, this time all the way to the top floor. The General and her posse don't come with us, just Griffin. He presses his palm against the grand, oak door, and the same Gorgon-headed sigil comes to life across the back of his hand. A heavy lock slides back, and he leads the way inside.

The library is a maze of towering bookshelves, lined up in neat rows. Torches burn low on the walls, filling the room with gold light. There are paintings of armored soldiers all along the walls, bordered by gilt framing. In the very center of the library, surrounded by small, low-burning candles, is a twenty-five foot tall sculpture, carved from smooth, clean ivory. It's the same woman from the conference room, Athena, only this time she wears a chiton that flows down to her bare feet. There's still a sword in her hand, aimed at the ornate gold circle at the center of the ceiling.

"Over here." Griffin waves us over to a dark wood table, where someone else has already left some of their books behind. "All right, what's the plan?"

Cass's voice is dry and mirthless. "Kill the dragon, save the girl?"

Griffin doesn't seem amused. He turns away from Cass and gestures to the rest of us. "What's the plan?"

"What are the chances that we could still just find the Fates?" Roman asks. "Because even if we find this Codex thing, how can we guarantee they won't just kill the Fates anyway?"

"Our guess is that whoever did this did it because they assumed the Fates would have the Codex, or at least some information about where to find it. Maybe that's why they've decided to keep them alive." Griffin should sound hopeful when he says it. He doesn't.

Olivia sits back, folding her arms. "But wait, if that's the case then how do you know anything we do will change that? It's fate, right?"

He's not so quick to answer this time. A vein jumps in his temple.

"We don't," he finally says. "By now, I'm sure you've realized that we really don't know anything. I wish I could tell you differently, but I can't."

Another long, swollen silence. I try to think, but my head hurts. It seems impossible that we could know where to start.

It seems impossible that we could change anything at all. If a room of commanders and generals has hit a wall, what makes them think we'll be able to get over it?

"The Codex." Olivia rights herself, letting out a long breath. "It's a book, right? Why would you kidnap someone for a book? That just doesn't make sense to me."

"It's gotta be one hell of a book," I say. I jerk my chin in Griffin's direction. "What *can* you tell us?"

He sits back in his chair to watch the domed ceiling above us. "I found an old journal in the Archives. I mean as old as ancient Mesopotamia. It was a trade receipt—oil and flour for this black book called the Codex Sanctus. I can't trace it after that and there's nothing else in any of our libraries."

"At least they won't get anywhere raiding libraries," Alessia mutters. She shrugs. "That's good. Doesn't really help us though."

Roman shakes his head. "How are we supposed to find something that doesn't leave a paper trail?"

Griffin leans forward on his forearms. "Think we might've missed something?" He asks. "We can comb through the library. It'll take some elbow grease, but that seems like our best shot."

Alessia yawns into her hands and answers for all of us. "Sick. Where do we start?"

There are dozens of bookshelves around us, each one so tall it seems to sway with its own height. There are at least a thousand books in here, if not more.

Griffin's smile is dim, like a dying lightbulb. "Wherever you want."

CHAPTER FIFTEEN

By THE TIME THE FIRST FEW rays of sunlight start trickling in through the roof, we're no closer than we were when we started. The room brightens beneath a new day. Above us, the sky is a pale, simmering pink, cleaved in two by the rising sun.

Baxter lounges in one of the velvet arm chairs, a half-open book in his hand. His snoring echoes against the walls. Alessia's on the floor, only a few feet away from him. She's trying to fight it, but the red rims around her eyes give her away. Olivia, the only one who doesn't look tired, flips through a book with a peeling cover. Beside her, Cassius is curled up on the floor.

Roman and I have been at this table with Griffin for hours. We've been sitting so still I'm worried I've turned to stone. First, we read through Minerva Squad One's incident report. The operation had actually been going according to plan. Griffin had successfully made contact with the Fates before they were spirited away by some kind of shadow. That's all it says in the file, and that's all Griffin remembers seeing. The soldiers guarding the Underworld covered their faces and wore all black. Whatever dark shadow swept the Fates away doesn't have a name.

After the incident report, we start trying to find anything on the Codex. Roman Googles it anyway, even though neither of us is very confident he'll find anything. And of course, he doesn't.

We spend an hour wandering around the library, searching for anything about a black book. There are myths, journals, and even textbooks on ancient Greek history, but nothing that dates back to ancient Sumer. Records of legends and myths are never exactly reliable, but the Codex might as well be a ghost.

Roman skims the last page of his book before pushing it away. "All right." He rubs his eyes, yawning deeply.

"I thought he was exaggerating," Alessia mumbles, eyes half-closed.

Griffin barely moves at the end of the table, his head resting against folded arms. "I never exaggerate. If there was something to find, we would've found it."

"So maybe it's not a book we should be looking for," Olivia says.

Cass waves his hand. "Say more words."

She comes over to the table carrying an old tome. It's a story about a hero and his quest to kill a monster. "What do you guys know about the Eye? The Graeae Sisters?"

"Perseus." Suddenly, Griffin pops up, his brow furrowed. "Olivia, you're a genius."

She smiles. "Seriously?"

"Seriously. I mean, they could tell us everything: who we're dealing with, what they want, what they're planning. Shit, they could even tell us where the Fates are."

Finally, Cass looks more awake. He leans over Olivia's shoulder to read the book in her hand. "Can they really do all that?"

"Yeah, can we get a refresher course on this?" Baxter asks. "I think I missed that part of the Greek God Crash Course."

Griffin ignores his jab. "The Graeae Sisters are the Keepers of the Sacred Knowledge. Their artifact, the Eye, gives them access to any piece of information you'd ever need."

"Artifact?" Roman asks.

"They're vehicles for divine power," Griffin explains. "Like the Trident or the Bolt. Your power belongs to you, and anything you bestow it upon becomes an artifact."

Cass still looks confused. "That makes perfect sense."

Baxter closes his eyes and lets his head hang back. "Does the book say how we find them?"

"Yeah. Some place called Cisthene," Olivia says. "It's an island."

"It's guarded by the Children of Dionysus," Griffin says. "I'll let them know you're coming so they don't try to kill you."

Olivia jerks back. "What?"

"If that's what we're doing then you guys need to come up with a plan," Griffin continues. "I'll present the op to the General, but I'm serious. Don't mess this up."

"It's comforting to know you have so much faith in us," Cass says.

Roman laughs a little, his smile strained. "So, do we get a code name too? Minerva Squad One is kinda sick."

Griffin shrugs. "I don't know. Maybe. How are you guys gonna do this?"

"Um . . ." Cass's voice trails off into snoring.

Alessia smacks him in the chest. "Look, I think we've all put in our best effort at this point." She gestures to the windows above us, where the sky has brightened into the soft color of peach skin. "Let's call it a night and regroup. Then, tomorrow we figure out how we need to do this. We'll be more productive if we're rested."

Baxter yawns. "Now that's a plan."

"Agreed." I drag my hands down my face. I can't remember the last time I stayed up all night like this.

"That works. I can take you guys home." Griffin laughs into his hand, a hint of mocking in his voice. "You guys should learn how to jump. It'll suck having to chauffeur you around all the time."

Alessia tilts her head. "Jump?"

"Oh shit." Roman's face brightens with fascination. "You mean teleportation?"

Griffin rolls his eyes. "If that's what I meant, then that's what I would've said."

"Whatever. How do we do it?'

"It's actually really simple," Griffin says. "You just have to breathe, visualize where you want to go, and be there."

"That's super helpful," Cass quips.

"Just try it. If it doesn't work I'll take you home. Where do you want to go?"

I point at Baxter with the toe of my foot. "His place."

Baxter nods. "That works. Let's try it."

No one leaves empty-handed. After we've all collected as many books as we can carry, we gather in the middle of the library again. I gaze at the double, gilded doors toward the back. The handles are secured by a long, gold chain.

"You got a monster in there?" I ask.

Griffin's expression is strangely serious. "It's the restricted section. And before you ask, none of us have the clearance."

Cass and Baxter actually look disappointed.

"All right," Griffin says. "Everybody close your eyes and listen up."

We do as he says. As soon as the world goes dark, it feels like I could fall asleep where I'm standing.

"Picture the house. Imagine how the walls sound with wind passing through them, how they creak. Imagine the porch, and the stairwell, and the front door."

I see it: a slightly smaller version of the more massive estate to its immediate left. The way the valley cradles it against the waiting arms of the forest. The white swing on the front porch, and the warm, frosted glass windows.

"Imagine that you're there," Griffin says. "You see the house, and then the wind carries you away."

A cold fist grips my sternum and snatches me into the dark. Just before I'm gone, I swear I hear laughter in Griffin's voice: "See ya later."

Freezing wind rushes around me, wrapping around my body like a glove. The darkness tosses me head over heels as I come down hard in Baxter's front yard. A quiet, cool morning rises around the sprawling estate. The house on the hill and all its coldness watches us as we right ourselves, brushing the dirt out of our clothes.

Alessia's laugh splits the air in half.

"We just jumped!" Cass cheers, smiling despite his exhaustion.

Roman doesn't look too happy about the verbiage, but he decides to let it go.

Our celebration is short-lived. In less than an hour, we've all showered and scavenged for clothes in the empty rooms. Baxter and Alessia bring down a mound of blankets from the attic.

We lay them out across the living room floor. Roman sets up a mound of pillows right beside me. It feels like a sleepover. Well, almost. When I was a kid, I wasn't worried about how I was going to save the world. Just how I was going to save myself from whatever boogie man was hiding in the closet.

Cassius brings us all plates of eggs and bacon. We sit on folded legs around the room to eat.

Olivia talks through a mouthful of egg. "I feel like we shouldn't just jump into this Cisthene thing. We need a strategy."

"Yeah, if we don't do this right we'll probably die," Baxter says.

I point between him and Olivia.

"You two are fast. If anything goes left, you'd be able to deal with it before the rest of us. And Alessia you're definitely a fighter, which is good. Things might get a little sticky."

"Are you volunteering my bravery?" Alessia scoffs. Then she shrugs and goes back to eating her eggs. "Whatever. It'll be nice to have some actual experience."

Something about the ways she says it unnerves me, like we're talking about gardening or something. I don't exactly know what to expect, but I know we've failed already if we don't anticipate danger. My dad would always say that, usually about things that were much more mundane. Knowing what I know now, maybe it was things like this that taught him that principle.

"What should I do?" Roman asks.

"You're the negotiator. If they're not willing to just give us the Eye, then you convince them."

"And if they can't be convinced?"

Someone should have an answer, but the room falls quiet. That's not a possibility I want to consider. I don't have the stomach for it.

"I don't know. It needs work," Olivia says, finally breaking the silence, "but it's a good start. When should we do it?"

"I have a project due soon—art history," Cass mumbles from his corner, his eyes half closed. "Oh shit. And Homecoming."

Roman's expression is searing. "Only if the world doesn't end first."

"Yeah, you're right." Olivia pushes her plate away and stares at her hands.

The end of everything: this tiny blue planet and the worlds beyond it too. It's still difficult to imagine. I've only ever known how to exist.

"Let's make a plan and get into shape," Alessia suggests. "Then let's go finish this shit."

Baxter's smiling, even though he looks like he'll pass out. "Yeah. *Then* we can worry about Homecoming."

"Exactly," Alessia agrees. "It's about priorities."

Ten minutes later, the sun conquers New River. The house fills up with natural light, but it doesn't matter. Cass goes first, and Alessia follows shortly after him. Roman's lazy, half-lidded smile is the last thing I see before sleep claims me too.

PART TWO:

HE WHO HUNGERS

CHAPTER SIXTEEN

ALESSIA FIGHTS TO KILL, HER EYES murky with deadly intent.

She swings her blade at my throat. Down toward my face. Across my ribs. I jump in and out of the arc of her arms, which move like vipers against me. Each time I manage to dodge her, it's always just barely. When I don't, the hot edge of her blade threatens to split my skin.

Dusk encroaches, washing the world in soft, yellow light. She's pressing me against the outer edges of the Yard's main clearing, her rhythm steady: *jab, swipe, jab, swipe.* I block her sword with the flat of my blade, pushing her back. Her eyes light up as she closes in again.

Another jab, this one aimed at my shoulder. I jerk back, sweeping out of the way just in time. She appears behind me. When she swipes at my ankles next, I'm less prepared. The pain is a bright flash of white light. My skin splits, and my left knee buckles.

She must notice, because she swings her sword into a spear, and jabs the glossy, wooden handle against my chest, launching me back. I'm not strong or fast enough to recover, so I land on my back in the dirt. She knocks my blade aside;

it vanishes in the air with a hiss. In the next second, the glossy red blade of her spear is aimed at my chest.

"Yield," she says.

"Fine."

Laughing, she lets her spear vanish and helps me up.

With Cisthene looming ahead of us, and the end of the world not so far behind it, we figured it would be best to actually figure out how to control our powers. Olivia and Alessia seem to be having the best luck, like they were made for battle. I, on the other hand, can't seem to get it.

"This sucks." I pull my sword out of thin air again, turning it over.

It's a long, silver blade, the hilt carved into the regal, deadly shape of a dragon's head. The silver serpent has two glittering rubies for eyes, so striking it looks like the blade can actually see. Carved along the blade's spine, in thin, looping Greek, is the inscription: *Lord of the Sky*.

The more time that passes, the more uncertain I feel. I've never been in a fight. Ever. I got close one time in tenth grade, but a teacher came to break it up before things could escalate. Aside from the otherworldly strength and speed, Alessia seems to have a natural predisposition to combat. When she swings a scepter into a sword, when she pivots on a dime in the air. It's more than talent. It has to be.

"You're so good at this," I tell her. "You and Liv. How do you do it?"

"It's cause you're thinking too much. Did anyone have to teach you how to make a storm?"

"No."

"Exactly." Her armor is gone now, but the spear in her hand still makes her look like a warrior. Not the fake kind, but the kind that could really kill you. "Baxter and I have this theory. We inherited the powers of these gods, and I think we inherited their battle experience too. But it's not like memories or anything. It's in our muscles, in our cells."

"Okay. I don't know. It doesn't seem like I got any of that."

She laughs. "That's because you never take the offensive. You're always anticipating my attacks, but you never initiate your own. It's because you're scared."

"I'm not scared."

Still smiling, she swings her spear so that the dull, blade-less end shoots out toward my face. Lightning charges my feet, and I slide back to the outskirts of the clearing. Her laughter echoes across the wide distance between us.

"That's fear, Ophelia, which is good, but you're not balancing it out."

Rolling my eyes, I trudge back to her. "What does that mean?"

"It means you have to attack just as much as you retreat. You're nearly as fast as Baxter and Olivia, definitely faster than me. That's why you didn't totally get your ass kicked. And honestly, you're probably the strongest out of all of us." She levels her spear at me, the pointed blade aimed at my face this time. "But you're scared, so you think too much, and you're blocking out your instincts."

"Oh." My cheeks burn. I'm not sure if I should feel complimented or reprimanded. "So what should I do?"

"Don't worry about that. Just move."

Faster than blinking, she swings the spear around and strikes me in the chest with the blunt end. The force sends me back to the edge of the clearing. She closes in the distance before I can react, falling into a similar rhythm.

Jab. Swipe. Sweep.

My legs fly out from under me. The world tilts, and my back hits the dirt. Before I can get up she's on top of me, the spear now a shining red battle ax. She raises it with both hands, leaving her stomach undefended.

I let my sword vanish and drive my fist into her gut. Her ax vanishes, and she crumbles at the impact. I don't give her time to recover. I hit her again, in the exact same spot. This time she rolls off me and scrambles to her feet. When she swings, there's a sword in her hand.

Our blades clang together, locking in a shower of sparks. I plant my foot and drive forward, breaking the hold. When I swipe at her chest, missing by an inch, she smiles. Red light shimmers over her body, leaving plates of armor behind. The eyes of the wolf carved into her breastplate burn with bloodlust.

We dance around each other's blades, the Yard rattling with the force of our blows. The lightning in my blood is frenzied. I press in, jabbing at her ribs. I give her enough space to leap to the left and sweep her legs out from beneath her.

She lands hard on her back. I aim the silver tip of my sword at her face.

"Yield," I demand, smiling.

But she's still smiling. Her hand flies out, and something cool and sharp coils around my ankle. She jerks the other end of the bullwhip, dragging me down to earth. Before I can get my bearings, she's standing over me. Sword in hand.

"Better," she says, smiling. "Now yield."

"Whatever." I knock the blade aside and kick my captured foot. "Get this shit off me."

Laughing, she lets the sword and whip disappear before helping me up. "I'm serious," she says. "That was much better. You really almost had me."

"But I didn't."

She shrugs. "Well, you can't have everything. Don't worry. With some practice, you'll be very dangerous."

"That's actually really sweet."

"You're welcome." Her expression darkens, something apprehensive there.

"What?"

She sighs. "I don't know, man. I just keep thinking . . . why didn't you tell us about your dad? I know it's not my business and I know how fresh it is, but you're my friend," she says, pointedly. "We don't have to hash it out, but I wanted to let you know that you didn't *need* to keep it a secret. Not from your friends. Okay?"

Her eyes are kind and so sincere it makes my throat pinch.

"Okay." I can't look her in the eye. "I mean thank you, Alessia. I mean it."

She shrugs me off. "Like I said, you're my friend. It's nothing."

Alessia and I leave in separate cars. I make the drive in silence, trying to clear that pesky, sentimental lump in my throat.

When I pull up to the house, the driveway is empty. It's nearly dusk, and it's a weeknight, but I'm glad they're not here. They'd have questions about my day and what I did. Those are getting harder to answer. I basically say the same thing every time, but how long can you really keep a secret?

Anger rushes into me like hot magma. I've only been keeping this from them for a few weeks, but their secrets are older than an entire lifetime. Out of everything, I think that's what's most frustrating. For everyone else, there's nothing connecting the fantasy to their real lives. They get to be gods and go home to their normal families, where at least one thing in their life isn't totally changed forever.

I don't get to say the same. Every single layer of my life is different, including the foundation. With each day that passes, I get the nagging sense that I didn't know my father at all. The more that feeling grows, so does the anger. I've never liked being angry with my father, and I especially don't like it now that he's not here anymore. It feels like I'm dishonoring the dead, but I can't help it. How do you honor the memory of someone you didn't actually know?

It's freezing outside, but the house is warm and dark. Something smells good in the kitchen. I follow the scent to a plate on the stove, wrapped in foil. The post-it note on top is a letter from Janus and Cherice.

Date night. Back at 11. Love you!

Sighing, I toss the note to the side. Janus made spaghetti tonight. I forgot how he likes to put sugar in it. That must be where my dad got it from.

I eat dinner in the kitchen before washing my plate. I take a shower and change into a pair of pajamas. By now, the house is completely dark and still. Cars drive by outside, their wheels splashing against a fresh onset of rainfall. I have no self-control. Instead of going to my room and going to sleep, which is absolutely what I should do, I walk down the hallway to their room. I look in the closet and notice a torn envelope sticking out from one of Janus's coat pockets.

It's from someone named Terrica Jones. The letter inside is written in thick, black ink, on heavy parchment paper.

Janus,

I'm so sorry. Jason was the very best of us.
As for the update you wanted: a few scouts at
the House of Brimstone reported seeing
Children of the First in Wales. Please be careful.
You know what this means.

I take a picture before putting the note back how I found it. I don't know what any of those words mean, but I am certain of one thing: whatever this is, it can't be good.

CHAPTER SEVENTEEN

LISTENING TO MR. HOUSTON'S LECTURE IS like having my teeth pulled, but maybe I'm just being dramatic. Being here feels strange. With the exception of a growing collection of Halloween decor appearing around the building, nothing else has changed in the past few months. Nothing but the quiet world between us, where gods and magic lurk beneath the shadows. And in our homes.

I couldn't sleep last night. I knew there'd be no point consulting Google on "Children of the First," but I had to try. After hours of pointless scrolling, I finally heard the sound of a car pulling into the driveway. Janus and Cherice were out much later than I expected. It was almost 1 am by the time they came inside. I'd gone down to meet them and managed to catch sight of the nasty bruise shining on Janus' cheek. Of course, that too had been "top secret" and "none of my business."

I'm still angry about it, even though I hadn't argued with them. There are more important things to worry about anyway. The first deadline looms closer: a date with Cisthene. I'm not sure what to expect.

Roman slides his foot over to nudge mine. British History is our only class together.

"You're scowling," he says under his breath.

"Nobody uses that word in real life." I nudge him back. "What do you have next period?"

He pretends to think. "Something I can skip."

"Cool. I need a study buddy."

He blinks. "Oh. For this class or . . . ?"

"No, genius. I brought some shit from the magic library."

"Right. We can go to the art room. It's unlocked."

"Yeah, that works."

Thankfully, the bell interrupts Houston's lecture. He doesn't look happy about it.

Roman and I head for the art room. He looks around like the secrets in our heads might be overheard by the students around us. I guess I don't really care as much about that. Even if people knew, no one would believe us.

"Hey, we're friends, right?" he says, surprising me.

I smile at him. "Well, actually I considered us eternal, mortal enemies, but I guess I like the idea that we're friends a bit more."

"You know, I can totally see the whole sworn rivals thing."

"Yeah. And it would be cool to have a nemesis." I bump him with my shoulder as we leave the main building. "Of course, we're friends. Why? What's up?"

"I've just been thinking about you," he says. "I know you're going through a lot, so I wanted to check in. See how you were doing?"

I shrug. "It's a day. There's another one after it."

"Yeah I know, but is it a good day?"

We climb the steps to the auditorium building and follow the main hall to a set of brown doors. Just as he said, the art room is empty. Fourteen black desktops stagger each other up and down the first half of the room, facing a lonely, brown desk. Through a breezeway to the left is the portrait room. Empty easels circle a plain wooden block in the middle of the room. Roman jogs ahead of me and drags a stool over to the block.

He's already taller, but he towers over me when we sit in the middle of the room. With sunlight spilling over him, it's easy to imagine that thousands of years ago, people would be clamoring to carve slabs of marble into his likeness. His hair falls in clean, black layers across eyes that shine like crystals.

It's not until he waves his hand in front of me that I realize I've been staring.

"Hey. Welcome to planet Earth," he laughs.

"Asshole." I reach into my bag for the first book.

I've been trying to work through the four I took from the library. The other three were mainly storybooks, but this one opens with a memo.

Archive: House of the Cursed Children, 1472
Sacred texts enclosed.

I read it again, but then the words start dancing across my vision, blurring into illegible characters. Roman must notice. He edges closer.

"What is it?" he asks.

I ignore him and flip through the page. The foreword is by General Sergeant Oscar Askis. He labels himself as a Child of the Void.

> *From the halls of our Cursed House, we engrave our history into the great tombs of time.*
>
> *To the Sacred Mother, She Who Walked First. Tyranny will never conquer the power of blood. Or bury these broken stories.*

"Ophelia," Roman says again, his hand hovering just above my shoulder.

I cower away from his touch. My body feels like a cut wire—charged and frayed.

"I've heard of this before." I flash him the first page. *"House of the Cursed Children.* My aunt and uncle have books about this in their basement."

"Seriously?"

"Seriously. And this photobook from the seventies. My family attended some kind of event, a banquet."

"Griffin did say that your father was some kind of war hero. That would make sense, right?"

It does, but it doesn't make me feel better. I keep flipping through the book, reading out loud. For the first few pages, the Sergeant tells the story of the First Goddess. She sprung from some primordial void and dragged everything else into being with the power of her hands. Her descendants filled the earth, living in its shadows. Always hunted by the Children of Paradise.

"Children of Paradise," he recites. "That sound familiar to you?"

I shake my head. "Not at all. Is Paradise some kind of god?"

"I don't know." He urges me on. "Keep going."

The next page is penned by a new author: General Maria Warcott, a Daughter of Ares. She writes about the fall of Olympus, and her grief is calcified into the dried ink. I read:

> *"The Great War ends with twelve empty thrones. The Lords of All Darkness and Suffering have been now and forever sealed in the belly of their Refuge, and shall never again stain the earth with their footsteps. Still, this great burden rests upon my heart. Who will carry the sun across the sky and call the oceans back from the shore? The earth mourns, and so do I. Would I trade the defeat of a great evil for the*

lives of our Fathers, even with it being clear that their lives were the immutable price of victory?"

She doesn't answer her own question, at least not in the journal. I wonder if she ever figured out the answer.

"Huh," Roman says, thinking. "That explains what happened to the originals, but I still don't get why we got their powers."

"Yeah. If they're dead, shouldn't their power die with them?" I keep flipping through the book, skimming the pages. There's nothing else about the Olympians. Not the Children of Paradise either.

I shut the book and toss it on the floor. "This is stupid."

Roman snorts and leans forward to pick it up. "Okay, maybe if we—"

The door opens in the other room and a clatter of footsteps sound into the art studio: teachers, and they don't look happy to see us. Not at all.

"You're not supposed to be in here," one of them says. He narrows his eyes at Roman. "I expect you to know that, Mr. Hartfield."

Roman's cheeks flush as we pack up our stuff. He apologizes for both of us, and we hurry out of the room before they can ask us what class we're supposed to be in.

"Sorry," he says on the way down the hall. "I thought it'd be empty."

"It's fine. That was just a . . . pointless exercise." I shrug. "It's whatever."

"I don't know. It might still be useful," he says. "Can I keep the book?"

"Sure. Go crazy." I fish it out of my bag and hand it to him. "What now? Do I have to go to class?"

"There's always the library."

That's where we spend the rest of the period. He's lost in the journal, but I don't bother.

The next time I see him, he's outside with Baxter and Cass. Baxter has the minister's map in his lap. He traces its lines with the capped end of a sharpie. Roman and Cass snicker amongst themselves at some private joke.

"'Sup." I sit on the other side of Baxter, jostling him with my shoulder.

Roman smiles at me, and Cass juts out his chin in greeting. Baxter says nothing, like I'm not even here.

I tap the map with my pen. "Didn't you already do this?"

"Don't you ever study?" Baxter asks, still not looking at me.

"Sometimes. Plus we already know where we're going, so what's the point?"

Cass lets out a breath through his teeth. I can't tell if his eyes are cautious or amused. "Here it goes."

Sighing, Baxter puts the map in my lap. There are four red Xs beyond the shaded cluster of a two dimensional forest. He draws imaginary circles around them with the marker. "So which X marks the spot? There are four of them. According to Fueves, this is the most updated map he could find. I'm trying to figure out which path is the right one."

"Yeah, but you can't really do that just by looking at the—"

"Ophelia, please." He hangs his head like I've actually hurt his feelings. "Can I just have this one thing?"

"What?"

"He's having a hard time," Roman laughs, clapping Baxter on the shoulder. "Remember man: accept the things you can't change."

Baxter's gaze is searing. He says something you'd never hear in a church as Olivia and Alessia come down the stairs.

Olivia sighs at the sight of the map. "Babe, why are you doing this to yourself?"

"I'm coping," Baxter chides, snatching back the map. "Isn't that what I'm supposed to do?"

"I don't think this is coping, man," Alessia says. "It's obsessive. It's not healthy. I'm kinda worried about you."

"I swear to God . . ."

I don't catch the rest of their conversation. Someone standing across the parking lot catches my eye. A boy in all black, with eyes like chunks of dull emerald. The people walking past don't seem to notice him, but I can't be imagining it. He's staring right at me.

"Hey." I nudge Baxter with my knee. "You see that?"

He and Roman follow the direction I'm pointing in. The boy doesn't move. The thick belt around his waist shines against the evening sun, marked with an arrowhead symbol. The blade of his sheathed sword is a bit harder to identify.

Olivia steps onto the sidewalk, tilting her head. "Who the hell is that?"

Alessia drops her bag and strides forward. "Let's find out."

She's stepping into the parking lot when the boy takes off. And he's fast, much faster than a normal person should be. And somehow, no one else sees him. No one but us.

A red blade appears in her hand, and she takes off after him. We follow, leaving the school behind. In seconds, we're miles away from town, in a dense cluster of green forest. He doesn't move like a man. He's a streak of shadow—darting between branches and dashing through underbrush.

Olivia and Baxter are faster. Just as they lunge for the hem of his robe, the boy soars into the trees. Their bodies collide, but Alessia's already leaping after him. I'm the second one up. The boy swings from branch to branch with one hand, and launches tiny, green daggers with the other. One of them scrapes across my cheek but I don't care.

"Stop!" Alessia shouts just ahead.

Streaks of silver and gold rush past me. Just ahead, a pale light parts the trees. I see a wide open clearing, stretching for miles. There's nowhere for the boy to go. No way for him to escape us.

Then the world goes black. In an instant, there's no more light. Only an impermeable darkness, stretching over the forest like a sheet of black film. I hear my friends shouting. I hear the creaks and groans of the trees. I stop in my tracks, balancing on a branch I can't see.

A second later, the sun returns. We scatter amongst the trees to search for the boy. When we don't find him there, we search the clearing. The forest is still and quiet, and the boy is nowhere in sight.

"What the hell was that?" Alessia demands, her cheeks burning.

Baxter looks around the clearing. "How the hell was he that fast?"

"I don't know." Roman shakes his head. "I couldn't see anything. It was so . . ."

"Yeah, me either." Cass tugs on his hair. He's got that look again, like he should be brooding in a dark window. "I don't like this. Why was he at our school?"

I look up at the trees. The boy moved through them at a speed so vicious it nearly blew the forest away.

Alessia kneels into a crouch, her brow slick with sweat. "Didn't those guards at the Sacred House have robes like that? Maybe they sent him."

Olivia shakes her head. "Why wouldn't they just tell us?"

"Yeah and why would he run?" Cass asks.

I don't have an answer. No one does. We watch the trees like they'll reveal his secrets.

CHAPTER EIGHTEEN

BAXTER AND ROMAN CIRCLE EACH OTHER hungry for blood.

The earth quakes each time their blades strike against each other. In the distance, gravel shifts at the impact. Baxter moves like a thief in the night, his body a streak of deadly gold. Arrows hurtle like falling stars across the Yard, always just barely missing Roman's body. If that scares him, he doesn't let on.

Cass and Alessia shout tips over the fighting. Olivia crouches on a log, watching the heaps of gravel around us like monsters hide beneath them. I can't blame her. The boy outside our school seemed to appear out of nothing. He vanished just as easily. After Cisthene, we'll bring it up to the Commanders. Who knows when he could show up again?

"No!" Alessia shouts. "On your left! The left!"

But it's too late. Baxter pivots to the right, trying to block Roman's falling blade. In a split second, his green sword swirls into a three-pronged spear. Roman flips it sideways, blocking Baxter's sword with one end. He sweeps his legs out from under him with the other. Baxter lands on his back, and Roman presses the blunt end of his spear against his chest.

"You cheated," Baxter accuses.

Roman laughs. "Expect the unexpected. It's the golden rule."

"That's not what the golden rule is," Cass says. A golden spear lounges across his shoulder, the tips of its twin prongs both beautiful and menacing.

Roman rolls his eyes. "Whatever, man. You're up."

Cass shrugs and steps into the middle of the clearing. Shiny black armor melts over his body. The gold-plated serpent across his chest looks like it's actually moving.

While they fight in the middle of the clearing, I'm hunched over a book from the Sacred House. I've seen the picture: a man devouring the body of his half-eaten child. The book explains it in much gorier detail, especially the part at the end, when Cronus's body is cut into pieces and tossed into the Pit.

There's an entry about the Sons of Cronus too, how they united the Titan's descendants in battle against the Children of Olympus. That was twenty-five years ago. Since their defeat, no one's heard from them since. There was the Battle on Mount Olympus, when the Saint of Blood smote them from the earth. The excitement in my heart fizzes out when the entry ends. I keep flipping through the book, but there's nothing else about my father.

I shove it in my bag. Searching for answers about my dad is useless. If he'd wanted me to know the truth, he would've just told me.

A tremor rattles the Yard, nearly knocking me over. Cass is on the ground, his spear gone. Roman stands over him, aiming the pronged edge of his spear at Cass' chest.

"You're done."

OF BLOOD AND LIGHTNING

Cass raises a hand, and his spear appears in an instant. Roman knocks it aside with his trident, laughing. "I said you're done."

Grumbling, Cass finds his feet and takes the walk of shame out of the clearing. Watching Roman now, I find it hard to believe that something so beautiful could be so dangerous.

"Lia." He calls, beckoning me with his spear.

Alessia cheers, urging me on, but I don't see the point. Out of all of us, only she and Olivia have been able to beat him.

I shake my head. "Oh no, I don't think—"

"Ophelia, come on," Roman says, pouting.

Alessia comes over to my log and pulls me up. "Just remember what we talked about. Don't think."

My throat is almost too dry to speak. "I'll try."

I step into the clearing as shimmering blue armor falls over me. Thunder rattles the clouds, and I unsheathe my sword—the Lightning Bolt.

Roman's eyes are bright with excitement. Somehow, it's more menacing than if he were glaring at me.

"You ready?" he asks, a strange softness in his voice.

"Whenever you are."

It's the wrong thing to say. In the next second, he's lunging, trident tips first. I surf a wave of lightning around the clearing, kicking up clouds of dust. *Swing. Jab. Slice. Sweep.* He's only a little faster than Alessia, but with nearly twice the force. I aim for the middle of his trident, knocking it off course each time he moves to attack.

When it swings into a sword, the blade sparks like the sun. Metal clangs as we dance around the clearing. Salt and ozone saturate the air. In a dance of sparks and ocean spray, the first blood shed is mine. He's aiming for my legs, but I'm too fast. The edge of his sword just barely splits the skin across the back of my knee but it heals in seconds.

I pivot and drive forward, pressing him farther out. Mountains of gravel crumble around us as our fight spreads deeper into the valley—over the hills, by the black iron gate, in front of the main station, all the way until we've made a complete circle. Back in the middle of the clearing, I swing my sword into a bolt and bring it down over my head. He jerks, like I expect. I swing the bolt back into a sword and knock his blade out of his hands. His sword vanishes, and there's nowhere to go.

"Yield."

He smiles up at me, his eyes wide and bright.

"I yield," he says.

The brittle texture of his voice makes my knees weak.

He stands up slowly, mindful of the blade at his chest. I can't read his eyes, something heady and unfamiliar. When the others flock over, he clears his throat and turns away from me.

"Anybody wanna dethrone the champion?" He asks, gesturing to me.

I let my armor vanish, and cool air rushes in like a salve. My skin is still hot from the lightning's touch. Yeah. It's just the lightning.

Baxter rotates his shoulder, grimacing. "Actually I think you dislocated my shoulder, so I'm good."

Roman shrugs. "It'll heal."

"Asshole."

"Oh shit." Olivia frowns down at her phone. "My parents need me at the house. They can't even plan a children's event without me."

"What's that?" I ask.

"My mom is on the PTA board at New River Elementary. She likes it when I help her plan things." She shakes her head and shoves her phone in her pocket. "Are we good here? It's almost eight." When we first got to the Yard, New River was still clinging to daylight. Now, a new night rolls in to take its place.

"Yeah, we should be," Baxter says. "Remember, we're meeting at my house in the morning. Don't be late."

Cass snickers. "I might sleep in."

Baxter ignores him.

We restage the clearing and head out together. Roman walks me to my car with that same hazy look in his eyes, but keeps a healthy distance between us.

"Drive safe," he says, opening the door for me.

"I don't know. I might wrap this thing around a tree on the way back. Just for fun."

He shakes his head, laughing, "Well, follow your heart then. I'll see you tomorrow, Lia."

I'm staring again. Dusk darkens his eyes, like a cool ocean in winter. "See you."

Laughing again, he shuts the door behind me. I don't stop watching his reflection in my rear view mirror until all that remains of the Yard is the fuzzy outline of a tall, black gate.

CHAPTER NINETEEN

BY THE TIME MORNING BREAKS OVER New River, I'm already up. Outside my door, the house is silent, like there's nothing alive in here but me. It's an appropriate sense of foreboding.

Usually, I wake up way past my first alarm. This morning is different. We're supposed to be at Baxter's house by nine, so there's a good stretch of time between now and the fate that awaits me. I try to shake myself free from that kind of thinking. This is a quest. Quests are fun. I'm going to a place that doesn't even officially exist. I should be excited, not sick to my stomach.

I move slowly. I can't remember the last time I made my bed, so I decide to make up for lost time. After smoothing out any creases or wrinkles, I start cleaning. I'm not that junky, but I'm not that neat either. I put clothes in their assorted baskets and drawers, and organize my shoes at the bottom of the closet. There's an empty rack of hangers dangling from the rail, so I give them purpose. When I'm done, I dust my drawers with Windex and wads of paper towel, before breaking out the vacuum.

My dad used to clean like this every Saturday morning. Eventually it became a habit for me too, but these past few months have thrown me off. It doesn't take as long as I hope. By the time I'm finished, it's only been an hour.

I move to the bathroom next and run the shower. I try to stretch it out for as long as possible, mostly because being beneath the warm, powerful spray of the shower head is the closest thing I have to peace these days. But eventually the water runs cold, and I have to get out.

I change in my room. I'm not sure what to expect, so I dress for hiking: a pair of olive green camo pants, a plain black shirt, and the clunky old hiking boots my dad bought for me a few years back during my nature phase. I did actually use them for their intended purpose before abandoning that era entirely, so the soles have already been broken in. I bounce back and forth on the balls of my feet to get comfortable before packing a bag.

My provisions are threadbare: an extra pair of socks; a notebook; the dull, chipped pocket knife that has my father's name on it; and a blanket. It's what I'm going with.

Downstairs, the house has finally come to life. I move past the fake cobwebs and inflatable witches to find Cherice in the kitchen. Cooking. Over the stove.

God save us all.

"Hey Phie," she greets, cheery as a dollop of sunshine. "I'm making oatmeal."

I glance at Janus, who shakes his head so slowly he might as well not even be moving.

"You hungry?" She asks. "I've got brown sugar, granola, peanut butter . . ."

"Yep." I take a seat at the table too, resting my bag at my feet.

It doesn't take long for smoke to fill the kitchen, but Janus and I aren't allowed to laugh. As it turns out, Cherice doesn't appreciate that kind of thing.

"Dammit," she hisses, scraping the pot out over the sink.

Oatmeal plops out in charred chunks. Janus opens the fridge and pulls out a carton of eggs; his poker face doesn't waver. Ten minutes later, Cherice sets the table, and Janus brings over steaming plates of grits and eggs.

He peppers kisses against her forehead. "Bon appetit, my love."

"Shut up." She grumbles, digging into her plate.

My uncle has talent. By the time we're finished eating, he's coaxed Cherice out of being upset by promising to pay for cooking classes. She hums a light tune as she clears the table.

"So," Janus pretends to wipe away a layer of sweat while she's not looking, "any plans today?"

A chill rushes through me, biting down to the bone. I ignore it.

"Yes, actually." I check my phone. If I don't leave in the next ten minutes, I'll be late. "I have a history project due in a few days, so we're working on it at Baxter's house."

He quirks an eyebrow. "Baxter?"

"The mayor's son, honey," Cherice says from the sink.

Janus still looks suspicious, but shrugs casually enough. "All right. When are you coming back?"

"Probably tonight. His mom might make us dinner."

Janus turns to smile at Cherice, who's just splashed a glob of soap against the front of her shirt. "So that means I get to make my crab pasta."

I shake my head. "No you don't. Not if I'm not here."

Cherice pouts. "Don't be like that. He hasn't made it in a year."

"Okay, fine, but can you at least save me some?"

"Maybe." Janus' smile is evil. "What's the project on?"

"Greek myths." I'm not really thinking about it, but it rolls right off my tongue. "We're presenting on the Fates."

Janus' expression doesn't change, but I don't miss the way Cherice tenses up by the sink.

"Hmm. Sounds fun."

"Sort of. You know anything that could help?"

I try to keep my tone light. I'm not fishing or poking at the fragile peace that exists between us. It's just a question.

"About the Fates or about Greek myths?" he asks.

I shrug. "Either one. We need all the help we can get." At least I'm not a liar.

"I don't know. Jason was the expert on that kind of thing." His expression is casual, but the air prickles with tension.

"Yeah. Well, thanks anyway." I stand up, scooping my bag with me. "And thanks for breakfast. I'll see you guys later."

It's a quarter past nine when I finally pull up to Baxter's house. Every light in the house is on. Alessia sharpens a knife loudly in the foyer. It's nearly the length of a sword, with a wide, vicious blade.

"That will be useful," I say.

She whirls the hilt across her knuckles, and the blood red stones along the blade's curved spine catch the light like fire. "This thing could slice a car in half."

"Well let's hope there are lots of cars on Cisthene."

In the living room, Roman and Baxter sit on the floor around the coffee table, heads bent over the map. Olivia flips through a book in the corner, and Cass fights sleep in the recliner.

He throws up a lazy hand. "Morning."

"Morning."

Roman pops his head up. The creases in his forehead are tense, but he's smiling. "Hey. I thought you weren't gonna make it."

"I'm never that lucky." I sit beside him, close enough to nudge his shoulder.

Baxter doesn't look up, but stays bound to the map in front of him. He's drawn purple circles and crooked stars in faded black ink.

"The circles might be other buildings," Roman explains, pointing across the table. "I don't think the Sisters would be there, but it's worth checking out."

"And the stars?"

"Danger," Baxter says, almost absentmindedly. "I think."

"What kind of danger?"

He shrugs. "No clue. I just figure it's best to avoid it." He throws an annoyed glance at Cassius, who still looks bored in his chair. "Which would be easier to do if we were actually looking at the map. Seriously."

Cass rolls his eyes, but drags himself out of the chair. He sits on the other side of the table and pulls the map closer.

"Pit of vipers? What's dangerous about that?"

"Well vipers are venomous, jackass."

Olivia snorts over the top of her book. It's bound in soft, brown leather, with dull indentations from what had once been beautiful artwork.

"What are you reading?" I ask her.

"*Tales of the Moon*," she says. "It's about Artemis. When we go back to the House, I want more books."

The shadow across Baxter's face is grim. "You know, it still bothers me that we don't know who that guy was."

"Maybe we can ask the Sisters," Roman says.

Leaning back on his hands, Cass says, "I still don't understand why we have the gods' power in the first place. Did they retire?"

"No, they died," I tell him. "Roman and I read about it the other day. They were killed in this huge war against other gods."

"Woah," Alessia says as she comes into the room, her blade gleaming. "Killed? By who? The Titans?"

Roman shrugs. "Maybe. The book referred to the other guys as the 'Lords of All Darkness and Suffering.'"

"Huh. Sounds like a very reliable group of people." Olivia closes her book. "Wait, maybe that's a tree to shake. Are they still around?"

"No." I shake my head. "The Olympians locked them away before they died."

For once, there's caution in Alessia's voice. "I don't know. People break out of regular jail all the time."

"Which is why we need to go." Baxter folds the map like he has a personal vendetta against it. "The sooner we talk to the Sisters, the sooner we get answers. Let's finish this."

We gather around him in the middle of the room. He holds out his arms, beckoning us to grab on. I'm not sure how tight my grip should be. When Griffin first transported us to the House, the world fell away like a house of cards. There was no color or sound, nothing to keep my body in place as the wind flung me into blackness. My stomach churns just thinking about it.

"Ready?" Baxter asks.

I nod. My mouth is too dry to speak.

He closes his eyes. It's just like being with Griffin in the Yard. Gold light blazes around his body and the entire world is plunged into shadow. It feels like his arms are ripped away from me. There's no anchor. Just a wall of ink and shadow, enclosing me in the palm of its massive fist. Wind rushes up against the back of my neck, but I can't tell if this is flying or falling.

A second later, my feet come down hard against a dune of sand. Behind me, black water erupts against a jagged shore. Giant rocks line the perimeter of the island, sharp at the edges like a row of black teeth. Clouds clog the sky, rattled with thunder and purple lightning. Gray sand stretches for miles along either side of the beach, all the way up to the scary looking forest in front of us. Trees with fat, black leaves sway in the wind like they're saying hello.

Baxter takes the map out of his bag, his eyes narrowed. "No, that's not right."

Roman leans over his shoulder. "Wait, where's the—"

"I know," Baxter says. He glances from the map to the wall of forest in front of us. "That's impossible."

"What's impossible?" Alessia asks. "Why do you look like someone pissed in your cereal?"

"There's supposed to be a big ass trail right there." Baxter points to the treeline, where there's obviously no trail in sight.

Alessia points in the same direction. "Like, right there? Because that's forest, Baxter."

"I can see that, Alessia. But the map—"

Cass takes it from him, his brows furrowed. After two seconds, he passes it back. "The map is wrong, dude."

"But we got that from the minister himself," Olivia says. "Why would he have the wrong map?"

"It is pretty outdated." I take a few steps to the left and crane my neck, but there are no trails to the east either. "It

OF BLOOD AND LIGHTNING

looks like the forest just filled itself out. If there was a trail here, it's gone now."

Groaning, Baxter crumples the map and tosses it into the ocean. Olivia gasps and smacks his shoulder.

"Why would you do that?"

"Because it's useless." He throws up his hands in exhaustion. "All right, what do we do?"

"We just split up," Roman says. "Ophelia and I can take the east, Alessia and Cass the west, and you two cut right through the middle."

"That's impossible," Cass scoffs. "Are we seeing the same shit? I mean, maybe the map is wrong because nobody actually lives here."

"Maybe that's the idea," Olivia says. "If you don't want people knocking on your door, make it look like there isn't a door."

"I really hate that that sort of makes sense." Cass reaches into the air and comes away with the handle of a two-pronged spear. "All right, Leese. You want the front?"

"Obviously." She's wielding the same, rubied blade as before. "We'll shoot up some sparks if we find anything."

"Hold up." Baxter says. "We don't have a useful map. We have no idea where we're going or what we're looking for."

"Well do you want the Eye or not?" And really, Roman's logic is flawless.

Map or no map, the Sisters are somewhere on this island. There's only one way to find them, and that's the hard way.

"All right." Baxter pulls a gold bow out of the air and stares up the beach. "Let's go."

We split three ways. When the trees swallow us, the darkness is nearly absolute. Heavy black branches criss-cross in front of us, so we have to cut them away as we hike. It's nothing like the trails my father and I would take at the nature preserves near our house. The earth is damp, so it gives easily beneath our feet. Wide, flat leaves block out any sunlight and trickle fat drops of rain onto our foreheads.

I listen for the sound of creatures stalking in the shadows, but the only footsteps I hear belong to us. Nothing chirps or chatters in the trees or breaks branches in the distance. There's just the steady slosh of our feet working against the mud and each clean swipe of our blades through the branches.

"This is creeping me out," Roman says. "We could be going in the opposite direction. And what if there are Burmese tiger traps?"

I stop in my tracks. "Why would there be Burmese tiger traps?"

"And that's exactly what everyone thinks right before they fall into one."

"Yeah, but I just don't get why—" I stop myself. "Okay Roman, I promise you there are no Burmese tiger traps. And if we're going in the opposite direction, we'll probably just end up going in a circle, so we'll find it anyway."

"Yeah, seems like pretty sound logic to me."

"Thank you." I bump him with my shoulder.

"Seriously, you really think we'll find them?" he asks, his voice low.

I don't know if saying what I think would be helpful. I'm not the optimistic type and being in the forest's belly doesn't help.

"I think our chances are better if we run."

He laughs, even though he doesn't look encouraged. "I think you're right."

We run for at least an hour, but it feels like almost no time has passed. By the time I finally have to catch my breath, I see no difference between where we started and where we are now. Each towering tree has the same face, and the foliage is just as thick on all sides of us. There are no openings, no paths, nothing to indicate that there's anything alive in this forest at all.

Roman slides into a crouch at the base of a tree, wiping his forehead. "You know, I ran track. I kinda hate that I quit. I'd be a star."

I sit across from him and fan myself with the neck of my shirt. "You'd be a cheater. No superpowers allowed, remember?"

"Well they don't have to know that. I could tone it down."

"Sure you could," I laugh. "You're a show off."

"I am not." He leans his head back, rolling his eyes. "Okay, maybe just a little."

"There we go. Honesty."

"Whatever. Hey, what do you think it would be like to just have these powers? No quest, no end of the world. Just the good stuff?"

"I don't know. I don't think you ever get anything good without paying a price. It's crossroads shit. You get ten years of wealth and prosperity and then an eternity of suffering."

"But why not?" He asks. "I've always wondered that. Why do you have to suffer just to be happy?"

"I don't know." I stare at the soil like it has the answer. "I think the only thing I really know is that nothing makes sense. It's not very comforting though."

"Maybe a little. Everything making sense means there are all these hard and fast rules and there's nothing left to discover. I like understanding things, but I also like leaving room for wonder."

I smile at him. "You're as optimistic as ever, I see."

"To a fault." He stands up and brushes the dirt off his jeans. "All right, you wanna keep moving?"

I let him help me up. "Lead the way."

We hike for another hour or so before the smell sets in. It's not the rotted, old fish from the beach. This time it's sickly and sweet, like the flesh is human. The more we hike, the more powerful it becomes, until a seam of light splits the trees ahead of us. It takes another twenty minutes of hiking and gagging for the trees to thin out, revealing a wide, jagged-edged clearing.

I've got a very bad feeling in the pit of my gut.

The smoldering, crushed husk in the middle of the clearing has to belong to one of the purple circles from Baxter's map. Whatever it was, it used to be big. Rubble and debris pepper the clearing's perimeter, still leaking smoke. There are shards of metal and bent arrows beneath our feet. The first body we see is propped up against a huge boulder, with a broken spear lodged through its chest.

Roman vomits into the grass.

There are at least a dozen more, all scattered around the clearing in various states of gore. Someone has an arrow through the middle of their face, and one of the bodies looks like it was torn in half by something with huge teeth.

"Oh no." My voice comes out in a breathless whisper. "Roman, this isn't good. Didn't Griffin say there were guards on the island?"

"Yeah." He takes careful steps further into the clearing until he's standing right over the body at the boulder. "I think we just found them."

He bends down and tears something away from the body. A bit of fabric. He holds it up to the light, revealing the symbol of a slashed, white eye.

I walk over to meet him, careful not to step in any blood. The boy used to be young and strong, with a crop of black hair hanging over a set of empty, brown eyes. The blood on his face and body has already dried, but the purple bruising along his arms and throat looks fresh. I bend down and press my hand flat against his shoulder.

"I would guess he probably died about two hours ago," I tell him.

Roman scoffs. "Do you think whoever did this is still on the island?"

I point to the building's remains, haloed now in fresh smoke. "Maybe. The fire's barely out."

"Okay." He holds a fist to his mouth to steady himself. "We need to check and see if any of them are wearing anything different."

My stomach turns, and I almost throw up for real this time. "Oh, Roman, I don't want to do that."

"I know," he says, apologetic.

We walk around the clearing, checking the embroidered patches on their uniforms. They're all wearing the same thing: black armored one-pieces, with slashed white eyes stitched into the shoulders.

The fear in my mouth is hot and rancid. If these really are the island's guardians, and they've only been dead for a few hours . . .

I swing my sword into a bolt, coaxing a rumble of thunder from the sky. I'm aiming it at the clouds when a shudder bites deep into the earth, rocking the trees so violently that a few of them snap and tip over. To the west, a beam of red light stabs the sky, funneling the clouds into a brilliant, churning vortex.

Roman spits a wad of bile into the grass. "We gotta go."

We make the journey to Alessia's signal at a run. The trees thin out again, revealing an even larger clearing, with a tall, crumbling tower at its heart. There's more smoke and more bodies, stacked in piles along the edge of the clearing.

Alessia's blade is buried in the earth and still belches crimson light into the sky. She jerks it free and smoke settles around us.

"This is bad," she says, no longer flippant or casual. "These are the guards."

"We know," Roman says. "We just found more to the east."

"What the hell is going on?" Cass demands, like one of us should have the answer. "They're not supposed to be dead."

"Well obviously." Roman shakes his head. "We need to be careful. Whoever killed them could still be on the island."

"Right." Alessia tugs at her hair. Her eyes go wide and her hand falls limp at her side.

Cass cuts wary eyes at her. "What is it?"

"If these are the island's guards, and they're dead, that means someone came here to kill them," she says. "Isn't it strange that the day we come here to talk to the Sisters, the island gets attacked? That's not a coincidence."

I hang my head. "Shit. Alessia that's—I mean obviously you're right, but that's insane."

"Who else knew we were coming here?" Cass asks. "Griffin, the Commanders, but who else?"

"Nobody." Roman shakes his head. "I know for a fact I didn't put it on a billboard, so this doesn't make any sense."

Cass breaks away from the huddle to watch the edge of the clearing. "Where are Baxter and Liv? Did they not see the signal?"

"Maybe they're in trouble," I say, feeling sick. "Those people could still be on the island. Maybe—"

In the middle of the woods, a second beam of light goes up, this one rich with sunlight. We only hesitate long enough to exchange panicked looks.

More trees, ripping past us with a vengeance. They thin out to reveal a manor at the heart of the forest. The crumbling house sits on a massive plot of scorched land, behind a black gate that looks like it was blown off. Bodies pepper the rugged edge of the clearing. They're piled up along the gate's singed perimeter and lead a bloody trail all the way to what used to be the front door.

It's a towering palace. Or at least it used to be. There's a crater in the roof, and the front doors look like they were torn right off their hinges. Olivia and Baxter wait on the lawn, with three body-shaped lumps in front of them, and a struggling boy between them.

His mauve robes have been torn to shreds, revealing a suit of black armor beneath it. His left eye is purple and swollen shut; there's a huge gash across the top of his right brow. Gold blood gathers in a pool beneath his bent knees, but I can't see the injury.

It's the bodies at their feet that stop me in my tracks. Three wrinkled women watch the sky through clouds of cataract. Gold rings glitter dully on each one of their bony, gray fingers, gnarled and struggling. Ichor gushes from identical wounds in their chests, right where their hearts should be.

I clutch a hand to my stomach, which churns violently. These can only be the Graeae Sisters, lying dead at my feet.

The boy seems proud of himself.

"What did you do?" I demand.

The boy smirks. Ichor dries in dark splatters across his face and in a thick golden ribbon down the corner of his mouth. "What was commanded. Her will be done."

Baxter jerks him around; the boy groans in agony.

"You don't get to gloat over this," Baxter hisses, but that just makes the boy laugh.

"Even dead men have their rewards," the boy says.

I ignore the violent shudder that rips through me. If I focus too hard on everything I see and smell—the sweet stench of charred flesh, the blood coagulating in the soil— I'll come apart. It's too awful. So I shove the revulsion away and replace it with rage. Hot and molten, like a viscous river beneath my skin.

"Does he have a name?" Cass asks.

"He wouldn't say." Olivia shoves away from the kneeling boy, disgusted. "Everybody else is gone. He's the only one here. I checked."

"Why would they leave him?" Alessia asks.

"Because he's already dead." Baxter drags the boy to his feet, leaning him against his body so he can stand. "They must have figured he'd slow them down so they left him to die."

The boy hisses, blood dribbling from his mouth. There's an edge to his voice, a harsh one, but he sounds like he's working for every breath. Now that he's standing, I can see the gruesome tear that stretches from his chest to the waistband of his pants.

I turn away, trying to catch my breath. This wasn't supposed to happen. We were supposed to come here and find the Sisters. We were supposed to fix this. And I guess, on some level, I'd hoped they could tell me something about my father, something my aunt and uncle aren't willing to. I'd come here for the truth, but all I have are the dead around me.

"Why'd you do this?" I demand, furious.

The boy looks me in the eye, smirking. It makes me so angry that I shove him out of Baxter's grip.

"You piece of shit!"

He flies across the clearing. Roman shouts after me, but I ignore him. I'm standing over the boy in an instant, lightning licking at my heels. He tries to roll himself away, but I plant my feet on either side of him. The arrowhead patch on his shoulder winks menacingly in the weak light.

I reach down to tear it away from his robe. "What's this symbol? Who are you?"

"I'm nobody," he groans, a touch of amusement still in his voice. "I'm dead."

I grab him by the front of his robes and raise him up so that we're eye level. "Actually, you're not yet, and I can make things a whole lot worse before you get there if you don't tell me who you are."

He must know I mean it.

"Okay, okay," he says, holding up a set of wounded hands. "I don't give out orders. I just go where I'm sent. I have no control over—"

"So who does?"

"The Mother." He says it like he's saying a prayer. "Our one true god. We do whatever she desires."

Alessia kneels down beside me, a black blade in her hand. "Who's 'we' and who's the Mother?"

He shakes his head. "All I know is that she wanted us to come here and cleanse the island. I mean, I've never even actually seen her. I told you. I'm nobody."

"I don't believe you," Alessia scoffs.

The boy laughs. "That's okay. It doesn't matter. She got what she wanted. Her will is done."

"And what will is that?" Roman asks over my shoulder. "What'd you do with the Eye?"

The boy sneers. "Hid it. Sorry."

I grind my teeth. "Hid it where, asshole?"

He doesn't say anything. He just smiles.

Alessia's hand shoots out like a viper, plunging her knife deep into his abdomen. He screams. She twists the blade.

"Hid. It. Where?" She demands,

The boy spits into the grass. "Okay. All right."

He blinks, the light in his eyes going dull now. He goes slack in my grip, but not before he can stare at me, stare through me, like there's nothing but sky in front of him.

"Caesar's." he says. His breathing rattles to a stop. He dies in my arms.

CHAPTER TWENTY

IT'S A LITTLE PAST NOON WHEN we reappear in New River. As soon as my feet hit the ground, my knees buckle beneath me. The world flips over, then lurches to the left. I think I'm on the ground.

I see the blurred shape of the guesthouse in front of me and the frenzied bodies of my friends. Someone shouts. Someone kneels down in front of my face. Roman.

"Ophelia!" He's shaking my shoulders. His voice is warped, like it's coming through a dirty puddle. "Are you okay?"

I sit up, shrugging off his hands. It feels like there's a pile of searing coals in the middle of my stomach. The dead boy's eyes stare back at me—first bright and burning with rage, then dull. I scrub my hands against my jeans, trying to rid them of that feeling. The boy's robes, his body heavy and slack against mine. The way his hands twitched against the scorched earth.

How could someone deserve death, even after doing something so terrible? And how could they just die in my arms? I hadn't done anything to him. Not really. Yet still, looking down at my hands, all I see is his blood. I was so angry, and for a second, just one, I could have crushed his heart.

I'm glad I didn't. I don't know if I would've been able to stomach it.

"Dude," Roman's voice yanks me back.

They're all staring at me, except Alessia, who's busy puking into a bush. There are hot tears on my face. I wipe them away and jump to my feet.

"Are you okay?" Roman asks.

"Yeah, I'm fine."

"Well, I'm not," Cass says, his face pale as a ghost. "That was awful."

Roman sniffs. "Yeah. I've never seen a—I mean, not in real life anyway."

"Me either," Baxter murmurs. "I didn't know people looked like that when they . . ."

His voice trails off. I close my eyes as a tide of memory washes over me.

The kitchen floor. My father. His wide, brown eyes, and the dread that filled my body when I realized he wasn't moving.

Alessia stumbles away from the bushes, groaning. She limps over to join us and wipes her mouth with a trembling hand. I try to ignore the blood drying across her knuckles.

"What do we do?" She asks. I've never heard her sound so small.

"We need to talk to General Davis," Baxter says. "They need to know that Cisthene was attacked."

"We have a bigger problem." I hold up the torn patch from the boy's uniform, ignoring the bloodstains. "You know that Watcher? He was wearing the same symbol. What does that sound like to you?"

Roman takes the patch from me to examine it. It looks like he's turning green. "Sabotage."

ON A SUNDAY AFTERNOON, THE SACRED House is buzzing. Everyone's outside. People lounge beneath the sun on towels and run after their children with water guns. There are bright, purple tents pitched all along the lawn. They brew stews in huge, black cauldrons, and turn meat over open-faced grills. On the left side, boys and girls who look a little younger than I am race each other on horses, fire arrows at straw targets, and spar in the middle of makeshift arenas.

To the right, children run barefoot in the grass, clobbering each other with fake swords. Whooping laughter fills the air as a fleet of Pegasi fly in from the woods, their riders dressed in silver fabric. Beneath the afternoon's high, yellow sun, they're bathed in a glorious light.

It's a terrible day for news like this.

We're about halfway to the Polis when Griffin comes riding in on the back of a sleek, black steed. He's dressed like a warrior, in a shining bronze breastplate, with armored grieves around his shins. He steps off the horse, but still towers over us. I'd forgotten how tall he was.

"Hey," he says, surprised. "What are you doing here?"

I flash the bloody arrowhead patch. "We need to talk."

It takes Griffin less than fifteen minutes to assemble the Commanders. We're back where we started: in the conference room, with four stone Athenas staring down at us.

General Davis runs her fingers across the patch, her lips pressed into a thin line. She's wearing jeans and a flowy white blouse. I hate to think that I'm ruining her day off.

"And where'd this come from?" she asks, her voice tight.

"Cisthene," Roman says.

She frowns. "I don't understand. This symbol doesn't belong to the Children of Dionysus."

"No, it belongs to the people who killed them," Alessia says. "By the time we got to the island, everybody was dead. Including the Sisters."

"They also took the Eye," Baxter adds. "It's gone. They stole it."

"Oh dear god." Minister Fueves clutches a wrinkled hand to his throat, his cheeks turning green.

The Lieutenant looks like she's seen a ghost, but General Davis keeps her composure.

"And you're sure?" she asks.

Olivia nods. "I helped pull them out of the rubble myself. It's true."

"Whoever coordinated that attack did it because they didn't want us to have the Eye," Cass says.

Alessia presses a tense finger into the table. "Do you recognize that symbol?"

The General passes the symbol to the minister, who shakes his head.

"It looks like it could belong to the Blessed Sisters of Artemis. Maybe." He shakes his head again. "I can reach out to them, see if they recognize it. I'll also circulate it wider around the network. Someone might know something."

"We also need to let everyone know what happened on Cisthene," the Lieutenant says. "We've had library raids, but this is different. They took out an entire house."

In the anger that gathers on the General's face, there's the shadow of a warrior. Someone who leads armies and leaps headfirst into danger's warm embrace.

The General curls her fist against the stone table, her jaw clenched. "Don't worry. We'll find out who did this, and we'll respond in kind. That's all."

Baxter shakes his head. "No, that's not all. Someone showed up at our school the other day, watching us. We tried going after him, but he ran away."

"We thought maybe it was someone that you guys sent," Olivia says.

The General shakes her head. "If we'd wanted to keep tabs on you, we'd just send Griffin."

Roman laughs, but there's no humor to his expression. "Yeah, that's what I figured."

"What do you mean someone showed up at your school?" Griffin scoffs. So far, he's just been glaring into the table like he wants to scorch it with his gaze.

Baxter tilts his head. "Those exact words. That's what I mean."

"Well that's—" Griffin massages his left temple; a vein jumps in his jaw. "Look, my guess is that whoever's watching you belongs to the people who attacked Cisthene. You're being surveilled, and that's not a coincidence. This is about the Codex. It has to be."

"But that doesn't make sense." I shake my head. "I get attacking the island and even taking the Eye, but why hide it? If they want the Codex, why not just use the Eye to find it themselves?"

"How do you know the Eye was hidden?" Minister Fueves asks.

"One of them got left behind," Olivia says. "We found him before he died and he told us. Some place called Caesar's.

"Caesar's? You're sure?"

"Positive."

"Maybe he was lying," suggests the Lieutenant. "That would make sense."

"No," the minister shakes his head. "This morning my artifacts team got a ping in Massachusetts, but I didn't think the report was that serious. Otherwise I'd have had them investigate immediately if I'd known that much power had been moved. I'm sorry."

"You know where it is?" I lean forward a little too eagerly.

He nods. "The Cambridge Museum of History and Culture. They just opened a new Roman culture and history exhibit a few weeks ago. Sometimes, divine artifacts get mixed in with the normal ones, but this was big."

"And you're sure?"

He almost looks offended. "Well, I'm rarely ever 100% certain, but given how recently we got the ping *and* what just happened with our friends on Cisthene—I'd say it's the perfect place to start. Why?"

"Look, I don't know if there was some kind of mix-up or what, but we couldn't use that map," Baxter says. "There were no trails on that island. None. The buildings were all over the place and it was huge, way bigger than the map said it should've been."

Now the minister really does look offended. "What are you implying?"

"Emilio," the General warns.

"I'm not implying anything," Baxter says, not backing down. "Look, we can't afford to go somewhere and not find what we need. That can't happen again, and it's not a knock against you, but I need you to be sure. So are you?"

The minister sighs but keeps his composure. "Yes, I'm positive. And I apologize about the map."

"Don't worry," Roman tells him. "We're back in the game now and we know where we need to go."

He sounds sure. Certain. At least somebody is.

"That's wonderful to hear. We are, of course, always here whenever you need our help," The General says, "but be advised, you're in more danger now than you've ever been in at any point in your life. That's where we are. You're being watched, and we don't know what we're dealing with yet. My personal recommendation would be to take lodging here at the Sacred House. We're better defended here."

Roman nods. "We'll think about it. Thank you, though. Really."

The General tips her head. "The Gods of Olympus are always welcome here."

I know she means it, but it just doesn't ring true. We're not gods. Not even soldiers. We're just a bunch of kids in over our heads. That much is obvious.

CHAPTER TWENTY-ONE

DEFEAT LINGERS ACROSS THE TOP OF my shoulders like a heavy, black storm cloud.

Griffin walks us back to the gate, scowling. People call out to him, inviting him to fire a flaming arrow or take a winged horse across the sky, but he just shakes his head. His shoulders are drooped and deflated, but he doesn't speak until we're well past the gate.

"You should have said something." His tone is accusatory.

"Um, we did?" Alessia scoffs. "Like, almost immediately."

"No, I mean, about the Watcher. Why didn't you come here first?"

"I—" she shakes her head. "I don't know man. The plan was to come here as soon as we finished on Cisthene; we didn't know someone was gonna beat us to it."

He doesn't look placated, but decides to let it go. "Well there's nothing we can do about it now. Just find the Codex and let us know as soon as you do. We don't know how much time we have."

"Would you know?" Roman asks. "Before they're killed—would you know?"

A beat of silence. Griffin's eyes are hard as flint. "Yeah, I'd know, but it wouldn't do any good."

"We'll find it." Roman assures him. "Don't worry."

Griffin's wave is half-hearted as he watches us leave.

It's dusk now. Baxter orders a bunch of pizza to his house. The sun fights a losing battle as it sinks below the horizon, blanketing New River in a sheet of dark blue. By the time the pizza gets here, night has nearly fallen but I feel too sick to eat.

"All right." Baxter sets the boxes down on the coffee table and sits on the floor. "Who all's staying the night?"

At first, no one answers. Olivia stares at the wall, her eyes foggy with something I can't quite place. Cass looks the same on the floor. The air in the room presses in on us, like the house is shrinking.

"I think I need to go home," I say.

Olivia nods. Slowly. "Me too."

Baxter watches her, frowning, but she doesn't say anything else.

"I'll stay." Cass leans forward to open one of the boxes.

"Yeah, me too," Roman says. "I want to know more about the museum."

"Tonight?"

"Yeah. Tonight. And we need to decide when we're gonna go get the Eye." He reaches into his bag and pulls out a laptop.

Out of everybody, he seems the most well-adjusted. Alessia's a different story. She swears and storms out of the living room. A second later, we hear the door slam behind her.

"She just needs some time," Cass says. He's on his third slice of pizza. "I think we all do. I don't want to jump back into this too soon."

Roman snorts, but there's very little humor to it. "Jump back into what? There's no in or out, Cass. Not really."

"Yeah, I know."

"You know there's something I still don't get," Baxter says through a mouthful of pizza. "Even if we were being watched, how'd they get the details? They would have to know exactly when we were planning to leave. Exactly where we were going."

His words leave an unpleasant chill in the room. Like so many other things, there are no answers. No way to know how and when we're being watched. No way to know how any of this is supposed to work out.

I shoot up from the couch and reach for my bag. "I need to go. I'm sorry."

I can't be here, not when the air is so full of fear and failure. It's hard to breathe.

Roman sets his laptop aside. "You want me to walk you out?"

"No, it's okay. I'll see you guys at school."

I'm waiting for the cold solitude of Baxter's front porch, but someone's already there. Alessia cries softly in the swinging chair, scrubbing her hands so violently it draws blood.

"Hey." I reach for her wrists. "Stop! What are you doing?"

She jerks away from me, hysterical. Her face is splotchy and red. She tries to catch her breath, but it keeps getting caught in her chest.

"I can't get it off," she whimpers. "I tried washing my hands, but it won't come off."

I examine her hands. The blood belongs to her, from the already healing scrapes along her fingers and knuckles. I grab her wrists again, more gently this time, and turn them over in her lap.

"It's okay," I tell her, even though it isn't. "It's just your blood. Your hands are clean."

"No they're not," she hisses. "I—god, he died. Right in front of me. No one's ever died right in front of me."

"I know. I'm sorry." I rack my brain for more things to say—something comforting, something encouraging—but there's nothing I can think of that isn't terrible.

He did die. And it was right in front of us. And I can't tell her it'll never happen again. I can't tell her that one day, someone will die and it won't be her fault. Because it might, and I can't promise her that.

"What do I do?" She lowers her head to her knees and really cries then. "I can't close my eyes without seeing his face. And my hands—I stabbed him. I didn't even think about it."

"He wouldn't have told us where the Eye was, not willingly."

"I know that," she hisses. "It doesn't matter. I never—I never thought I could be the kind of person who does shit like that, even when it's necessary. But I did, and it felt so . . . easy. And it makes me sick because I've been treating this like a costume. The weapons and the fighting, the idea of fighting. But it's real. People die. And I'm the reason."

I finally let go of her hands and take a seat on the ground. "You weren't. He was gonna die anyway."

"I know that too."

"And there was nothing any of us could do to keep that from happening."

She rolls her eyes. "Yeah, but I wasn't thinking, 'Maybe I should help him.' I didn't care if he was in pain, or if he was sick, or any of that. I didn't even care that he was a person. I just wanted an answer, and that was more important than his life."

"Well think about it like this: why was he there? He'd probably killed so many people already, and he didn't care at all. Even when he was dying. It's not like you hurt someone who was innocent, Alessia." I feel gross just saying it. The ideas are rational enough, but does that make them right? She looks devastated, and I know I've only made things worse.

"One day it will be someone innocent." She sniffs and stands up, towering over me. "I'll see you later, Ophelia."

"Leese—"

"Goodnight." She goes back inside the house, letting the door shut hard behind her.

I only let myself leave the porch after staring at the wall for a minute. She said it like prophecy, like the death of an innocent at her hands was a sure thing. A thing none of us can stop.

I try to convince myself that she's wrong on the way back home, but all I can think about is my father. Griffin said he was a great warrior, that everyone on this side of the world knew who he was. They called him the Saint of Blood. How many people slipped into the shadows at the edge of my father's sword? Did he grieve for each one of them, or did he grow cold and detached at some point? Did it become easy?

I pull into the driveway with the weight of the whole night dragging at my shoulders. My body aches, even though I barely did anything. I'm walking up the driveway when I notice a dark silhouette watching me from across the street. It's the stocky shape of a tall man, dressed in all black, with robes billowing around his ankles. Even from here, I can see the shape of the sword that dangles from his waist. He's standing just outside the streetlight, half-crowned in shadow.

Rage catches my feet like fire. I storm down the front lawn, glaring across the street. The man doesn't move, but I'm close enough to see his smile now—it's not exactly a smile. There's too many teeth. It's more like a lion baring its awful, bloodied maw.

"Who are you?" I demand. I don't care that I'm shouting. The man doesn't answer. His shoulders tremble, like he's laughing softly at some joke I can't hear.

I plant my feet at the edge of the sidewalk. It takes all I have not to cross the street. I pull my sword from the air, igniting the sky above into a devastating storm. Black clouds coil into a bed of electrified snakes; thunder rolls over New River in waves. I aim my sword at the man's chest. I could throw it, and I wouldn't miss. I'm sure of it.

"What the hell do you want?" I scream.

He shrugs. The motion is so casual it nearly makes me drop my sword. "Never mind what I want."

I'm stepping into the street when the darkness behind him deepens into a wide, sprawling curtain. Ribbons of shadow spring from his back and latch onto his body. One second he's laughing, and then the next he's gone. The shadows swallow him into nothingness, leaving only an empty strip of pavement behind.

I'm so shocked I loosen my grip. The sword vanishes, but the storm remains. Each quick hammering beat of my heart sparks a new rumble of thunder. I watch the empty space where the man once was in shock, my mouth open. I think I'm waiting for him to reappear, to spread his hands wide like he's just cut a beautiful woman in half. But there's no magic trick. No illusion. He really is just gone.

"Ophelia?"

The voice comes from behind me. I jump, yelping lightly, but it's just Cherice. She's standing outside the front door, squinting beneath the porch light.

"What?"

"Ophelia, honey, who were you talking to? And why are you standing outside?"

I look back across the street. The shadows look normal, not like they could spring to life and spirit a man away. Not like they're holding him now, just barely out of sight.

"No one." I shake my head and start walking back up the lawn. "Thought I saw a cat. Sorry."

She doesn't look like she believes me at all, but she doesn't push. Just before the front door closes behind us, I swear I see something twitch in the shadows.

CHAPTER TWENTY-TWO

CHERICE SETS SOMETHING DOWN IN FRONT of me, snatching me out of the haze.

I'm not sure how long I've been sitting at the table. I remember waking up and stumbling through a shower. I remember the walk down from my room, but nothing else. It's like being caught in an endless dream, one where I'm always standing at the edge of the sidewalk, or crouching at the top of the stairs.

It occurred to me last night, when I'd listened in on Janus and Cherice's meeting, they were talking about attacks. Organized attacks. A nameless, faceless "they" and a trail of violence and deaths.

I don't know who Ankippi and Surias are, but I'm willing to bet Zeus' bolt that they have something to do with divine children. Well, had, because if it's what I think it is, none of them exist anymore.

And then there's the man. His presence was unmistakable. He wasn't a trick of the light, or anything I could have imagined. He spoke to me.

Cherice waves a hand in front of my face. "Hello? You in there?"

She's set down a plate in front of me, and a bottle of Irish cream coffee liqueur I laugh as I take my fork. The sound is much too forced to be mirthful.

"Yeah. Still waking up."

"Well, drink your coffee," she says. "We're going out today."

"Oh?" I tip a bunch of creamer into my mug. "For what?"

"I have some errands to run and I don't feel like doing it by myself." She sits on the other side of the table and starts cutting into her French toast. Thankfully, they were pre-frozen. "Obviously, you don't have to, but I figured you wouldn't mind getting out of the house."

I shrug and take a sip of my coffee. I can't pretend being alone in this house wouldn't unnerve me, not after last night.

"I'm down. What do you have to do?"

Something in her eyes darkens. "Well, I have to go by the bank. And then I'm gonna pick up some prescriptions. Oh, and Janus has some suits at the dry cleaners; I got the call this morning. But," she pauses to wipe her mouth, "there are some things that used to belong to the twins, and I think it's time to donate them."

"You're donating their stuff?" I don't mean to sound so forceful. I definitely don't mean to sound betrayed, but that's how it comes out.

I don't miss the flash of hurt across her face, but she tries to ignore it. "Not all of it. Just a few boxes. They're taking up too much space in the basement, and Janus and I thought it would be a good idea to give them to people who can actu-ally use them."

"Oh. Where is he?"

"They called an emergency meeting at the Station. The Fire Department wants to make sure the safety protocol for

176

the Halloween bash is up to date." She goes back to her plate but stops short. "And Ophelia, I promise you, I would never just give away all of their stuff. It's all I have."

I look down at my plate. I can't stand the wounded look in her eyes, like I've twisted a knife.

"I know," I tell her. "I'm sorry."

After breakfast, we clean the kitchen together. Her mood must have lifted a little, because she hums in my ear as I dry the dishes. She washes them carefully in lemon-scented soap.

When we're done, she retreats upstairs and comes back down with a ring of old keys. She passes me an unsure look as she goes to stand in front of the basement door.

The lump in my throat hardens into a ball of cold candle wax. Janus was very clear that I was never, ever allowed back into the basement under any circumstances, but I guess this time it can't be helped.

"Don't tell your uncle about this." Cherice pulls the door open and the hinges whine in protest.

She pulls a string in the corner of the walkway and a pitiful lightbulb springs to life.

"Not a word," she presses.

"Definitely."

The boxes we're looking for are beneath the staircase, at the back of a narrow, dusty room. There are broken bits of ornament by the door and more boxes that have been wrapped carefully in layers of yellowing manilla tape. One of them has my father's name on it.

I pretend I don't see it and follow Cherice deeper into the cellar. The ink on the boxes is fading, but I can tell it's Iris and Irene's handwriting. Irene's name is written in a neat, looping script; the I is dotted with a crooked, black heart. Iris' handwriting is thin and scrawly, like a chicken wrote it.

Cherice laughs, her eyes glistening with tears. She rubs them away with her wrist before laughing again.

"I remember this," she says. "It was after their first year of school. We were moving. Irene insisted on writing her own name, so of course Iris had to. She always wanted to be just like her sister."

I clamp my mouth shut. I know I should say something, and I know exactly what it should be.

I'm so sorry, Aunt Cherice. A mother should never have to bury her children.

The words sit on my tongue like coals of molten lava. It's too painful. Iris and Irene should still be here. It was painful enough to think that they'd been taken away by a whim of fate, but to know that someone decided to end their lives, to know that they were—

Upstairs, someone rings the doorbell. It echoes throughout the house like a haunting.

Cherice wipes away more tears. "Shit. I forgot the internet guy was coming to drop off the new router. Can you wait here?"

I struggle to find my voice. "Of course."

"Okay."

She leaves the cellar and then her footsteps pound above me, all the way out of the basement. I run to the box with my father's name on it and split the tape with my fingernail. It smells like old jasmine and fading eucalyptus. I swear under my breath. There are layers and layers of books and blank paper, a glass paperweight in the shape of Medusa's head, and a small, bronze mail knife. I keep rifling through it, my heart pounding in my throat, until my hands close over a leatherbound journal.

I can tell its age and wear by its broken spine. The leather is soft and faded, but I can still read the label on the cover: *property of Jason Johnson.*

Upstairs, I hear the front door close. I vanish to my room and hide my father's journal beneath the comforter. Downstairs, the house creaks as Cherice moves through the living room. There's a thump as something hard lands on the floor. In the next second, I'm back in the cellar, standing in front of the open box. Cherice's footsteps land above me. I switch the box on top for the one on the bottom and shove all three of them back toward the wall. Cherice returns just as I reassume my position in the back.

"Sorry about that," she says, shaking her head. "That idiot almost got the wrong house."

"Oh, that's okay. Did you want to go through some more stuff?"

She stares hard at her children's belongings, locked away in soft, old boxes. It's disturbing that everything that ever belonged to them is just a relic of ancient history now. They were supposed to have decades. They were supposed to take things and leave them behind in time's indiscriminate current. It wasn't supposed to be the other way around.

"No," she says. "Let's just take these and get it over with."

It takes us two trips each to clear out those boxes. We load up Cherice's car, and make the silent drive into town. Even the air is heavier, like it's resting its whole weight against my shoulders.

Cherice stops in front of a tiny, storefront building. "New River Thrift" is written in light blue chalk on the building's glass face. Someone took out the time to draw cartoonish flowers and a crooked-faced bunny.

I help Cherice take all the boxes inside and wait at the desk with her. The girl working on the other side looks younger than me. Her eyes are blue like Roman's.

"Welcome to New River Thrift. How can I help you?"

Cherice gestures matter-of-factly to the boxes by the door. "I have some things I'd like to donate."

It's not what the girl wants to hear. She eyes the boxes with unveiled malice, before reaching under the desk for a stack of papers.

"All right. We'll have to go through them, make sure they're up to standard. It'll probably take half an hour, so you can sit in the waiting area. Whatever we don't take will have to go back with you."

Cherice sucks her teeth but tries to smile. "Okay."

"And," the girl passes her a stack of papers. "You'll need to fill these out."

"Of course. Thank you."

We sit in the waiting area, which is just a bunch of mismatched chairs in the front right corner of the building. A rickety old table sits between them, covered in magazines. Beneath it, a chipped fountain gurgles cloudy water.

"God, I hate this place," Cherice mutters. "I'm sorry about the wait."

"Oh it's fine."

It's absolutely not fine. There's nothing worse than waiting rooms.

Cherice starts on the paperwork, and I try to find interest in my phone. Usually, mindless scrolling is a decent pastime, but I can't focus. My mind keeps getting pulled back to the quest, to the horrors on Cisthene. The strange man outside my house, and his quiet implications.

I hear Baxter's voice in my head. *We're being watched.*

Cherice swears under her breath. "This is the worst. There are like a million pages."

I look up and freeze. Outside, in the parking lot, there's someone watching me. There's no mistaking it. He's standing by my aunt's car, sneering through the glass.

"Hey Aunt Cherice, I'm gonna get some fresh air."

"Okay," she says, not looking up from her papers. "Don't go too far."

"I won't."

A bell jingles as I open the door. At a time like this, I'd expect at least half of the town to be at one of New River's massive churches. The plaza's parking lot is nearly empty, save for the man standing on the sidewalk.

"Beautiful weather, isn't it?"

I recognize his gaudy black robes, but nothing else. It was too dark to make out anything about his face. Something about his voice though, its warm, menacing timbre, is familiar.

"I love fall," the man says, not moving. "I always think that people have the wrong idea about death. Fear, repulsion, avoidance—it's the wrong attitude. When the leaves die, they decay into pieces of gold, and pave our streets. Death is beauty."

My stomach drops. I do know that voice. It floated across the street last night to tickle my ears.

"What do you want?" I ask him, just like I did last night.

He smirks. "You already know what we want. I'm sure the Vessel told you."

"So this is about the Codex?"

"What else, Lighting God?"

"My name's Ophelia."

Another smirk. "I know. I know lots of things. I know your destiny."

I ignore the frightened chill that lopes down my spine. "And what's that?"

"To die, at Her command. An honorable destiny. I almost envy you."

"And who's that?" I ask, ignoring the jab. "Your one true god?"

His laugh is cold and rattling, like a serpent. "Some think so. Others not so much. But she is our queen, and her will is the law. What she wants, Lightning God, is your life. In due time."

"So tell me who she is. I'll lay down my life right now."

"That's funny. Honestly, I'm surprised you don't know. Aren't you Jason Johnson's daughter?"

A wall of fire pushes up my throat. "You don't get to say his name."

He quirks an eyebrow. "Oh? From what I gather, I'd say I knew him better than you did. You knew a facade."

"Shut up."

He presses on. "I knew who he really was. I knew that he was their hero, and I know that heroes die."

He slides two fingers across the hood of Cherice's car as he crosses over to the sidewalk.

His robe billows in the wind, revealing the hilt of a sword and a storm builds in my blood.

"Easy," he laughs, watching the sky. "I haven't come for blood. I just wanted to see the Lightning God for myself. That's all."

"And?"

He shrugs. "I'm unimpressed."

The door opens with a jingle, and Cherice steps out in front of me. Her shoulders are squared, her feet spaced evenly apart. I can't see her face, but I'd imagine there'd be fire there.

The man's eyes brighten with delight. And recognition too. "Ah, sweet Lydia. Your beauty stands the test of time. How kind are the gods of our birth."

"Get out of here, Alex," she demands, her voice low and cold.

He seems amused at that, but doesn't say anything. He looks over her shoulder, locking eyes with me. They twinkle with something dark and threatening.

"I'll be seeing you. Ophelia," he says. He nods at Cherice, bowing at the waist. "Goodbye, Lydia."

Then he turns and walks away. When his robe flutters behind them, revealing the sword belt around his waist, the embroidered shape of an arrowhead patch winks in the sunlight.

Cherice watches him until he disappears down the main road. When she turns back to me, her eyes are blazing with fear. There are so many things I want to say, but my tongue feels swollen.

"Get in the car," Cherice says.

"What?"

"Don't ask me questions, Ophelia. I said get in the car. We're going home."

I look back at the shop, where the clerk pretends not to watch us. Then back to the main road. Just like last night, there's no trace of the strange watcher. Cars hurtle past, and he's nowhere in sight.

I don't argue with Cherice. She unlocks the door and I slide into the passenger seat. She locks it back before going into the shop. Ten minutes later, she comes back with a single box. Her eyes cut around the lot suspiciously before she finally puts the box in the trunk and gets behind the wheel.

I shudder as she pulls out of the parking lot. We both survey it carefully, but it doesn't help. If I've learned anything, it's that you don't have to see something in order for it to see you. Could he still be watching? Is he waiting for something? Why did he really come here, and why did he know my aunt? Why did she know his name?

"Who was that?" I demand as we hurtle past New River's old fashioned firehouse.

We're going much faster than we're supposed to. Her fingers clench so tight around the steering wheel that her knuckles turn white.

"No one," she says.

I scoff. "I'm not stupid. You knew each other. You said his name."

She cuts her eyes to me, but doesn't say anything. The block of fear in my stomach quickly melts into a hot, boiling rage.

"That guy's been following me around," I tell her. "He showed up outside the house last night. If you know who he is you need to tell me."

She slams on the breaks, and the car goes lurching to a violent stop. The car behind us blares and swerves around.

"He was at the house?" She asks, her eyes wide as satellites. "That's who you were talking to?"

"Why's he following me?"

"Ophelia." She presses her knuckles against her temple. "I can't—I'm sorry, but I can't. We just need to get home."

"This is getting so old. He knew who my dad was. He said he knew him better than I did." I do my best to keep my voice level. "Why won't you just tell me the truth?"

"For your own good!" she yells, surprising me. "We've made a lot of mistakes, your father made a lot of mistakes, and unfortunately there are people who think you should pay for them. I wish I could tell you more, but I literally can't. I know that's not the answer you want to hear, and I'm really sorry, but you just have to trust me. Okay?"

I roll my eyes and turn away from her, pressing my forehead against the window's cool glass. I'm blazing hot all over, like there's a hot spring at my core. I want to yell or drag thunder across the sky, but there'd be no point. Their secrets and lies have met me face-to-face, and they still won't tell me the truth. If it weren't so infuriating, I'd admire the commitment. If I want the truth, I have to take it for myself.

"So I guess that means you won't be telling me who 'Lydia' is either, huh?" I murmur.

She's quiet for so long that I think she's ignoring me. When she finally speaks, her voice is thin and weak.

"Like I said, we've all made mistakes."

CHAPTER TWENTY-THREE

WE EAT FROZEN STEAK AND GOUDA pizza off paper plates, and no one speaks.

Janus wasn't in the best mood when he got back from work, and his expression is dark and stony now. He picks at his pizza, disinterested, with trembling hands. Cherice and I have decided to ignore it.

"Got some things out today," Cherice mumbles, looking down at her plate.

Janus doesn't seem interested, but he answers anyway. "That's good. I wish I'd been here to help." He glances at me. "I hate that you had to do all that by yourself."

Cherice shrugs. "It's okay. I managed."

I watch her in disbelief. Perhaps it had been too much to expect an explanation from either of them. Maybe the person I'm really mad at is myself. What I hadn't expected was for Cherice to just lie to him, especially about something so serious.

I bring my hand down into the table, rattling our plates. "Actually, I helped."

"Oh." He keeps his tone mild, but a vein jumps in his temple.

"Yeah, we went to the thrift store in town. There was this guy outside, in the parking lot."

"Ophelia." There's warning in Cherice's voice, but I don't care.

"He carries a sword. Very old-fashioned," I continue. "He showed up at the store, just like he showed up outside the house last night—for me."

"Ophelia," Cherice shouts, angry now.

"What? You were gonna lie to him too? Pretend it never happened?"

"I was going to tell him. Me!" She jabs a finger into her own chest. "Ophelia, why can't you just trust us?"

"Why can't you tell me the truth? Don't I deserve to know?" I say, standing up. "I had to find my father's dead body, and you don't think I deserve to know who he really was?"

Janus' voice is flat and searing. "Enough! You're a child, and I'm not doing this. We've already told you everything you need to know. The rest is none of your business."

"Bullshit!"

Cherice jumps to her feet. "All right. That's completely inappropriate."

"I'm being *followed* around town by a guy who wants me dead. What's appropriate about that?" I point at Cherice. "And *you* knew him. You knew him, and what?"

"We will handle it," Janus says, still trying to stay calm. "Right now, you need to go to bed. You have school tomorrow."

I lock eyes with him, outraged. He holds my gaze and says nothing.

"Unbelievable," I scoff.

I resist the urge to throw my chair or crack the table in half and just go upstairs. I hear thunder rumbling outside my window. I want to scream. I know it wasn't a good idea to start a fight down there, especially with how hard today's been, but I can't believe it. Everything that's happened, and they still don't trust me. They'd rather sustain the integrity of a lie than prepare me for what's coming.

Because something is coming. I can feel it in my bones. That man said death was my destiny. Technically, everyone's going to die, but there was a strange weight to his prediction. Like my death is soon and imminent.

My father's journal is still where I left it. I make sure my breathing is slow before opening it. I hate how everything with his name on it feels so heavy.

I lock my door and sit up reading for hours. The front cover is labeled "Index Mythologia" in my father's faded script. The entries are handwritten. The drawings too. Monsters dominate the pages in smudged, black oil, some with hissing heads, others with ghastly, webbed wings. About halfway through the book, there's a drawing of a woman with grass-green skin.

Gaia.

The name is familiar, along with all the others that follow. *Erebus. Uranus. Eros. Nyx.* The Firstborn: ancient gods older than the Titans and the Earth itself. It's the last name that's unfamiliar, and his drawing takes up two pages.

His body is a frightening mass of smudged black ink and fiery red paint. He has six red eyes, and a mouthful of razor-sharp teeth. My father's handwritten label identifies him as: *Kreos, God of Hunger.* His entry tells the story of a jealous god, who wanted to rule the Earth. He challenged Olympus with the might of his army, the Children of Paradise, and his queen at his side—Nyx, the Goddess of Endless Night.

I snap the book shut and lunge for my phone. The line rings three times before Roman answers, still on the edge of sleep.

"Lia? Are you okay?" He mumbles, his voice thick.

"How fast can you be at my house?"

"What?"

"I know it's late, but—"

He cuts me off. "I'm on the way."

Five minutes later, he appears at the foot of my bed out of thin air. He's still in his pajamas, and he's wearing a pair of glasses I've never seen before.

"Sorry. I figured you wouldn't want me using the front door," he says, holding up the book

"Right. Come here." He sits down beside me, and I try to ignore that I technically have a boy in my bed. This is not the right time at all to be so aware of his shoulder against mine, or how he smells like a fresh shower.

I open my father's journal between us, right on Kreos' page.

He winces. "Who's that?"

"Kreos—King of Paradise. He's the king of this older race of gods, ones who challenged the Olympians."

He sits back, furrowing his brow. "Hold on." He vanishes and reappears an instant later with another book in his hands, the one I let him keep. He flips through it to the General's entry. "Do you remember that day in the art room? When we were reading about how the originals died?"

"Yeah, yeah. Holy shit, the Children of Paradise." I flip through the journal again, to my father's entry about

Scions. "These Children of Paradise. Think about what that boy on Cisthene said, about fulfilling *her* will. They're the children of these older gods, and I bet that's who's been following us around."

He grimaces down at the journal. "Any clue on who the '*she*' is?"

"Yeah, actually." I show him the gray-skinned woman with black eyes. "Nyx—Goddess of Endless Night. I just don't get how that's possible though. They're all supposed to be locked away."

"Maybe it's not the gods themselves. It makes sense for their descendants to want revenge," he says. "It would explain why they've been attacking demigod houses. And why they've been trying to kill us."

I shake my head. "But those attacks weren't just about killing people or destroying things. They were looking for the Codex but I don't get how the Fates factor into that."

"Maybe the Fates are just collateral?" he suggests. "Or an incentive?"

"Yeah, but for who? If it's an incentive for us, why hide the Eye so we can't use it?"

He rakes a hand through his wayward hair, sighing. "I don't know. Like you said, none of this makes sense, but at least we know who we're dealing with now."

I flop back on my bed. "I hate this. Why does it have to be so complicated?"

"Because then it wouldn't be fun," he snorts.

"I'm gonna hit you."

"That's okay."

I sigh and bump him with my shoulder. "Thanks for coming, by the way. I know I woke you up."

"It's nothing." He shrugs. "I'll always come when you call."
Warmth floods my cheeks. I turn away so he can't see the
stupid grin that splits my face. "Thanks. You don't have to do
that though. Really."

"Tough. You're stuck with me. Sorry."

In the low light of my room, his smile is dazzling. I notice
the clarity of his eyes, each wayward tousle of his silky hair.
His glasses have slid low on the bridge of his nose, and I can't
help myself. I reach out and push them up with a gentle
nudge of my finger.

"Whatever. You're very sweet."

"Thanks." His cheeks are flaming red. "So, I'll see you at
school tomorrow, right?"

"Maybe, maybe not." Alex's warning flashes through my
head and I realize that there may be more truth to my words
than I realize.

He frowns. "What's wrong?"

"When I got home last night, this guy was watching me
from across the street. He was dressed like the attackers on
Cisthene—same patch and all. And then today, Cherice and
I were in town, and he showed up again. He was saying all
this weird shit about how my destiny is death, and then
Cherice told him to get out of there. They knew each other."

His brow furrows again. "What'd he do?"

"He just left. Just like that."

"Ophelia, why didn't you say anything? What if he did
something to you?"

I wave my fingers, sparking lightning between them. "I'm
not exactly defenseless."

"No, I know, but these people are dangerous. They killed an
entire house of demigods. Just promise me you'll be careful."

"I will."

"*And* promise me you'll call me if you see him again. Or if anything like that happens again." He shakes his head. "Honestly just, if you *ever* need me, for anything, please just call. I'll answer."

I search his face, but I can tell that he means it. I reach out for his hand. I'm not really sure why. He reaches back, loosely connecting our fingers.

"Promise." I squeeze his hand. "Thank you."

He squeezes back. "Of course. I'll see you tomorrow, Lia."

"See you tomorrow."

He vanishes, and the last thing I feel is the warm grip of his hand in mine. I stare at it, my palm still tingling. When did I become this person? When did seeing him make every part of me feel fuzzy and warm? And how is any of that even possible, given all these terrible circumstances?

I flop down on my back, sighing. The hummingbirds in my stomach are restless. It's stupid. It's so, so stupid. But it's the best feeling I've had in months. Something wild and warm, breaking the ice around me. Something new.

CHAPTER TWENTY-FOUR

I MAKE A POINT TO WAKE up early to avoid Janus and Cherice. It almost works, but I'm still in the foyer putting my shoes on when Cherice comes downstairs in a pencil skirt and blazer. Janus is in his pajamas. He looks at me like he wants to say something, decides against it, and goes into the kitchen instead. A part of me, a guilty part, wants to apologize for disturbing the peace. It doesn't have nearly as much intensity as the rest of me, which blisters and stews with a persistent rage. I could see past the thinly-veiled apathy on Janus' face last night, but it doesn't matter. How could he look at me like that, like I was being unreasonable? Like I'd stepped out of line? I'm just as entitled to my family's truth as he is, so why would he keep it from me?

Cherice looks like she's going to try to make peace. I wish she wouldn't bother.

"Ophelia . . ." she starts.

"It's okay. I don't care anymore," I tell her. I put my hand on the doorknob but she stops me.

"Please, just let me say this."

I sigh and turn back to her. She takes my silence as agreement.

"Look, I understand how frustrating this must be, but please know that we only want the best for you. When we do tell you everything, we don't want you to have to worry. That's all."

"Too late," I scoff. "I'll see you later."

I don't let her say anything else. I leave the house and storm down the walkway.

AT SCHOOL, BAXTER AND CASS ARE waiting on the porch steps, a book between them. I plop down on the other side of Cass without a word, and glare down at my shoes. My vision blurs. For a dangerous second, I'm so angry I think I could cry.

"Well good morning to you too," Cass quips, nudging me with his knee.

"I'm not in the mood," I mutter.

"Everything okay?" Baxter asks.

"No. No, it's not." I tug on my fingers before crumpling both of my hands into fists. "My aunt and uncle know something and they won't tell me."

"Something about what?" Cass asks.

"All of this," I wave my hands around. "I found a journal that used to belong to my father. He was writing about harpies and hellhounds. He was writing about gods, but older gods."

"Oh. Like the Titans?"

I shake my head. "Older." I reach into my bag and pull out the journal, flipping to Kreos' shadowy, black figure. "My dad called him the God of Hunger. Apparently, this guy is their King—the King of Paradise."

Baxter frowns down at the journal. The wrinkles in his forehead deepen as his brow pinches. "Well that's horrifying and all, but what does it have to do with our thing?"

I flip through the journal again, landing on the page about Scions this time. I ignore the tremor that runs through me, brittle and freezing. "You know how Olympians create lines of demigods when they reproduce with mortals? The immortal line isn't diluted by human blood. It's the same concept with the Firstborn, and it would explain everything: Cisthene, the watcher."

"That guy that's following you?" Baxter says. "It would've been nice to hear that from you, by the way. We can't afford to keep secrets."

Alex ghosts across my brain like a cackling shadow. Roman must have told them. It would explain that too. The way he talked about my destiny and his fealty to the Mother. Nyx. She'd sent him to me each time, just like how she'd sent the watcher to our school. Just like Cisthene.

"I know. I'm sorry."

"Seriously," Cass adds. "If you see him again, say something."

Alessia comes in from the parking lot, her shoulders drooped and low. She sits on the ground in front of us, leaning her back against the base of the staircase. At the sight of the journal in Baxter's hands, she hangs her head.

She gestures at it with a wary finger. "That doesn't look good."

"Oh it's not." Cass' voice is biting and sardonic. "Turns out, the people targeting us are the descendants of much older gods. Like the first gods ever."

"That's not funny, Cass." She mutters.

He laughs again, a bitter, coughing sound. "I'm not joking, Alessia."

"Hey, we've been busting our asses at the Sacred House,"

she counters, irritated. "How come nothing we've read has mentioned older gods?"

Cass shrugs. "Who knows? If they're really that old, I wouldn't imagine there'd be a lot written about them anyway."

"Yeah, that makes sense." Baxter says, pinching the bridge of his nose. "It doesn't really do much good though. We still don't know why they want the Codex."

"Or where it is," Cass adds dryly.

"Or where it is," Baxter agrees.

"Don't worry. We're gonna find the Eye," I tell them. And then, with some strange surge of conviction, "Today."

"Today?" Alessia scoffs.

Cass doesn't sound like he's taking me seriously. "Funny."

"I'm sick of sitting around," I say. "We got nowhere last weekend because they were one step ahead of us. We don't know when they're watching or how they're figuring out what we do, so we should go today. Like, right now."

"You're insane." Baxter shakes his head. He pulls his lips together like he's just bit down on a lemon wedge. "But you're right. It should be today."

"What should be today?" Roman walks up to join us, his bag half slung across his shoulders.

He's not wearing his glasses anymore, and his hair looks neat and brushed. I try to pretend I'm still the same person as I was before seeing him in his pajamas. I don't think it's working.

Olivia comes up only a few paces behind him, wearing a pair of black camo pants. Her braids look fresh and fall down her back in neat, black layers.

She points to the book in Baxter's lap. "You know, I feel like I'm not gonna like whatever this is."

"We should go to the museum today," I say. "We need the

Eye, because now we know who's watching us, and it'll only get worse if we drag this out."

She lets out a low whistle, shaking her head. "Yeah, I don't love it."

Roman shrugs. "Well, I'm in."

"Of course you are." Alessia rolls her eyes.

"Look, it's not a terrible idea," Baxter says. "Regular people wouldn't be able to see us, and it's not like we have to catch a plane to get there. It's a field trip. It's fun."

Cass' smile beams with disbelief. "Field trip. Incredible."

"What about school?" Alessia asks, albeit a bit halfheartedly.

More people arrive and walk around us to get inside. There's a ball of fire in the pit of my stomach, and its hunger can only be satiated by action. Not sitting in a classroom all day. Not being content with the carefree life my aunt and uncle think I live. Today, I have to get something done.

"What about it?" I shrug. "You'll probably have third period with a bunch of Scions, anyway."

"That's sick," Alessia chides.

Cass drags a hand down his cheek so he can groan into the heel of his palm. It's an exaggerated sound, but he really does look exhausted. Like he hasn't slept in weeks.

"All right, whatever," he says. "I'm in. It's less boring than calculus."

Olivia leans against the wall, chewing on her lip. Her eyes are distant, but her voice is like steel. "I'm in."

Alessia casts irritated looks around the circle, but doesn't protest. "Whatever."

We sit on the steps until the first bell echoes out the front door. Baxter and I lean over his laptop, tracing an online directory of the Cambridge Museum of History and Art. It's right downtown, next to the water. There's a 3D-walkthrough of Babylon's floating gardens and an entire exhibit on how the Ancient Egyptians mummified their dead. The third floor is dedicated to Ancient Mesopotamia and its fertility goddesses. And the fourth, at the very top, is a Roman history and culture exhibit, outfitted with actual relics from the ancient city itself and life-sized sculptures of their gods.

"It's definitely the fourth floor," Baxter says. He takes a red sharpie and draws a huge circle across the map.

"Why Roman gods though?"

He shrugs. "Maybe they have a sense of humor."

After studying the museum's illuminated position on the wide corner of a city square, they all gather around me at the base of the steps. Alessia doesn't look any more excited than she did ten minutes ago, but she doesn't say anything. Roman's eyes are oddly trusting as he watches me: I think that might be more terrifying.

They latch onto my arms, and I close my eyes. I see the front, paneled face of the building, the way it dominates the corner and overlooks a busy city. I see the smooth, neat letters of the sign, carved out of black and white neon. The wind catches around us, soaked with a pungent stench of ozone. A second later, New River High falls away, and the wind drops us right in the middle of a busy street.

Three cars jerk and swerve around us, nearly sending the eighteen wheeler on the other side of the divide careening into a line of brightly colored shops. The intersection is wide and freshly paved, but the surrounding buildings are much older. They're nearly stacked on top of each other and line the road like brick-and-mortar sentries. Unlike New River, Cambridge is bustling.

People don't even seem to notice as we run onto the sidewalk, nearly knocking them off their feet. As soon as we get close, it's like their eyes gloss over.

Armor melts over us as we step onto the sidewalk. I unsheathe the Lightning Bolt, provoking a groan of thunder from an otherwise beautiful sky.

Four yellow school buses pull up right in front of the sidewalk, delivering children from Cambridge Middle. I can hear them shouting through the windows. The last bus screeches to a stop, and a flood of children spill onto the sidewalk.

"Oh no," Olivia mutters. She's watching the museum's dark face like the sight of it makes her sick.

"What's wrong?" Baxter asks, catching her elbow.

A bead of silver light comes on in her right eye. "This is definitely it, because I just got the worst feeling. There's something in there."

"Yeah. The Eye," Cass says matter-of-factly. I hit him in the chest with the back of my hand.

"Something else," Olivia says, ignoring him. "Something evil. And hungry." She doesn't sound afraid when she says it, just cautious.

I look around, checking the street for anyone who looks like they should be at Comic Con. I don't notice anyone watching from across the street, but that doesn't mean they aren't there. At this point, they could be anywhere. Watching us from any distance, with any number of terrible things in mind.

I shake off the chill. It sort of works. "Let's go," I say, pushing ahead to the doors. "We can start on the fourth, but we need to search every floor."

"Sounds like a breeze." The hitch in Roman's voice is hard to miss.

Cass claps him on the back. "It's nice to see you haven't lost your cheerful disposition."

We vanish into the building's main foyer, past the ticket line. It's a wide, high-ceilinged room with intricate patterns carved into aged ivory. A chandelier of glass and crystal hangs from the ceiling, scattering shards of brilliant, gold light. The floor is flat and smooth, a rich dark mocha. In the middle of the room, standing behind a barricade of red rope, is the 20-foot tall, marble figure of a woman.

She's wearing armor: grieves, a breastplate, and the helmet beneath her right foot. The light spills over each smooth groove of her muscled arms—the left one, as casual as stone can be at her side, and the right one, gripping a massive white sword. The sculpture is clean and dazzling, like it was polished recently. I feel tiny in front of it

"Minerva," Roman mutters. He points to the tiny sign in front of the red rope, which advertises the exhibit in bold, bronze lettering. "That's where we're going, right?"

I study the statue. It's beautiful, but something about it suddenly makes me feel sick. I nod.

Four arched doorways lead out of the foyer. We take the left one to a set of elevators. There are six floors, but the last two are password accessible only. On the ride up, Olivia's expression grows more severe. The light in her eye seems to grow stronger the higher up we get. When the elevator lets us out on the fourth floor, she steps out with an arrow in one hand and a bow in the other.

"Something's not right," she says. "I wish I knew what it was, but . . ." She shakes her head.

Ruefully, Alessia pulls a blade out of the air: a long, red sword with black jewels down the spine. We walk into the exhibit's gaping, dimly-lit mouth. There are at least a dozen people here, but nobody seems to notice the group of armed teenagers.

Pieces line the exhibit's wide arch: yellowed pages of parchment in display cases, weathered book spines, dull swords and dusty, crookedly carved shields. Mannequins assembled in a stagger of rows model the peak of Ancient Roman fashion: pale togas and full-suits of heavy-looking armor. One of the mannequins clutches a tall spear in its right hand. The other, dressed in a gray tunic, holds a plastic hand to her chest, right beneath the clunky, eye-shaped jewel that dangles around her neck. It's a foggy chunk of diamond that's roughly the size of my uncle's fist with dull green emeralds outlining the edges. In the center, embedded deep in the diamond's heart, is a cluster of amber and some other jade green jewel.

"Well, that was easy." I reach out to snatch the necklace away when Olivia screams behind me.

"Ophelia don't!"

I hear the heavy swish and thunk of an arrow flying. In the same instant, my hand stalls against an invisible partition. The air splits down the middle, and something's ugly, black talon swipes at my wrist. I jump back, splattering gold blood across the museum's beautiful chocolate floor.

"Get back!" Olivia yells.

Something invisible roars in agony. The entire building trembles.

A black creature steps out of the air on massive, pawed feet. Its fur is coarse but sleek. It gazes down at us through the green eyes of a woman—haunting and beautiful. Black braids fall past her feline ears, but her body is the powerful, menacing form of a lion. She's easily much taller than the Minerva statue downstairs, so her head just barely scrapes the exhibit's high ceilings. A single paw is the size of a Mini Cooper.

She makes an exaggerated show of stretching out her massive, shadowy body, head rolling from side to side. There's a cold intelligence to her eyes. Her tail, heavy and black, swishes back and forth behind her. The light catches the reflective surface of what has to be a pattern of scales. When a red-eyed serpent jerks around, nearly snapping off my face, I realize it's not a tail at all. The serpent has the same kind of awareness in its eyes as it hisses at me through a mouthful of fangs.

"*Who dares to seek this treasure?*" Ancient Greek rolls off the Sphinx's tongue in a tangled chorus.

I feel so small standing in front of her, even with the sword in my hand and this lightning in my blood. It takes everything I have not to take another step back. My wrist throbs. The gash across the top of my hand heals slowly, so I'm still bleeding.

"*The Gods of Olympus,*" I shout, mostly as an experiment. It doesn't really sound like I believe it. "*We need the Eye.*"

She purrs. There's something especially violent about the softness of her voice. Beside her, the serpent hisses with laughter.

"*Those that hunger need bread. Fools need sense,*" she says, laughing. "*What makes your need so special?*"

Roman comes up beside me, breathing hard. I can tell by his trembling hands that there's more fear today than courage.

"If we don't get that Eye, we won't be able to save the Fates. They'll—,"

The Sphinx throws her head back into a deep, rumbling yawn. The entire exhibit rattles, but no one else seems to notice. A group of kids our age come right up to the mannequin's display case, only an inch away from the Sphinx's massive paws. She ignores them.

"*Yes, yes,*" she sighs, still yawning. "*If the Fates aren't rescued, they die. If they die, the world ends. Very dreadful business. Not very exciting.*"

Olivia steps forward with four arrows notched in her bow. Silver armor glows against her body, the same color as the light that fills her brown eyes. If any one of us actually looks the part, it's her.

"*I'm not interested in what bores you,*" she says, her voice flat and cold. "*I'm interested in the Eye. You can give it to us, or we can take it. Either way, we're leaving here with it. Today.*"

Finally, something like excitement flicks on in the Sphinx's eye. She pads forward a little, into the full light of the exhibit. On all four paws, she towers over us, as horrifying as a monster should be. The serpent behind her titters curses in Ancient Greek as she walks, howling with laughter.

"*Oh, fair Huntress,*" she purrs. "*There are only two ways to obtain what you seek. Blood. Or thought.*"

"What?" Cass scoffs.

I sigh, remembering. My father told me this story too. It's just so different seeing something in real life when you've been led to believe that it was always only a story. "She wants us to answer her riddle." I shake my head. "Is that it? We play your game and then we get the Eye?"

She hums pleasantly. "*You're already halfway there. Yes. Play the . . . game, get what you want. Lose or refuse, and death will be your reward.*"

The air splits beside him, and Cass pulls out his bident by its long, golden handle. He aims it up at the Sphinx's massive body, defiance raw and unyielding on his face.

"We're gods," he says. "If we say move and give us the Eye, then you move and give us the Eye."

"*Oh? Is that so, little god?*" She sits back on her thick, muscled haunches and lowers into a crouch, like a house cat.

I hold up a hand, but I'm not sure who I'm trying to hold back—Cass or the monster. "Look, we'll play your game. Just give us the riddle."

Still lounging on her haunches, she rolls her head from side to side, pretending to think. When she splits her lips to smile, each one of her fangs glints in the light. Her teeth are like rows of pearly white daggers.

"*You have one guess. From the moment you're born, I know your name. I am your one true destiny and your ever loyal shadow. There is no place to hide where I will not find you,*" she says. "*What am I?*"

Roman pulls us into a huddle. Olivia still has arrows notched in her bow, and Cass watches the Sphinx with a threatening gaze.

I am your one true destiny.

"Ease up," Baxter tells them. "As long as we solve the riddle we should be fine."

"That's what we said the first time." Cass' voice is bitter, like he's spitting acid. "'As long as we go to Cisthene, we'll be fine.' They're playing us. Again."

A smirk curls at the ends of Roman's mouth. "No. If they could use it, they'd have it."

Alessia scoffs. "Right, but they don't. Instead, they hid it here and set a monster to watch it. Because they can't use it, and they don't want us figuring it out either."

I press cold fingers against my temple, tuning them out. A rush of hopelessness plunges down the slope of my spine. What had Alex said to me? They were almost those exact words.

I am your one true destiny.

"Okay let's figure this out," Roman says. He recites the riddle again; his Greek is smooth as honey.

"Maybe it's about bodies," Alessia says, but she doesn't sound convinced. "Your body is always with you, and I mean, if we're getting philosophical—that almost makes sense."

"Yeah, I guess you could argue that your body is your destiny," Olivia adds, grumbling, "in a weird, abstract way. But how would it know your name?"

"How about a soul?" Roman asks. "The soul is your destiny because it belongs to you. It knows your name because no one could know you better, and it's your loyal shadow because it can never leave you."

Cass shrugs. "Okay. That's an option, but what if we're wrong?"

Olivia grimaces. "According to the myths, if you don't answer the Sphinx's riddle correctly, she eats you alive."

"So either way we might have to kill her." Cass whirls his spear into a long sword, then back into a spear. "I'm not exactly against that. It might be faster."

I look back at the Sphinx, who smiles pleasantly, with her head resting against her paws. She runs a large pink tongue across her teeth.

Alex. His unwavering calm. The way he spoke so softly, like he didn't want to disturb the pebbles beneath his feet. Of course, that had only been on the surface. There was the casual cruelty of his smile—empty hands that had been shaped in the image of violence. I'd asked him what my destiny was, and his answer was so simple. So simple and so certain, like the jaws of something inescapable.

"It's death," I say, almost like I'm in a daze.

Roman quirks an eyebrow. "What?"

"It knows your name from the moment you're born. It's impossible to escape." A deep freeze blossoms across my ribs. It feels like I'll never be warm again. "Death is your destiny."

"And you're sure?" Cass asks.

I nod. My mouth is so dry I can barely swallow. "I'm sure."

When we gather back in front of the Sphinx, she purrs in excitement. "*So soon?*" she asks.

"We're ready." I say, ignoring the hungry flicker of her eyes.

"*Good. What am I?*"

My voice sounds empty and cold, and not unafraid. "Death."

At first, she looks disappointed, and a spasm of terror ripples through me. Her massive head tilts to the side, so that she's resting her left cheek against a taloned paw.

"*Oh no,*" she muses, sucking her teeth. "*That's correct.*"

Alessia narrows her eyes. "What do you mean 'oh no?'"

The Sphinx raises up to sit on her back legs, revealing each of the long, deadly claws in her front paws. She smiles, but this time, there's nothing pleasant about it. "*No one's ever answered correctly before. But now I'm going to have to eat you anyway. It's sad.*"

"What the hell?" I demand. "We had a deal. We answer the riddle, you give up the Eye."

"*You didn't even make me swear on the Styx. How serious could you be?*" She raises a paw and waves a single, black claw at me, going *tsk tsk.* "*Oh, but Ophelia, dear, don't worry. I only intend to make feasts of your friends. After they're dead, you and I will be making a short journey. I'm afraid you're expected.*"

Cass sighs beside me, a resigned sound. "I hate it when I'm right."

The Serpent lunges at my chest with the speed of lightning. I only just barely avoid the harsh snap of its teeth. We scatter as the Sphinx leaps into the air, cackling as she cracks the exhibit's carved ceiling. The building trembles and rains down clusters of dust and drywall. People escape in screaming clusters, but I'm not sure what they see.

A massive black paw lands in front of me as the exhibit fills with echoes. A volley of arrows has gone flying, each finding their home in a pocket of the Sphinx's flesh. All it takes it a wide sweep of the Serpent's head to knock Baxter and Liv off their feet.

Cass and Roman stab their spears into the Sphinx's front paws, just as the Serpent lunges for Baxter's limp body. I slide across the exhibit on my knees in just enough time to slash my sword through the Serpent's meaty body. Its head hits the floor with a wet thunk. Black blood gathers around me.

The Sphinx wails, but I don't wait for her to attack. With her feet still pinned to the floor, I run up the twitching slope of the Serpent's body. A heavy, black paw hovers over me, but I leap out of the way before the Sphinx can bring down her claws. I land on her back, buried up to my calves in stalks of coarse, black fur. I run to the base of her neck, raising my sword. The Sphinx brings down another paw. I'm not fast enough.

Her claws catch my shoulder, tearing three deep gashes right into my armor. Six silver arrows fly over my head as the word lurches out of frame. My legs slip out from underneath me, and I fall to the hard, polished floor with a thud. I feel the clean, agonizing snap of bone in my chest.

The Sphinx thrashes just above me, howling in pain and rage. The Serpent's body still bleeds behind her, scattering black blood all along the walls. Alessia swings a heavy, double-sided ax through the Sphinx's back right leg, severing it at the foot. At the same time, Roman swings the trident into a sword and starts hacking away at her front leg.

My armor's gone. I push myself up despite the sharp pain in my chest and switch my sword to my left hand. My right shoulder throbs worse than my wrist did. I try not to look. I wouldn't be able to stomach the sight of oozing ichor and mangled flesh.

Baxter fires an arrow that lodges deep in the Sphinx's left eye. He skates off the wall in a streak of gold light just as she swipes at him. Her front leg is mangled, and snaps off with a final swing of Roman's sword. She roars and slams her head into his body. He goes flying out of sight.

I rear my sword back, melting the sword's metal into a rod of hot blue lightning. The Sphinx roars as Cass mounts its back, hacking it open with his sword. She shakes, jerking him off.

"Get back!" I shout, my blood boiling with heat.

At the least second, they all clear out of the way. The Sphinx levels her one good eye on me; the other gushes black blood down her face. She roars, the sound rattling the entire room. As she lunges, I launch the lightning bolt across the space between us. It meets her halfway, scattering her body in a sickly shower of matted fur and thick, black blood.

Finally, the exhibit is quiet.

Cass raises bleeding arms in sardonic triumph. "Yay. We did it." He winces and clutches a hand to his ribs.

"That's what you get for being a smartass," Alessia mutters. She limps to his side to examine the wound.

Ignoring the pain in my shoulder, I step over bits of charred lion to the same mannequin as before. When I reach out for the jeweled eye around its neck, nothing intercepts me. I pull off the heavy, silver chain and shove it carefully into my pocket.

"In hindsight," I say, still trying to catch my breath, "we should've just listened to Cass." I press a hand to my forehead in disbelief. "Oh god, I can't believe I just said that."

Olivia sits down hard on the floor, nursing her wrist. "I think hearing it just made me nauseous."

Cass rolls his eyes. "Ha ha. Can we get out of here? I need to throw up."

Roman gestures to the carnage around us. The cut across his chest looks shallow, but I can't say the same for the long gash down the side of his right arm. Blood drips from his hand in fat, golden drops.

"What about all this?" He asks.

It's not just the blood or severed paws either. Deep cracks carve along the exhibit's wall. Bits of dust and chunks of drywall rain down on us from the crumbling ceiling.

"I say we do nothing." Olivia pushes herself up from the floor. "All in favor?"

All around the room, we chant *aye*.

We latch onto Baxter's bleeding arms as beads of gold light come on in his eyes. In the next instant, the Cambridge Museum of Art and History is nothing more than an awful memory.

CHAPTER TWENTY-FIVE

As soon as we appear inside Baxter's house, my legs fail me. I latch onto Roman's good arm to keep from falling. His hand snakes around my waist, and he leans my weight against him. Cass runs as fast as he can on an injured foot to the kitchen; a second later, we hear the sound of him vomiting.

If I weren't in so much pain, it might be funny. Unfortunately, nothing about this is funny. It was easy to push my body forward in the exhibit, back when I felt nothing but lightning and adrenaline. Now, I just feel empty. My muscles are tight and sore, and the gashes along my shoulder throb with fire. Every time I breathe, it feels like a knife twists in my chest.

"I think I need to sit down," I mutter.

"Not on the couch," Baxter cries, throwing out a panicked hand. "Hold on."

He pushes the couch out of the way before disappearing into the kitchen. Five minutes later, he comes back dragging two different dining tables behind him.

"Hold on," he says again and vanishes into thin air.

Cass hobbles out of the kitchen, wiping his mouth. "I think I broke the garbage disposal. I think there was blood in it."

Olivia laughs, before wheezing and hanging her head. She leans against the bottom of the banister, clutching a hand to her side. "Shit. This isn't fun at all."

"I feel lied to and misled." Alessia pulls her shirt up to examine the gash along her navel. It's not deep, but it's still bleeding. "Aren't we supposed to be indestructible?"

"Who told you that?" Roman asks. "She was a monster. Maybe wounds inflicted by magic don't heal the same."

Baxter reappears with a bundle of white sheets in one hand and a pile of first aid kits in the other. He spreads the sheets across each table carefully.

"Okay, who's hurt the worst?" He asks.

Alessia jabs a finger at Cass. "There was blood in his vomit."

Roman nudges my head with his. "Her ribs are broken."

Baxter hisses and jerks his chin in Olivia's direction. "Liv, how you doing?"

Her eyes are closed, but she shakes her head. "I'm better than them. I can go last."

"How'd you know my ribs were broken?" I ask Roman.

He presses gentle fingers against the side of my chest. Even though his touch isn't harsh, pain spreads through me like wildfire.

"I can feel 'em. Come on."

He walks me over to one of the tables. I'm surprised when he scoops me up and lays me across it.

"I could have—"

He interrupts me, smiling. "I know."

While Baxter starts on Cass, who has a patchwork of dark purple bruising across his torso, I examine the long gash down Roman's arm. He lifts his sleeve to reveal how the wound starts as a jagged half-moon at the top of his shoulder and carves a crooked line all the way down to his wrist.

"It doesn't even hurt that bad," he says, his face white as a fresh patch of snow.

"Shut up. It looks awful."

He sighs, dropping the facade. "Yeah, it kind of is."

"You can go ahead of me," I tell him.

He shakes his head, his eyes going wide. "Absolutely not. Let me see your shoulder."

"Okay."

He helps me turn on my good side, before cutting away the sticky, torn fabric over my left shoulder. I wince as he peels it away, exposing the wound to cold, open air. I hear him hiss.

"How bad is it?" I ask.

He hums thoughtfully. "Well, let's just say it's best you don't look at it."

"You have an incredible bedside manner. Have you ever thought about med school?"

"Sorry," he says. "Baxter's almost done with Cass. Just hang in there."

A few minutes later, Baxter migrates over to me. He balks at the sight of my shoulder too.

"It looks like something tried to eat you," he says.

"You're so terrible at this," I mutter.

"Yeah, yeah. Give me a second."

His hand hovers over my back. A tide of warmth trickles through me, soothing the throbbing pain into nothing. Something tugs at my skin. It takes me a second to realize that it's closing.

"How'd you even figure out you could do this?" Roman asks.

"I read," Baxter says simply. A second later, "All right, turn around."

Roman helps me onto my back and lifts my shirt. If I crane my neck, I can see the dark bruises along my own chest. I can't look long though, because now it feels like I'll faint.

Baxter holds his hand over me again. Gold light fills his hand and falls over my body in a misty, bronze haze. The pain ebbs away and whatever was loose in my chest mends itself. When I sit up, it feels like nothing ever happened in the first place.

"Thanks," I tell him.

Baxter shrugs. His face is bruised and there's a thin scratch along his left temple. Other than that, it doesn't look like he caught the worst of it.

"Just don't get yourself killed. There's probably nothing I can do about that."

I ignore the grim nature of his words and let him heal my other shoulder.

He moves on to Roman next, and I step into the bathroom. I almost scream at the sight of my own reflection. My clothes are splattered in globs of oily, black blood, except for where my left sleeve was. That entire portion of my body is caked in dried ichor. It looks like I just stumbled out of a horror movie, something where aliens come bursting out of people's chests.

I run the sink and fill my hands with warm water, trying to scrub as much blood from my skin as I can. My head is light and loopy. Knowing how my body hit the floor takes me back to the time my dad had to rush me to the ER in fifth grade, when I accidentally swallowed a baby lizard and the way my dad and I panicked, but now it is different. I've never been in this much pain before. Ever.

I keep seeing the Sphinx's gaping maw, rancid with the stench of old bodies. I can't imagine how many people have found death in the dark cavern of her jaws. That could've been us. It could've been our destiny.

I catch myself on the edge of the sink. It's too similar to ignore, even if it feels like a stretch to correlate that. The Sphinx had told us death was our destiny in nearly the exact same way as that man Alex outside the thrift store told me my destiny was to die. It could be a coincidence, but I know better now. Maybe Alex's threat wasn't a clue after all. Maybe it was a prophecy.

Someone knocks on the door. I flinch, but it's Roman's voice that comes through.

"It's just me," he says, sounding exhausted.

I unlock the door and let him in. He closes it behind him and leans against it. His eyes are closed, so at first it looks like he could be sleeping. His breathing gets more shallow with each quick rise and fall of his chest.

"Roman?"

He doesn't answer. He just presses both hands against his face as it crumbles.

"Hey." I'm reaching for his shoulders before I can think about it.

It feels natural, so I just go with it. Pulling him into me feels natural too. So does holding him as he hyperventilates. I don't know why, but I want to keep him close, where monsters and trained killers can't get to him. The feeling is foreign, this urge to protect something.

"I'm sorry," he mumbles into my neck, his breathing still strained. "I was just so scared."

"Me too," I tell him. It's the truth.

For a second, when the Sphinx leapt into the air, when she was the largest, most powerful thing in the world, I thought we were going to die. Nothing else mattered: not our powers, or our strength. I saw death in each powerful stride of her body, and it seemed inescapable.

"I'm sorry," he says again.

"Stop apologizing. It's okay to be scared."

He laughs. It sounds a little hysterical. "No, it's not. Not really."

I pull away just enough to look him in the face. His cheeks are flushed with hot blood, and there's a wild, panicked sheen glossed over his eyes.

"Who told you that?"

He takes another second to slow his breathing. "That's just life. Sometimes things suck, but being scared doesn't fix anything."

"It's not supposed to," I tell him. "You're still a person, Roman. You can still feel things, and no one's gonna think any less of you for being afraid."

"Promise?"

I hold out my pinky. He links his through mine, and we let them dangle between us.

"Thank you," he says, leaning his temple against mine.

It feels good to have his weight against mine, but I don't tell him that. I rub circles into his back until I feel his breathing even out.

"Don't thank me," I tell him. "You'd do the same for me."

Our eyes meet. A smile tugs at the corner of his lips. "I would." He clears his throat. "Well, on the bright side, today wasn't totally pointless."

I pluck the old jewel from my pocket. It looks a little less cloudy in the clear light of Baxter's guest bathroom. Up

close, I can tell that the center is a striking cluster of amethyst. It prickles against my fingers like something in the
clunky silver chain is alive. Looking at it fills me with a sick
sense of trepidation.

"I kinda thought it would be an actual eye," I mutter.

"Yeah, me too. You ready?"

"I don't think I really have a choice."

We all gather back in the living room. The tables have
been shoved to the side, and Baxter's in a fresh pair of
clothes. Cass and Alessia sit on the couch, him sleeping
against her shoulder with a pillow clutched to his chest.
Olivia's on the floor, with one of her legs lounging across
Baxter's thigh.

"I had one rule," Baxter groans when he sees us.

I furrow my brows. "What are you talking about?"

Alessia shrugs, a barely-contained smile splitting her face.
"I just didn't know that narrowly escaping the clutches of
certain death could get someone in the mood. No judgment
though."

Cass, who must not really be sleeping, laughs against her
shoulder.

"Oh, shut up," Roman says, plopping down on the other
side of her. He moves to make room for me.

I roll my eyes and hold up the Eye. It was carved in harsh
strokes, with a rough hand. Its chain is old and worn, like its
silver has been gradually shaved down by every hand that's
touched it. Although, I wouldn't think that it's changed
hands too much until recently. That's Nyx's fault.

It's strange to put a name to something I've never seen. It's
even more difficult to believe.

"Can I see it?" Roman asks.

I hand it to him without a word. He holds it up against the light. "You know, if Alex was giving you a clue, that means they wanted us to find the Eye, which means I was right."

Cass scoffs. "It's like Halley's Comet."

"Shut up."

"Right about what?" Baxter asks.

"They needed us to find the Eye, us specifically." He says, "Maybe they can't make it work, but we can."

Alessia doesn't look as hopeful. "But if they couldn't figure it out, why should we be able to?"

"No, not 'we.'" Olivia points at me, her eyes calculating. "You. The Sphinx wanted to eat the rest of us, but not Ophelia. For some reason, she wanted to keep you alive."

"Yeah, that's right." Roman passes me the Eye. "But why though? Maybe that Alex guy told you how."

"No, he just gave me a clue about the riddle." I shake my head. "That's it. But it's a necklace. How hard can it really be?"

I'm grateful that no one puts in the effort to answer my question.

I drape the Eye over my neck. It feels much heavier than I expected, like I'm wearing a lump of gold. It's warm too. I press my fingers into the rough diamond, waiting. I'm not sure what to expect, but it certainly isn't the dull buzz of nothingness that follows in the seconds after I put on the necklace.

Olivia frowns. "Is it working?"

"Maybe." I tap the Eye with my finger, then swat at it with my hand. Still nothing.

Cass rolls his eyes. "It's not a jukebox, Ophelia."

"Well then what's your idea, Cass?" I counter, sharper than I intend to.

The wave of victory that had washed over me when we killed the Sphinx retreats rapidly, leaving behind a sprawling shore of disappointment. I frown down at this useless, stupid thing. It's just a piece of decoration, and it's not even pretty.

"Oh," Roman says, his voice low with defeat. "Maybe it's because the Sisters are dead. Griffin said they were the Keepers of the Sacred Knowledge. If they're dead, then maybe no one can access it ever again."

"But we still have the actual Eye," Alessia protests, her tone searing.

Roman shrugs, but there's nothing casual about it. Something about his eyes is tortured. "We have the vessel but I don't think we have its power."

I tear the Eye away from my neck, breaking the chain. Alessia gasps, but I ignore her.

"This is bullshit." I push up from the couch.

I'm going to leave the room, but Olivia's phone rings. She studies the screen, and a film of horror slowly falls over her face. She didn't look anywhere near this afraid when we were facing down the Sphinx.

"What is it?" Baxter asks.

She ignores him and answers the phone. She grimaces, pressing her eyes shut, before speaking.

"Hey, Mom."

CHAPTER TWENTY-SIX

TODAY, WE HAD OUR FIRST REAL brush with death. Somehow, the thirty-second conversation Olivia has with her mother is so much worse.

I check my phone for the first time since we left. It's about halfway through the school day. By now, everyone should be leaving their lunch period. I have history, or I would if I were there.

"Mom, I can explain—" but Olivia cuts herself off, because she can't. Not really.

Janus and Cherice might be an unfortunate exception, but no one else would believe us if we told them what happened to us today. Even if we showed up with the Sphinx's severed head to prove it, they literally wouldn't be able to see it. As it turns out, battle and bloodshed aren't acceptable excuses for skipping school.

Olivia's mom must be loud, because I can hear her garbled voice on the other side of the room.

"Okay," Olivia murmurs. "Yeah, I hear you. I know. Okay."

Another second passes, and she finally hangs up. Before she can speak, Roman's phone rings next. Then Alessia's. A bundle of dread crawls up my throat when I feel my own phone buzz in my pocket. I pull it out and grimace down at my uncle's face, flashing across the screen.

We all decide to let them go to voicemail. By now, we get the gist.

"So all of our parents are waiting at the school," Olivia says, her voice low.

Baxter throws his head back, dragging a hand down his face. "Oh my God."

"We have to get our stories straight," Alessia says.

Cass looks shell shocked, like he's seen something terrible. "What about our clothes? What are we gonna tell them?"

"The truth," Roman suggests.

Olivia bucks her eyes at him. "Are you crazy?"

"It was a suggestion."

"We definitely cannot tell them the truth," I say. "We need to change our clothes."

Olivia laughs. It's too sharp to be genuine, like she's losing it. "We need to change our identities."

"Liv," Baxter says, his voice soft now. "We just killed something that was three times bigger than a building. We can figure this out."

"If we change our clothes they'll know something's up," Roman says, his arms folded. "They all saw us leave this morning."

I pick at the tattered shred of fabric that used to be my left sleeve. "We look like *this*. How do we explain that?"

"Okay so obviously we were skipping school," Alessia starts. "We go with that. We tell them we went to the Yard."

"How'd we get like this?" I ask. "We're covered in blood."

She rubs her forehead, exhausted. "It's oil?"

Cass pinches the front of his shirt. It's filthy with smudges of the Sphinx's blood and flecks of dry ichor. "They wouldn't buy that. Even if it's not red, it behaves like blood. We look like we killed somebody."

"He's right," Baxter mutters. "Okay, so we have to change, and we did skip school. We have to say we did something really bad, but like, normal bad."

"The Leap of Faith," I suggest. "We skipped school to go to the woods and we went cliff diving. We planned it beforehand, so we brought a change of clothes."

"That could work," Alessia says. "So we meet at the school in fifteen?"

"Yep." Roman tugs on his hair. He doesn't look as rattled as he did in the bathroom. "I bet they're so pissed."

"*I'm* pissed." I shake my head. It's stuffed full of fog. "We did all that work just to be back where we started. And now we have to deal with this."

No one says anything. I know I don't have to point out our failure. Its gravity sits at the center of the room, sucking each of us into its belly. Maybe saying it was supposed to make me feel better, but it only drives my disappointment into a bar of hot rage. I don't know at who I should be more mad—the Scions or myself.

For a second, I'd thought Alex had been trying to help me. Of course it was toward the effort of his own sick agenda, but it seemed like a step in the right direction. When I took that Eye from the mannequin and felt its power, I thought we'd finally gotten our first win, but it's just more of the same. The same failure, sitting in our laps a second time.

"So what are we gonna do about it," Roman asks. "What do we do next?"

His voice is so calm it irritates me. How can he just stand there and act like this is okay?

I resist the urge to tell him so and plop back down on the couch. The Eye slides down my hand, the old silver chain cutting through my fingers like water. It has the look of something powerful, but now I know the truth.

"You know what," Olivia scoffs. "We do the walk of shame to the Sacred House and tell them we hit another wall. Then we waste our time in the library reading thousand-year-old books that won't help us do jackshit."

The bitterness in her voice surprises even me, but I can't say she's wrong. The Sacred House reached out to us because they thought we could help. I can't help feeling like all we're doing is proving that they made a mistake.

"Wait, no." Cass sits up in his chair. It looks like he's having an epiphany. "If the Eye's lost its juice, why go to the trouble of hiding and guarding it? It doesn't make sense."

Baxter seems a bit more hopeful. There's almost a wistful glean to his face now. "Because maybe they figured out they couldn't use it, but they figured we still could."

"Why?" Alessia sits back, exhausted. "That's a lot to assume, and I can't see any reason why we'd be able to use it and they wouldn't."

Baxter leans forward on his knees, suddenly full of conspiracy. "I don't know. There could be a lot of reasons. Maybe—"

My phone buzzes again. An angry text from Janus flashes across the screen, but I choose to ignore it. Today's been hard enough.

I clear my throat. "We've got bigger problems guys."

And just like that, Baxter is back to baseline. "All right," he says, picking at a skin tag on his thumb. "Let's face the music."

It's not at all what I want to do, but I agree anyway. Some things are just unavoidable.

We leave Baxter's house to go our separate ways. At home, I wash up in the sink, and quickly throw on new clothes. There are specks of ichor dried in my hair, but there's nothing I can do about that.

Roman, Baxter, and Alessia are waiting by the front steps when I appear at the school. Despite what Alessia said earlier, their grim expressions still bother me. I find myself with a bowling ball of dread sinking in my gut. Janus and Cherice are already on edge, and I can't imagine that this makes things better. A part of me doesn't care. Unfortunately, there's no place for that part of me here. If I'm going to convince them I'm not lying, I at least have to pretend to be sorry.

"My mom's actually gonna kill me," Alessia mutters, almost like she's talking to herself. "I won't even be able to go to prom."

"Maybe a hellhound will kill you first." Baxter's voice falls flat around us.

"Dude," Roman winces.

Baxter blinks. "Sorry. I'm spiraling."

The others appear a few minutes later, looking just as grim. We exchange looks, none of them reassuring, before taking slow steps up the stairs. It does nothing to slow time around us, and there's no time to prepare before we have to walk into the office.

Somehow, seeing a group of angry adults waiting in the front office is worse than seeing a giant Sphinx step out of thin air. This feels more real, and there's nothing that having superpowers can do about it.

A woman who looks exactly like Olivia steps to the front of the group, but my eyes go to my aunt and uncle. It doesn't make it any better that she had to leave work. They both look pissed. There's no room for doubt. I flinch and turn away from their hard gazes.

Thankfully, Principal Smith steps out of his office and into the waiting area. He levels a disapproving gaze at all of us, lingering on Roman. He hangs his head.

"Well, let me just say that I am very disappointed in all of you," he says. "We expect better of our seniors here at New River High. You're here to set an example. Now what do you have to say for yourselves?"

Olivia's mom folds her arms. "Yes, please explain yourself. I would like to know what possessed all of you to do something so stupid."

I can't find my voice, but Roman speaks for us.

"We wanted to go cliff diving." He sounds small, not at all like he's the person who wields Poseidon's trident. "So we skipped, and we thought we could sneak back in. It was stupid."

I chance a look up. Everyone else throws their hands up in exhaustion, but I can tell Janus and Cherice don't believe me. They don't say anything, but it's evident in the hard set of Cherice's chin and the incredulous look on Janus' face.

The principal scoffs. "That's ridiculous. *And,* unacceptable. You all have detention after school. Two weeks. And if anything like this happens again, you'll be looking at expulsion. It won't be tolerated. Not here."

"Thank you, Principal Smith," Cherice says. She locks eyes with me. They're full of fire. "We'll take them home."

Cherice drives my car home, and I ride back with Janus. At first, he says nothing. He feels cold beside me, like I'm riding with a block of ice. I brace myself. I know what it feels like just before a storm hits.

It hits about fifteen minutes into the drive. Janus passes the turn into our neighborhood and keeps going down the long back road. I glance back, but he doesn't say anything. In the next ten minutes, we're still driving.

"Where are we going?" I ask, keeping my voice low.

He takes so long to answer that I start to think he must be ignoring me.

"I don't believe that story," he says.

"What do you mean?"

He cuts a look at me. "You skipped school because you wanted to go cliff diving? I'm not stupid, Ophelia."

"I didn't say you were."

"Where were you?" He asks. "Where'd you go?"

I look away from him, staring hard out the window. I can't fight the hot wave of indignation that rushes through me. He doesn't believe me? And he actually expects me to tell him the truth?

"Why won't you tell me the truth about my dad?"

He groans and throws his head back. "We're not talking about that. I already told you."

"Then we're not talking about this. I went cliff diving. Believe me, don't believe me. That's what happened."

"Fine," he grinds his teeth, before spinning the car in a haphazard U-turn. "You're grounded. No more friends, no more adventures. You go straight to school and come straight back home. The car has GPS, so I wouldn't try me. I mean it."

"Okay," I tell him.

"Okay," he says.

SOMETHING WAKES ME UP IN THE middle of a dream: a dull tapping at the window.

I glare blearily at the clock. It's the middle of the night, and someone thinks throwing rocks at my window is a good idea. I sit up too fast; my brain still isn't awake yet. At first, I consider ignoring them. They'll get the message soon enough. But the tapping persists, more forcefully this time.

I groan and throw my legs over the edge of the bed. My body aches. Baxter might have been able to heal my wounds, but there was nothing he could do for the strain on my body. My muscles are tight and sore now, even worse than earlier.

I hobble over to the window and throw it up, frustrated. I'm expecting Roman or Cass. Not the man with the mocking expression, the one has a name now: Alex. His robe billows importantly in the wind, but all I feel is disgust. He winks up at me and strides out of sight.

I tug on my sneakers and vanish from my room. I appear at the head of the driveway, just as he's walking past my car.

"What are you doing here?" I demand, trying to keep my voice down.

He's undeterred by the vitriol in my voice. "I came to congratulate you. You all must have been pretty smart to figure out the Sphinx's riddle."

"You gave me a hint." I say it like an accusation. *"Death is my destiny."*

He looks amused. "That was a prophecy, and it wasn't for your benefit. I promise."

"Then what are you *really* doing here?"

"I wanted to continue our conversation. We were interrupted."

"Yeah. We were." I narrow my eyes at him. "How'd you know her?"

"I don't think I understand."

"Yes, you do. Stop playing dumb."

He laughs. "I like talking to you, Ophelia. You're very quick. As for your question, I've known Cherice for quite a while, long before she was 'Cherice.' At least, I used to."

"How?"

"We were very close friends. We fought together. Lived together. I wish things were different."

I shake my head. "You're lying. I don't believe you."

He shrugs. "Believe what you want. Our history is already set in stone. In a way, so is yours."

"What are you talking about?"

"Does your place in this web of mystery and magic not seem strange to you?" He asks.

"Aside from the usual, not really." But I'm lying.

It does bother me. Why would Alex single me out like this, and why would my family be involved?

"I knew your father. He didn't have the gift, but there was something in his cells, something promising." He laughs. It's a disturbing sound. "We've been watching you for a very long time, Ophelia. Most of us were certain when you inherited Zeus' power, but I wasn't so sure. I am now."

"So what? This is a test?"

He sneers at me, his teeth coated in grime. "Ophelia Johnson—always so quick. And I'm sorry about that, by the way. Tests are annoying, but as I said, we had to be sure."

"Sure of what?" I demand, but I'm already hearing a woman's ghostly voice.

When Cass pulled my Grandma Rosy from the ether, she'd told me she had already seen what was coming. She'd said that only I could stand against it.

"Purpose, Ophelia. Everyone has a purpose, and we wanted to be sure you could live up to yours." He takes a step toward me, his hands still at his side. "Mother will be very pleased."

I take a step back, shaking my head. "Why don't you just say her name? I know what you are, and I know who you serve."

He's smiling in earnest now, but there's nothing pleasant or kind about it. His teeth remind me of the Sphinx's.

"You only know what you think you know," he muses.

"Then explain it to me. Why do you want the Codex?" I demand. "And what do you want with me?"

"Oh, Ophelia. All we want is to go home. Unfortunately, you're the key."

Before I can ask anything else, his sword is flying through the air. He moves so fast I don't see him lunge, and he's standing over me in seconds. I don't have time to tug my sword free or even move back. I throw out my arm, and a jet of lighting hurtles through his chest. He flies back, his body barely missing Janus' side-view mirror, and rolls all the way down to the street.

I run down to stop him before he can roll into the road. His eyes are wide open in shock. It's the last expression he'll ever make. My hands shake as I search his robes, but all I find is a small, jade green dagger. There's an inscription carved down the blade's spine in Greek: *To Endless Night*.

Lightning surges in my hand, and I melt the blade down to nothing. When I'm done, I hold both hands over the man's body and char it to dust. It takes much longer than I expect, and the smell nearly makes me vomit. When I'm done, all that remains is a pile of sandy ash. I stand back and watch the wind carry it away, down the street and out of sight.

CHAPTER TWENTY-SEVEN

A WEEK PASSES WITH THE HOUSE perched on another precarious peace.

I keep my head low. I don't do anything to make Janus and Cherice even more angry than they already are. I go straight to school and do my homework in detention. I get home at the same time everyday and spend most of my time in my room.

Janus refuses to speak to me. Cherice is little more than a reluctant moderator. Sometimes she'll look at me, and a white hot rage will flash across her face. It's undercut by a deep sense of worry.

I don't mind the silence. In fact, I'm glad. Something about this feels more authentic. Before, we were just pretending. Each moment we spent together hinged entirely on my own silence. Now, I don't have to play the part. I can stew and brood as much as I want.

And I do. I skip breakfast and eat dinner in my room. When I come in from school, I greet them out of obligation only, and I don't put in the effort to sound happy about it. The only downside is that they circle me like hawks. I have to call whenever I get to school and let them know when I get home.

I try not to think about the Codex. There's nothing I can do to beat back the vicious grip of failure. The Eye sits in my bedside table, hidden beneath a notebook I haven't used since the fourth grade. I tried one last time to get it to work. I haven't looked at it since.

Like usual, I'm up early this morning. I shower and get ready well before I start hearing my aunt and uncle moving in the hallway. I freeze as someone's footsteps trek past my door, but they continue on downstairs.

I PACK MY BAG QUICKLY AND take the stairs two at a time. The coffee pot gurgles in the kitchen, my uncle sings about candy rain. My hand is on the door when Cherice appears behind me, calling me back.

She's standing with her arms folded and her shoulders squared. Clearly, she means business.

"I need to talk to you," she says.

I turn back, sighing. "Okay."

"I know you're not gonna tell me the truth, but I find it hard to believe that you'd actually skip school to go cliff diving. You're smarter than that."

I shrug. "I don't know what to tell you."

"Look, there are things you don't understand, things you can't understand, but it's not safe to lie. Not now."

I study her face, but it gives nothing away. That same surge of indignation rises in me, prickling across my tongue.

"I'm not lying. I did a dumb teenager thing because I'm a dumb teenager. I regret it, but I can't change it. And I can't tell you anything different."

She purses her lips. "Can't or won't?"

"Can't. Can I go now?"

Red heat flares beneath her cheeks. It's not the right thing to say.

"Actually, as a matter of fact, you're gonna stay here until you tell me the truth," she says, each word stilted and searing. "The *entire* truth, and you will not lie to me."

I narrow my eyes at her. I know it's immature and unproductive, and I'm just making things worse, but those are distant thoughts. She has the audacity to demand the truth, when that's all I've been begging for since August. Each time they've denied me, but now I'm supposed to tell them everything? If I weren't so furious, I'd laugh.

"You first," I say, my voice flat and cool.

"That's not fair."

"It's not? Because from my perspective, we're doing the same thing, only *I'm* the one who's wrong."

"This is *not* the same," she hisses. "If only you knew."

"If only I knew *what*?" I press.

"This isn't about me," she says. "We're not talking about me."

"Of course not." I roll my eyes. "Every time I bring it up you shut me down. You act like I've done something terrible, when all I want is the truth. You're right. We're not the same. You're worse."

I hear my voice raise, but I can't stop it. Janus comes up behind Cherice, appearing docile for once. In contrast, Cherice is livid.

"If only you knew how selfish and ungrateful you sound," she shouts. "If only you knew the things we've gone through to keep you safe. You would never say that. And yet you can't even give us the benefit of trusting us."

Janus watches her warily. "Babe, ease up." He places a hand on her shoulder, but she shrugs it off.

I jerk my head back. The perimeter of my vision has gone fuzzy with dancing, black lines. "And what's that supposed to mean?"

"Exactly what I said. You're ungrateful. You think you know everything, but you don't. You have no idea. Your father sheltered you too much, and you don't get it." She shakes her head. I can't tell if she's more disappointed or angry.

Her words hit me square in the chest, with all the force of a slew of bullets. My anger fizzles out into something worse, something more pathetic. It's wounded and small and wells up in me like the fierce jet of a hot spring.

I'm seeing everything, the entire slew of violence and tragedy that's followed me for the past three months. The shredded body of the Sphinx. The boy who died in my arms. My father's listless form on the kitchen floor, the chestnut emptiness of his eyes.

"Ophelia!" Cherice's voice is shrill, like she's been calling me for a while. "Answer me. Tell me the truth."

I blink away the hot tears forming in my eyes. I can still feel my rage, hot and boiling, but I've lost all my conviction.

I shrug, throwing up my hands. "Look, I'll tell you like I told Uncle Janus. I went cliff diving, and I'm an idiot. That's what happened."

She narrows her eyes at me, but doesn't say anything else. Scoffing, she turns, pushes past Janus, and disappears into the living room. His eyes are apologetic.

"You're gonna be late," he says. For once, he doesn't sound angry.

"Yeah." Without looking at him, I leave through the front door.

My face burns even as I step out into New River's mid-autumn freeze. Icy wet drops melt against my cheek and white flurries fly past my face. Halloween's only a few days away, and already the first snowfall has come to blanket New River. Normally, snow fills me with a warm, childish glow. I can remember every single time my father would shake me awake to show me a coated lawn. Today is different. He can't show me anything, and something about this snow fills me with dread.

I drive to school in silence, not bothering with the radio. I walk over to our usual spot and sit on the steps. I'm the only one here. Snow falls in thick sheets now from a cotton white sky. It's an infinite kind of sky, with no beginning or end. It wraps its hazy white arms around us, blocking out the sun.

When I walk through the night my father died, I remember the knife more clearly. Of course there'd been a knife. I'd leaned down to examine its thin, etched symbol.

I press harder, trying to remember, but the memory dissolves into watercolor.

The others slowly trickle in. Alessia sits on the other side of Cass. They're both lost in murky, distant thought. Baxter and Olivia are next, deep in conversation. When Roman arrives, he looks tired. He sits by my feet, at the base of the steps, and loops his finger through my shoelace in greeting.

The air sours between us. My throat tightens around each breath. Finally, Alessia sniffs to break the silence.

"I have a proposition" No one responds. "No quest shit today."

Baxter shoots his hand up. "I vote yes for everybody."

"I vote yes for you voting yes," Roman says.

Cass' glazed look persists. Alessia waves her hand in front of his face, but he pushes it out of the way.

"Stop that. I'm thinking," he says.

"Does it hurt?"

233

He shoots her an icy look, but ignores her.

"Seriously," she says. "What's up?"

He shrugs and sits back to rest on his elbows. "I don't know. I just feel like today's gonna be a bad day."

Olivia grimaces. "Are you sure you're not catastrophizing?"

He rolls his eyes. "That's not a real word. And no. It's not in my head."

"Can we ignore it?" I ask.

Roman chuckles at my feet.

Cass shrugs. "Probably."

By now, a flood of students moves around us. The first bell sounds in two short spurts. Cass shakes his head like he's trying to clear it.

"Forget I said anything. No quest shit." he says.

"No quest shit." I repeat it like a mantra. Like I'm trying to ward off something evil.

THERE'S A SAYING ABOUT MEN AND laughing gods. Nothing ever goes as planned, even when there isn't really a plan.

I sat with my friends at lunch, and the same dismayed sludge from earlier settled between us. Cass hadn't lost the dull haze in his eyes, and it made me think of that night in the woods, when he summoned my grandmother out of blood and fire. I tried pressing, but his answer only left a bitter taste in my mouth.

I have a bad feeling, he'd said. At this point, I've learned to take those words as prophecy, even if I don't understand them.

It's not until halfway through my history class that a bundle of dread drops into my stomach, too. Goosebumps chase each other along my skin, and all I can hear is the steady pounding of my own heart. Snow still falls outside, but suddenly the room is scorching hot. I press a hand to my throat, where sweat gathers in a thin sheen.

Fear trickles through me like venom. There's no mistaking it.

I raise my hand, and Ms. Paulson stammers to a stop. Her lips go thin and white, but she tries to smile as she acknowledges me.

"Yes, Ophelia?"

I ignore the sixteen pairs of eyes bearing down on me. "I think I need to go to the nurse. I don't feel good."

It's true. My head spins with some strange anguish. My stomach coils into sickening knots.

She doesn't look pleased. "All right," she says. "You're excused."

I yank my bag over my shoulder and stand in the same motion. Murmuring rustles around me as I leave the classroom, but I don't care. I make it two hallways down before a strange figure makes me pause. He blocks the door to the staircase with his hulking figure, and he definitely doesn't belong here. His skin is the color of porcelain; the scaled patches along his shoulders and ribs catch the light like rainbows. White hair falls in neat layers over a pair of piercing, silver eyes. His face is a beautiful work of delicate, rounded features and sharp cheekbones, but there's something malicious about him. Whatever he's come for, it can't be good.

I repeat the mantra in my head. *No quest shit.*

"You're in my way," I tell him.

He smiles, revealing a set of perfect, white teeth. "Forgive me, just this once. It can't be helped."

"And why's that?"

He leans back against the doorway, shoving his hands in his pockets. He wears baggy, black cargo pants, with rows of silver chains dangling from his hips. His boots are heavy and faded, with dull, silver toes.

"You're expected," he says. "It would break Her heart if I came back empty handed."

My heart plummets. I don't have to ask who he's talking about.

"Raincheck." I try to keep my voice level. I gesture around at the empty hall, which has never been more quiet. "I'm at school."

"Yeah, I noticed." He studies his nails. They're black and smudged, like he'd dipped his fingertips in a tub of tar. "Forgive me, but I have to insist. Mother isn't known for her patience, and she's been waiting a very long time to meet you."

I take a step back. I can't help it.

"You don't even know me." But I know I'm lying even as I say it.

Alex had known me, just like he knew my aunt. Just like the Sphinx had known me.

The stranger smiles. Something about his youth is other-worldly. He's beautiful, but there's something awful and twisted about it.

"I know lots of things, Ophelia," he says, pushing away from the doorpost. "I know you have the Lightning God's power. I know what you're capable of, and I know it won't be enough. Nothing you do can stop what's coming, so why not be kind to yourself?"

"What do you mean?"

"I'm talking about purpose. Our destinies were set in stone long before we were born. I am fated to be a dutiful son, and the Gods of Olympus are fated to die. Always."

In the next instant, he lunges at me. Black talons slash at my face, and I roll out of the way. I pull my sword out of the air, and swipe down. Flesh tears, and something hot splatters against my legs. I don't look. In the next second, the fire alarm goes off, but none of the students that spill into the hall seem especially terrified. Lucky them.

I disappear into the flood of students that descend down the staircase. I fumble with my phone, frantically typing a message. I have to warn the others, and I have to find a way out of here. This isn't like the watcher in the woods, or even the attack on Cisthene. Whatever that thing is, it's not human.

I burst out of the staircase and take off down the main hall. Teachers direct students out the front doors in the usual orderly fashion. I've nearly made it outside when a strong hand yanks me off my feet. I go flying all the way down the hall and then right through someone's door. Glass and splintered wood sprinkle around me, and my whole-body aches.

My lip throbs. I spit out a glob of ichor. "Goddamn it."

I make it to my feet just as he lands in front of the door. I don't know if he's a man or a monster. Long black talons hang from his fingers. His beautiful face is warped into something haggard and evil; sharp fangs fill his mouth, jutting out of his jaw at strange angles. There's a shallow wound along his ribs where my sword cut him, bubbling with black blood.

"You know, I'm kind of glad you made it exciting," he says, laughing. "I never get to do anything fun."

"You're insane."

He rolls his shoulders and black blood races beneath his skin. It travels from his fingers, to the harsh lines of his jaw. Dark sludge drips from his mouth, dribbling down his chin. "That's an opinion."

I reach for the lighting bolt and rear back with a hissing blue rod. I launch it across the space between us, and time slows to a crawl. The bolt hovers only a few inches from his face. Just before it collides with him, a long silver sword appears in his hand. With nothing more than a casual swipe of his sword, he knocks the bolt aside.

I stagger back, speechless. The bolt vanishes before it even hits the ground, returning to me, and he doesn't even look startled. The sword in his hand whirls in a blazing silver arch, catching fire. He aims it at my chest, chuckling.

"By this holy blade, by the vow of Endless Night, I commit thee to the Mother's grasp. Accept your fate with dignity."

"Eat shit."

Laughing, he lunges. I meet the harsh swing of his blade with my own. We fly up and down the main hall in huge, bounding leaps, pressing each other forward and back. He swipes at my clothes, tearing open gashes in my skin. His black blood boils against my blade, but the pain must not faze him. The more we fight, the more he cackles. His face grows more monstrous, more distorted by shadow and evil.

He pivots to the left, swinging his sword up against my side. I parry and swing my other hand down, full of lightning. He catches it in an iron grip. Lighting licks at his fingers, blistering his skin, but he doesn't scream. He swings me around his body and launches me to the other end of the hall.

My body crumbles into the wall, leaving a massive crater behind. My ankle throbs. As he saunters toward me, his steps devastatingly slow, I realize I was wrong. He's a monster, but not in the way that I thought. His malice comes from something else, something deeper. He's not like the Sphinx, and yet he's not like the Scions either.

OF BLOOD AND LIGHTNING

Thick white horns grow from his shoulders in ridged sta-lactites. His shoes are gone, and gnarled black talons leave marks in the wood where he walks. Ichor drips from his blade and marks a trail behind him.

"What the hell are you?" I wheeze as I struggle to my feet. I'm worse off than I realize. I have to drag one of my legs behind me, and I'm bleeding everywhere.

"*I am Somnus. Wherever there is fear, I am their god.*" He holds out his arms, revealing each scaled patch on his chest. "*Behold.*"

I'm beholding. It's terrible. And it's beautiful. He walks the road between dreams and nightmares, bridging them both.

I hold my sword out with my left hand. My right is thick and swollen, and I can't feel my wrist. Smiling, he lowers his blade. Just as he lunges, a volley of jade green arrows slams into his body. He turns away and a silver blur slams into him. I think it must be Olivia.

Relief rushes through me like a river. I'm hobbling over to help her when another shape comes through the doors, impossibly fast. Two figures dance around the monster now, working in tandem. They slash at his ankles, across his back, and at his side. Black blood stains the floor, and the monster roars in agony. Neither of them is Olivia.

I can't move. I can't convince myself that what I'm seeing is what I'm seeing, because it can't be real. Cherice is an unstoppable force in a suit of silver armor. Janus is nearly as fast as she is. They fight with a trained confidence, like they've been here before.

I have to be dreaming. There's no way this is real. Not this vicious monster and certainly not my aunt and uncle, who both fight like they were born for the blade.

Cherice shouts. The monster whips out a blackened hand and sends my uncle careening through one of the glass doors. She shouts his name as he disappears, and the monster raises his sword. She can't see it, because she's not looking at him. There's a murderous glint in his eyes.

Finally, I snap out of it.

"No!" I shout, the sound making my ribs ache. Cherice turns her head as the monster lunges at her.

I hold my hand out, but it's not lighting that answers. Something else, something brimming with heat and blood, floods my limbs. I feel each atom of the monster's body. I feel the bonds between them. The heat in my body swells in the center of my palm, building into a supernova.

The monster stops. Finally, he looks afraid. He eyes my palm warily and throws out a frenzied hand.

"Don't!" he shouts.

It's too late. I squeeze my palm shut, and the air around his body goes bright with shreds of purple light. They pulse around him like globs of living matter, before erupting against his skin. He screams. Strips of white flesh peel up all across his body, leaving behind jagged, black wounds. Cherice ducks for cover. His agonized roar rattles the entire building; I nearly trip from the force of it.

"*Brother!*" someone screams.

Behind me, another monster comes barreling around the corner. His skin is pitch black, with rows and rows of white Greek lettering dancing across his body.

LET THERE BE TERROR IN SLEEP.

He barrels past me on glossy goat hooves, knocking me aside. It's so forceful that I leave another crater in the wall, right beside a bleeding Cherice. Her eyes are closed, her head limp against the wall.

"Aunt Cherice!" I shake her good shoulder, trying to rouse her.

The new monster collects his brother, who screams in his arms. The other one is injured too. There are deep slashes across his chest, and it looks like he's missing a hand. He levels a hard gaze at me, scowling though a row of yellow teeth.

"Hey!" Another voice at the end of the hall.

It's Roman, bloodied and bruised. He rears back the trident and lets it fly. By the time it reaches us, the two monsters have vanished. His spear lodges itself in the wall, right where Somnus' head would have been. The monsters leave nothing behind but a pool of steaming black blood.

"Shit," Roman hisses, hysterical.

He races down the hall and drops down at my side. He gently prods my body, checking my wounds. I don't have the stomach to look.

"I'm fine," I say, waving him off.

"Obviously not."

He helps me to my feet and leans my body against his, just like last time. He asks me if I'm okay, but I ignore him. I can only gape at my aunt, who's slowly waking up beside me. My uncle limps in through the shattered door, but he doesn't look any better than Cherice. He kneels down beside her and holds her face.

"Hey, honey," he says, stroking her cheek with his thumb. "Eyes up. Look at me."

My uncle tears off a strip of his robe and presses it against the wound. When he looks back at me, his eyes are full of devastation.

"I'm so sorry," he says.

It feels like I'm going to throw up.

"Ophelia, we can explain everything," Cherice wheezes, her eyes fluttering. "Please."

A rumble of footsteps sound around the corner. Four people in bloodied armor step into the main hall, brandishing weapons. I only feel a little relief at the sight of my friends, injured, but still walking. At the sight of us, they stop short.

"Thank god," Alessia sighs. Her hair is sticky with wet ichor. "We couldn't find you guys. We thought—"

"They're okay," Roman says.

I spit again—more blood. "I'm not sure about that. What happened to you guys?"

"We got attacked in our classrooms," Olivia says. "That . . . thing just walked right in. I thought pulling the fire alarm would help. I'm sorry."

"Who's this?" Baxter asks, gesturing to Cherice and Janus. "Wait, they can see us?"

"That's my aunt and uncle," I murmur. "And yeah, they can see us."

Alessia steps forward, glaring down at Cherice's prone form. "Why's she dressed like that?"

"Ask her."

"Like I said, I can explain," Cherice says, struggling to her feet.

"So start." My voice is cruel, but I don't care. "What the hell are you doing here?"

"You said you were in trouble," Janus says. "You texted me."

"It was an accident," I say sharply.

He looks past me to examine my friends. More devastation rolls over his face. There's a cold resignation there, like he's finally accepted something terrible.

"Ophelia, we need to get out of here," he says, "I know you're angry and I know you don't trust me, but—"

"Why would I wanna go anywhere with you?"

It hurts when I say it, but I don't care about that either.

"You wouldn't, and I understand that. We made a mistake," he says. "We shouldn't have lied to you, but I promise that's all over now."

I scoff, rolling my eyes. "Right."

"No, I mean it," he says. "Please. Come home, and we'll tell you everything."

CHAPTER TWENTY-EIGHT

WE RIDE BACK TO GREEN GROVES in a long, five-car caravan.

I leave my car in the parking lot, and ride in Roman's passenger seat. He keeps cutting glances my way, but I ignore him. Now that the heat of battle has receded, I can feel every tear in my skin. Ichor stains my clothes the color of bronze where it's dried and bright gold where the blood is still fresh. It'd be pointless to try and stop it; there are too many places to apply pressure.

When I thought about finally getting the truth out of Janus and Cherice, I hadn't thought it'd be like this. A part of me wants to disappear before they can tell their story, but I know that's just me being dramatic. This is all I've wanted for the past few months. Why can't I just be happy about it?

We follow Janus' SUV into the driveway. Olivia and Cass park behind us. Baxter and Alessia park on the street. Everyone hobbles in a single file line up to the front door; Janus unlocks it with a bleeding hand.

A light comes on in the foyer, stabbing my eyes. I raise a grubby hand to shield them.

"Sit. I'll get some supplies," Cherice says.

She disappears into the kitchen and starts fumbling around in one of the cabinets. Janus eases into the recliner in the corner and props his left leg up. The armor is shredded by a blade's criss-crossing pattern, revealing mangled skin underneath. Ichor drips down the side of his leg, as gold as mine; he must not care about the couch.

Cherice comes back with a first aid kit and starts dressing the gashes down Janus' leg.

Baxter gives me a pointed look. I nod, urging him on.

"I think I can help," he says, doing his best to smile.

Now that he's not in his armor, I can see how injured he is. He clutches a swollen hand to his chest and casts the other one over my uncle's leg.

"What the hell are you doing?" Janus demands, jerking painfully.

"Just relax," I tell him.

Shimmering waves of gold mist fall over my uncle's leg, mending the flesh beneath his shredded armor. He watches in astonishment, clearly not believing it. When Baxter is done, my uncle gazes up at his face, where two twin suns still burn in Baxter's eyes.

"Are you—?" He starts, but he can't finish.

My aunt runs her hand over Janus' leg, her mouth hung open in shock. "Not even a Sun Child could do this." Then she gazes reproachfully up at Baxter, like what she's seeing can't be real. "What are you?"

Baxter glances around at the rest of us, but I wave him on. Might as well, since we're finally being honest.

"Three months ago, I inherited Apollo's power," Baxter says. He gestures around at us. "We each inherited the powers of an Olympic god."

My aunt and uncle lock eyes with me. I don't say anything, but I don't look away. I limp over to the couch and take a seat, wincing at the stress on my wounds. There are gashes all over my body. I'd managed to block some of Somnus' attacks, but he moved too fast. It was like he had two blades and two sets of hands.

"Ophelia—" my aunt starts, horrified.

I cut her off. "You first. Talk. Tell me everything."

Baxter goes around the room, healing wounds. My aunt and uncle tell their story.

"We come from a cursed bloodline, Ophelia, a divine one." Janus says.

"The House of the Cursed Children," I murmur.

"That's right," he says. "Our line has been targeted by other Scions for centuries, which is why we're members of the Demigod Council of Houses; being alone is too dangerous. Hundreds of years ago, when the Olympians were fighting the very war that they would die in, our ancestor, Khaos, decided to betray her comrades in order to protect the human race. She sided with the Olympians and locked the Firstborn away forever in an underground prison. One they can never escape from.

"Doing it cost her her life, but she saved humanity from a terrible fate. Scions are known for holding grudges, and they've been holding one against Khaos' descendants ever since her death. Wherever we go, we're hunted."

I can't find my voice. Slowly but surely, I've been realizing that my boring, regular-ass family wasn't so boring and regular after all. I thought tragedy was the only thing that set us apart, but it turned out to be the symptom of something bigger. Something divine, and it's been living in my blood this entire time.

"About two hundred years ago, descendants of Khaos had nearly been hunted to extinction. We formed an alliance with the Demigod Council of Houses for survival," Janus says. "Our family was very powerful. It all began with your grandfather, who sat on the Council as the Cursed House's Chief Representative. When he became General of the Cursed House, he passed the seat to your father; Jason had just turned twenty-one."

He says it with a distant bitterness, like it's something he hasn't quite gotten over.

"Anyway, your father represented our House for a long time." More darkness in his voice, dragging each word down with the weight of a millstone. "Until your grandparents. And Iris. And Irene."

I have to choke back my own vomit. He doesn't have to tell me this part, but I do need to hear it.

"It wasn't an accident," I say, half-question, half-admission. "Right?"

Cherice pulls her knees up to her chest, her eyes glossy. Janus looks like he wants to reach for her, but he doesn't.

"No. There was a car accident, but it was orchestrated by the Children of the First," he says. "There was nothing anyone could do, and your father couldn't take it. He left the Council, he left the House, and he moved away with you. Far away. He was protecting you."

My fingers prickle with negative energy. I have to hit something. Break something to pieces. But of course, the anger is only vapor thin. Grief for each of them bursts wide open in my chest, like water flooding a broken dam. I want to curl into myself, but there's not enough room on this couch.

"We're still active members of the Council," Janus says. His voice is strained now, but he presses on. "After your father abdicated the position, I became Chief Representative and Lieutenant General. That's why we've been sneaking around. About eight months ago, demigod houses started getting raided. It wasn't until about five months ago that we confirmed it was Scion activity. Since then, we got pulled into it, and we've been investigating the raids. There was another one a few weeks ago, on Cisthene."

Cass scoffs. "Shit."

"What?" Janus asks. "That mean something to you?"

"Yeah. We were there," Cass says.

Janus and Cherice stare at me like I've grown another head.

"What were you doing on Cisthene?" Cherice demands. "Do you have any idea how dangerous that could have been?"

I shift in my seat and lean forward, resting my elbows against my knees. "Yeah. I also know how dangerous being here is. I had to find something so I went looking for it. By the time we got there, the Scions were already gone. Most of them anyway."

"What were you looking for?" Janus asks.

My blood boils at the thought of that useless hunk of diamond sitting in my bedside table. It's so ugly and cloudy; I couldn't even sell it at a pawn shop.

"The Graeae Sisters," Roman answers. "We were just hoping to talk to them, but the Scions got there first."

"Yeah, we saw." Janus narrows his eyes at us. "How'd we miss you? We sent a crisis team out later that night."

Roman shrugs. "We're fast."

He sounds exhausted when he says it.

"All right." Janus rubs his hands together. His eyes are weary. "Now that was our story. I need to hear yours." He gives me a pointed look. "Obviously, you've been keeping secrets too."

"Uh-uh." I point at Cherice, who's busy dabbing at her eyes. "You. How'd you know that guy who was following me around? And why'd he call you Lydia?"

She looks down at the sprawl of her silver battle robes, stained black with Somnus' blood. Something about the way her thumb glides across the fabric makes me so sad.

"I'm a Scion too, but I'm not a Child of Khaos," she says. It's a rueful confession. "I'm a Child of Uranus, or at least I used to be. When I met Janus fifteen years ago, I abandoned my brothers and sisters. I abandoned my name too; Lydia was my great grandmother. Before that, Alex and I had fought together many times. I guess we sort of became friends."

"Then why'd you desert them?" I don't mean to sound so harsh, but she doesn't seem to mind.

"For love." She gazes fondly at Janus, and then a cold darkness rolls over her face. "And because they're evil, every last one of them. Scions are raised believing that the god's commandments are the law, and nothing is above the law. But the Firstborn are pure evil, and they want to do nothing but infect the earth with blood and darkness."

"*Endless night,*" I murmur.

Roman frowns at me. "What was that?"

"Right before Somnus tried to kill me, he said something over his blade, like an incantation."

Cherice beats me to it. "The Vow of Endless Night. It's the highest vow a Scion can make, and once they make it, they have to fulfill it." She hangs her head, swearing. "What exactly did he say to you?"

"By this holy blade, by the vow of endless night, I commit thee to the Mother's grasp." I brace myself for something, some cold conviction, but it doesn't come. "I thought he was just threatening me."

Janus and Cherice exchange looks again, both of their expressions fixed in anguish. Cherice looks like she's going to be sick.

"What?" Roman asks, an edge to his voice. "What does that mean?"

Janus sits back with a heavy sigh. "It means now that Somnus has vowed on the Mother to kill you, he has to fulfill it. And he will."

Surprisingly, hearing that doesn't make me any more afraid than I already was. The heat that burns in my stomach comes from rage.

"Didn't really look that way to me," I say, remembering how he'd wailed in agony. "We ran them off."

"Yeah, and they'll come back," Janus says. His voice hardens into steel. "Now. The truth. Everything."

He's asking me, but we go around the room and piece together our story. I start at the beginning, with the very first dream I had. Then I tell him about the night that Khaos and Zeus came to me. Knowing what I know now, knowing what's in my blood—there's no room for doubt. The woman who drove her sword through my heart was my ancestor, as fierce and alive as ever, even if only in a dream.

"The Sphinx didn't care that we got her riddle right. She was gonna eat us anyway, so we had to kill her," Cass continues. He tells the story like it exhausts him. "But of course, it didn't work, and we're basically back where we started."

Cherice's jaw hangs open. Janus has leaned forward on the edge of his seat. For a second, neither of them says anything. I try to imagine what it would be like to hear all this as a story, as opposed to actually experiencing it. I don't think I'd believe me either.

Cherice is the one who breaks the silence. "That explains a lot."

Alessia laughs. "Does it?"

"Well for one, when our crisis team didn't come back with the Eye, we were worried it'd been stolen by Scions," Cherice says. "I guess great minds just think alike."

"What doesn't make sense," Janus adds, "is why *you* were looking for it in the first place."

Baxter furrows his brow. "We just told you. If we don't find this Codex the Fates—"

Janus cuts him off, scowling. "No, I mean, the Fates' disappearance is highly classified information. I have no idea how you'd even know they were missing. Honestly, I have no idea how you'd even know they existed. Look, the Council has a crisis team working on this, so it doesn't make sense for a bunch of children—no offense— to be involved at all. How'd you get roped into this in the first place?"

Alessia doesn't bother to hide her indignation. "All I know is that the Vessel of Destiny found us and practically begged us to help them. They attempted a rescue op in the Underworld a few weeks after the Fates went missing, but it failed so they needed us."

Cherice jerks her head back. "You've met the Vessel of Destiny?"

"You haven't?" I ask.

She rolls her eyes. "No one gets an audience with the Vessel, ever, unless it's extremely serious. You don't find him, he finds you."

"Exactly," Baxter says. "He was working with the Sacred House and he found us. That's why we're doing this."

Janus and Cherice match gazes, their mouths hanging open. It's almost funny.

Janus turns back to us. "Have you figured it out? Who took them, I mean."

"Yeah, actually." Roman's expression is dark; he tugs absentmindedly on a loose thread. "We were thinking it was just the Scions, but those people who attacked us today—they didn't even look human."

"Because they're not. That was Hypnos and Somnus—the Princes of Paradise," Cherice says. "They're Children of the Firstborn, but they're completely different from Scions. They were both born to Nyx and Kreos, so they're not human at all."

"Kreos?" I think of the shadowy figure that had taken up two pages in my father's journal. "I thought all the Firstborn gods were locked away."

"Well that's the official story, but it's not true," Cherice says. "When Khaos sealed Paradise, she trapped some of them, including the King, but Nyx and a few of the others have been free ever since."

Janus snaps his fingers. "Which must be why Makena went over our heads. She'd never be able to present that theory to the Council, so she reaches out to the gods directly, one of whom just so happens to be my niece." He studies me curiously, like he's trying to make sure I'm real. "I knew I sensed something different, but I just thought it was your divine blood. I had no idea you inherited Zeus' power. I didn't even know that was possible."

I squirm beneath his gaze. It makes me feel like a specimen.

"Why would General Davis go over the Council?" I ask, trying to change the subject.

"Yeah, and she didn't even mention the Firstborn," Alessia says. "When we first spoke, it didn't seem like they knew much more than we did."

The grim expression on Janus' face deepens. "She wouldn't. Demigods have a very rigid philosophy; their society is built on tradition. Traditionally, the story goes that the Firstborn were all locked away when the war ended. For Cursed Children like us, we know the truth, but for them, that's considered heresy."

"That's dumb." Cass says it unkindly, but Janus doesn't look like he disagrees.

"Obviously, but now things are different," Janus says. "Two of the Firstborn were here in the flesh. The Council won't be able to ignore this."

Janus flies around the room, searching for something. "All right, I need to notify the Council." He pulls a silver flip phone from a dresser near the foyer before freezing. "No. No, I need to contact the Sacred House. I need an audience with the Commanders."

"Well that's pointless," Cherice shrugs. "I had to wait a week to get an audience with Makena last time."

"Don't bother," I tell them. "We need to go there anyway, so you can come with us."

Janus laughs. "Unless you have an audience or an escort, you won't even get past the gates."

"Yeah we will. We have clearance."

He frowns at me. "You have clearance? What level?"

"Alpha-B," I tell them.

Cherice looks furious.

"What? Ophelia, these are the kinds of things you tell people," she says. "The Sacred House never just gives out security clearances, especially not Alpha-B. There are like ten people max who're cleared that high."

I shrug. "Sorry. I didn't know that you two were into this kind of thing. I thought Uncle Janus was a firefighter."

He rolls his eyes. "I am a firefighter, but you're right. None of us can change the past, but from this point on, I promise to be one hundred percent honest with you. It was wrong of me to keep you in the dark, but please know I only did it for your father. He didn't want you growing up with all this stuff, especially after what happened to our family. We thought we were protecting you."

A hard lump forms in my throat. This would be a terrible time to cry, so I don't.

"Right," I say, clearing my throat. "Well, we need to figure out how we move forward, and that means finding the Codex. That ring any bells for anybody?"

And to my dismay, Janus and Cherice look like they have no idea what the hell I'm talking about.

"Not at all," Cherice says. "It came up in our intel, but we can't find anything on it. That's why we were looking for the Eye."

"I just wish we knew why they wanted it," Alessia sighs. "Right now, the plan is to find it before they do and lure them into a trap, but it might not be the best idea to let them get that close to it."

"What about the Eye?" Janus asks. "If you have it, it could probably tell us."

"Oh we have it," I scoff. "It's useless. We already tried, but it wouldn't even turn on."

Janus squints, thinking. "Were you wearing it right?"

Baxter blinks. "As in around the neck?"

Janus nods. Baxter massages his forehead in exasperation.

"Well, we were all there when Ophelia put it on. She didn't do it wrong," he says. "Roman thought it might have been because the Sisters are dead."

Janus shrugs. "Maybe. If the fabric of reality can be dissolved when the Fates die, it's not a stretch to think that the Eye would lose its power when its vessels die. I really don't know enough about it to say for sure."

"So what should we do?" Olivia asks. "We don't have any other leads."

"Okay how about this." Cherice massages one of her temples. "Today's been a lot, so let's wrap this up. We can meet with Makena tomorrow and make our next move. Now that we can prove the Firstborn are still around, we can get the full weight of the Council behind this."

"Yeah," Janus says. "We can order some pizza and you guys can stay here for the night. I think it would be best for everyone's safety. I know you guys are gods and all, but if Hypnos and Somnus came to kill you personally, then you're in more danger than ever. And please tell your parents where you'll be."

Alessia shrugs. "I'm fine with that."

The others go around the room, murmuring their agreement, but I can't speak. My stomach turns with something awful.

"I need a minute."

I push to my feet and walk into the foyer. The front door is a welcome sight. Someone calls after me, but I ignore them and let myself out of the house, into fresh, cool air.

CHAPTER TWENTY-NINE

I COUNT EACH OF THE LINES in my fingers. Out loud.

The world softens and tears around the edges, and everything that's happened in the past few hours finally crashes over my head. As soon as the door shuts behind me, both my knees buckle. I catch myself on the rail with a trembling hand and ease myself down on one of the porch steps. At first I'm hunched over, my face in my hands. The only sound around me is the rough whisper of each digit I count. Then something pinches in my chest, and I have to throw my head back to catch a full breath. It sort of works.

My chest rises and falls with each heaving breath. By the time I realize I'm hyperventilating, I can't stop it. I try to stand, not entirely sure why, but I can't get my legs beneath me. Baxter's healing hands have fixed everything wrong with me physically, but there's something else, something much deeper. It coils around my heart like the cruel, scaled body of a snake.

The door opens and warmth washes over me. Distantly, I can hear chatter inside the house. Roman's broad-shouldered figure fills the doorframe. He's watching me like I'm the most pathetic thing he's ever seen, like it physically hurts to look at me. I turn away from him, trying to hide my face.

"I'm fine. You can go back inside," I tell him. I can't keep the quiver out of my voice.

He crouches down and sits on the steps beside me. I feel his hands on my shoulder, slowly turning me toward him.

"You're a shitty liar," he murmurs, studying my face. His fingers are warm against my jaw; I think he might be checking for bruises.

I laugh, trying not to meet his eyes. "I really am okay. Sometimes I just need to cry. For fun."

"That's okay. I just don't want you to cry alone." And he says it like he means it.

I think back on every night I've cried myself to sleep, with nothing there to comfort me.

"I'm really good at it," I tell him.

He frowns. "Yeah, I know," and presses my face against his chest.

I don't fight it. As soon as I'm sequestered against the warmth of his body, every defense I have is useless. He holds me until my breathing settles and my hands stop shaking. Then, he holds me up until New River's blueberry sunset deepens into a pitch-black night.

Finally, when we've been sitting here for so long that we should turn to stone, he pulls back just enough to look me in the face. I study the gentle slope of his heart-shaped lips and the straight bridge of his nose. Concern makes his eyes murky and frenzied, despite how calm he felt against me.

"Better?" He asks.

I can't speak. Instead, I fall back against his chest. His arms are just as tight this time, and he rubs a wide circle into my back.

"I know," he says, even though I haven't said anything.

Something about those two words, or maybe how softly he says them, pushes against the levy in my chest. My face burns, and I feel tears welling in my eyes. I pull away from him just as they splash against my face, but he doesn't let me go. He frowns as he brushes them away with the pad of his thumb.

"What do you need?" He asks.

"A coma," I mutter, swiping at my eyes.

"No, I mean from me," he says. "What can I do to make this easier for you?"

I shake my head. I wish I could stop crying, but the tears just keep coming. There's no stopping them.

"I don't think anything could make this better," I tell him. Beneath all the grief welling up against my ribs, I feel a rage I've never known. "He was all I had."

It's so unfair that they took him from me, especially considering how far he went to escape that life. He moved us across the country and cut us off completely from everyone else in our family. At the time, I didn't understand, but now I get it. The idea that he could lose me to the demons of his past drove him away. What hurts the most though is knowing that his efforts to protect me could never have spared him.

"I'm so sorry," Roman says. "I know saying that doesn't do anything. I know that there's nothing anyone could say to fix any of this, but I'm so sorry. I really am. You shouldn't have to go through this."

He sounds so sincere when he says it, and it still isn't enough. I lean away from him and wipe my face. Gradually, the grief tempers into something like magma. I stare at the empty street ahead, remembering how I'd melted Alex's body into ash. It's one life weighted against a loss I'll never recover from. That too isn't enough.

"You don't have to be sorry," I tell him. "It's not your fault, it's the Firstborn. Cherice said it. They're evil."

Roman shivers, but he tries to hide it. When he speaks, there's something like resolve in his voice. "I don't think they're gonna stop. Your folks said they've been at this for centuries."

"Yeah. They won't." I hold my hand out, and lightning dances from my elbow to the tips of my fingers. The air shimmers, and the silver, dragon-headed hilt of the Lightning Bolt appears in my palm. *"Justice."*

"What?"

"There's no justice in this world, Roman. You have to forge your own." I turn the blade over, letting it catch the light. "The Old Gods have to die. *That's* the only justice my father can have, so that's what I'll do. I'll kill them all, starting with *her.*"

Roman and I sit on the steps until a blue Honda pulls up outside the house. Two teenage boys stumble out, balancing two large pizzas in each of their hands. I point to the front door; one of the boys looks annoyed as he knocks. My uncle comes out to pay in cash. Baxter and Cass help him carry the boxes inside.

Janus lingers in the doorway, eyeing the two of us suspiciously.

"You guys all right?" My uncle asks. "It's pretty cold out."

I try not to shiver as he says that, but the cold is getting to me. Before the pizza arrived, I had my fingers curled against Roman's side. Now they're numb and frozen.

"And I mean, cold pizza really doesn't live up to all the hype like that," he adds. He casts a wary look out across the neighborhood, which is quiet and still. "It's just not safe to be outside like this."

"Yeah, I agree." I stand and help Roman up too, even though he doesn't need it.

Janus shuts the door behind us once we're inside, locking it.

We all eat our pizza down in the living room, and then take turns in the shower. I use the one in my bedroom and slip into an old pair of sweatpants. Something about scrubbing the day off of me makes me feel better, even if it's just a little.

Downstairs, the living room buzzes with conversation. Olivia and my aunt talk about archery in the corner, while Baxter, Alessia, and Cass argue with my uncle over the best way to kill a Nemean lion. I don't have it in me tonight, but I find the idea of being alone just as terrifying as Somnus' blackened hands.

I sit on the loveseat, and Roman sits with me, close enough to press our thighs together. Eventually my head gets heavy, so I lounge against his shoulder. He's warm and soft against me, and solid too, like I'm leaning into steel. He wraps an arm tight around my shoulders, and everything that's wrong suddenly feels a little less so.

I pick at my fingers in his lap, tugging at each strip of loose skin around my nails. He makes a disapproving noise and separates my hands with one of his own. I curl my fingers into the soft curve of his hand and run them across his calloused palms. Wielding a sword hasn't been kind to him.

He starts humming something, a song I don't recognize. I close my eyes to focus on the rich, warm tone of his voice, how it vibrates in both of our chests. The melody is light and whimsical, like a waltz between fairies.

I don't realize I've fallen asleep until I wake up in someone's arms, with the house's black darkness hanging over me. I'm moving up the stairs, but I'm not walking. Someone's strong arms are carrying me. I jerk in surprise, but recognize Roman's voice when he shushes me.

"What's going on?" I can hardly get the words out. Despite my surprise, I have to fight to stay awake.

"You fell asleep, then so did everybody else," he says. "I'm taking you to your room."

"Oh, okay."

He laughs at how my words run together. I don't have the energy to defend myself. I just press my face deeper into his chest, where all the warmth is, and close my eyes.

When I wake up again, the light in my room is on, and he's easing me into bed. I pull my body into a tight coil as he drapes the sheets back over me, tucking me in.

"Thank you," I mumble, my eyes half open.

And then, just when I think I can never be surprised by anything ever again, he leans forward and kisses my forehead. "Of course. Goodnight, Lia."

He reaches for the lamp, but I throw out a weak hand to stop him.

"What?" He asks, smiling down at me.

"What if I have a nightmare?"

He crouches down beside the bed so that our faces are level. My bedside table casts gold light into his cerulean eyes, and I can't help myself. Smiling like a drunk idiot, I reach out with my index finger and poke his cheek, right where his dimple is. I hadn't noticed he had dimples until now, or the thin white scar that cuts across the top of his full, pink lips. I hadn't noticed the long, black swoop of his eyelashes either, or the crookedness of his smile.

"I can stay with you," he says. "I don't know how good I'll be at protecting you from nightmares, though."

"You can try your best," I suggest.

He laughs and slides in beside me. "Yeah, I can."

He pulls the sheets back over us both, and I instantly burrow into his side. His warmth rushes through me, a gentle salve over everything that hurts. He reaches for me too and rolls over onto his back. I rest my head against his chest, listening to the quick hammer of his heart.

I laugh into his shirt. When he laughs too, it ripples through me like ocean water.

"What's up with you?" He asks, still laughing.

"Your heart's beating really fast," I say. "Are you nervous?"

I look him in the eyes when I say it. Red blush floods his cheeks, and I can't stop myself. I actually giggle into his chest. A mischievous look crosses his face, briefly, before he rolls us over. His weight is warm and comforting against me, and it's like I'm seeing the sun for the first time.

The light washes over the back of his head, creating a dazzling corona around his face. He's so close that his hair tickles my cheeks, sending goosebumps raising all over my skin. One arm is beneath my neck, supporting my head. The other hovers just above my hip; his fingers are blazing hot against my skin. My heart pounds so hard it could jump out of my chest.

"At least that makes both of us," he says, but I'm not listening anymore.

I'm not thinking either. I bring my thumb up to trace the soft outline of his mouth. I haven't even made it to his bottom lip when he's kissing me. First it's tentative and soft, like he's not sure. I wrap an arm around his neck, pulling him closer. His lips fall open against mine, and he's kissing me with more urgency now. Like there's not enough time in the world.

When I pull away to breath, he rolls onto his side and leans back in for more. We kiss until our lips are numb, and then until we can barely keep our eyes open. He presses his lips to mine one last time, soft as peach fuzz, and falls asleep in my arms.

PART THREE:

THE
GODENDER

CHAPTER THIRTY

WE'RE STANDING IN THE SAME MASSIVE clearing, with a wall of empty air in front of us.

A second later, the wall splits, revealing the Sacred House's black gate and the bustling compound that waits beyond it. The last time I was here, children and their parents chased each other with water guns along the front lawn. Now it's blanketed by thick white snow; the guards at the front are wearing long, black trench coats.

They don't question us as we approach. They simply bow as the doors break open.

"Where's Griffin?" Baxter asks one of them.

The guard looks terrified. "In the Polis," he says.

Janus and Cherice look astonished as we cross onto the grounds. There aren't many people out. A squad of people who look younger than I do are led in a single file line around the property's perimeter marching, but that's about it. Warm lights are on in the residential quarter, but the Sacred House's public square is a ghost town.

We have to let ourselves into the Polis, where the Vessel of Destiny sits on the stairs with his head in his hands. He jerks to his feet when we walk in, and is only slightly relieved to see that it's us. He actually looks nauseous.

"Oh no. Oh no," he groans, dragging his hands down his face.

"What ever happened to 'hey, how are you?'" Cass quips. "Does the coffee maker not work around here, anymore?"

Griffin ignores him and points fingers at my aunt and uncle. "What are they doing here?'

"They're my aunt and uncle." I say simply.

He groans again, like he's gonna be sick. "Why would you bring council members here? Why?" He tries and fails to smile at them. "No offense."

"Not at all," Janus says, his expression mild.

"Well it would've been nice to know we were disobeying the Council of Houses," I shrug. "Also would've been nice to know that there was a Council of Houses."

"It was irrelevant." Griffin rolls his eyes. "Plus, they'd just try to shut us down. They wouldn't like our working theory."

"Which is?" Baxter asks.

Janus holds up his hands, beating Griffin to it. "Let me guess. The Gods of Paradise, right?"

Griffin goes pale. "How'd you know?"

"They were attacked by the Princes of Paradise. At their school." Finally, there's some heat to his voice. "Why would you bring children into this?"

"Are you serious?" Griffin asks. "They're not just children. They're the Gods of Olympus, and we need them. Let's go somewhere to talk."

Once again, I find myself sitting in the stone meeting room, under the watchful, stony gaze of Athena. The commanders sit across from me, not looking nearly as pleasant as the first time

I met them. Which wasn't very, to be honest. They throw dirty looks at my aunt and uncle, who return them in kind.

"Makena," my uncle says, breaking what's been a tepid, nearly minute-long silence.

"Janus," she says back, history bloated in her voice. "You look well."

"Likewise." Another tepid silence, and then Janus sets his teeth. He gestures to Griffin, who's white as a sheet. "So I'm guessing you didn't think it'd be a good idea to tell the Council you'd met with the Vessel of Destiny."

"It was my idea," Griffin says simply. "I didn't know who I could trust, but when Makena and I had the same suspicions, I knew it was better if we kept things quiet."

"If you suspected the Firstborn, why didn't you tell us?" Baxter asks, his tone accusing. "It would have saved a lot of pain and suffering."

"And time," Roman adds, unkindly.

"I suspected Scions," Makena says, breathless. "I didn't think in a million years that the Gods of Old themselves were behind this. I certainly didn't think they'd have the Council in their pockets."

Cherice scoffs. "Makena, what the hell are you talking about?"

"Emmanuel Martin," she says, just the name. "When I first suggested a recovery operation, he shot me down. I confronted him after the meeting, and he tried to intimidate me."

"Should we know who that is?" Alessia asks.

"He's the Council Magistrate," Cherice says. "He's the only one on the council with any kind of veto power."

"Yes, and if you'll remember, my proposal was the one that got all the votes," the General chides. "Seven others voted against me, and Emmanuel was the one who shot it down. He said he'd take care of it, that none of us should worry. Guess who all was appointed to Martin's specialized operation team?"

"The ones who voted against you," Janus says.

"Exactly. And guess who also hasn't made any progress since the day we went to the Underworld?" By now, the General's voice is searing. She levels her eyes on my uncle, whose expression I can't read.

I've seen my uncle angry. I've seen him irritated. This is something else entirely, something like authority.

"So what are you saying?" he asks.

The General leans forward, folding her hands. "Just that—to me—it would appear that the Council Magistrate actively blocked my action plan, knowing he didn't plan on doing anything about it himself. You might call that incompetence. I prefer sabotage."

My uncle scoffs, but Griffin raises his hand in the General's defense.

"It doesn't make sense otherwise," he says. "How'd the Fates even get kidnapped in the first place? They were supposed to be guarded by the Children of Ares, but somehow, no one noticed they'd been infiltrated? Not one person?"

Alessia perks up at that. "Children of Ares?"

"They were charged with protecting the Fate's realm," Minister Fueves says, his voice a dull, bored drawl. "The night the Fates were taken, they didn't report an intruder until after the abduction. And no one was killed or injured."

Cass sucks his teeth. "Yeah. That sounds like sabotage to me."

Cherice rolls her eyes, but I can't say she looks unconvinced. "Can you prove it?"

The commanders exchange annoyed looks. It's the Lieutenant that breaks the silence.

"Not yet," she says. "I've contacted the Council Magistrate several times to request an audience, but he hasn't returned my correspondence. We're being ignored."

"That doesn't sound like proof," Janus says, his voice heavy. "But it does sound suspicious. Look, I'll keep shut about this, but you need to get me something concrete. If Martin really is working with the Firstborn, then we're all in a lot of trouble." He points down the table, where the six of us watch with bated breath. "Secondly, I don't appreciate you soliciting children to do your grunt work, Makena. If you suspected Martin, you should've come to me. Why not ask my House for help?"

Something like disbelief flashes across the General's face. She laughs, but there's no humor to it. "Janus, I didn't solicit children. I turned to the Gods of Olympus, *our* gods, because I know the Scions are stronger than us, and they're acting under the organization of their own gods. If we don't do the same, we won't survive. That's the reality, and it's time you start living in it." She looks over at the six of us, that same fire burning in her eyes. "Now, where are you? On the Codex?"

It feels like my teacher's just asked for the homework, but I didn't do it. Shame moves through me, quick and vicious. I'd wanted to have better news. Instead, I'm no closer than I was before.

"We found the Eye, but it doesn't work," Roman says, his voice feeble in the great, stone room. "We couldn't use it to find the Codex."

"Impossible," says Minister Fueves.

Roman blinks. "Well I mean, we tried it and it didn't work. Seems possible enough."

The minister shakes his head. "No, I mean—the Sisters were only the messengers. The Eye is the vessel of the Sacred

Knowledge, and whoever gives it blood can access its secrets. Now, not everyone is able to use it; children of the gods wouldn't be able to, neither would mortals. But as gods yourself, you should be able to access its truth."

It's so quiet you could hear a pin drop. Coupled with all the shame, I mostly feel like an idiot. A huge idiot. Somehow, it hadn't occurred to me that maybe, what the ancient magical artifact really wants is blood. Unbelievable.

"So just like . . ." Cass makes a flippant, one-handed gesture. "Bleed on it. That's it?"

The minister nods. "Yes. That's it."

"Goddamn it," Baxter mutters, hanging his head.

"I still don't like this, Makena," Janus says. "You should have come to me directly."

"Perhaps, but that's not what happened." The finality in the General's voice chars the air around us. "Regardless of what should and shouldn't have been, everyday we don't find the Codex is another day closer to the Fate's imminent demise. So I would politely request that you pick up the pace, and I'll work on proving my theory on Martin. Understood?"

No one says anything, but her order is clear enough. It falls in the room like we're soldiers in her charge.

"Oh, and one other thing," she says, now with a note of warning in her voice. "Be very careful, all of you. It's not safe in New River, a fact with which I'm sure you're now intimately familiar."

No one says anything. I think about my father's journal, and the way he'd drawn Kreos. Like something boundless and evil. Something that couldn't be stopped.

CHAPTER THIRTY-ONE

AFTER THE GENERAL LEAVES WITH HER posse, Griffin walks us back to the main gate. My teeth chatter at the wind, which teases winter with each freezing gust. The lawn is strangely quiet, like even the earth knows its days are numbered.

At the gate, my uncle offers Griffin his hand.

"I apologize that we aren't meeting under better circumstances," Janus tells him. "I'm Janus Johnson, Chief Council Representative of the House of Cursed Children."

My aunt, who looks sick, offers her own hand. "And I'm Cherice. Just Cherice. It's nice to meet you."

Griffin laughs, even though worry weighs his shoulders down. "Oh, I know who you are," he says. "For whatever it's worth, you're a legend in my book, Cherice. It takes courage to reject the station of your birth and choose what's right. And Janus, I've heard the stories about you and your brother. I was sad to hear that he'd passed. He was a hero, a real one."

I turn away, because I don't want to see the look of half-veiled agony that crosses Janus's face. When he speaks, thankfully, his voice is steady.

"Thank you," Janus says. "It means a lot to know that the Vessel of Destiny regards my brother that highly. I only wish . . ."

He trails off. I look away again. I hear Griffin speak, his voice soft.

"So do I," Griffin says. "We always find ourselves wishing that our heroes had more time. It isn't fair."

His voice breaks near the end. I finally look at him, at his pale, tortured expression. His eyes are distant and dark, not filled with a pensive, white light. He shakes his head, clearing it, and tries to smile.

"Thank you for visiting," he says, clearing his throat. "Oh, I almost forgot."

He pulls a tiny flip notebook out of his pocket and scribbles something down with the small, black pen strapped to its cover. He tears the sheet out and passes it to me.

"From now on, if anything happens, you call me," he says, his gaze piercing. "And for the record, the General's invitation still stands. You know New River isn't safe."

Without explaining himself any further, Griffin turns on his heels and heads back to the Polis. My uncle watches him grimly, like there's a shadow at his back.

We vanish and appear again in New River, at the foot of my aunt and uncle's driveway. I watch the dark, grand faces of each house that lines my street. Right now, everyone's either at work or school, so Green Groves sits beneath a near absolute quiet. It was in a quiet just like this one that I'd first seen Alex. It was in a quiet just like this one that I met a monster face to face. Griffin was right. This place isn't safe anymore. Maybe it never was.

"I think we should take the General up on her offer," Olivia says. "Being here freaks me out. I don't like that they can just find us at school."

"Which was?" Janus asks, raising a single, suspicious eyebrow.

"We leave New River," I tell him. "The General offered us room and board at the Sacred House a long time ago. I wasn't really on board at first, but I don't think we have a choice anymore."

"You're talking about living at the Sacred House?" Cherice scoffs. "Absolutely not. That's extreme."

"Is it?" Baxter asks. "They attacked us at school. If we hadn't pulled the fire alarm, someone could've gotten hurt. Someone innocent, who has nothing to do with this. We're not just putting ourselves at risk by being here."

Janus steps back in surprise, but he's lost for words. He rubs his eyes like he's exhausted. Already it feels like it's been a long day.

"Okay, how about this," Janus says. "It's up to you, obviously, but if you stayed we'd protect you. We know what we're dealing with now; we can help."

I shake my head. "We're not the only ones we're trying to protect. It's not safe for you either."

There's something like amusement in his eyes, then despair. "You don't have to protect me, Ophelia. That's not your job."

But he's wrong. He's so wrong. The Firstborn have already taken so much. I can't let them take anyone else from me.

"Yes, I do," I tell him, crossing my arms.

"Then let us come with you," Cherice says, pleading. "We *can* help you. And the General too."

I look around at my friends, but they all just shrug. I guess I shouldn't want anyone to disagree with me. I shouldn't want my aunt and uncle to be anywhere other than where I am, but things are different now. Where I am isn't safe. With Somnus's vow unfulfilled, there's nowhere I can go where he won't try to kill me. The people I love will just be empty collateral in the greater effort of his mission. He won't care that I'll grieve them, and he won't care about what he's taking from me.

It would be better for them to be away from me. It would be better for everyone to be away from me, but I know that's not realistic. So the next best option is to stay together and keep them where I can see them.

"Can you help the General get proof on Martin?" I ask.

"On Martin directly, probably not," Janus says. "But he's fairly open with his inner circle and one of them might be easier to nab. We'll see what we can do."

"Yeah, I know one of the guys on the Council's crisis team," Cherice adds. "He thinks we're friends. I can work with that."

I don't like it. I don't like it at all, but I really would hate to leave them here. I wouldn't be able to forgive myself if something happened to them.

"All right," I say. "Okay, but we leave in half an hour. The less time we spend here the better."

The others go home to make their preparations. Something about it feels like the last rites before a funeral. I've only lived here for four months, and I'm already leaving this place behind.

Before Roman leaves, he pulls me behind my uncle's truck so that we're just out of view. His expression is frenzied, like he's thinking of a million things at once. His hands are like blocks of ice and tremble around my wrists as he pulls me closer to him.

"Are you all right?" He asks.

I nod. "Yeah, I'm great."

The corners of his lips twitch with amusement. "That's very convincing." He kisses my forehead. "I won't be gone long. I just need to talk to my mom. Is that okay?"

"Of course," I tell him. "But don't rush, please. Take your time."

His face softens into something rueful. "Yeah, you're right. I'll see you in a bit. " He kisses my cheek this time before vanishing in a spray of jasmine and sea salt.

The only one of my friends that remains is Cassius. It's not until I see the bags he's carrying that I realize he's just the first one back. He's got a backpack slung over his shoulders and a bulging duffel bag in his left hand. He sits on the front steps with a stony expression. He watches the street ahead like he's looking for ghosts.

I nudge him with my foot on the way up. The door is half open, so my aunt and uncle must already be inside.

"Are you gonna sit out here the whole time?" I ask him.

He shrugs. "Maybe."

I pull the door open with my foot and gesture to the empty foyer. "Nope. It's not safe. Get in."

He looks back at me, cracking a smile. A wicked light casts over his once shadowy expression. "Are you worried about my well being? Am I hearing that, right?"

"Cass, you know I'll kick your ass. Get in the *house*."

Laughing, he pushes up from the steps and starts walking inside. With his foot halfway over the threshold, he stops to smile down at me. For once, nothing about this smile is mischievous or biting. His eyes are unguarded, sincere too.

"Thanks, Ophelia," he says. "For caring."

I swat him on the shoulder. "Shut up. You never have to thank me for caring. Now get in."

Cass sits in the living room after I let him go inside, and I run up to my room to change. I can hear my aunt and uncle moving around in their bedroom, both of them speaking in voices too low to hear.

I fish a duffel bag out of my closet and start packing it with as many clothes as I can. The last time I packed like this, I was getting ready to leave Austin behind. These circumstances are so much different, but it feels strange packing my life away again. I raid the bathroom for toiletries and then stuff an extra pair of sneakers into the bag before forcing the zipper closed. After setting the duffel bag by the door, I start working on a backpack next. I pack my father's journal, the books I kept from the Sacred House, the old scrapbook my grandma made of me when I was a baby, and then, finally, the Eye.

I turn the cloudy, diamond necklace over in my hands, watching how light struggles to pierce its armor. I don't put it in my bag. It belongs on my neck. I pull out the Lightning Bolt, melted into a sleek, silver, blade, and prick my finger against its pointed edge.

I cut deep, creating a short incision across the pad of my finger. Ichor trickles down my hand in a warm stream, splashing against the Eye in fat, splattering drops. At first nothing happens. Then, a white light blazes from within the diamond's cloudy center, casting my room in jagged shadows. A cold, invisible hand comes up behind me and yanks my head back. My room disappears, and I'm staring into an empty black void.

It's too dark to see anything, but I can make out the faint shape of thick, black clouds. That same cold hand pushes me forward, propelling me through the clouds.

"Lightning God, Child of Khaos—what do you seek?" a voice asks.

There's no one here, certainly no one that should know who I am. I try to look around, but my head is fixed in place.

My voice feels heavy and slurred. "The Codex Sanctus."

My stomach plunges. Dread fills my body in a wild, freezing river. I can feel my chest rising and falling. I can feel panic unfurling in my stomach like a venomous snake. There's nothing good about the thing I seek.

The clouds part in front of me as the cold hand at my back pushes me forward. Finally, I can see the wide, sprawling landscape of a dark forest. Wide-leaved trees sway violently in the wind. They slap me in the face as the hand lowers me down into the forest's belly, right at the doorstep of a crumbing temple.

The stone is dark and wet with rain. It doesn't look like anyone's prayed here in centuries. In fact, the last time someone did, it couldn't have gone well. There's a large crack webbing up the stone staircase, all the way to an open set of double doors. At least they used to be. There are two stone slabs on either side of the walkway, each cracked in half. The hand seems to urge me forward, but I don't want to go in. There's something terrible in that temple. Something that should never be free.

But I do enter the temple. It welcomes me with a cold draft. The foyer is wide and empty. There are shards of crushed glass all along the floor and huge splattered pools of what has to be ichor. The ceiling is a domed skylight; it was shattered a long time ago. Words carve into the walls in a language I can't read, but I can tell it's much, much older than Ancient Greek.

I follow the hand's goading up a long set of stone steps. Wet ichor trails up the steps in dark splatters. The higher I climb, the sicker I feel.

The hand guides me to a room on the third floor of the temple. The room is splashed with gold: gold paint, piles of ancient stone jewels and chains. There's a gilded throne in the middle of the room, behind a high stone altar. The building is ancient, but the four candles that burn at each corner of the altar have to be fresh. Jewels spill over the altar's edges, around the worn leather book in the center. It doesn't have a title or a cover, but I can feel its power tugging at something deep in my stomach.

I'm stepping forward to touch it when I hear footsteps behind me.

My sword is out in an instant, rippling with pale blue lightning. She's taller than me, and the calm, powerful expression on her face is familiar. A million suns blaze beneath her skin. When she walks, liquid gold seeps out from her bare feet. The first goddess, coming down to meet me once again.

I jerk back, but the altar's behind me. "It's you."

"No," she says. "It's you, Ophelia. It can only be you."

"I don't know what that means."

"Perhaps not, but hear me well. The Order of Ruin is your birthright. You will slay him and turn his kingdom to ash. It is written."

"What are you talking about?"

She's so close that I can see the galaxies swirling in her dark eyes. There are billions of them, each as brilliant as the last, with bright quasars at their center.

"What is this?" I mutter, half-mesmerized.

She lifts her hand. "The First Temple. Find it, and most importantly, never let them take you."

"Wait—"

She presses a finger to my forehead, and the whole world goes black.

CHAPTER THIRTY-TWO

I WAKE UP ON THE FLOOR. The first thing I notice is the pale slat of sunlight falling over me.

I notice its warmth, how the strange, black space of my vision had been anything but warm. I clutch a hand to my chest, where my heart hammers against my palm. Sweat forms in small droplets along my skin, freezing cold. My room is empty, but the air is charged with something else, something alien and alive. I find myself searching for that woman—the woman I know. The woman whose name is thick and hot in my throat, like vomit. My ancestor, whose power lives in my blood just as surely as the Lighting God's.

Khaos. I'd seen her, just like I'd seen her the night Zeus gave me his power.

I tear the Eye away from my neck. I don't care that I snap the chain. It's hot in my hand like a lump of burning coal. I shove it into my bag, far out of sight. It takes me another second to really find my feet, and then one more to calm myself down.

Everything about the vision felt so real. The desolate temple, and the odd shadows that painted its barren walls. Its stone stained with ichor. The heaping piles of jewels and the path they carved to that empty throne. *The First Temple.* I'm not sure if the name is for decoration or the statement of a simple fact, but I know it's where we need to go.

After I slow my breathing down, I do one last check around the room. I know I won't see it again. I'm not sure for how long. Maybe forever, but that feels too final. A sense of unease slithers beneath my skin, but I push it down. For better or worse, there's no going back. My only option is to move forward, no matter how terrible the future might be.

Downstairs, most of my friends have made their way back. Roman and Cass talk in low voices on the couch, while Alessia broods on the loveseat.

"Hey," I kick Roman's foot as a personal greeting. "I have something to tell you guys." I pause. "Where's Olivia and Baxter?"

"She wanted to talk to her mom," Cass says. "Baxter went with her, but they shouldn't be too long." His eyes are wary. "What is it?"

"It's good news," I tell him. "I don't want to say it twice so I'm gonna wait."

"Is everything okay?" Roman asks, worried.

Cass rolls his eyes. "She just said it was good news."

"Exactly. Since when do we ever get good news?"

I ignore their bickering and set my bags down in the foyer, where everyone else has done the same. When I sit beside Alessia, at first, she tries to ignore me.

Or maybe not. Maybe she's just so caught up in thought that she really doesn't notice me plop down beside her. I wave my hands in front of her face; she blinks and looks at me like she doesn't recognize me.

"Do you smell burning toast?" I ask.

She rolls her eyes, but the corner of her mouth lifts a little. "Sorry. I didn't sleep well."

I sit back in the loveseat, my chest suddenly very heavy. "That's not it."

She throws me a dirty look, but it quickly fades into something resigned. She leans back too, shrugging in surrender. "It's so stupid. I used to hate this place; all I wanted to do was leave. And now that we have to, I can't even be cool about it."

Her eyes glitter like a cluster of sun-stained diamonds. I reach out and press a hand to her forearm. Homesickness might as well be my mother tongue. Next to grief, it's the one thing I know better than myself.

"It's only for a little while," I tell her. "Once it's safe, we'll come back. I promise."

She scoffs. "You don't get it."

"Okay, then explain it to me."

Her eyes darken. It's like a storm cloud has rolled in over her shoulders. "The Firstborn want war. They won't stop until they get it, so there is no 'after.'"

I look away from her, my eyes burning. I know I'm not angry at her, not really. I just hate that she's right.

"No there will be," I tell her, even though saying it feels like a lie. "We're gonna find the Codex and when the Firstborn come for it, we'll kill them. It's simple."

She rolls her eyes. "You know you don't believe that."

Footsteps thunder down the stairs. My aunt and uncle come down with duffel bags and drop them in the foyer too. They're both dressed for hiking, with the same bulky black boots on their feet. Both of their belts secure the long swords that dangle from their waists.

Cherice sets a hand on her hips and takes in the house. Her expression is so resolved, I almost miss the sadness underneath it. But it's there, in each line of her face.

Janus pulls a wrinkled sheet of paper out of his pocket. "All right, I know we've got clothes, shoes, and armor. I packed a bag of first aid supplies and emergency rations too."

"Did you get the maps? And the contact journal?" Cherice asks.

Janus nods. "Yep. Got those too." He frowns her and leans in close to say something I can't hear.

She nods. When he doesn't look convinced, she just shrugs. I look away now, because her armored expression falls away, for just a second, and it's the most vulnerable I've ever seen her.

Alessia nudges me with her knee, her expression almost cruel. "There's no after for them either."

It hurts to hear her say it, especially after all that I've just learned. When you're born into it the way they were, when it's in your blood, there's no such thing as an end. The cause, if it can be called that, is the beginning and end of everything.

Janus and Cherice leave to talk in the kitchen after offering weak greetings. By the time Baxter and Olivia appear in the living room, they've been talking for twenty minutes.

Baxter looks ready for anything, in a rough pair of faded jeans and combat boots. Olivia, however, just looks ready for a stroll beneath a flurry of fresh snowfall. Her orange sweater is the color of dying leaves, and her boots aren't made for hiking.

"Sorry we're late," Baxter says. "I wanted to talk to my father."

Roman's voice is full of sympathy. "How'd it go?"

Baxter sits down in the love seat; Olivia sits on the armrest and lays a hand on his shoulder.

"Don't worry about it," he says. "They just don't get it."

Cass furrows his brows. "They don't get what?"

"Why I have to leave," Baxter says. "I told them the truth. It just felt right."

"And what'd they say?" I ask, but I can already tell by the defeated slump of his shoulders.

"What any well-adjusted and responsible adult should say. They thought I was crazy," he chides. "And I kept trying to show them my bow, but they couldn't see it. I tried to jump them through the house, but they couldn't come with me. They didn't even register that I'd gone anywhere. I looked crazy."

"No you didn't," Roman says, shaking his head. "They're just—"

"Normal." Baxter says it like a prayer. "I'm the one who's the freak. I knew how it was gonna go, and I said something anyway. I'm an idiot. I shouldn't have told them anything."

"You're not an idiot, Baxter. You shouldn't keep things from the people you love, even if they don't believe you," I tell him.

He tries to smile, but I know he doesn't believe me. "I hope you're right."

It's another twenty minutes before we're finally ready. I don't like the idea that we were stalling, but something about leaving New River makes the bottom fall out of my stomach. It feels like we're hurtling out to space, with nothing to hold onto but a cold, black emptiness.

I force myself to remember the Eye and the way my blood fell over it. We're not floating aimlessly, and I'll prove Alessia wrong. There won't be a war. After we're done, there won't be any more bloodshed. The Firstborn will think they're coming to claim a prize, but they'll only be coming to die. I'll make sure of it.

Janus and Cherice come out of the kitchen with grim expressions. They try to keep their voices light, but I'd be able to recognize that dark cloud hanging over them anywhere.

"Rock and roll, I guess," Janus mutters as we gather in the middle of the living room.

We link hands around the circle. Cass's smile is bitter, like he's sucking on a peach pit.

"Please keep all hands and feet inside the ride at all times." He doesn't say it like he's joking.

His eyes glow the color of blood, and the smell of pomegranates fill the room. A second later, we're hurtling away from New River's gravity.

The forest is freezing and splashed in twilight. When the air splits in front of us, we're met with the warmth and glow of torch light. Tiny fires blaze all along the large black gate, illuminating the perimeter of the Sacred's House massive estate.

A sprawl of house lights shimmer in the distance like a fiery horizon. As we pass the dark, empty lawn, the city opens up to a complex network of gridded streets. Shops line the city like rows of teeth, built from red brick and dark glass. Deeper into the city, I can see the paneled, slant roofs of townhouses.

The Polis is no less formidable at night, with all its lights dimmed. The emptiness of the foyer seems to blanket us in layers of deafening silence; a harsh chill fills its vaulted halls.

Dim torches light the Polis's dark hallways. Guards stand sentry in the shadows.

"Where's the General?" I ask one of them. "We need to talk."

"The General is away on business," he says, keeping his eyes forward. "Her return isn't expected for the next few days."

"Wonderful," Cass mutters under his breath.

"Where's Griffin?" Alessia asks, impatient. "Can we speak with the Vessel?"

The guard nods. "He can be summoned."

"Good. Have him meet us in the library," I say.

I'm surprised that I've memorized the way there. Our footsteps echo throughout the empty building as we climb the stairs. Moonlight trickles in through the floor-to-ceiling windows on each landing, painting us silver. Climbing these stairs reminds me of the First Temple, and the cold dread that slithered into my stomach.

There are more lights in the library. Low candles burn in the building's massive chandelier, and torches glow warmly all along the walls. Roman, Baxter, and Olivia sit at the table, but Cass plops down in one of the maroon armchairs near the fire. By now, twilight has surrendered to night, making way for the sheet of stars that beams down on us through the glass-paneled ceiling.

"All right, out with it," Alessia says. "What'd you see?"

Janus frowns at me. "Did I miss something?"

"I got the Eye to work. I bled on it," I tell them. "And now I know where we need to go: the First Temple."

"It was that easy?" Baxter scoffs.

"Well I didn't get a map or anything, but I'm sure that's what she said," I say. A shudder runs through me. There were more stars in her eyes than any in the sky above me. "I saw Khaos. She told me I had to find it."

I don't include the rest of her message, the parts I didn't understand. Twice now she's mentioned "The Order," and twice now she's affirmed that whatever it is, it belongs to me.

My uncle leans forward. "You saw Khaos?"

The library doors burst open, and Griffin walks in on heavy feet. He's wearing a matching set of red flannel pajamas, and he doesn't look happy to see us.

"You woke me up," he mumbles as he pulls out a seat at the table.

"Sorry, Sleeping Beauty," Cass says. "This is important. We know where to find the Codex."

Griffin furrows his brows, but he doesn't look any more awake. "Are you sure?"

Alessia looks at me. I roll my eyes.

"Yes, god, I'm sure." I massage deep circles into my temples. "The Eye asked me what I wanted to know, and when I said the Codex, it showed me the First Temple."

Griffin sits back, a calculating look on his face.

"What is it?" Cherice asks.

"I've heard that name before. In a book." He shoots up from the table and crosses the library much faster than a human should.

We watch him climb the ladder, and go down a row of books on the top row of the leftmost section. Finally, he pulls out a thick, leather-bound volume and races back to the table.

"What's that?" I ask.

He doesn't answer. He flips through the yellowed pages before finally stopping near the middle. "*And silver waves do kneel at that great shadow. Skies cower at the First Temple's gilded crown.* It's from a poem about worship."

"Does it tell us where to find it?" Roman asks. "Even a hint?"

Griffin scans the page and all the fire in his eyes goes out. "No. It's just a line, but I knew I'd read it before."

Janus looks pleased as he roots around in his bag. "But I know someone who can tell us." He pulls out a tiny notebook, with the word CONTACTS sprawled across the label in blue ink. He flips to the exact page like he has it memorized. "Madame Sarai. She's a historian, and she owes me a favor."

Griffin rolls his eyes. "Not that witch."

Cass hisses. "Ouch."

"What do you have against witches?" Cherice laughs.

"I don't have anything against witches. I just don't trust that one." Griffin shuts his book and slides it away from him. The circles around his eyes are the color of plum skin. "Look, if the Madame can help, all power to you. Just be careful. Love them or hate them—witches can be tricky. Very tricky."

After another hour spent in the library, to the avail of no effort in particular, Griffin reluctantly volunteers to show us to our rooms.

Unfortunately, we don't get to head back toward the glittering city, which is still teeming with life. Our rooms are in the Polis, on the top floor. We pass through a door that's been marked with the same sigil as the one the Lieutenant carved into our hands. Griffin presses his palm against it, and a serpent-haired woman appears across his knuckles in blood red ink.

The door breaks open, and we're let into a dimly lit hallway with shining hardwood floors. There are no guards here. Just a row of wine-colored rugs and long wax candles burning with warm light along the walls. Chandeliers of clear, shimmering glass douse us in more light. The vaulted

OF BLOOD AND LIGHTNING

ceiling is carved from smooth ivory, and colored scenes sprawl above our heads. A goddess hovering over a burning city, wielding a red-tipped sword. A woman in mauve robes standing over someone's split skull.

As Griffin leads us down the hall, I study the statues and paintings we pass. There's a grizzled old man, carved from stone, and a statue that's just like the ones that watch us in the conference room, only smaller. We go down the main hall and take a left. We don't stop on this one either, and instead go through a set of towering double doors. Griffin opens them with the flat of his palm.

These doors let out into a wide common area. There are two sofas and a bunch of arm chairs in the middle of the room, each arranged around a low burning fireplace. There's the same vaulted ceiling, only this one is made of glass, and lets in the light of countless stars. Three narrow hallways lead from the common area to rows of what have to be bedrooms.

"Welcome." Griffin holds out both hands in a weak gesture of welcome before collapsing into one of the chairs. "We're roommates, by the way. Don't keep me up all night."

"Wouldn't dream of it," Cass says. "I wanna go see the city."

"Wait, so which ones are ours?" Olivia asks, ignoring him.

Griffin shrugs. He's cuddled up against one of the pillows with his eyes closed. "Just pick one. This is a private wing for important guests only, so we're the only ones who sleep here."

Laughter floats down the hall as Cass and Alessia race to look at the rooms. My aunt and uncle seem less enthusiastic, but the dark clouds from earlier are all gone now. As Griffin dozes in his chair, Olivia and Baxter break off to pick out a room. I sit on the couch, exhausted, and let my bags land by my feet. I hadn't realized how tired I was until I felt how soft this couch is.

Roman plops down beside me and leans his head against my shoulder. I pinch his chin with a lazy hand and laugh when he tries to bite my thumb.

"All right, we're going to bed," Cherice announces from the doorway.

Janus covers his mouth with a fist, yawning deeply. "Goodnight. Don't stay up too late."

"Goodnight," Roman mumbles, his voice thick.

I flash them a thumbs-up. Griffin snores on the couch.

Another ten minutes has passed before I realize Roman and I have fallen asleep on the couch—his head on my shoulder, my cheek pressed against his hair. I jerk awake against him after something soft hits me in the chest. Griffin stands over us, another pillow already in his hands.

"What?" Roman mutters, his eyes cloudy with sleep.

Griffin tosses the pillow back on the couch. "Go to bed," is all he says, before starting down one of the long hallways.

It takes more strength than I expect to stand and pick up my things. It's a long walk to the room we decide to share. It's at the end of the third hallway, with a single, king-sized bed. Dark red curtains hang from the bedpost, the same color as the fuzzy, long-haired rug at the edge of the bed. There's a black couch and a desk in front of it toward the front of the room, and two vanities pushed up against the wall on either side. The room is dim, lit only by the low burning lantern on the bedside table.

As soon as the door closes, Roman's kicking his way out of his pants.

"Sorry," he mumbles, his words strung together. "I'm just changing."

Normally, the idea of Roman taking his clothes off in the same room as me would send me into shock, but I'm too tired to care. I change my clothes in the middle of the room too before sliding into bed beside him. He's not wearing a shirt, so when he reaches for me, and I melt into him, all I feel is skin, warmth, and boy.

"Goodnight," I mumble into his chest.

He peppers a lazy path of kisses across my temple. "Goodnight."

I'm asleep before I've even fully registered his scent: jasmine, clean soap, and something else, something citric.

CHAPTER THIRTY-THREE

A VOLLEY OF FLAMING GREEN ARROWS cuts across the sky. And then another. And another.

I sit with my legs folded on the front lawn, watching a new morning unravel above the Sacred House. The sun is a bloody red smear as it crawls over the horizon, splashing the world in rays of pink and gold. Unlike last night, the city is quiet. All the action is on the lawn.

A squad of kids in black robes fire arrows under the watchful eyes of their instructor. They have to be no older than fourteen, but they handle the weapons with a trained precision. Across from them, another group of kids march along the front perimeter of the lawn with javelins hoisted over their heads. They march in a rigid phalanx and launch the javelins at straw targets.

When I first woke up here a few days ago, it felt like I was living in some kind of dream. It surprised me to find daylight streaming in through a strange window, or pouring over the edge of a desk that didn't belong to me. Roman had been the only familiar thing in sight.

Being here is like being in a dream, a forbidden one. If my father hadn't tried so hard to protect me, this would've been

OF BLOOD AND LIGHTNING

my life. I would've been just like the kids on this lawn, training in the early hours of the morning instead of getting ready for school. I'm not sure which is better: sacrificing your entire childhood to become a warrior or being blindsided by the truth. Maybe there is no better option. Only the one that's chosen for you.

After the day has fully broken, I see my aunt and uncle coming down the Polis steps. They're dressed like council members, with long black robes and glossy boots.

"Hey, we couldn't find you," Janus says. "Everybody's almost ready to leave. You all right?"

"Yeah." I push up from the lawn and turn to go with them. "I just wanted some air. Are you waiting on breakfast?"

Cherice shakes her head. "No. After we meet with the Madame, Janus and I have to get with Makena on the Martin thing. I still think it's crazy, but I wouldn't put it past him."

"What makes you say that?" I ask.

She exchanges a dark, irritated look with my uncle, who rolls his eyes.

"When he first joined the council he tried to have the Cursed House excommunicated," my uncle says. "That was back during your grandfather's later years. He didn't get the votes then, but he tried again when he became Magistrate. Even to this day, he hates that we're part of it. I never knew why."

"Maybe it's because you're Scions," I suggest. "Demigods and Scions aren't exactly best friends."

Cherice scoffs. "Martin isn't stupid. He knows how beneficial this alliance is to the demigods. They wouldn't be able to build fortresses like this if it wasn't for the Children of Khaos. They would've gone extinct a long time ago."

I stop in wonder and look around like I'm seeing everything for the first time. I hadn't really questioned the invisible wall that surrounds the Sacred House, concealing it from view. With everything else going on, it just didn't seem especially remarkable. I never could've expected it was the work of Scions though, much less the ones I share an ancestor with.

"Seriously?" I ask.

Janus beams with pride. "Every time demigods need any kind of protection, they ask us to fortify the land. Most of our squads are exclusively for defense and fortification." The pride flickers out, leaving something sour behind. "Not for long, I guess. War and whatnot."

The others are already waiting in the foyer. During the day, the large, paneled glass overhead washes the room in pale, clean light. The fireplace is an empty hearth, but there's more than enough sunlight to make me feel warm.

Roman reaches for me when he sees me, pouting.

"Hey, where'd you go?" he asks.

I lean into his side and linger there with my cheek against his shoulder. "Outside. I was just sitting, so I didn't want to wake you up."

"Okay, but next time you can," he says, pecking my cheek. "I like just sitting with you."

I think about the water tower. It is a great pastime.

"Yeah, me too," I tell him.

Griffin clears his throat by the coffee table. He doesn't look nearly as exhausted as last night, but there's something off about him. Like there's a weight that we can't see tied around his ankle.

"So," he says. "Madame Sarai. Who's going?"

Cass frowns. "All of us?"

He shakes his head. "No, you're not. The Madame doesn't like visitors on a good day and she doesn't care if you're gods or not."

My uncle shrugs. "Well, I'm the one with the favor."

"I'm related by blood to the one with the favor," I say, raising my hand.

I've never met a witch before. Like so many other things, I didn't think they were actually real.

"I wanna go," Roman says, beating Baxter to it.

My uncle laughs. "All right, you two, Griffin, and I think that's it. If we overwhelm her, she won't help us."

"That's so not fair." Baxter looks devastated.

Olivia taps his shoulder with her forehead. "There's always next time."

He rolls his eyes. "Is there though?"

Cass sits forward and grabs him by the shoulder. "Look, when else have you ever had unrestricted access to a demigod city?"

Finally, a slight smile tugs at the corner of Baxter's lips. "You know, I don't think I have."

"Exactly."

Alessia squeals. It's the most excited I've seen her look in a while. "There's a training center, right? And we can get in?"

"Don't break it." Griffin says, pointing a stern finger at her.

It might as well be white noise. Alessia races off without responding, a mischievous glint in her eye. Cherice laughs at the defeated look on Griffin's face.

"I'll keep an eye on them." she says.

After saying their goodbyes, my aunt leaves out with the rest of my friends in a buzzing frenzy of conversation. Griffin joins our party with a distrusting expression. It's the same one he had the other night, when Janus first mentioned the Madame. Like I said, I've never met a witch. I'm not sure what to expect.

"Are you gonna throw up?" Roman asks.

Griffin cuts impatient eyes at him. "Does it look like it?"

Roman shrugs. "Kinda."

He rolls his eyes and holds out his arms. "Whatever. Just grab on."

We latch onto his arms. In the next second, the Sacred House is washed out by a blaze of white light, and we're standing on the candy green lawn of what looks like a fairy cottage. Dense wood surrounds us in spirals of emerald trees. We're at the end of a cobblestone walkway, which marks a path to a rounded front door, cut from panels of oak. The house is corn yellow, with glittering, oval windows, and a drape of vinery sprawled across its bricks. The porch is overflowing with strange, bulb-like flowers, and the only one waiting for us is a fat, black cat, sleeping on his paws.

"So she's a hobbit," Roman says.

"You're disrespectful," Griffin says, but he's smiling. It fades quickly. "Okay, seriously. Be careful and pay attention."

"Is she also a thief?" I ask.

He laughs. "Very funny. Let's go."

Griffin leads us down the walkway, but we've barely crossed onto the porch when the door slowly creaks open. There's no one behind it.

Roman furrows his brows at me, but I just shrug. Smirking, my uncle strides forward, through the door, without another word. We follow him into the house's rounded foyer. The floor is a gleaming stretch of dark wood, with creme-colored walls rising to meet a high, carved ceiling. The house is flat and cozy, with the smell of baked cookies filling its walls. Strange flowers with glowing, purple bulbs and shards for teeth purr by the front door. Blue vines hang from the ceiling, curled around tiny orbs of white light. At the very end of the foyer, where the hall steps down into a rounded living room, waits a witch with flaming red hair.

Her skin is the color of dark mocha. She wears a long, black robe, cut low at the top, with splits running up her thigh on each side. There are crystals in her dark fishnets, and her thigh-high boots clack importantly as she comes to meet us.

"By the gods, to what do I owe such dazzling company?" she purrs. There's a pulsing glow in the middle of her green eyes. "Janus Johnson, I thought you'd forgotten about me."

My uncle smiles, something restrained in the set of his jaw. "Well, I'm sure that's what you were hoping, so I hate to be the bearer of bad news."

"Nonsense." Another glint in her eyes, this one with mischief. "I was hoping I'd see that pretty face again."

I narrow my eyes, staring between the two of them. Janus's expression has hardened, but the Madame has the hungry, alluring eyes of a housecat.

"You know Cherice sends her regards," is all he says.

Madame Sarai scoffs. "I have a rule about wives in my house, Janus. As long as you're in here, I won't hear about it."

"Then lucky we won't be here long," he says. "Remember Crete?"

Her expression falls flat, into something hot and bitter. She smiles, but her lips are strained. "Of course. I forget nothing."

"Cool. You owe me a favor. I've come to collect."

She looks around at the rest of us, thinking. Her eyes bore into me, green and vicious and calculating. She smirks, clicking her teeth.

"Oh, what a pickle you're in," she mutters. Her eyes widen pleasantly at the sight of Griffin, who still looks uneasy. "And hello, Stranger. You keep interesting company."

"Occupational hazard," Griffin answers simply.

Still smiling, she turns her eye on Roman. "You must be the Sea God." She lowers herself into a deep curtsy. "An honor to meet you, and a privilege to walk this Earth with you."

Roman looks uncomfortable, but he tries to smile. "It's just Roman, but thank you."

"You're adorable," she laughs, before turning her eyes on me.

A pinprick of light comes on in her left eye. She looks at me like she knows something, some secret or inside joke that I'll never be able to figure out. She lowers into the same deep curtsy as before, not taking her eyes off mine.

"Lord Zeus," she greets, her voice slithering. "Do forgive me for saying, but you're the spitting image of your mother."

I don't remember what I was going to say before. My mind goes blank. I've gotten used to people mentioning my father, but it's the first time anyone's ever told me that I look like my mother.

Janus clears his throat. "Are you gonna help us or not, Sarai?"

She taps her chin with a black-nailed finger and pretends to think. "I suppose, but first—tea! Come."

She turns in a whirl of spinning, black fabric and takes off into the living room. Griffin and my uncle exchange grudging looks before following her, leaving Roman and I with no other option but to do the same.

The living room is filled with incense smoke: frankincense and bergamot. Tapestries and fairy lights hang from the ceiling, and the walls are lined with rows of old book shelves. She gestures for us to sit on the long, black sofa; it feels like the cushions are trying to swallow me.

"One second," she muses, before disappearing into the kitchen.

The room is a haze of light and smoke. There's an acid green rug in the middle of the floor, right in front of the roughly cut coffee table. Huge crystals glitter in rows along a table on the far side of the room, next to a collection of mason jars.

Roman nudges me with his foot, pointing. "Is that an ear?"

I look closer, and sure enough, a pale, severed ear floats in a soup of chunky red fluid. "Why'd you make me look?"

"I'm sorry."

The Madame glides out of the kitchen with a silver platter suspended in the air, right above her open palm. She sweeps her hand in a graceful, downward gesture, and the platter lands on the table in front of us. With another flick of her wrist, a grand chair with red velvet upholstery appears in front of us. She eases into it and folds her legs.

"One second." She holds up both index fingers like a conductor and traces invisible lines over the table.

A silver pot moves on its own and fills five cups with steaming, black tea. Four arrange themselves in front of us, and the fifth floats into the Madame's waiting hand. Pleased with herself, she leans forward and dumps in four cubes of sugar.

"Help yourselves," she says.

Roman takes his tea black, but I fill mine with cream and sugar. Griffin and my uncle both opt out.

"To what do I owe the pleasure of your visit?" the Madame asks.

Janus tries to keep his expression pleasant. "Like I said, it's time to cash in on that favor."

Sarai rolls her eyes, but appears resigned. "Yes, yes, the favor. That's all you care about. It just better be good."

"We need to find the First Temple," Janus says.

She freezes with the tea cup at her lips, her eyes murky now. Something dark rolls over her shoulders, a storm cloud. She narrows her eyes at my uncle.

"What do you want with the First Temple?" she asks.

"That's my business. I just need to know where it is. I figured you could help." He gives her a pointed look, his eyes hardening.

She takes a thoughtful sip from her cup and sets it down gently. "Of course, I know where it is. I'm surprised you don't."

"And why is that?"

"Well, it's built in the honor of *your* ancestor, so I don't think it should be too much to expect you to know your own history." The mischievous light in her eyes returns. "The First Temple, literally, was the First Temple ever built in a god's name. Khaos was that god. It's as much a divine artifact as it is a place of worship."

"So how do we find it?" I ask.

"Not easily," she says. "You must cross the Uncrossed, which will be treacherous, even for you."

"What's that?" Roman asks.

Griffin looks pale. "Exactly what it sounds like. It's a place of monsters and death—you wouldn't find it on any map. You can't be serious."

"Oh I'm very serious," Sarai says. "And I can draw you a map, but I must warn you. The First Temple is bloody business. Whatever it is you're looking for—gods bless your poor souls."

"It doesn't matter if it's dangerous," I say. "We have to go."

The Madame smirks. I can't tell if her eyes are malicious or not. "Your mother's beauty and your father's courage—impeccable. Jason would be so proud."

Janus tenses beside me. I look from him to the Madame, at the invisible tether of history that unravels between them.

"How'd you know him?" I ask her. "And my uncle too."

She gazes ruefully at Janus. "They saved my life. That's why I'm doing this. Your uncle doesn't think I have a heart anymore. He hasn't for a long time. Guess I'm still trying to prove him wrong."

For a long time, it's quiet. Finally, Janus clears his throat.

"The map, Sarai. We need the map."

She waves her hand, and her teacup disappears. "Right."

I sip tea with a knot in my stomach as Sarai sets out a piece of parchment paper and bleeds over it. Her dark ichor forms lines along the page, carving a path that cuts through a vast, inky ocean. Griffin leans his head over the map, tracing its lines with his finger.

He scoffs and passes the map to my uncle. "It's on the other side of the water."

My uncle hisses, a shred of memory caught in his eyes. "Well, it could be worse." He tucks the map away and offers Sarai a hand. "Thank you. Our debt is done."

303

She winks at him. "Not hardly. If I didn't owe you any-thing I'd never see your face. So just consider this an act of kindness." She doesn't shake his hand.

"Right." With nothing else, he stands and starts heading for the door, leaving the spread of tea forgotten. Griffin bows at the Madame and stands too, which is our cue to leave. She clears her throat after we've just barely reached the foyer, something playful and wicked in her eyes.

"Ophelia." When she says my name, a millstone drops into my stomach.

"Your uncle believes I am cruel and unkind, but he's wrong." She casts a sardonic look at him. "So when you want to know more, you know where to find me."

"More about what?" I ask.

Green light flashes in her eyes. "Your destiny."

CHAPTER THIRTY-FOUR

It's a quiet walk back to the Sacred House's library, and I take each step like my shoes are full of cement.

All I can think about is my mother. As soon as I was old enough to understand, my father told me that our family only had two people: me and him. My mother left the day I was born, and she hadn't looked back. When I started middle school, I decided that I was going to find her myself. But there was only so much I could do as a kid, and of course, I learned that the hard way. Even with the entire internet and a nearly limitless supply of willpower at my disposal, it was impossible. My mother was committed to remaining a mystery. That was the year I learned not to pressure my dad to help either. Some things were just too painful for him, and he wanted nothing to do with it.

I got over it. From that point on, I'd embraced the fact that it was just my dad and me, and that was enough. Or at least I thought it was. I was fine with my mother being an empty shadow, something without a name or a face. She still doesn't have a name, but for the first time in my life, someone's told me I look like her. No one's ever done that. Not my aunt and uncle, not even my grandparents. In fact,

I don't remember anyone else but my father ever talking about her.

And the witch, the one who has some kind of history with my uncle.

The others make it to the library around the same time as we do. They're in considerably better spirits. Baxter and Alessia have been smeared in glittering gold paint, and Olivia has bundles of tiger lillies clustered in her hair. They're each wearing mauve togas, with rough leather sandals strapped around their feet. Cass has a triumphant light in his eyes that I haven't seen in weeks; the trail of smeared lipstick running along his collarbone must be why.

Cherice comes up behind them like a parent chasing their children at Disney World. Loose flower petals are scattered in her hair, and she looks exhausted.

"They're really fast," she huffs. "I mean they can never just walk. Always running, all the time."

"So it looks like you guys had fun," Griffin says, his observation blunt.

Baxter doesn't seem to notice. "This place is great. I say we just stay forever."

"Sorry. We're leaving tomorrow," I tell him and walk ahead into the library.

I drop my bag by the door and collapse into one of the chairs at the long, wooden tables. It feels like I'm going in circles.

The others file in and take seats around me. Already the light in Cass's eyes is fading. I almost feel bad.

"Wait, that was quick," Alessia says. "What's the catch?"

My uncle passes the map around the table, his expression murky. "That's where you need to go. As for the catch, you never know with Sarai."

Cass examines the map, tapping it with his index finger. "How do we get there? Can we jump?"

Griffin shakes his head. "Not directly to the First Temple. The port's guarded by the House of Demeter, but they'll let you through. I'll have the Commanders contact them. I hope you like sailing."

Alessia laughs, but stops when she realizes that he's serious. Her cheeks darken to a sickly shade of green. "Holy shit, you're serious."

"Are you afraid of boats, Alessia?" Griffin asks, a smirk tugging at his lips.

She throws up her hands. "I think it's perfectly reasonable. "

Roman laughs. "Wait, this is news to me. You're really afraid of the water?"

"What about Cisthene?" Olivia asks. "We were surrounded by water. And dead bodies."

"Yeah, but we weren't *on* the water," Alessia counters.

We all laugh, even though it's very serious to her. It feels good to laugh, almost as good as it feels to have a plan. It's bittersweet, but I just try my best to enjoy it.

We give ourselves a few days to prepare. I spend most of them consumed with thoughts of my mother. Even when I'm trying to focus on the Temple, or that strange ancestral power in my blood, she's always at the back of my mind.

I try not to sit still too long, even though I'm restless. One night, Griffin takes us out to explore the city. The Children of Athena lavish us in lillies and heavy gold coins. I'm reluctant. It feels counterproductive to pour any energy into recreational activities, but I quickly change my mind. The city is a cluster of glittering lights. People crowd around us, dressed in purple robes, with bundles of flowers and heavy baskets of loose drachma. The air pulses with plucky music, and the sweet perfume of incense and honey. The Children of Athena smear their hands in gold paint and reach out to touch us as we walk in a processional down the street. They're chanting voices rise over the music, their conviction an all consuming fire.

HAIL THE HOUSE OF OLYMPUS.

The next morning, it's back to business. Roman and I pack quickly as the sun rises to light the world. It's so early that the entire House is quiet. The only people out on the lawn are the guards and the children that have been training since summer.

Leaving this room is easier, even with my fond memories of the city. At first, letting go is like pulling teeth, but if you do it enough, eventually you can't feel it anymore. At least I hope it works like that.

We're the last ones to join the huddle at the base of the Polis's steps. My aunt and uncle are here too, dressed casually. Griffin's in his pajamas, still yawning into the heel of his hands.

"'Bout time," he mumbles, his voice nearly too thick to understand. "I can't go back to sleep until you leave."

"No one said you had to see us off," Cass says, smirking. "It almost sounds like you care about us."

"You should get your hearing checked," Griffin retorts, but there's no malice in his voice. "All right. You have the map, right?"

Baxter pulls it from the front pocket of his bag. "Check."

"What about emergency supplies?" Janus asks. "We don't really know what to expect from the river."

"Seems pretty obvious to me," Griffin mumbles.

My uncle ignores him. "Just always be prepared for anything. You never know what to expect."

"It's not us you should worry about, Mr. Johnson," Alessia says. I'd say the look on her face is smug, but there's something disturbed underneath it. "We killed the Sphinx. No problem."

Cass quirks an eyebrow. "No problem? I distinctly remember coughing up my own blood."

"You lived."

Cherice laughs. "I hear you guys. I do. Most divine children train their entire lives to be warriors, but it just comes to you naturally. It's impressive, but just be careful. Remember who we're dealing with."

"We will," Roman says. "We'll be fine. Just find something on Martin and get the council on our side."

Janus nods resolutely. "Makena comes back today. I've got something up my sleeve that I want to run past her. Just focus on the Codex. Without that, everything else is for nothing."

Griffin snorts. "No pressure. Break a leg."

I don't bother commenting that someone actually might.

Baxter scans the map again before shoving it back in his bag. We wave goodbye, and gather around Baxter's outstretched arms. The gold light in his corneas is brighter than the rising sun, but Griffin calls out to us just as the world begins to blur at its edges.

There's a single beam of silver light in his right eye, and he's looking at me.

"Ophelia," he says, his voice heavy with the thrum of prophecy. "Be clever. *Never let them take you.*"

A chill rolls down my spine. My mouth is dry as bone, but I force myself to nod. "I won't," I tell him.

With a bitter taste in my mouth, I hold on tight to Baxter's shoulder as the world falls away and a wall of inky blackness falls over everything. We're hurtling through a storm of empty air, so violent that it tears at my clothes. I can't even feel my own body, but I know something's wrong.

There's a musty, earthy stench in the air, which is moist and thick, like cold soup. An invisible wall of glass slams into my body, knocking the wind out of me. I'm thrown back so fast I can't even scream. Light and color slowly fill the darkness around me. As my back hits a hard deck, a dark gray sky takes shape above me. I can hear water rushing so violently it roars. Drops of cold rain splash over my face. And it smells like smoke.

I scramble to my feet and take in the smoldering island. Green fires rage defiantly beneath a gentle onslaught of rain. There are overturned chariots in the street, with snapped weapons scattered among the debris. I've learned to recognize the way death sets into a body. Even from here, at the edge of the dock, I can see piles of charred shapes, twisted in agony. A single flag remains untouched, flapping violently from the hollow roof of a building: corn yellow, marked with the flaming, black shape of a cornucopia.

"We're too late," Cass hisses, tearing at his hair.

He's staring out over the dock, toward the river, where flaming ships disappear in a haze of thick, gray fog. The river is so wide that I can't see what's across it, or what's on the other side of its long, snaking spine. It disappears around the jutted edge of the island, into a blurred landscape of harsh cliff sides.

Baxter tries to control his breathing, but I don't think it works. "There's no way. Only four other people knew we'd be coming here. We haven't left the House in days. They couldn't have possibly . . ."

But he doesn't finish his sentence.

Alessia's jaw twitches. It looks like she could spit fire. "That witch. The one who gave us the map. Griffin said we couldn't trust her. We can't even trust the Council of Demigods, and their own people are dying."

A horrible thought comes to me. "The Commanders knew, too."

Cass shakes his head. "Yeah, because they *wanted* us to come here. They asked for our help. That doesn't make any sense."

Olivia disappears into the village in a streak of silver light. She's back in seconds, clutching a scrap of fabric. The symbol stitched in white thread is an arrow's head, stained with ichor.

She swears and crumbles the scorched fabric. "If they did this to the island then they're probably already on the water. At this point, we can assume they know what they're doing, and we already know what they want."

"They're not far." Roman says. He's crouched at the edge of the pier, with his fingers swirling in the water. "This is salt water, so I can track them. If the city's still on fire, then they haven't been gone long. They're only an hour away from here."

A light flicks on in Baxter's eyes. "This thing's like 6,000 miles long. We could beat them there."

Alessia scoffs. "How? We can't jump across the river, and they burned all the boats."

And then, while I'm thinking about how to reverse the impossible, Roman dives headfirst into the water. I'm moving before I can even call out to him. I get as close to the edge as

I can, with my face just inches above the river. It's so thick and murky that I can't see through it, but something with a silver, knife-like fin gets close enough to the surface to break it.

I jerk back, yelping. A second later, a hulking shadow cuts through the fog. I scramble back as it gets closer, until the odd shadow sharpens into the massive, glistening body of a ship. Plumes of black smoke rise from the crest of the bow, but the ship is mainly intact. Two heavy white sails dangle from the mast, full of wind. The hand-painted eyes decorating the ship's hull are smeared with ash and stare out with an empty kind of malignance.

The ship moves so fast I'm afraid it won't stop. At the last second, Roman soars out of the water like a swan. He lands on his feet right in front of me, clutching a frayed rope. Despite having just emerged from the river, he's completely dry.

"We have a boat," he says, proud of himself.

I'm staring at him in awe. For a second, I'm scared my jaw is hanging. "You're insane."

"I solve problems. I'm a problem solver." He shrugs, but the blush in his cheeks is telling. "Come on."

CHAPTER THIRTY-FIVE

OUR SHIP CUTS THROUGH THE RIVER like a blade's serrated edge.

Roman commands the bow, his hands cast over the water as Baxter mans the helm. We're moving fast. Wind fills the sails in dramatic gusts, and the world streaks by in smears of black and gray. From this distance, I can't even see the island anymore. Somehow, the stench of blistering flesh sticks with me.

I'm perched on the rim of the ship's edge, staring ahead into the river's open face. Olivia crouches on the other side, a bag of silver arrows flung over her back. Alessia and Cass patrol the deck, their armor wet with ocean spray. Nearly an hour has passed, and the only ships we've seen were the burning carcasses the Scions left. Their shapes were quickly swallowed up by the fog.

I hook my legs over the ship's edge and watch the water churn by beneath me. In my favorite memory of my grandfather, we were on a river but it was nothing like this. The water stretched out on all sides of us like a glittering plate of smooth glass. Our boat glided across like it didn't want to disturb any of the sleeping life forms below. The memory changes shape a lot. Sometimes that sky is clear and blue in my mind. Sometimes it's a vortex of gold clouds, caught up in a glorious sunrise. I can never remember how early we used to go out there.

Back then, the most exciting thing I knew about my grandfather was that he had been a Marine. He was a large, broad-shouldered man up until the day he died. His sons would inherit his strength, and the rich, mocha of his skin. They got their dark hazel eyes from their mother though. My grandfather's were deep and black, like twin abysses.

I find myself thinking about the last picture of him I saw. He was nothing like the gentle guide that taught me how to bait a hook or reel in a catch without slipping on the deck. In that photobook, he looked like a warrior. His sword wasn't much different than mine, and he held it like he meant to challenge heaven. As much as I'd have liked to know him, I'll never get to meet that man.

We sail so far and so long the silence calcifies around us. There's only the dull gurgle of water as the ship cuts through the river, and then the light pattering of rain. It's only mid-morning now, but the sky is a dark, ominous gray. If it weren't for the restless tension aching in my joints, it might be beautiful. Like how a cemetery is beautiful sometimes.

"Yo, how far out are we?" Cass calls from the deck. His armor is gone. He sits with his elbows resting on his knees.

Roman hasn't lost his statuesque focus. Sea green light casts spotlights over his face as he guides the ship. "Not far. There's something up ahead. On the water."

He doesn't elaborate, but his warning is clear enough. I slowly ease out of my sitting position and settle into a crouch. Perched on the edge of the ship, I can see how staggering mountains rise in the distance. Strips of dark trees smudge along the river's embankment, tearing violently in the wind. Things with fins and tooth-like tails bob against the surface of the water, but none of them get close to the ship. For Uncrossed waters, I'd say we're doing pretty all right.

For a second, the fog thickens into a dense wall ahead of us. I peer into it, but I can't see anything else. The sky darkens with the sun's disappearance, and the only major light comes from the search towers in Roman's eyes.

"Shit," Olivia hisses, her shape cut out by the silver glow of her armor.

And then, just as Roman tenses, the fog thins into silver ribbons. A dark shape cuts through—a hulking ship, charging ahead on the water. At least forty people are crowded onto its deck, each wearing suits of black armor. There are more in the masts, wielding flaming green arrows. Their boat looks like ours: double masted, with hand-drawn eyes staring darkly from the hull. A tattered yellow flag hangs in the wind, its black cornucopia smudged by ash and dirt.

I know they see us. As soon as we're close enough to make out the Scions in the yards, the ship puts on a jolt of speed.

"Faster," I call to Roman and our ship lurches forward.

Water rises on either side of the bow in foaming white walls. The distance between our ship and theirs shrinks, despite their desperate speed. The air splits. A volley of flaming arrows sail toward our deck like falling stars. Baxter and Olivia answer in kind, dispatching the arrows before they can meet us.

Someone shouts orders on the other ship. Metal groans as long canons glide out through slats in the ship's polished hull. Armor melts over my body, charged and buzzing with the frenzy of lightning.

315

A second later, the first rounds of cannons fire at our ship. Roman jerks the wheel to the left, violently. Bombs sail past the ship's mast, exploding in the sea behind us. Jets of water knock our ship around and I nearly plummet into the water below.

Metal groans again. We're close enough now that I can hear the order to reload. I hold my hand out, but I'm not reaching for lightning. Instead, I focus on each plank of wood in the ship's body. The thick cotton of the sails, the ancient iron bolts holding its boards in place. I feel them all in my hands, hot and frenzied, like the atoms are squirming in my skin.

"Ophelia, get down," Roman shouts. "I'm pulling it."

"No," I call. "Get in closer."

"What?"

Thick heat builds in my stomach.

"Are you insane?" He shouts.

Another volley of cannons comes hurtling toward us. Roman jerks the ship, exposing its left-hand side to a wave of devastation. Olivia fires six arrows from her bow. They explode in showers of silver sparks on contact, incinerating the cannon fire to ash. Baxter loads six more in his own bow and aims them at the ship's hull.

"Wait," I shout, because the heat in my hand has built into a fire.

The Scions advance. There are dozens of them, and they all have the same hungry eyes. A stocky girl with long red hair shouts for another load, and archers behind her set green fire to the tips of their arrows.

"Ready?" The girl calls.

Violet globs of plasma gather around the ship in a pulsing web of matter, pinching the air. I clench my hand into a fist, and the ship craters in on all sides. The pulsing webs bite into the hull, chewing up thick boards of wood. The double masts split right down the middle, and then again into splinters. Scions scream as their ship erupts into a mushroom cloud of purple flame. The force of the explosion sends a tide of rushing water toward our ship, nearly tipping us over. A wall of water rises right in front of me, swallowing the destruction whole. What's left behind is the quiet, rippling surface of the river and a soup of charred debris.

Roman gazes up at me in what has to be a mixture of fear and awe.

"Since when could you do that?" He asks.

I hop down from the ship's perch and land flat footed on the deck. "It's complicated. I just had to see if I could do it again."

"And what exactly was that?" Baxter's still gaping in shock at the floating pile of debris.

"It's how I wounded Somnus," I tell them. "I think it's because of Khaos, but I'm not sure. I'm still figuring it out."

Alessia whistles, looking impressed. "It's like the air just crushed in on itself. I'd hate to be on the wrong end of that."

I look down at my hands. Heat prickles in my fingers. I feel each wet molecule of the river. The particles that compose our ship's hulking structure. Each buzzing bulb of matter in the air, clouds, and mountains. A second later, the heat trickles out of my palms. I feel nothing.

Eventually, the debris and rubble that used to be a Scion ship is swallowed by fog.

We sail in silence through a world that grows steadily more gray. Thick black clouds hang low above us, blocking out the sunlight. The water churns violently as wind rushes in swooping gales. Thankfully, the waves calm under Roman's outstretched palm. He doesn't speak much. When he does, his voice is heavy and low, like he doesn't want to disturb the water.

It gets so dark that I can't see anything in front of me. Olivia and Alessia disappear below the ship's deck and return with a dozen kerosene lamps. We string them all over the ship, but the light is a meager effort. The trees surrounding us sway like a wall of dark shadow. If I stare too closely, the shadows grow talons and teeth and faces.

For a while I stay up front with Roman, crouched on the edge of the ship. I watch the empty fog around us for danger, and he cuts wary glances at me. When I can't stand the silence anymore, I step down into the deck to sit on milk crates with Cass and Olivia. She reads an old, leather bound volume by the light of her own glowing irises. Cassius crouches over the edge of the ship with his bident, watching as scaled creatures ghost the surface of the water.

"Do you think Artemis hunted everything she was supposed to?" I ask, not really sure why. "You know, before she died?"

Olivia's eyes pulse like quasars. "No. There are still things to hunt. There always will be." She sniffs in the dark, but I can't read her expression. "It's a shame."

"How can you know for sure?

She shrugs. "Nothing's in the water, but there are things out there. Hungry, bloodthirsty things. Evil things. I can feel them, like a sixth sense. When we went to that museum, as soon my feet hit the ground I got this wave of dread. The same thing happened at the school that day. I get it now, but I wish I could've figured it out earlier."

She goes back to her book, and I join Cass at the ship's starboard side. He's perched on the rim of the boat, his bident long and glowering above the water. Something with a six-foot tail and two metallic wings folded against its body goes whizzing beneath the river's surface. It disappears, or so I think. Cass lowers his spear and strikes the water. A shudder rocks the ship, sending violent ripples through the river. I have to steady myself against the wall, but Cass keeps his balance as he pulls his spear back. Clearly, he's pleased with himself.

The oddly translucent creature hangs limply from Cass's spear, its massive, silver eyes foggy now. Gray blood drips down the spear from a gash in the creature's chest, where the spear has gone through its heart. I don't want to call it a fish, even though its scaled body shimmers in the weak lamplight. Its tail, which is only a few feet shorter than Cass's spear, flails in the wind like a listless flag. Webbed wings dangle from its back, glittering in sheets of rainbow.

Olivia retches. "What the hell is that thing?"

It looks like a melting fairy with tiny, clawed stubs for fingers. "Cass, that's disgusting."

"I think it's cute." Cass frowns down at the creature. "I wasn't trying to kill it though. I was aiming for its tail."

Roman calls out from the bow. "I need light."

A vague silhouette cuts across the sky ahead. A dark, hulking shape, its outline layered like a cluster of mountains.

"Got it," Baxter shouts.

A dozen gold arrows sail across the sky, bulbs of light pulsing in their blades. All twelve of them explode into showers of supernova. White light races across the entire world, rinsing it clean of the fog and dark clouds. The noon sun and a clear blue sky are all that remains.

"Ah, shit! I overdid it," Baxter says, scratching his head.

With no more fog or shadows, it's impossible to miss the empty, pebbled shore looming ahead. The river banks against a beach of dingy white stones, before smoothing into rough, yellow sand. The beach is a thin strip along miles of empty land, and then everything gets swallowed up into a cluster of dark forest. Beyond that, black mountains hang in the sky, tipped white with snow.

Roman steers the ship to a smooth stop at the river bank. He drops the anchor, and we make land. As soon as my feet hit the ground, the same heat from before erupts in my chest. Purple light snakes beneath my skin, curling up along my wrists and throat. The island goes quiet, and all I can hear is the sound of my own beating heart.

I'm staring into the sand. It dances and swirls in front of me, even though the wind is mild. A fissure bites into the earth, and a pit opens up at our feet. A set of iron stairs leads down into absolute darkness. I gaze into the pit and the pit gazes into me.

"I have to go in," I say, my voice low.

The heat in my chest is a crackling campfire. Each of the island's atoms sits in the middle of my palm.

"Okay," Roman says, his voice wary. "Lead the way."

I take the first few steps into the pit. Walls of pure shadow rise around me, like the earth is swallowing me, and the world is falling away. It takes a few seconds to realize that the earth really *is* swallowing me. My friends shout my name as sand closes over my head. I try to run back, but my feet are rooted in place. The shadows swallow me, and the sun disappears.

The same cold hand that gripped me when I was wearing the Eye takes hold of me now. Through the darkness and shadow, down each iron step, until finally I'm standing in the belly of a gulping, dimly lit cave. Slick walls of black stone rise all around me, inlaid with shreds of jade, ruby, and amethyst. The jewels glitter against a weak flood of torchlight. Lanterns line the long hallway in front of me, which leads to the fractured steps of a gray temple.

Dread still rips through me, but I step into the temple anyway. Even with that cold hand at my back, I'm sure this isn't a dream. My feet swish roughly against the battered stone. When I run my hands over shards of stained glass, they cut my fingers. Something terrible happened here. Gold statues of an armored woman are overturned on each floor of the temple, some of them sliced right down the middle. Every altar I see is defiled with sickly splatters of ichor. There are weapons at every turn, some destroyed, some simply forgotten.

Finally, on the third floor, in the very last room, I see it. In real life, the room of golden treasures glitters like a million suns. There are piles of gold cups, plates, and silverware. Open chests of glittering drachma and racks of gold weapons: swords, arrows, and spears. I follow a red carpet to the altar at the front of the room, which is not so magnificent in comparison.

Ichor and black blood stain the white ribbons that dangle from the altar. The bronze bowls of spices and offerings have been burned and turned over. There's an inscription carved right into the altar's wood:

IN THE NAME OF HE WHO HUNGERS.

It's the book in the middle of the altar that has my attention. It's a modest black volume, bound in moleskin. A bulky black chain binds its pages.

A familiar voice settles in, soft as a church mouse.

"Lightning God, take that which you seek."

I recognize my ancestors voice within a command that can only mean one thing: I've found it. Finally.

As soon as I touch the book, the cold hand yanks me away. Out of the room of treasures. Away from the defiled Temple. Through the rushing darkness and back onto land, where my back hits the beach so hard it knocks the wind out of me. I gasp, shocked at how full the air is up here. I hadn't noticed how thin it got the closer I was to the Temple.

My friends swarm me, talking at the same time. Their voices tangle together so bad it makes my head hurt. I hold my hand up to stop them and feel the full weight of the Codex in my lap. It's still bound in those heavy, black chains.

I was half afraid that I'd imagined everything, but this book is real. As real as the salty water crashing to shore.

Alessia doesn't just pump her fist and start shouting like a crazy person. She jumps to her feet and runs along the beach's thin strip shouting like a crazy person. Cass and Baxter join her, while Olivia shakes my shoulders. Under the brightness of a new sun, on the other side of the Uncrossed Waters, we celebrate in earnest for the first time.

Back at the Sacred House, meeting with the commanders is bittersweet.

Roman tells them about the Children of Demeter and the destruction the Scions levied against their village. A moment of silence lingers in the room. How many demigods have been killed by Scions so far? How many Cursed Children? I don't like thinking about the number. It makes me feel sick.

Still, sickness or not, the cause for celebration is right in front of me. The Codex isn't as big or grand as I thought. I'd imagined one of the beautiful, velvet bound volumes they have in the Sacred House's library. This one is just plain and black; the only spectacular thing about it is the chain that keeps it closed.

"Well done," Makena says. "I'm deeply grateful for the effort you've all put in. Truly. I know this hasn't been easy, but this would never have happened without you."

"Now I think we might just stand a chance," says Minister Fueves. "At this point, we can contact an ambassador of the Firstborn and arrange an exchange. Once the Fates are secure, we can kill the Firstborn."

My uncle frowns. "How do we know they won't just send more Scions? Or that they won't be one step ahead of us? Very proud of everyone, but this almost went the other way."

"Janus is right," Cherice says. "The Codex is really our only advantage. We still don't know why they want it, or how they always seem to know what our moves are. We need to be careful."

The minister bristles with impatience. "If anyone should know the answer to that, I'd think it was you."

Cherice narrows her eyes. "Actually, we've got plants on everyone in Martin's circle right now. They don't know they're being watched so they'll slip. When they do, we'll have everything we need on him."

Minister Fueves tenses, but says nothing.

"Excellent," the General says, her tone landing with authority despite her smile. "We need to move forward, because as long as the Fates are with the Firstborn, the whole world is at stake. That doesn't mean we have to be foolish.

Tonight everybody get some rest. Then take the next few days to come up with a plan. I'd like to hear it before the week ends."

After she's said her piece, the General bows in parting and leaves with a flank of her Commanders. It's like all the tension goes out of the room, and everybody collapses in their chairs. Roman tears through his hair. He watches the Codex with apprehension and awe.

"All that fuss over one little book," he says.

Griffin scoffs, his eyes piercing. He sits forward like he's thinking about touching the book but changes his mind. Instead, he looks at me, smiling.

"Whatever happened to those Scions anyway?" He asks. "They're not still out there, right?"

I shake my head, remembering how the explosion had nearly capsized our own ship.

"Of course not," I tell him. "They've gone to be with their gods."

CHAPTER THIRTY-SIX

THE CHILDREN OF ATHENA ARE HUNGRY for war.

I'm not sure how fast it usually takes things to spread around here, but by midmorning the next day, the mood on the grounds has drastically shifted. The Sacred House flies six, mauve banners high, displaying the ugly, severed head of Medusa. Troops run drills on the lawn and flyers balance on horseback as they practice flinging arrows from the sky. The world outside is a muffle of orders and marching feet. Metal too—swords clang as soldiers spar, and silver arrows sail home to their straw targets.

Janus and Cherice left the morning after our trip through the Uncrossed. My guess is that wherever he is, Council Magistrate Martin is in a lot of trouble.

I don't focus too much on him though. I spend most of my time in the Polis, either in the library or conference room. One night, Baxter and I sit with our heads bent over a drawing of six stick figures, leading a horde of hastily drawn smudges. It's supposed to be battle schematics, but neither one of us is actually any good at drawing things. The idea is simple enough—the Sacred House will amass as many soldiers as they can, and we'll lead them into the Cisthene.

When I'm not agonizing over battle schematics, I'm outside on the lawn. Ever since I stepped into the First Temple, that ancestral heat returns with more ease. I feel it bubbling up beneath the lightning in my blood, spreading through me like a vicious serum. Demigods arrange straw targets in front of me, over and over. I spend hours pulling on the part of me that comes from Khaos. It answers in destructive force each time.

Despite all that, it's not Khaos's power or even the idea that we could face the Firstborn soon that eats at me. It's not even the strange, searching look Griffin gives me whenever we're both in a room at the same time. It's the book, and the muffled power that lurks in its bound pages.

Every night I stare into the book's cover, wondering what kind of secrets it conceals. There are no clues, no blurbs or summaries. I don't bother searching the internet; I know that would only disappoint me. I've gone through the library twice, but there's no mention at all of any kind of Codex. Even after all this time, it's still a mystery.

I'm in the library this morning, nursing a cup of tea. I sit with my father's journal, going over the page about Kreos. I can't forget the inscription I'd seen on that altar: *In the name of He Who Hungers.* I hate that my father hadn't written more about him. Or anybody for that matter. Killing the Firstborn seems easy, but the God of Hunger is an even bigger mystery than the Codex.

The door opens and Cass steps into the library with a long piece of parchment paper.

"What's up?" He sits across from me and spreads the page out across the table.

"Hey." I gesture absentmindedly. "What's that?"

"Articles of the Dead," he says. "I found it in here yesterday. I thought I might've been too tired or something but it really is just a list of names, old names."

He starts listing them and a cold chill slithers into my stomach. He shudders too before stopping, so I know I'm not just imagining it.

"That's bad news," I tell him.

He shrugs, grimacing, and pushes the paper away. "I don't know. It's not connected to the Firstborn at all. The byline says that whoever these people are, they're sealed under the authority of Hades."

"As in *you* Hades or *Hades* Hades?"

"I don't know," he says. "The book I found it in was about the Underworld. I was reading about the Pit."

"The Pit?"

He sits back in his chair, trying to relax. "You know the story about the Titans? How Zeus chopped Cronus up into a bunch of tiny, fun-sized pieces?"

"Oh that Pit." I nod. "Yeah. My dad told me the story a few times. Bedtime stories."

"That's one hell of a bedtime story," he says. "Anyway, the Articles of the Dead were just folded up in the book. It doesn't seem related to anything."

I wag my finger at him. "Those words are a curse, Cass."

"Yeah, I know," he laughs. "Famous last words."

The library door opens again, and Griffin sweeps in, wearing a set of black robes. These make him look official, like he's the kind of person you want to stand up straight around. Of course, Cass doesn't bother.

"'Morning," he greets.

Griffin bobs his head at him before turning to me.

"Ophelia, your uncle and aunt should be back later tonight. Apparently, they've got something."

"That's good," but there's a lump in my throat, because he's looking at me like he's seeing something else.

He shakes his head, trying to clear it. "Also, both of you, the General wants to meet tonight. She wants a final work up of the plan."

"Sounds good," Cass nods. He tilts his head. "What's with the face?"

Griffin frowns, his eyes troubled. "I've got this feeling. I don't know, it's weird."

Cass tries to sound undisturbed. "You seem like the kind of guy who gets weird feelings a lot."

Exasperated, Griffin rolls his eyes and starts walking toward the door. "Whatever. We're meeting at eight tonight," he says. "Don't be late."

My aunt and uncle get back a little after dinner. A snow-storm rolled in a few days ago, and it won't leave. Thick flurries fly around my face as I cross the lawn to meet them. They're both dressed in all black, with heavy coats over their robes. When they left, they looked like they were going for a trek through the surrounding woods. Now, they look like a pair of assassins. Assassins who smile when they see me.

Despite their grim attire, they both seem to be in good spirits. Cherice pulls me in for a hug, her body heat feverish. The lanterns burning along the House's gate make her eyes unusually bright. Either that, or she's really in that good of a mood.

"Be honest, if you two had been cloned by bodysnatchers, would you tell me?" I ask, raising one of my eyebrows.

My uncle laughs. It's a good hearty laugh, one that carries all the best notes of my father's. For a second, I'm imagining the two of them as boys, laughing together, like everything around them would go on forever.

"Seriously," I say, willing the image away, "what's going on? You two are smiling, and I thought you forgot how to do that."

"We just met with all our contacts," Janus says. "Most of Martin's men are too smart to slip, but apparently his assistant isn't. He's a young kid, barely older than you. One of my guys tapped his phone. Apparently the kid had a friend who died on the Uncrossed. Yesterday, he makes a call to somebody, crying about how guilty he feels for lobbying against Makena when he knew what Martin was about to let happen. He was vague enough, but we got the gist."

"Damn. Who was he calling?" I ask.

Cherice shrugs. "We don't know yet. We're having the number traced, so we should have a name by tonight."

"Great, because the General wants a final work up of the plan," I tell them. "I'm actually headed to the meeting now."

They walk with me across the lawn, on either side of me. I never get used to how impossible this is. For months, they were sworn to keep this part of themselves a secret. Now, we walk in the same world, side by side, and it occurs to me that this isn't a new world at all. It's the world I always should've been part of. Who might I have been if I grew up knowing that magic was real, and more importantly, that it lived in my blood?

"So," my uncle says, "how are you feeling? I know you're not familiar with our customs yet, but most kids don't get opportunities like this. The days of the quest are long gone."

"Seriously?" I ask.

He nods. "In ancient times, most people who took a quest didn't survive to see it through. People wanted their kids to stop dying, so the Council established an age limit—nineteen and up only, and it had to be approved by a special committee. Under ordinary circumstances, this would've gone up the ladder a long time ago." He says it with a painful edge of regret to his voice. I look away, trying to hide the shadow that falls across my face. "That's what should've happened."

"But these aren't ordinary circumstances," I tell him. "Griffin came to us personally because the Council is too corrupt to fight its own battles. And before that, Zeus himself gave me his power. They killed my dad. This is my quest, Uncle Janus. It was always going to be."

"I know." He says it like it's the saddest thing in the world, "I know you're right, and I know you're strong. I get that before it seemed like I didn't know that, but even then, I promise you, I've always known. And it's not just because you're Jason's daughter. Your strength—your courage and defiance—those are all you."

My eyes sting, but I won't cry. I squeeze my uncle's shoulder as I hold back the tears. "Thanks Uncle Janus. That really means a lot to me."

"It's the truth," Cherice says. Her eyes glisten like mine. "Lord Zeus was the King of Olympus, the most powerful god in his Pantheon. I believe you inherited his powers for a reason, and you're proving it everyday."

When we make it to the conference room, everyone else is already here, except for the General herself. My aunt and uncle sit on the right side of the table. I sit on the left, between Roman and Olivia. He slides his foot around mine and taps the toes of his sneakers against my ankle. I pat his thigh, trying to smile. Janus's words are still loud in my mind, instilling a sense of pride that makes it hard to swallow.

"You okay?" Roman murmurs, just loud enough for only me to hear.

I squeeze his leg. When I smile, I feel more tears welling up in my eyes. "I'm great."

This time, I know he believes me.

Makena's wearing slacks and a white blouse today, with her hair pulled into a tight bun behind her head. She sits at the end of the table and calls the meeting to order with a pleasant smile.

Janus and Cherice give the same report they gave me at the gates. I expect the General to look pleased. I'm not prepared for the deep sadness that rolls across her face.

"I certainly had my suspicions, but I guess I hoped they weren't really true," she says. "Martin and I actually have quite a long history together. I'm not sure why he'd do this."

"Now that I think about it, it does seem strange," Cherice says. "Aside from the fact that there's no way he could've gotten away with it, why would a demigod ally with the Firstborn anyway, especially against his own interests? It's bothering me."

The Lieutenant shakes her head, disappointed. "What could a demigod possibly gain by siding with the Firstborn? It just doesn't make sense."

Baxter jumps in. "You know, there's something else I don't get. There was only one way to know where the First Temple was, and we're the only ones who had the Eye. Yet, there were Scions on the water and they were ahead of us; they knew where they were going and they knew how to get there."

"I'm telling you. It was the Witch," Alessia says. "She's the only other person, aside from the people in this room, who knew where we were going."

Cherice grimaces. "Look, I'm never one to take up for Sarai, but she just wouldn't do that. Scions killed her mother. She hates them as much as we do."

"So who did it?" Olivia throws up her hands. "This is bigger than just the Council of Houses. None of us have had any direct contact with anybody on the Council, aside from Mr. and Mrs. Johnson. Even if they're watching us, even if they're corrupt, somehow, someone's getting information directly from us to them."

"So what are you saying?" Minister Fueves asks, his eyes sharp like flint.

"I'm saying you have a leak, Minister." Olivia jabs a finger into the table. "You have a leak *here*, in this House. I can't see any other way that this makes sense."

The Minister turns green. His hand trembles as he dries the sweat on his forehead. "I must confess that that's deeply unsettling. I couldn't imagine anybody in this House selling out to the enemy. It's unconscionable."

Janus sets his jaw. "Then it's a good thing we're tracing that call. By tonight, we'll know exactly who's doing this and they'll pay for it. I promise that."

"Thank you, Janus. Thank you, Cherice. I appreciate all you've done toward this effort. It's overwhelming," the General says. She clears her throat. "So, the Operation. How do we precede?"

"We've asked the Firstborn for an exchange at Cisthene," Minister Fueves says. "Should they agree, we'll send an unassuming convoy ahead to confirm the Fates's presence."

Alessia reaches down and pulls a stack of papers out of her backpack. There's an air of importance in the set of her shoulders and the way she speaks. "At that point, Baxter and Olivia will be in charge of extracting the Fates as soon as possible. After we confirm the Fates's evacuation, Cass, Roman, Ophelia, and I will jump an army to Cisthene." She sets the papers down, pleased with herself. "Then, the Firstborn will die."

A fire burns in each fiber of my body. The Firstborn are entitled to a single prize, a single future—death. It is certain.

After the meeting ends, my friends make plans to celebrate in the city. I'm too tired, so I tell them to go ahead without me. When I vanish, I take refuge in the still silence of my room.

It's not really my room. The bags in the left corner belong to Roman. We share this bed every night, and I've gotten used to the feeling of another warm body beside me. Roman is good, solid ground. You could build a house on it, and the waves would never wash it away. It would never disappoint you. That's just how he is.

My mind races, so I take a shower. I find peace beneath the warm spray of the water, so I just stand there. Even with all the certainty and confidence, peace is hard to come by. I'm becoming increasingly sure that my only future is at the hilt of a sword. I'm not sure how to feel about it. On the one hand, this blade—this life of battle and blood—is my birthright. On the other, I know how far my father went to escape this life. Does walking this path defile his memory, or is it the only sure way to honor it with any kind of justice?

I turn the shower off and wrap my body in a towel. Roman's back in the room, sitting on the bed. He tries to squirm out of his shirt, but it appears to be fighting back. I laugh as he tugs blindly.

He sighs. "This is ridiculous."

"Incredibly. Hold still." I stand between his knees and gently tug the shirt over his head.

It tousles his hair as it falls away, leaving it in wild, over-grown locks. His eyes are bright and curious, like he's seeing me for the first time.

"Thank you," he says, hooking his hands around the back of my knees.

I shuffle closer and take hold of his shoulders. I feel hard muscle beneath layers of soft skin. Baxter healed our injuries, but the long gash down his arm is still a thin white scar. There are more scars too, scattered along his collar bone, across the top of his right shoulder. I trace a line down the strong slope of his jaw with my finger, laser focused.

He tenses beneath my hand before scooping me into his lap. My legs straddle his waist.

"We should go somewhere," he says, his voice low and broken, "after this is all over."

I tangle my fingers in his hair. "Yeah? Where?"

"Anywhere," he shrugs. "Wherever you want. I'd go anywhere."

"Hmm," I pretend to think. "I've never been to Ohio."

He laughs and tugs me closer, his hands on my hips now. "Okay, we'll go to Ohio. Then Italy and Aruba. Maybe Greece. Let's go everywhere."

"You don't want to finish high school?" I ask him. "What about college?"

"Well, before all this, I didn't really know what I wanted my life to be, but now I do." His hands slide up to my waist. "I figured it out that night, when you were talking about justice. They've hurt so many people—brought so much suffering—and we can make them pay for it. That's why we have these powers, so that's what I'm gonna do. I don't know if that counts as purpose, but I have a choice, so that's what I choose."

He tugs me even closer. "And then, when that's done, when it's really over, I just want to be with you. I don't care where we go—not really. As long as you're there, I'm there."

Warmth bubbles in my chest. His eyes are bright and enchanted, as clear as the blue water I leapt into the day we met. "Even if it's just Cincinnati?"

"Yes, even if it's just Cincinnati. I mean it—anywhere." He leans forward and presses a kiss to my chin. "You're so beautiful. I'd follow you anywhere."

The only thing between us is this towel wrapped around my body. I can feel the warmth of his hands and chest, pressing against me. His lips trace a light path from my jaw to my collarbone. They sprawl across my chest, as his hands slide beneath the towel, exploring the bare skin along my back. For the first time today, my mind goes blank, and I find how incredibly easy it is not to care about the Fates, or the Firstborn, or that goddamn book.

I take his face in my hands, kissing him. He falls back on the mattress, and I fall with him. He grazes cool fingertips along my thighs, up and down the slope of my spine. I plant both hands in the mattress to deepen the kiss, but there's no such thing as close enough.

He mumbles something against my mouth—my name—before flipping us over. His weight against my body sends me into a frenzy. I ghost my hands across the waistband of his jeans. It takes him two seconds to tug them off, tossing them to the side.

My legs circle his waist like I'm trying to keep him grounded to the earth. His hips move against mine, and my whole body goes weak. There might be evil and darkness lurking all around us—crouching in the shadows, just out of sight—but there's no place for any of that here. Here, in the infinitesimal space between us, there's only skin and warmth. His body against mine, my name on his lips. These plumes of desire burning through me like an unquenchable fire.

He says my name again, trying to sound more steady.

"Is this okay?" He asks, his pelvis resting against mine.

I nod. "Mm-hmm." It's not at all the intelligent response I'm going for.

He laughs and bends down to kiss me again. His breath is heavy and desperate in my ear as the mattress jerks beneath us. I unravel like a blooming flower at the tender mercy of the winds around it.

CHAPTER THIRTY-SEVEN

I'm dreaming about fields of fresh flowers, a clear-eyed sun, and miles and miles of skin.

It's a good dream, probably the best one I've had in months. All the others have been filled with cruel shadows and monsters with bloodied teeth. I like the change of pace, and the idea that in a dream this pleasant, I might catch a glimpse of Roman's face.

Then, all I hear is shouting. Distant and urgent, like it's on the other side of a wall.

I wake up to Roman shaking my shoulders, the harsh light of a lantern cast over his face. When I went to sleep, he was soft and open, like I could run my hands through him with no resistance. Now, all the tense lines of his face are drawn tight. His hair is wild from sleep, and a pair of sweatpants hangs low on his hips.

"Ophelia!" Finally, his voice sharpens into focus, rousing something deep in my chest.

"What happened?" I mutter, my head still foggy.

I look around the room for some sign of danger, but all I see is what's always been there. His clothes are piled on one side of the bed, my towel forgotten on the other.

"Something's happening outside," he says. "We have to go."

No sooner than he says it, a devastating explosion sounds outside. The Polis rattles so hard it feels like I'll fall out of bed.

"Shit." At least now I'm awake. I slide out of bed, taking one of the sheets with me to wrap around my body. "What was that?"

He shakes his head and starts kicking out of his pants. "Come on, Lia. We gotta go."

We dress quickly in the dim light of the room. I nearly trip over my own feet as I tug on my shoes. We're both heading for the door when another explosion sounds, this one right on top of us. I shout Roman's name just as the ceiling caves in. The floor gives beneath my feet. I slip and curl in on myself as chunks of stone and glass fall like rain.

A black sky emerges above me, lit with thin strands of moonlight.

I think I'm dead. I only ever feel this sense of displacement when I jump, and I'm sure I didn't jump. I have no body—no voice or hands. Not until the slate of shadow above me splits down the middle, revealing Roman's smudged face and a sea of rubble.

"Oh god," he says as he pulls me out, crushing me to his chest.

He tugs me to my feet and doesn't stop moving until we're no longer standing in the pile of rubble that used to be the Polis. Globs of green fire rain across the sky like shooting stars. The entire world is burning. Ugly, black creatures scatter throughout the grounds, their fangs oozing with black goop. One of them charges me on shiny, reptilian legs. I can't tell if its body is flesh or shadow. It makes odd, janky movements, like a puppeteer is slinging it around. But the fangs, talons, and rippling, batlike wings at its back are definitely real.

It closes in, screeching something awful. I flick my hand, and a long arc of lighting falls from the sky, vaporizing the monster's body. It leaves an ugly black smear in the grass.

"What the hell is that thing?" I gag at the smell, like sulfur and rot.

More advance on us. I call lightning down in blazing pillars, scorching the hoard. It doesn't matter. Hundreds of them pour in through the Sacred House's open gates. Its hinges are seared and twisted, like something powerful blew them off. Scraps of debris litter the lawn, sizzling hunks of metal, chunks of stone and marble. Black smoke gushes from the burning city. The screaming is the loudest sound in the whole world.

Soldiers in black robes advance through the gates by the dozen. First are the swordsmen, then the spear bearers. The archers march in to flank them. The soldiers halt their march in the center of the lawn, their expressions empty.

Footsteps sound behind us. My heart drops, but it's only the Children of Athena, coming to match the foreign army with their own. They're outnumbered, and that's without the horde of monsters laying waste to the Sacred House. I count at least seventy soldiers, dressed in traditional Greek armor; dozens more stream in from the city. The General leads them, a massive broadsword in her hand. The Lieutenant is at one side, the rest of my friends on the other.

It's so quiet that all I hear is the crackle of flame and screaming in the distance. At the arrival of the army, the monsters have gone still. Like they're waiting for something.

Roman and I take slow steps backward until we're standing in line with the General. Her back is long and straight, and she greets our invaders with a smile.

"*Children of Shadow and Death*," she calls, her voice projecting across the lawn, "*you have trespassed on sacred grounds. This land is blessed by the Blood of Her Holy Might—Mother Athena. I'm afraid I must ask you to leave, and I will only ask once.*"

A woman shouts from the army's right flank. "*We recognize the might of no other Mother. Behold.*"

Someone toward the back of the army blows a horn. It rings something awful through the Sacred House. First, the shadow creatures drop to their knees in a show of reverence. Then the swordsmen, who sheath their blades in the earth. Then the spear bearers and the archers too.

In the middle of the lawn, beneath the horn's awful chorus, a ribbon of shadow splits the air. It billows out in long, sweeping strands, before expanding into a dark, swirling portal. Two men step out on horseback—one alabaster, one obsidian. One with beautiful, white horns and black talons at his fingers. One with goat legs and dancing white letters moving across his skin.

Somnus and Hypnos.

I take a step back. The God of Fear smiles at me from across the line, a cruel promise twinkling in his eyes.

The two brothers step to the side, making way for a tall man in a pinstripe suit. His skin is the color of sickness, his eyes sunken and yellow. He's not thin, but his face is so ghastly it's like I'm seeing a skeleton move and breath. The dead horse he rides in on is at least seven feet tall.

A gray-skinned woman is the last to come through the portal. She rides on the back of a live, white Pegasus. Her sweeping, black gown doesn't seem fit for a battlefield. Neither do the sandals that strap up to her knees. She's beautiful, in the way that only something terrible can be beautiful. Her eyes are two bottomless pits, and long, black talons curve out from her fingers. She rides to a stop beside the ghost-faced man. The portal behind her vanishes, and the awful chorus finally goes quiet.

All at once, the army speaks. The monsters too, and if I listen close enough, even the shadows.

"*Hail the Mother of Endless Night,*" they chant. "*May her reign last forever and ever.*"

I let out a shaky breath. I know her, just as surely as I know the two monstrous gods at her side: Nyx, the mother of shadow—Queen of Paradise.

The drawing in my father's journal was eerily accurate. He got her features perfectly: the thin, sloping nose, her empty eyes. The way her lips curve into a mirthless, reptilian smile.

"*Greetings to the Children of War,*" Nyx calls, her voice light and pleasant. "*Tonight, you have each earned a rare privilege. As you have proven yourself worthy to die at the hands of the Blessed Army, tonight you shall each make Elysium's golden shore. Submit to your fate with honor, for you are the chosen few.*"

Again, in grating harmony, the army chants. "*Hail the Mother.*"

Nyx continues. "*Gods of Olympus—your predecessors had the honor of dying at my hand. Tonight, I shall claim the Codex Sanctus and grant each of you the same kindness. Truly, it is an honor like no other.*" Then, impossibly, she says my name. "*Ophelia Johnson, our destinies will at last align. You will serve your purpose, and you too shall know my kindness. As your father knew it. As your ancestors. This is my will. So let it be done.*"

"Hail the Mother."

My vision goes spotty. Rage builds like a hot typhoon in my chest as lightning scatters across the sky. The clouds churn into a terrible storm, and thunder pummels the earth. Nyx smiles up at the sky, her cheeks dimpling.

I'm stepping forward. I'm not thinking. I don't care. I was going to deliver death to Nyx's doorstep, but it's fine with me if she'd rather come collect it herself.

The General jerks me back, her grip like iron.

"Let me go," I snap.

The blue light from my eyes flickers across her stony expression. There's no fear there. No anger. She's just a soldier.

"No," she says, her voice low. "Find the Codex, and then get it and *yourself* as far away from here as possible. Do you understand?"

"But I—"

"Go. Now. I will not ask again."

She says it with the full weight of a general's authority. I look at my friends and then at the army that's so much bigger than ours. The General's eyes are burning, and I know I don't have a choice. Without another word, I duck past her and take off toward the crumbled remains of the Polis. I turn back just long enough to watch Nyx raise and lower a pointed finger. The two armies charge, and I force myself to run in the opposite direction.

The Polis isn't far. From here, the battlefield is a wild smudge of fire and inky black shapes raging across the lawn. I see the wide, flat blade of what has to be Alessia's battle ax cut through a hoard of monsters. A volley of silver arrows explodes across the sky, raining down shards of flaming metal.

Dammit.

I run to the far right end of the rubble. All I know is that this is roughly where our room was. I start flinging chunks of stone away. I've only been looking for a few minutes when I start finding bodies—mangled corpses with twisted limbs, exposed bits of bones, and bleeding stumps.

Gagging, I start dragging the bodies away. I try to be as gentle as I can and line them up as far away from the battle as possible. I can't look too closely at their faces. Each one is my father or my grandmother. Janus or Cherice, who I haven't seen since earlier this evening. They're all I have left.

I'm searching the rubble desperately when I see the outline of a man's shape on the other side of the debris. He's hunched over, his hands struggling to move a heavy slab of stone.

"Hey!" I shout.

He staggers back as I approach, but doesn't move away. As I get closer, his features sharpen in the light. It's Minister Fueves, his robes tattered and stained with blood. Ichor gushes from a deep gash against his temple, but he looks fine otherwise.

"Oh, it's you." I wipe my hands on my pants, staining them with dust and blood. "Have you seen my aunt and uncle?"

He points toward the city, his expression mild. It doesn't seem like anything really excites him. "The last I saw your aunt and uncle, they were fighting the Queen's creatures in town."

"But they're all right, right?"

He nods. "Yes, as far as I know."

I gesture to his torn clothes and the blood on his face. "And what about you? I thought you'd be where the action is."

He looks out at the battle, where a gold spear sails across the sky like a spinning needle. His expression is oddly glib. "I could say the same for you. Nerves?"

I snort. "No. I'm looking for the Codex. The General wants me to find it."

He steps forward, suddenly alert. "Ah, I see. Let me help you. Four hands work faster than two."

I shrug. "Sure. Just be quick."

I go back to the right side of the rubble, while he searches the left. There are more bodies beneath each layer of stone. I keep lining them up behind the Polis's crumbled grounds. Behind me, the world rattles beneath explosions. The air is so thick with smoke that breathing makes my throat hot and raw.

Ten minutes go by. I'm still digging, my only support the creaking pile of rubble beneath me. I lift a long slab of stone over my head and launch it into the shadows. Finally, a black book emerges, intact. I tug the book free and call out to the Minister, who's digging through stone with bleeding hands.

When he sees the Codex in my hands, his face goes soft with a look of relief. It's the most pleasant expression I've ever seen him make, which isn't saying much at all.

"Excellent," he says, his voice soft as he closes the distance between us. "Ophelia, you have no idea. I thought we were done for. Really. We can't thank you enough."

"No problem." I tuck the book under my arm. "I guess I have to leave. The General wants me gone."

He quirks an eyebrow. "Gone?"

"Yeah, I don't know. She just told me to get as far away from here as I could."

He nods, quiet for so long that I don't think he'll say anything at all. Then, as casually as if we were talking about the weather:

"Yes. Makena's a very smart woman. Were our interests aligned, I'd recommend listening to her. But, alas."

"What?"

The Minister lunges at me, a knife suddenly clutched in his bleeding hand. I step out of the way; his blade catches empty air. I'm about to bring my fist down, into his face, when a sharp pain sets fire to my ribs. The arrow stuck through my side is already stained with ichor. The archer who sent it steps out of the shadows, into the light. He notches another arrow and aims it from behind Minister Fueves, who's smiling like a shark.

"What?" I mumble, my mouth hot with blood.

The archer fires again. The arrow sails into my shoulder. I scream, dropping the book. Minister Fueves scrambles forward to pick it up.

"Ah," he sighs, examining the cover. "*Codex Sanctus*—the original holy book. Truly, Ophelia, believe me when I say thank you. Without you, none of this is possible."

"You piece of shit." I grip the arrow in my ribs and rip it out. The world goes white, but I don't pass out. "Why would you do this?"

"You were raised among mortals, lived as a mortal," he says. "I don't expect you to understand what it's like to exist in the shadows, with not one ounce of power in the world around you. Mortals worship false gods in their temples and churches; they walk past us without a single shred of reverence. Our leaders would have us take this in stride, but I refuse. I am not a traitor, Ophelia. I'm a revolutionary. When Kreos enlightens the world, when he is freed from his cage and claims the Order for himself, the world *will* know peace. But first, it will know wrath. The mortals will finally understand their natural station, and we, the Divine Children, will ascend to our rightful place. Isn't it beautiful?"

I spit into the grass, aiming for Emilio's feet. "You're insane."

"So was Galileo," the Minister chuckles. "Then, nearly four hundred years later, history judged him as a genius. I believe history will judge me in kind."

The archer taps Minister Fueves with a menacing finger. "Enough of this. The book, Emilio. I am to recover it and take the girl to the Refuge."

The Minister hands the book over. "Right. I assume that's our next stop, then."

In the archer's hands, the book vanishes in a plume of shadow. Here one second, gone the next. He smirks. "Something like that."

His hand shoots out like a viper, sinking a blade into Emilio's heart. The old man gasps as his legs slide out from underneath him and gold blood spreads beneath the fabric of his shirt.

"Why?" He croaks, his cheeks a violent red.

The archer shrugs. "You were needed. Now you are not. *Rest in the Mother's will.*"

The Minister claws against the earth, but it's all the fight he has in him. The archer watches him die, and I finally muster the strength to rip the arrow out of my shoulder.

"Hey!" I unsheathe my sword and aim it at the Scion's chest. It hurts to walk, to hold up this blade, but I do it anyway. "Where'd you send it? Tell me."

He smirks. "Where you'll never find it." His expression is eerily resigned, almost delighted. "You might as well just kill

OF BLOOD AND LIGHTNING

me now. I'll never tell you where, and it's an honor to die under the Queen's conscription."

I can tell he means it. I let my sword vanish. "I believe you, but what do you want with me? You already have the Fates. You already have the book. What more could you want?"

He smiles. There's nothing unkind about it. "Everything, Lightning God. Your life, and everything you have, and everything you value. Nothing less."

He moves to unsheathe a sword; I vaporize him in a pillar of lighting. More footsteps sound to the left of me. I've pulled my sword free in a second, but the battered figures approaching are familiar. Janus and Cherice, in shredded robes, with black blood staining their swords. Cherice carries two.

"Oh thank god," I mutter.

They run across to meet me, but I don't let them hug me. I pull back the torn fabric of my shirt. My wounds are bad. My head spins, but I have to stay steady.

"Have you seen Emilio?" My uncle demands, furious. "We got the paperwork right before the attack started. Martin's assistant was making that call to Fueves, just like he has for the past eight months on a regular basis. It's him, it's the Minister. He's our leak."

"I know." I point to the Minister's dead body and the pool of ichor around him. "Look, he's dead but they got it. Some guy came by and just . . . magicked the thing away. I don't know. It's gone."

"Oh shit," Cherice says. She glares out at the battle. It pushes closer and closer to the Polis's crumbled remains, which isn't a good thing. "Okay, we can deal with that later, but this isn't good. We didn't have enough numbers in the city, and we definitely don't have enough here. We can't turn this around."

"Have a little faith," Janus says, but there's no conviction in his voice either.

"I'm gonna kill her," I hiss, my hands shaking. "She has to die. I have to kill her."

"You have to be careful," Cherice says.

"I don't care and none of you can stop me," I say. "I'm doing it."

Janus looks wary. "Ophelia, please. Don't do this. I know you want revenge and I know it hurts, but you have to be smart. Sometimes you don't win every battle."

Silver armor melts over my body, shielding my wounds from the harsh elements. I say nothing.

My sword melts into the long rod of the lightning bolt. I rear it back behind my head, far enough to avoid the fighters on my side. I throw my leg forward and launch the bolt into the air. I'm jumping after it, soaring so high that the battle opens up beneath me like a yawning, black mouth. Lighting rains upon a horde of Scions, and I come down in the middle of the battlefield, landing on my feet.

The stench of earth and blood nearly makes me sick. I can't make out any of the squirming black shapes around me to separate demigods from Scions. I only know I've seen one of my friends when the earth rattles violently and an arc of blazing light goes off like an explosion. Really, the only one I see, the only one I recognize—is the Queen.

She hasn't moved from her white Pegasus, where the ghost faced man stands quietly at her side. I surge forward, slashing my way through a squad of advancing Scions. She picks me out of the crowd with a taloned finger, beckoning, and all I can think about is my father.

His still body. The dull, lifeless eyes. The stench of sulfur and rot filling the kitchen.

I cross the distance between us in one infinite bound. Lightning strikes as I come down in front of her. She doesn't flinch, even though the man watches her sideways. Her expression is still pleasant, like she can't smell the blood and burning around us.

"*Ophelia Johnson, at long last we meet,*" she muses. "*I must admit that while you've certainly inherited your father's hubris, you've also been blessed with your mother's delicate features. She's a beautiful woman.*"

"What do you want from me?" I demand. "You kill my family, you kidnap the Fates, and for what? Some dumb book."

The man scoffs, but she holds up a hand to stop him. Still, she appears amused.

"*Is that what you believe about your ancestor's only living relic?*" She scoffs. "*How dreadful?*"

"What are you talking about?"

She slides off her Pegasus in a movement so fast and graceful it's like water. I take a step back, my sword still held out. There's something menacing about how beautiful she is, something awful in her graceful stride. She stops a good distance away from me, her hands open and empty.

"*Do you think the stars perch at their posts by chance? Or that a bird's song is just a random assortment of notes and sounds?*" she asks. I can tell she's not expecting an answer. "*Everything, my dear girl, has its place. Even the weak, creeping things. I know your father tried to keep you away from this world, but it's your destiny. That is why I have come tonight, Ophelia Johnson. I didn't just come for some dumb book. I came for you.*"

I tighten the grip on my sword. My heart hammers so hard it could jump through my chest. "No. You came to die."

I'm bringing my sword back when my chest explodes with fresh agony. My armor dissolves, and the slick edge of a sword tears through me, just beneath my sternum. The air is sweet with honey and rot. Someone I hadn't noticed before leans in close behind me, so that their hot breath curls down my neck.

"Hello, Little God," Somnus purrs.

He pulls his sword free and kicks me to the ground. Nyx looks pleased as he comes around me, his blades dripping with bright ichor.

"Very well done, my son," she says. *"Get her to the Refuge and don't let her out of your sight."*

I kick out as he advances on me, but there's only so much I can do. I slip in a pool of my own blood, which gathers quickly beneath me. I'm confused. Why is the world blurring at the edges? Smoke, blood, and earth mingling into one horrifying image.

Somnus kicks me in the chest and I go flying across the lawn. Gold and silver sparks rain down on me. Something in the air is sweet with jasmine and sea salt.

The monstrous God of Fear takes slow steps toward me. He looks disappointed. *"I do hate that you wasted my evening. This was supposed to be fun."*

I dig both hands into the soil. Atoms prickle in my fingertips: the earth, each blade of grass. Every pebble. I will not let them take me. I won't give Somnus the satisfaction of having my blood on his hands.

A flood of heat rushes through my limbs. Violet plasma snakes through the air, stretching from the open gate to the

Polis's rubble. It sets over the Sacred House like a cage of living, searing matter. The earth trembles, and everything goes quiet. No more fighting; everyone watches the sky as it splits and pulses. And then a portal of shadow opens where the gate used to be and everyone moves at once. Floods of Scions and beasts rush past me to escape through the portal. Through the chaos, I stare at Nyx.

"I'll kill you," I shout; lighting prickles in my teeth. "You're dead, Nyx. You hear me. I *will* kill you."

Somnus freezes, horrified. The pleasant mask on Nyx's face finally falls away. She takes a step back, baring her teeth.

"*You have no right,*" she says. "*The Order belongs to the King.*"

Somnus spits into the grass. "*We have to retreat. Now.*"

Nyx stands over me, watching, with Somnus waiting impatiently at her side.

"*Hear me, Lightning god,*" she hisses. "*I will return. I will take the Order of Ruin, and you will die. This is my will.*"

She reaches for me but I throw out a bleeding hand, and a purple rod of lighting chews through her shoulder. Her scream rattles the world as she staggers back into Somnus's arms. In the next second, they're both gone, lost in a plume of shadow. The earth trembles as the rest of her forces retreat and the portal ripples closed. Silence falls over me, and I have nothing left. The heat in my body flickers out, vaporizing the web of sizzling plasma.

I try to get up, but I can't stand. I slip on my blood and then onto my back. The only thing that moves through me now is pain, and then eventually darkness, as the razed grounds of the Sacred House finally bleed out of view.

CHAPTER THIRTY-EIGHT

Here, in this quiet black chamber, I look for my father.

The room has no walls or corners. No ceilings or floors. It's as narrow as a tiny hallway, with no lights illuminating the dark corridor. Shadows billow out all around me, and the whole world feels like frostbite. My feet are heavy, but I stagger forward anyway. Each step takes me closer and closer to the beaming white light at the end of the tunnel, cut out in the shape of a tall door. I'm desperate. I have to make it there.

At the very end, where the door is rinsed in light, I see the outline of my father's shadow. I walk faster, but I can't run. I can smell his cologne and the black soap he'd buy at the farmer's market. His laugh floats down the hallway, a chorus of ghostlike bells. I'm so close now that he's no longer just a fuzzy, black outline, but a strong man standing tall against the light. I can't tell if he's facing me or not. I can't tell what he's wearing. But I'm moving, my arm stretched out. His name on my tongue like some cruel weight of gold.

Nothing matters. Not sickness or death, or disease or blood-shed. Not any of the terrible things that happen to men on Earth, and then again in the afterlife. Because here, my father

*is laughing, just down the hall, and death is a door so thin I
could split it with my fingertips.*

Here, death is vapor.

WHEN I WAKE UP, ROMAN IS the first thing I notice. He's
sleeping in one of the chairs by my bed with a red quilt
draped over him. My aunt and uncle are beside him, leaning
against each other on a loveseat. On the other side of the
room, Olivia and Griffin are asleep too.

I blink, trying to remember something, anything. I don't
know how I got here, or even where here could be. There's a
soft mattress underneath me and a heavy, black quilt thrown
over my body. I don't recognize the room, or any of the furniture. Only the pain in my body. That's familiar.

When I try to move, it feels like a needle slices through my
chest. I gasp, going still. Roman stirs in his chair and rushes
to my side, his eyes wild.

"Hey, love," he says, his voice soft. "You have to stay really
still. You were in pretty bad shape."

For the first time, I notice the tightly wound bandage around
my torso. I want to tear it away and look at the wound underneath, but I know that's stupid. I also don't have the strength.

Pain jogs my memory. I see green fires raging across the
lawn and hoards of shadowy creatures laying waste to the
Sacred House. I see an army and their undead steeds. I see
gods that look like monsters, and chunks of silver fire raining
from the sky. I close my eyes, wishing it was just another
nightmare.

"How many?" I ask, my voice low.

The others wake up at the sound. They lean toward me,
watching with worry in their eyes.

"How many what?" Roman asks.

"How many people died?" I ask him. "I need to know."

Silence craters in on us. Griffin answers, as low and dejected as I've ever heard him.

"Four hundred and forty-five," he says. "We lost half the House."

I'm too sick to speak. I wonder how many Scions died, but I know there's no point. Even if I could kill every last one on the planet, it wouldn't make up for what happened here. I remember the bodies I saw, how they were mangled and twisted, their expressions forever frozen in agony.

My stomach turns. Roman manages to get a trashcan in front of me just in time. When I'm done throwing up all the bile in my stomach, I wipe my mouth and shove the can away.

"The good news is that we finally have the Council's backing. They've got infantry from the Houses of Ares and Aphrodite coming in to help us." Uncle Janus says. "As for Martin, I confronted him with the phone records a few days ago, and he's been thrown out of his seat."

I furrow my brows. "A few days ago? Wait, how long has it been?"

Cherice rubs her hands together like she's trying to wring them out. "Almost a week."

"What?" I try to sit up, but my wounds force me back down. "What the hell happened? Why would you let me sleep that long?"

Roman takes both of my hands into his like he's holding a dying bird. "You almost died, Ophelia. I tried waking you up—it wouldn't work. There was blood everywhere, and you wouldn't talk to me. We didn't know if you were ever going to wake up."

His voice breaks off and he hangs his head, hiding his tortured expression. I rub my thumbs over his knuckles. I wish there was something I could say to comfort him, but anything I say would probably make it worse. I don't care about dying. I know that now. Lying in that grass was the closest I've felt to my father in months, and I'd trade it for almost anything. Almost, because the only thing better would be cutting out Nyx's heart.

"Hey, I'm not going anywhere, and I'm fine. I am," I tell him, even though everything still hurts.

The heat in his voice surprises me. "You almost got yourself killed when you weren't even supposed to be there in the first place."

"That was my only chance," I tell him, my hands trembling. "I could've killed her. She was right there. What else was I supposed to do?"

"Live," Olivia scoffs, throwing up her hands. "You're supposed to live, Ophelia. Are you insane?"

"That's not the point." I snap. "She's nearly killed everyone in my entire family. Am I just supposed to be okay with it? Does she get away with it?"

Roman comes forward to comfort me, but I shake my head. I don't need comfort or tenderness. I need retribution. "Okay. So what now? Did we quit?"

Griffin's expression is grim. For a second, I'm afraid he's going to say yes, but it's worse than that. "Actually, no. Two days after the attack, the Firstborn sent an emissary. In forty-eight hours, they'll send another to collect Ophelia. If she doesn't go willingly, the Fates will die."

"Okay." I'm already nodding. I've already made up my mind.

I search myself for fear. There's rage and a misery so deep it lives in my bones. But there's no fear. Not at all.

My uncle jerks up from his seat. "Okay? Do you hear yourself?"

"What else am I supposed to do?" I roll my eyes. "If I don't go, they'll kill the Fates."

"Maybe, but let's not pretend that's what this is about." He jabs a finger at me. "You'll be going on a suicide mission, Ophelia, and you know that. You know that. I understand where you're coming from, but getting yourself killed won't help anybody and it's certainly not what Jason would've wanted."

"I know that already," I shout. My father's name makes me ache. "Look, the fact of the matter is that the Fates are going to die and we don't even have the Codex anymore. I'm the only bargaining chip left, and I might be able to kill Nyx before they kill me."

Griffin shakes his head. "It's not that simple. They don't just want to kill you. They want to use you. Do you remember what I said to you, before you left for the Uncrossed?"

I recite his grim warning like I'm bored. "Yeah. Never let them take you, but they wouldn't be taking me. I'd be turning myself in." A sick thought comes to mind. "Look, if it comes down to it, I'll make sure they can't use me for anything."

Roman turns away. "That's not funny. Not at all."

"I'm not joking. It's a solution to a problem."

"And what does that solve?" An anger I've never seen before flashes across his face. "If you go there and you kill yourself, they still have the Fates and the Codex. The world still ends. Nothing about this situation improves if you die, Ophelia."

I stare at the wall across the room. As long as I get to kill her, I don't care what happens to me. But there's no point telling him that, so I just say nothing.

Roman scoffs and looks around at the others. "Can Ophelia and I have a minute? Alone?"

They don't look happy about it, but the others file out the door. Cherice lingers to watch me, teary-eyed. She's halfway through the door when she walks over to my bedside and presses both hands to my face.

"I need to tell you that I understand, Ophelia. I know what you're feeling," she says. "I know how angry you are. I know you want to burn the world so bad you'd set it on fire while you're still inside, but that's not the way. We can fix this and we can avenge Jason, but you dying has no place in that equation. Do you hear me?"

I don't look at her. Her words hit me like a wall of fire. "I hear you."

She watches me for a second, so I finally look her in the eye. When I do, I recognize the wave of sadness that crashes in her eyes. She kisses my forehead, and it almost breaks me. "That's all I had to say. Just think about it."

"Okay."

She leaves the room then, and it's just me and Roman. He sits on the edge of my bed with his head in his hands. I watch the rise and fall of his shoulders, how they tremble as he tries to catch his breath.

I don't know how things could have changed so quickly. We were just happy. *I* was happy, but maybe I should've known better. I'm not built for tenderness or trips around the world. I'm an instrument of war. I know that now.

"I'm sorry," I tell him, even if I'm not totally sure I mean it. I am sorry, but it doesn't change anything. My mind is made up. "I didn't mean to upset you."

He finally looks up at me, shocked. "I'm not upset, Ophelia. It just scares me that giving up your life is so easy for you."

"But Roman, if I don't go, the Fates—"

"I don't care about the Fates." Anger washes over his face again. "I don't even care if the world ends anymore. If you go there and die, I definitely won't. Even if we save the day, you'd still be gone and that's not a win to me. I wouldn't trade you for that."

"But it's the whole world, Roman. You can't say that."

"Yes, I can. I do." He takes my face in his hands so that all I see is the burning fury in his eyes, the resolve. "I'd so much rather save you than the Fates. It's not even a question. I know that's not the right way to feel, but I don't care."

He looks so distraught it makes my chest ache. I don't recognize the anger in his eyes, anger I don't think is directed at me anymore. I wrap my hands around his forearms and press my forehead to his. A feeling rushes up in my chest, but it's not the warmth and light I've come to expect. It's vicious and desperate, and I know the worst time in the world to tell someone you love them is right before you die.

"Promise me something," he says, and I already know I'd promise him anything.

"Yeah."

"Just don't be the hero this time." he says, closing his eyes. "For my sake."

I hear what he can't say: don't die.

"Okay. I promise."

Relieved, he leans down and touches his lips to mine. A second later, someone knocks at the infirmary door.

Baxter comes in with a defeated expression. "I'm sorry," he says. "I just wanted to check the dressing."

Roman moves back, nodding. He watches silently as Baxter checks my wounds. They've become thick bands of scarred flesh. I'll probably have them forever.

"It's healing fine, but I don't like that it took so long," Baxter says. "My guess is that these were vowed blades, but I'm not sure."

Roman gives him an exhausted look. "But she'll be okay, right?"

"Yeah, man. She'll be okay," Baxter makes an effort to sound reassuring, but he scowls at the door like he's trying to burn holes through it. "Look, I know Nyx is sending Scions to come get you, but you don't have to go. If you want to fight it, I'll fight with you. I mean it."

I sniff, but I refuse to cry. "Thanks, Baxter. I really appreciate it."

He shakes his head. "It's nothing. Your fight is my fight."

As he leaves, I feel a pang of guilt. I wish I could tell them the truth. I wish they understood. This is no one's fight but mine. No blade but mine will erase Nyx from this world, and I know now that that's not a path they can take with me. They care too much. They would let Nyx live if it meant keeping me alive, but Nyx can't live. Even if my life is the price I have to pay.

I've made up my mind.

After Baxter gives the okay, Roman finally lets me leave the infirmary. He's not talking much, and I can feel his anger like a quiet furnace. He doesn't let me walk. After

MICKI JANAE

strapping on his backpack, he scoops me out of the bed and the room vanishes.

We appear in a bedroom. It's smaller than the one we had, but the four-poster bed with dark curtains is the same. There's a black, leather chest at the end of the bed, and a vanity desk pushed up against the left side of the room. There's a stack of towels and a basket of supplies on the desk. I recognize my backpack leaning against the mirror and my father's journal beside it, both caked with white debris but still intact.

"I went through the rubble at the Polis and I found some of your stuff." He's still speaking in that same flat voice.

"Okay." I drag a hand down my face. "Hey Roman, I think I need a minute. You know, to process."

I try to make it sound like I'm not kicking him out, even though that's exactly what I'm doing.

Thankfully, it doesn't seem like my words wound him any further. "I understand. Just come find me when you're ready, okay? Please?"

I nod. Another pang of guilt, but I try to ignore it. "I will. Thank you. For everything."

He kisses me again, maybe for the last time. I try to hold him there, which makes him laugh. "You're welcome. I'll see you later."

I smile. It feels like I'm holding up the world with my shoulders. "See you later."

My body still hurts, but it doesn't matter. As soon as he's gone, I spring into action. My body is still caked in dry blood and grime, so I scrub myself clean as quickly as I can. I find fresh clothes in my bag and tug them on like there's a clock in my head, slowly counting down.

360

My heart hammers, but I try to ignore it. When I dig through my bag again, my hand closes around the cool, clustered shape of the Eye. I pull it out with a flood of relief. I wasn't sure if it had survived the assault on the Polis. I don't know what I would've done if it hadn't.

I do feel bad about this. I feel even worse for lying, but it can't be helped. Nyx has to die, and they can't come with me.

I unsheathe the Lightning Bolt and make a long incision across my palm. Ichor drips over the Eye's dull face and the room bleeds out of view.

The great rushing dark, whirling past me. Clouds of infinite blackness frame the world around me. There are no bodies, no earth, no sky. Only shadow, and a voice crying out from the dark.

"Lightning God, Child of Khaos—what do you seek?"

"Nyx," I say. "Show me Nyx."

The hand at the back of my neck pushes me forward. Through the pit of black shadows, over an expansive cavern, and then over the spiky arms of a tall, black gate. A black river runs the length of the whole world, separating a long line of people from the sprawling kingdom on the other side. Rigid black towers form a dark city miles beyond the river. Hordes of people burn in a tar pit on the left hand side. I want to close my eyes, but the hand keeps pushing me forward.

I rush over miles and miles of dark sand. There are people everywhere, some walking in chains, some bathed in gold. I think I've gotten to the very end of the kingdom when the wall of shadow in front of me splits like rippling silk. And beyond it, bathed in a blaze of torchlight, is an even bigger kingdom, surrounded by walls of black brick. A massive castle overlooks a city of houses and the monstrous hoard that inhabits it.

*Troops of shadowy creatures, rows of Scions in black armor.
The blazing ball of white light in front of them dims to reveal
the battered shapes of three ancient women.*

*The hand lowers me down into the city's belly, until I'm
standing across from the army. A gray-skinned woman leads
them, her reptilian smile as cold and cruel as a dagger.*

*The voice washes over me, more command than invitation.
"Take that which you seek."*

I WAKE UP GASPING. I GIVE myself two seconds to catch my
breath, and then I'm flying around the room. There's parchment in one of the vanity drawers. I find a pen in my bag. It
takes me thirty seconds to write the letter, thirty more to
finally stop crying.

"I'm sorry," I mutter, even though there's no one around
to hear my apology.

I don't bring my bag. I take nothing with me. I leave the
note on the bedside table and let the room vanish around me

CHAPTER THIRTY-NINE

I APPEAR ON THE SHORES OF a black river, beside an infinite line of the dead. It stretches farther than my eyes can see behind me. Each member waits with a single silver coin, at a pier that bobs in the water. I see a towering black gate on the other side, guarded by a massive dog with three, snarling heads. Despite the dog's obvious ferocity, it whines affection-ately as a man in black robes reaches up to pet one of its snouts.

Twelve people hobble through the open gates, into the dark kingdom. The gates close on their own after letting them through, filling the black void with the grating sound of metal on stone. There's no sky above me, just an endless expanse of shadow and darkness. Beyond the gate, I hear a man's booming voice, someone screaming, the screeching of invisible creatures that must be anything but human.

The Land of the Dead sprawls before me, but it's not what I've come for.

I walk over to the pier as the man on the other side steps back into his skiff. The dead scatter as I approach. They're more skittish than anything.

The man crossing the pier has an ancient face. His black robes are too big for him, but he doesn't seem to mind. A white beard hangs low past his waistline, and his eyes are empty black pits, filled only with two orbs of hazy, blue light.

Charon, the Underworld's ferryman.

He latches his skiff to the dock with a fraying rope before stepping onto the pier. He bows deeply.

"You don't have to do that," I tell him.

He raises a single, white eyebrow. *"All meager creatures must pay fealty to the Divine, My Lord."*

Those two words make me squirm. There's too much reverence.

"My name's Ophelia. I'm no one's lord." I gesture to the long, scattered line behind me where the dead whisper in low, frantic voices. "You're hardly a meager creature."

"I must disagree. I am merely a sailor. That being said, My Lord, I must tell you that this is no place for the living."

"Maybe not, but I'm expected," I tell him. "I've come here for Nyx."

It seems impossible that he could get any paler, but he does. At the mention of her name, he looks across the dock like he expects her to appear.

"Forgive me, my Lord, but I must advise against that. The Queen of Shadow is not one you come to willingly."

"I know that already. I don't need a preamble. I just need you to take me to her. Now."

He hesitates. His pit black eyes burn with devastation. "Very well."

We load onto his skiff and sail across the River Styx. Ghostly faces linger just beneath the surface of the water, wailing in noiseless agony. I recognize a few of them: Thomas Jefferson, Christopher Columbus, and a man who looks like Vlad the Impaler.

"What are they doing here?" I ask.

Charon's smile is anything but pleasant. *"They tried to escape. No dead man who crosses these shores shall ever again pass into the land of the living. No mortal man, anyway."*

As we get closer to the other side of the shore, I feel Cerberus's three-headed snarl in my chest. No amount of living with the impossible really prepares you for the sight of a giant, three-headed dog. He relaxes as Charon approaches, but watches me with apprehension. When I look him in the eye, he whimpers and lowers his head.

"Don't mind the dog," Charon says. *"He's really just a baby."*

Charon leads me through the Underworld's rusted gate, where billions of people split into three lines. One trails deeper into the kingdom, over a dune of black sand. In another, everyone in the line is connected by a long set of rattling chains as they stand before a man's floating head. He's a king, with giant, glittering jewels in his crown. A massive gavel floats in the space between him and the people he judges.

"Guilty," he shouts. *"Amadius Clade, I hereby condemn you to an eternity in the Fields of Punishment."*

The man screams as three hag-like shapes drift down from the sky to carry him away.

The third line, directly parallel to the second, stands before a whirling, gold portal. The floating head in front of them belongs to a green-eyed queen. When her gavel falls, the man in line raises his hands in triumph.

"May the Fields of Eternal Pleasure welcome you," the Queen says, her voice like silk.

My heart clenches painfully. How long would it take me to search these lines and find my father? Is it even possible?

"*My Lord*," Charon calls ahead of me, his face still pale. "*I must ask, are you sure you want to do this?*"

I ignore the wave of doubt that crashes over me. "I'm certain. Let's go."

He holds out a bony hand, beckoning me to grab on. As soon as I feel the papery texture of his skin, we're soaring through the air. I can see everything: the pale blue river that cuts across the length of the dead man's kingdom, The Fields of Punishment, washed in fire and blood. A castle comes into view as we fly farther south, its windows dark and hollow.

"What's that?" I ask, pointing down.

"*Queen Persephone's estate.*"

It's only when we've gotten to the Underworld's southernmost border, where the large black gate comes back into view, that we float down to earth. We land just beyond the gate, in front of a wall of pure shadow. There's nothing here but a dark emptiness, like I'm staring into deep space.

Charon frowns. "*Unfortunately, this is as far as I can accompany you. I am not permitted to enter the Refuge. You will forgive me, yes?*"

"You've done enough," I assure him. "Tell me something. How long have the Firstborn lived here?"

"*Since the Fall of Paradise, My Lord. After their King was locked away, the Children of Paradise made their home in the Underworld's belly,*" he says. "*Queen Persephone hasn't left her manor in centuries, as she is now just a queen in name only. Only one queen truly rules the Land of the Dead, and that is the Queen of Shadow.*"

He pulls a short dagger from the folds of his robes. I step back, but he only drags it across his own palm. Ichor pools in his hand as he presses his palm to the wall of shadow. A shudder rocks the sand beneath me. Gold light spreads out across the border in a shower of sparks. The shadows part like a red sea, revealing a towering, brick wall beyond it.

It's exactly how the Eye showed me. A million torches burn along the wall, adding weak light to the dark kingdom. A horde of Scions stand watch at the Kingdom's entrance, arrows and swords drawn.

I nod at Charon. "Thank you," I tell him.

He looks ill. *"Do not thank me. I have done nothing but deliver the Crown of Olympus into the jaws of certain death. It is not admirable."*

Without another word, he vanishes.

There are dozens of Scions at the Refuge's border. An army larger than Nyx's invaders has come for me. Each blade has only one purpose.

"Lightning God," one of them shouts, her voice booming. *"Surrender yourself to the Mother's will."*

I clench my fist, and lightning falls from the sky, scorching the front line to heaps of ash. I don't wait for the gate to open. I cross it in a single, bounding leap. More guards wait beyond it—on horseback, in flaming, green chariots. The army charges at the same time, their war cries echoing like the roar of a dragon.

Blue armor melts over me as more lightning rains down. The air is rancid with ozone and the stench of blood. I unsheathe my sword and slash my way through the charging armor. I don't stop until I'm standing on the other side of a mountain of corpses. It's not retribution fully realized, but it's a start.

In the distance, perched on the edge of a dark mountain, is a black castle. It's twice as big as the one I saw in the Underworld and is surrounded by a hoard of soldiers. More stream in from the city, shouting orders to each other as they advance. Creatures of shadow pull themselves out of the earth, their teeth glistening like shards of firelight.

I run until I'm standing at the edge of the mountain, with a trail of destruction behind me. Children of the First stream down the mountain face, unphased by the deaths of their comrades. Beads of green light stare back at me. It's not until they're flying at my face that I realize they're arrows. Hundreds of them fall from the sky. I scream as I feel their burning tips pierce my skin.

I stagger back, holding up both hands to shield my face. Then I'm on the ground with feet trampling over me. A million hands tear at my clothes, hoisting me onto their shoulders. I try to twist out of their grip, but it's too painful to move my body.

Suddenly I see him—the God of Fear himself, stalking through a break in the crowd.

"Hail the meager might of Lightning Gods." His fist flies out, striking my face. The Refuge goes dark.

My head pounds as I come to. I'm in a small, stone room, chained against a wall. Candles cast dim light against the darkness. The long rug in front of me is knitted from old, red wool. It looks like a room I know, from the First Temple, except there's no treasure. Only an altar in front of me, burning with black candles, and a set of dirty, iron doors behind it. Hand prints in black paint smear down the length of the door, which is shrouded in clusters of black roses.

I try to stand, but the green chains around my wrist are bolted to the wall. The skin around my wrist is already worn and slick with ichor. There are burns along my arms and legs. Each move sends jolts of pain rushing through me.

"*You have to know how deeply foolish it was to come here on your own. You aren't as powerful as you think.*"

Nyx sits on a cushioned throne in front of the altar. Her black gown sweeps down to her ankles, revealing her black sandal straps. Glittering silver chains wrap around her arms, casting bulbs of crystalized light all over her body. She looks like an angel, but that reptilian smile on her face is a mark of the evil within.

"It was a calculated risk."

"*Well, at least it all worked out for me.*" She sits back in her chair, folding her legs. "*I want to tell you a story, Ophelia Johnson. I need you to understand.*"

"I do understand," I tell her. "You've killed over a thousand demigods in the last five months. You've defiled sacred grounds, you kidnapped the Fates, and you killed my father. What's there to understand?"

"*The why,*" she says simply. "*You don't understand why any of these things were necessary. Without the why, I am nothing but a tyrant who rules with baseless cruelty. I wouldn't agree that that's accurate.*"

I shrug. "I would, but sure. If it makes you feel better."

"*Years ago, before the dawn of man or Titan or Olympian, there were no other gods before us,*" she says. "*We, the Firstborn, ruled over a quiet Universe, under the authority of our king, my husband Kreos. Then the other gods came, and man sprawled across the Earth. By then, they'd forgotten us. No one remembered the Gods of Old. They only wanted to worship your predecessors, the Olympians.*

"*Now, Kreos had a vision. He saw a world where humanity knew and revered the gods of their history. They would lavish us in worship and sacrifice, and the world would know peace. With Kreos in power, there'd be no war or death or sickness. He had a plan, and he could do it. All we had to do was purge the Gods of Olympus. We were so close."* Rage sparks against her beautiful face. *"And then my sister, your ancestor, betrayed us."*

"Khaos was your sister?" I ask.

She scoffs. *"My oldest. When we first waged war against the Olympians, she fought at our side. We could've ushered in a new world with her help, but she didn't have the stomach for what needed to be done. We were going to win. Then she turned on us. She sided with our enemies, and locked our King away in a sunken tomb. I would've killed her with my bare hands, but she'd already sacrificed herself."*

"It sounds like she was smart," I say, despite the vicious chill rushing down my spine.

"She was a fool," Nyx corrects. *"And she only prolonged the inevitable. Since the day the Codex Sanctus was written, I've been waiting for you, Ophelia. It only answers to the Order of Ruin, so I've kept my patience for thousands of years, until you could emerge. Until I could bring you here, bathe these doors in your blood, and finally free him. At last, my time has come."*

My head spins. There's a long knife on the altar, a bronze goblet, and a book in chains.

"The Order belongs to the King," I mutter, remembering.

She smiles. *"Oh yes. My sister's most sacred power was the Order of Ruin. She could turn atoms into living bombs. My husband was going to harness it for himself to usher in an age of peace, but she gave it away to a lesser god. I could never understand the merit in binding her greatest gift to the Lightning God, but it doesn't matter now. I have you."*

I see the cage of pulsing matter that sat over the Sacred House. How it chafed and peeled at the air. I see a ship in the Uncrossed waters, splintered beneath my closed fist. I have to keep her talking.

"What do you mean she bound her power to the Lightning God?"

She narrows her eyes at the question. *"Exactly that, Ophelia. Within you, there are two great divinities. The Lightning of Heaven and the Order of Ruin, bound together by blood and destiny. But I do not answer to destiny."*

"The Order belongs to me," I tell her, remembering Khaos's words. "You can't have it."

She pushes up from her chair so fast I almost don't see her stand. She's a tall woman. When she walks, it's with a graceful, sweeping terror. Like you wouldn't even want to run away. She crouches down in front me and takes my face in a taloned hand.

"Oh sweet girl, I already do." She stands and walks over to the altar, where she takes up a thin, black book: The Codex.

"Even if you kill me, you won't kill my friends," I hiss. "And they won't stop until you're all dead. Even Kreos will die."

"Oh," she says, like she's looking down at a stupid puppy. *"Ophelia, I don't think you get it yet. I would've thought your father had educated you, but it appears not. You are the Godender. Without the Godender, the Holy Seven have no power. As soon as you're dead, they will merely be children once again, and I will claim their lives too. There are no other gods before us, and there will be none after."*

She comes forward with the Codex, still bound in chains.

"Open it," she hisses.

"Okay. I will. Just tell why my Dad had to die?"

"Personal grudges aside—it was a matter of necessity. Everything I have done has been to bring you here, kneeling before me."

I clench my fists around the chains. Purple light snakes through them, and they shatter. She watches in astonishment as I rise to my feet and unsheathe the Lightning Bolt.

No more speeches.

By the time I've crossed the short distance between us, she's holding a long blade of pure black shadow. Darkness billows out around her feet as she meets my sword with her own.

Each strike of my blade is for my father, and my grandmother, and my grandfather. Iris and Irene, and the four hundred forty-five Children of Athena that were killed two nights ago. I fight for the Fates, and the Codex, and then finally, for my own grief. When I bring down my blade, I bring it down with all the ugly, black weight that's lived in my heart for the past few months.

My vision blurs. Time moves as a searing arc of light. We fight until I'm bleeding all over, until her blood covers my blade in a slick layer. I'm closing it to slash at her neck when a searing pain comes alive in my thigh. My left leg goes numb and buckles beneath me.

I land on the floor, with only a second to scramble away as something black and hissing snaps at my face. The shadows at her feet have become a pit of black vipers. Their eyes are beads of bright rubies. I try to stand, but I can't feel my leg. My armor is gone and ichor gathers beneath me in a shimmering puddle.

Nyx cackles. *"Hubris is the downfall of all men: the mighty are only blessed with despair. I would tell you to remember that, Ophelia, but I think it's a piece of advice you won't need. Today, you've achieved your purpose. You should rejoice."*

I spit a wad of blood at her feet. I can feel venom moving through me. Each second that passes is dimmer than the rest, like all the light in the world is slowly bleeding out.

Just then, a three-pronged spear sails into Nyx's chest. I look back to see my friends: Roman, Cass, and Griffin.

"Get out of here," I shout at them. There's a ball of heat building in my palm.

Every atom in the room buzzes with ruin. They can't be here.

They move fast. Griffin dashes toward the altar, takes up the chained book. Then he's gone in a shower of white light.

Roman runs forward, his sword held out. Cass comes up behind him. Nyx blocks the pronged-tip of Roman's spear, and Cass drives a gold sword into her side. He twists the blade, his teeth gritted, before wrenching it out. Nyx howls. Her sword and goblet clatter to the floor. The vipers at her feet dissolve.

Nyx collapses, blood pooling around her. Her jaw distends as she screams, filling her mouth with rows of carnivorous teeth. "You arrogant, meddling children," she screams. "I'll kill you all."

Cass and Roman ignore her. They each grab one of my arms and lift me up. The world blurs around me. My stomach clenches with awful nausea. I try to fight them as they drag me toward the door, even though there's no strength in my limbs.

Nyx pushes herself up onto a bended knee. Her hair hangs in damp, bloody strings around her face. *"Here me well, Gods of Olympus. As I slew your predecessors, surely you will die at my hands. Your blood will wash the earth, and the whole world will know that Kreos is King."*

Nyx vanishes, her voice echoing after her. Cass and Roman ignore my protest as they carry me through the palace—up flights of stairs, through long corridors and finally through a set of double, oak doors. Soldiers and monsters gather at the castle's edge, armed with bloody intent. We stop outside of the gates. I hold my hand up toward the palace, feeling each atom in its dark edifice.

Green light comes on in Roman's eyes. The world is falling away. But just before we vanish and the darkness claims us, before we're gone and the Firstborn city of refuge melts into shadow, I close my fist.

The last thing I see is a cage of molten plasma closing its jaws over Nyx's castle, crumbling it to nothing.

CHAPTER FORTY

A BULB OF GOLD LIGHT HANGS over me, its warm, dazzling face pressed up against mine.

Everything else is a smear of paint swatches: soft pinks, a striking, blood orange, and a million dancing streaks of fiery red. The sun hangs right in the center, above my head, brighter than anything else. It drags across the sky, away from my face. I feel its warmth hovering over my right leg, and then this feeling that I'm being soaked through with its light.

As a soft heat rushes through me, the world sharpens into focus. The swatch of fiery colors fades into a slab of sunset, sprawled across the chain-linked shoulders of silver mountains. A cliff face stares down at me, dark figures perched along its edge. I'm on my back in a plot of grass, with a host of faces looking down at me.

I vomit a reeking, black fluid into the grass. Cherice rubs my back. Baxter crouches at my right, a ball of yellow light in his hand. When I'm done throwing up, he scans that same hand up and down my body, mending wounds.

He doesn't look happy. Cass crouches down in front of me, scowling. Behind him, Roman kneads his eyes with his knuckles.

"What the hell is wrong with you?" Cass demands.

Baxter glares at him, his eyes alive with gold light. "Cass, she's hurt. You can at least wait until she stops bleeding to death."

I look down at my torso as Cass says something I don't hear. My armor's gone. My shirt is a bloody shred of fabric. "Shit," I mutter, my head pounding. The mending flesh underneath is a gruesome sight.

Janus's voice is loud behind me. "All right, everybody needs to clear out. We have to get her inside."

An argument breaks out. Their voices tangle together like a cluster of barbed wire.

"Enough," Janus shouts. "I get it, but she needs to rest. She can't do that with ten people shouting in her face, so back the hell off."

Roman's voice is low and searing. "I'm not going anywhere."

Janus sighs. "Fine. Just you. But that's it."

In the distance, someone screams. A long, loud, horrible scream that casts its misery over everything. My body hurts, but I crane my neck up just enough to see who it is.

The Lieutenant, running across the grass, holding a limp body. She falls to her knees, her hair bloody and tangled around her, and cradles the dead woman to her chest. Her sobs clatter throughout the valley, crashing over us like acid rain.

"Oh god." Janus, a hand clamped over his mouth, takes off running to crouch down by the Lieutenant.

Cherice's expression shatters. Tears glisten in her eyes. "Oh my god." She looks at Baxter and Roman. "If you take her to that two-story building right over there," she points in a direction I can't see. "There should be an infirmary. Do *not* let her out of that bed."

"We won't," Baxter says pointedly as he pulls his hand away. "I'm done."

Roman comes forward. He's wearing the same tortured expression as the night I made him a promise, only now he looks betrayed too.

"I'm—"

He cuts me off and takes me into his arms, cradling me to his chest like a baby. "Don't." He stands and starts carrying me away.

I can't take that look on his face, so I look over his shoulder to peer out across the wide open fields of the valley. Wounded soldiers surround us in clusters—nursing their wounds and tending to their dead. Smudged figures advance down the long, dirt road that leads from here to the city. Gray mountains form a staggering ring around the massive clearing, watching the Lieutenant as she sobs over the brown-skinned woman in her arms.

The brown-skinned woman in mauve robes, with her hair slicked back. The woman who doesn't move, even though I can hear the Lieutenant begging her to wake up from here.

I press my hands against Roman's chest and scramble out his arms. He protests, but I ignore him and run across the field with lightning at my feet. I don't care that my whole body burns with pain. I drop down to my knees at the Lieutenant's side.

"Ophelia, what are you doing here?" Janus demands. He glares up at my friends, who've come up behind me. "You had one job, man."

"You really don't know her at all if you think she listens to anything I say," Roman chides.

"Shut up," the Lieutenant shouts, hysterical.

She turns the General over in her lap, revealing the bloody gash torn into the dead woman's chest. Her robe is open, the punctured armor beneath exposed to sunlight. She doesn't look like the General. There's no fire or resolve in her open eyes. No impossible calm. There's just nothing.

"We got separated," the Lieutenant sobs. "I just found her, and . . ."

The rest is clear. Cherice tries to console her, and their voices fade into a muffled blur. Rage rushes through me, hot and unforgiving. I see the Refuge crumbling at the beck and call of my closed fist. I see Nyx too, vanishing into a budding rose of black shadow. She got away.

I slam my fist into the earth as I stand, cratering the hard soil beneath it. I turn away from them, like I'm going to walk into the ring of trees across from me, and then right through the mountains beyond it. I'm so angry it feels like I really could.

Then, a shimmering voice consumes the earth.

"*Peace child,*" a woman says. "*Tonight, she rests in the golden splendor of Elysium, and has such been avenged by eternal pleasure.*"

The voice startles me, but I'm arrested by a cool sense of calm. Three women appear in front of us, with Griffin standing beside them. Purple bruises form on his face, and ichor dries in a stream from his left ear. By comparison, the three women beside him are shrouded in clouds of white light. Their white chitons are pure and unblemished. Their dark brown skin flashes like halos against the light. They don't walk. Each of them hovers just above the grass, resting on air.

As soon as I see them I know them. Clotho. Lachesis. Atropos. It's not from a story or anything my father told me. It's with an ancient sense of familiarity that I recognize the three Fates, finally here in the flesh.

The Lieutenant stares at them, her mouth gaping wide open. Atropos, the tall woman in the middle, smiles down at her. There's an ancient kindness in her eyes that makes me ache.

"*Be not dismayed, Atalanta of Kenes,*" she says. "*The time has come to stand in your teacher's stead. Will you carry this burden and walk as she did?*"

Atalanta's still teary-eyed, but something like steel hardens in the set of her jaw. She nods, slowly, deliberately. Like she means it. "I will."

"*Very well.*" Atropos looks out at the rest of us, a serene expression on her face. "*Daughter of Uranus, Son of Khaos— once again our paths align. It is a delight to see you both in good health. I do hope you're prepared for what's to come.*"

I jerk my head back in surprise. For the first time, I see that Janus isn't struck with awe. There's an ancient familiarity in his eyes too.

He smiles, something small and painful. When he speaks, it's in his mother tongue. "*I've been preparing all my life. I think I understand now.*"

Lachesis smirks, something mischievous. "*As I said you would.*"

Finally, the three Fates turn their beaming white eyes on me and my friends. Until now, nothing has felt sacred or divine. Nothing but the three women floating in the air above me, warming my skin with their radiant light.

Lachesis spreads her arms, mischief still in her eyes. "*The Holy Pantheon, at last reborn in the world. We extend our deepest gratitude for your service. We cannot thank you enough.*"

Cass, slack-jawed, searches for the words but doesn't find them. I don't know what to say. It never occurred to me that I'd get to meet them face-to-face.

Roman's cheeks are flushed like rubies. He bends his left knee, lowering himself to the ground. Clothos points a finger at him, her eyes sharp.

"*Do not kneel, Sea God,*" she orders. "*The Gods of Olympus rule all and kneel to none. You will need to remember that. I apologize that there isn't more time to prepare, but the time has come. A Holy War is upon us, and you are our spear and rod. You must never bend, kneel, or bow. Understood?*"

We nod.

"So what are we supposed to do?" Alessia asks. "I mean, maybe we got lucky and Nyx is already dead."

My chest burns with an unquenchable fire. I curl my fingers into the earth, tearing up soil and grass. "No." My voice trembles. "No, she got away."

"*Indeed, she is free. And the House is incomplete,*" Lachesis says. "*When Khaos gathered with the Olympian remnant at the First Temple, there were seven surviving gods: Zeus, Poseidon, Hades, Apollo, Artemis, Ares, and Athena. You must find the Priest of War, and bind the House if you want to succeed. There is no other way.*"

Atropos gazes down at me. She lowers herself so that her feet crush the dead grass beneath her and cups a hand against my cheek. Something breaks in my chest, a splintered levee releasing a flood of grief and misery. For just a moment, my heart is so empty it feels like my ribs could cave in around it.

"*Ophelia,*" she says. "*I know you have suffered. I regret to tell you that there is much more suffering yet to endure. The Holy Seven are the rod and spear, but the Godender is our sword. The fate of Paradise is at hand. Will you answer?*"

And really, there's no other answer. It's already written in each tiny nucleus of my cells. In the gold ichor that stains my clothes, and the hot lightning that boils in my blood. In the grief rushing out of my heart, and the rage settling in to take its place.

"I will," I tell her.

Pleased, Atropos dips her head and floats back up to join her sisters. They smile at us, their eyes flaring. White light flows out from their bodies like streams of silk. As they're enclosed in a rippling cocoon, Clothos smirks down at me.

"The Codex will open to Ruin and Lighting."

With that, they disappear, leaving a shower of sparkling mist in their wake.

A long pensive silence settles around us. Then, with the General's body balanced on her knee, the Lieutenant kneels. All around us, soldiers take a knee. The wounded. The bloodied. The beaten. The soldiers approaching from the city halt in a staggered formation, and kneel in one, seamless motion. With that look of familiarity still warm in his eyes, my uncle kneels too, and then my aunt. There's a smile on Griffin's face, which is washed over with pride. He takes a knee and chants in a booming voice. His call spreads over the valley. All around us, soldiers answer in a roaring chorus.

"Hail the Gods of Olympus—rule all, kneel to none."

As dawn breaks the next morning, we bury our dead.

Every soldier, farmer, and god in the city gathers around a raised funeral pyre. The sun creeps out from the mountains, bathing the House of the Cursed Children in fresh light. Under its gentle glow, children of divine blood watch the bodies of their brothers and sisters burn with green fire.

Clothos told us that a Holy War is upon us. Looking out at the Sons of Apollo, the Daughters of Aphrodite, and the Children of Ares, I feel its breath fanning over me. These are the warriors Janus called in through the Council. They fought with us, died with us, and now, side by side, we mourn the people we loved.

I see Paris, the General's son, for the first time. He eulogizes his mother from behind an oak podium. Grief sags against his shoulders, but he stands tall, like she would've. When he speaks, it's with all the authority she carried.

"Today, our dead are the best of us," he says, his voice carrying out like a ghost over the hollow grounds. "We remember soldiers, warriors, and the bravest among us. We also remember our mothers and fathers, our sons and daughters. Tonight, each of them rests in the golden splendor of Elysium and have such been avenged by eternal pleasure. They will never cry, bleed, or hurt again. They will always know nothing but peace."

"We hereby put them to rest, freeing them of earthly burdens. They are where the agonies of men can touch them no longer. To this, we celebrate." He raises his hand in a straight line.

Archers in mourner's robes step out from the crowd. They set their arrows ablaze against the small, rough stones in their hands and aim them at the sky.

"To our fallen Children, by the Might of *Our* Holy Mother, may the Fields of Splendor keep you warm always," he says.

All at once, the archers fire. Their arrows dash against the sky like rushing, green ghosts. Then they plummet back to earth, landing in the pit of bodies. A green bonfire rages between us, blazing with the light of a stolen sun.

There's a reception after the funeral, but we forego it. Instead, we gather in a dark conference room in the Cursed City, lit only by a single lantern, with an unassuming black book between us. I'm sitting in the middle of the table, with my friends gathered around me. Griffin stands off to one side, and my aunt and uncle are across from me. The room is so quiet, I can hear my own heart pounding.

I wrap a hand around the old chain, making a fist. Purple light webs through the iron shackles, before the chain vanishes in a shower of black dust.

Cass throws his hands up, rolling his eyes. "Why can't we ever be in the know whenever something's that easy."

Alessia swats his shoulder, shushing him. She gestures to me with a nudge of her chin. "All right get on with it. What does it say?"

Tension builds in my stomach. I open the book to pages and pages of inked passages, but I can't read any of them.

My shoulders drop. "I have no idea."

"Of course," Olivia mutters as she drags a hand across her forehead.

"Hold on. Excuse me." Griffin pushes his way to my side. He takes one look at the book's first page and laughs.

"What is it?" My uncle asks.

"It's written in the Oracle's language. You'd have to have a direct connection to Destiny to understand it, but hold on." He casts a beaming hand over the book, and the Oracle's language dances into Ancient Greek. "You should be able to read it now. And it should be you."

I nod and swallow the lump in my throat. The language is different, but these words haven't lost their power. The label written across the top of the page reads, *The Godender Prophecy*.

I clear my throat and read, "*A Cursed Child will inherit Lightning and Ruin. The Holy Seven will walk the Earth. He Who Hungers shall sever the ties of his chains with the Arm of War. An Everlasting Night will reign upon the Earth, and the Hoards of Paradise will make feasts of men. Ten thousand suns will wash the Earth in Apollo's wrath. The Huntress's might will scourge the Sons of Paradise. Children of the Old Blood and the Hosts of Olympus, the Heirs of Death and the Beasts of the Sea, will unite beneath the Staff of Ruin and wage a Holy War against the Hordes of Paradise. It is written, on this the Codex Sanctus.*"

My whole body goes numb. The Codex's words are alive in the air, alive in each one of us. It's been months, but I recognize the Oracle's words for what they are. This is destiny, here in my hands

"So he does get out," Roman says in disbelief, his face a mask of horror.

"No." I shut the Codex. As soon as I take my hands away, a new set of chains materializes to bind its pages. "He won't, because we're going to stop them. This war doesn't start after he gets out. It starts right now."

CHAPTER FORTY-ONE

ONCE AGAIN, I HAVE A NEW home. With the Sacred House empty and scorched, and New River tainted with the presence of Scions, the only other place to go is the land of my father. A single House, the only one of its kind, nestled in the palm of quiet, blue mountains, just an hour east of Baker City, Oregon.

The Cursed Children are not a defeated people.

My new room is in the city, in the corner of a small, brick cottage, on the second floor. It's just like any other house and I share it with Roman. The first night, he refused to talk to me, and all day—through the funeral and the meeting—he hasn't said anything to me.

I know I wounded him. I could see it when I woke up on the outskirts of the Cursed House. I just didn't know how much. Every time he looks at me, he looks devastated.

He comes into our bedroom and doesn't say anything. I watch him rifle through his bag for something, wordlessly, until I can't take it anymore.

"Roman, I'm sorry," I tell him.

He sighs without looking at me. "I don't want to talk about it, Ophelia."

"So you're just not gonna say anything?" I scoff. "Super mature, by the way."

He drops his bag and turns to face me, his eyes burning. "I already said everything I had to say and you lied to my face. Why would you make me that promise if you were going after Nyx anyway?"

"Because you'd try to stop me," I tell him.

He scoffs, a bitter look washing over him. "Yes, because I want you to live. I didn't know that was such an outrageous thing to want."

"It's not about me! If I don't kill her, she gets away with everything she's done, and then goes on to do a whole lot worse. I'm sorry I lied, but I saw an opportunity and I took it. Sue me."

He groans into his hands as they drag down his face. I can't remember a time when he was ever frustrated with me, let alone angry.

"God, Ophelia, I almost watched you die, and I just don't get why you'd put me through that again. I can understand wanting Nyx dead, but why do something so dangerous? Why'd you just leave me here?" He closes the distance between us to hold my face, his hands gentle despite the anger in his eyes. "I know you don't care if you live or die, but I do. So what am I supposed to say?"

The passion and anger in his voice rolls over me, and I don't know what to say. All I can think to do is apologize, but that doesn't change anything for either of us.

Defeat crashes over him. He kisses my forehead and pulls away. "I need air. And space," he says. "I'll see you later."

He heads for the door. Panicking, I call out to him. "Are you coming back?"

A pause. "I don't know." And then he's gone.

After the door shuts behind him, I sob into my hands. I don't know what's worse. What he said or the fact that none of it changed my mind. He's right. He'd do anything to keep me from dying, and I'd do anything to kill Nyx, even if it means I die with her. We're at an impasse.

Downstairs, someone knocks on the door. I wipe my face as I go down to answer it, but I know my eyes are still puffy. To my dismay, it's Janus, carrying a battered, brown box. He furrows his brows at the sight of me.

"What's wrong? Who did it?" He asks, craning his neck to peer into the house. "Do I need to kill that boy? 'Cause I don't care who he is."

"Nothing. And nobody." I shake my head. I change the subject. "What's that?"

He doesn't look convinced, but he lets it go. "Just some things I think you should have. Can I come in?"

I let him inside and we sit in the living room. He sets the box down on the coffee table and slices it open with a box cutter. Inside is the photobook, as dusty and worn as it was the day I found it, and a small, golden dagger. Chiseled into the dagger's leather-bound hilt is the image of a rising sun. The inscription carved into the blade's spine makes my chest ache. *The Saint of Blood.*

Janus picks up the dagger and presses it into my palm. The blade's been nicked and scratched, but it doesn't look dull. The rough leather of the hilt is so worn it peels.

"When your father was twenty-six years old, he faced an army of Scions with just that dagger. It was the last time he fought in the Cursed House's name," my uncle starts. "When he was twenty-eight and he had you, he told me to keep this with me, for safekeeping. For you. He kept you in the dark because he wanted to protect you, but he also thought you should know where you come from."

My hand trembles around the blade. It's not just another thing my father owned. I can still turn the pages of his books and find his scent, but this is different. This is a side of my father I never saw, the real side. The side that killed monsters and slew dragons. The side that was deadly and powerful, not gentle and kind. I don't think this blade is the reconciliation of those two people, but I so wish it could be.

I close my fist around the dagger's handle. Lightning flickers between my fingers, washing the blade in hot blue light. I don't know where the words come from, but they're at the tip of my tongue. I raise the flickering blade to my lips, whispering over it in Greek.

"*I bless this blade by the power of Zeus.*"

Thunder rumbles outside, and now my father's dagger is an artifact of holy war.

Janus gazes at me in astonishment. "What'd you do?"

"I'm not sure."

Lightning threads through the blade's inscription, bringing it to life. My father—the Saint of Blood—immortalized in six inches of lightning and gold.

I remember five months ago, when Cassius summoned my grandmother. She told me that everyone was fine. That my father was good and happy. I hold the blade up to my lips and mutter over it anyway.

"*May you rest in the golden splendor of Elysium.*"

My uncle echoes me. "*May you rest in the golden splendor of Elysium.*"

THE END

ABOUT THE AUTHOR

MICKI JANAE IS AN AUTHOR ON a mission. Tired of growing up with scant representation of young Black women in fantasy, Janae took matters into her own hands to craft *Of Blood and Lightning* (the first book of The Godender Saga), a compelling novel full of intricate world-building, electrifying storytelling, and diverse characters. Currently, Janae is studying at the University of Alabama, Birmingham, where she continues her passion for literature and explores visual creativity as a budding filmmaker with an eye on expanding the voices of young Black women in both fields. Currently Micki Janae lives in Birmingham, AL.

RECENT AND FORTHCOMING BOOKS FROM THREE ROOMS PRESS

FICTION

Lucy Jane Bledsoe
No Stopping Us Now

Rishab Borah
The Door to Inferna

Meagan Brothers
Weird Girl and What's His Name

Christopher Chambers
Scavenger
Standalone
StreetWhys

Ebele Chizea
Aquarian Dawn

Ron Dakron
Hello Devilfish!

Robert Duncan
Loudmouth

Amanda Eisenberg
People Are Talking

Michael T. Fournier
Hidden Wheel
Swing State

Kate Gale
Under a Neon Sun

Aaron Hamburger
Nirvana Is Here

William Least Heat-Moon
Celestial Mechanics

Aimee Herman
Everything Grows

Kelly Ann Jacobson
Tink and Wendy
Robin and Her Misfits
The Lies of the Toymaker

Jethro K. Lieberman
Everything Is Jake

Eamon Loingsigh
Light of the Diddicoy
Exile on Bridge Street

John Marshall
The Greenfather

Alvin Orloff
Vulgarian Rhapsody

Micki Janae
Of Blood and Lightning

Aram Saroyan
Still Night in L.A.

Robert Silverberg
The Face of the Waters

Stephen Spotte
Animal Wrongs

Richard Vetere
The Writers Afterlife
Champagne and Cocaine

Jessamyn Violet
Secret Rules to Being a Rockstar

Julia Watts
Quiver
Needlework
Lovesick Blossoms

Gina Yates
Narcissus Nobody

MEMOIR & BIOGRAPHY

Nassrine Azimi and Michel Wasserman
Last Boat to Yokohama: The Life and Legacy of Beate Sirota Gordon

William S. Burroughs & Allen Ginsberg
Don't Hide the Madness: William S. Burroughs in Conversation with Allen Ginsberg
edited by Steven Taylor

James Carr
BAD: The Autobiography of James Carr

Judy Gumbo
Yippie Girl: Exploits in Protest and Defeating the FBI

Judith Malina
Full Moon Stages: Personal Notes from 50 Years of The Living Theatre

Phil Marcade
Punk Avenue: Inside the New York City Underground, 1972–1982

Jillian Marshall
Japanthem; Counter-Cultural Experiences; Cross-Cultural Remixes

Alvin Orloff
Disasterama! Adventures in the Queer Underground 1977–1997

Nicca Ray
Ray by Ray: A Daughter's Take on the Legend of Nicholas Ray

Stephen Spotte
My Watery Self: Memoirs of a Marine Scientist

Christina Vo & Nghia M. Vo
My Vietnam, Your Vietnam
Vietnamese translation: *Việt Nam Của Con, Việt Nam Của Cha*

PHOTOGRAPHY-MEMOIR

Mike Watt
On & Off Bass

SHORT STORY ANTHOLOGIES

SINGLE AUTHOR

Alien Archives: Stories
by Robert Silverberg

First-Person Singularities: Stories
by Robert Silverberg

Tales from the Eternal Café: Stories
by Janet Hamill, intro by Patti Smith

Time and Time Again: Sixteen Trips in Time
by Robert Silverberg

The Unvarnished Gary Phillips: A Mondo Pulp Collection
by Gary Phillips

Voyagers: Twelve Journeys in Space and Time
by Robert Silverberg

MULTI-AUTHOR

The Colors of April
edited by Quan Manh Ha & Cab Trần

Crime + Music: Twenty Stories of Music-Themed Noir
edited by Jim Fusilli

Dark City Lights: New York Stories
edited by Lawrence Block

The Faking of the President: Twenty Stories of White House Noir
edited by Peter Carlaftes

Florida Happens: Bouchercon 2018 Anthology
edited by Greg Herren

Have a NYC I, II & III: New York Short Stories;
edited by Peter Carlaftes & Kat Georges

No Body, No Crime: Twenty-two Tales of Taylor Swift-Inspired Noir
edited by Alex Segura & Joe Clifford

Songs of My Selfie: An Anthology of Millennial Stories
edited by Constance Renfrow

The Obama Inheritance: 15 Stories of Conspiracy Noir
edited by Gary Phillips

This Way to the End Times: Classic & New Stories of the Apocalypse
edited by Robert Silverberg

DADA

Maintenant: A Journal of Contemporary Dada Writing & Art
(annual, since 2008)

MIXED MEDIA

John S. Paul
Sign Language: A Painter's Notebook
(photography, poetry and prose)

HUMOR

Peter Carlaftes
A Year on Facebook

FILM & PLAYS

Israel Horovitz
My Old Lady: Complete Stage Play and Screenplay with an Essay on Adaptation

Peter Carlaftes
Triumph For Rent (3 Plays)
Teatrophy (3 More Plays)

Kat Georges
Three Somebodies: Plays about Notorious Dissidents

TRANSLATIONS

Thomas Bernhard
On Earth and in Hell
(poems of Thomas Bernhard with English translations by Peter Waugh)

Patrizia Gattaceca
Isula d'Anima / Soul Island

César Vallejo | Gerard Malanga
Malanga Chasing Vallejo

George Wallace
EOS: Abductor of Men
(selected poems in Greek & English)

ESSAYS

Richard Katrovas
Raising Girls in Bohemia: Meditations of an American Father

Vanessa Baden Kelly
Far Away From Close to Home

Erin Wildermuth (editor)
Womentality

POETRY COLLECTIONS

Hala Alyan
Atrium

Peter Carlaftes
DrunkYard Dog
I Fold with the Hand I Was Dealt
Life in the Past Lane

Thomas Fucaloro
It Starts from the Belly and Blooms

Kat Georges
Our Lady of the Hunger
Awe and Other Words Like Wow

Robert Gibbons
Close to the Tree

Israel Horovitz
Heaven and Other Poems

David Lawton
Sharp Blue Stream

Jane LeCroy
Signature Play

Philip Meersman
This Is Belgian Chocolate

Jane Ormerod
Recreational Vehicles on Fire
Welcome to the Museum of Cattle

Lisa Panepinto
On This Borrowed Bike

George Wallace
Poppin' Johnny

Three Rooms Press | New York, NY | Current Catalog: www.threeroomspress.com
Three Rooms Press books are distributed by Publishers Group West: www.pgw.com